P9-DMM-205

HOW TO BREAK A BOY

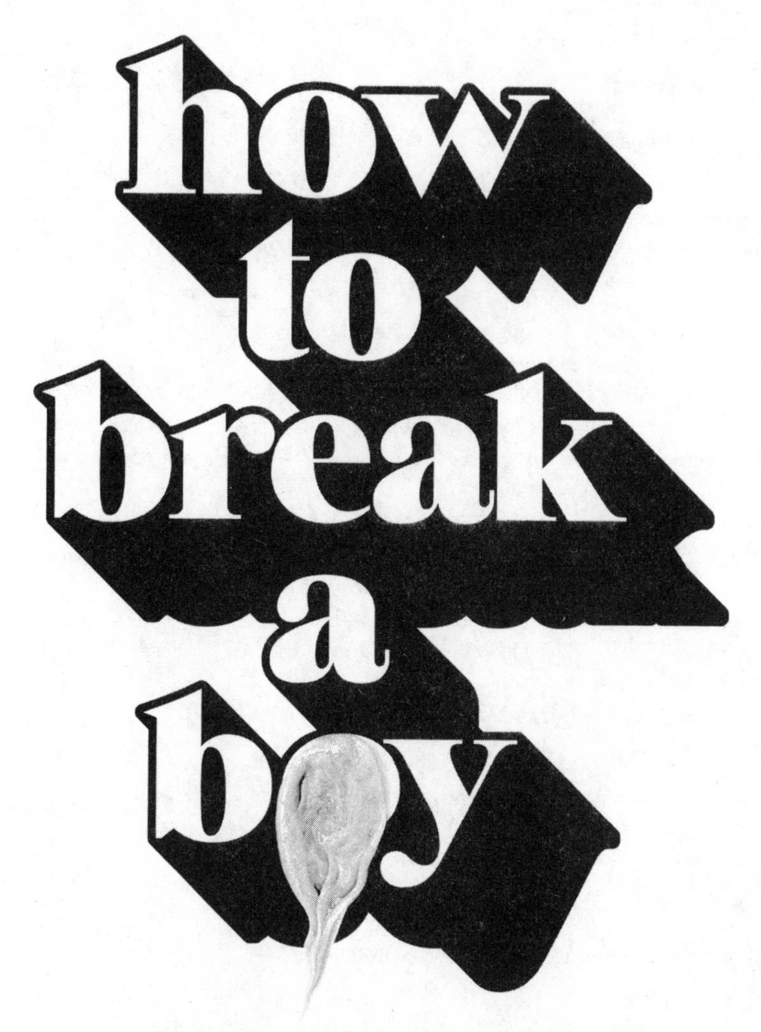

LAURIE DEVORE

NEW YORK

[Imprint]
MAKE YOUR MARK

A part of Macmillan Children's Publishing Group, a division of Macmillan Publishing Group, LLC

Library of Congress Cataloging-in-Publication Data
Names: Devore, Laurie, author.
Title: How to break a boy / Laurie Devore.
Description: First Edition. | New York : Imprint, 2017. | Summary: "A cheerleader questions whether she can quit her mean girl ways—or if she is just rotten at the core"—Provided by publisher.
Identifiers: LCCN 2016015265 (print) | LCCN 2016042639 (ebook) | ISBN 9781250082862 (hardback) | ISBN 9781250082879 (ebook)
Subjects: | CYAC: Cheerleading—Fiction. | Self-perception—Fiction. | High schools—Fiction. | Schools—Fiction. | Friendship—Fiction.
Classification: LCC PZ7.1.D489 Ho 2017 (print) | LCC PZ7.1.D489 (ebook) | DDC [Fic]—dc23
LC record available at https://lccn.loc.gov/2016015265

Our books may be purchased in bulk for promotional, educational, or business use. Please contact your local bookseller or the Macmillan Corporate and Premium Sales Department at (800) 221-7945 ext. 5442 or by e-mail at MacmillanSpecialMarkets@macmillan.com.

Book design by Natalie C. Sousa

Imprint logo designed by Amanda Spielman

First Edition—2017

10 9 8 7 6 5 4 3 2 1

fiercereads.com

For Billie Jean Andrews Devore, the only person in the world who wanted this as much as I did. Miss you, Grandma.

1

If you're riding up from Columbia on I-20, get off at Exit 98 and drive northeast for about forty-five minutes, past a bunch of cows and historic battlefields and bullshit, and you'll hit Buckley, South Carolina. It's a blink-and-you-miss-it town, minus there being anything to miss. When you see a sign declaring the BUCKLEY HIGH GOLF TEAM STATE CHAMPS and a water tower with some faded spray paint, you're there. If you hit the Gas-n-Go, you've gone too far.

We moved to Buckley after I finished sixth grade. Mom bought a tiny house on Main Street, with no explanation as to why we were moving from the middle-class suburbs of Charlotte to a shithole town whose residents live for beauty-salon gossip and the repeal of separation of church and state. Her mouth would flatten into a line of distaste when her eyes hit the ridiculous headlines of the one-man biweekly newspaper, and even though she never said it, she expected better of us than to act like everyone else in Buckley.

Just because you're in the zoo doesn't mean you're an animal.

Buckley liked to maintain an aura of historical importance. Here, a plantation where Jefferson Davis once spent the night. There, a monument for a fallen Revolutionary War soldier, right on the spot he died.

They'd have you believe that Buckley was a perfect—if smaller—representation of southern gentility; another Charleston or Savannah, nestled in the flatlands of eastern South Carolina.

But underneath it all lurked the same nasty streak that marked so many small southern towns. The windows filled with defiant Confederate flags, the sexual rumors whispered behind closed doors, and the firm belief that Buckley was the finest place on God's green earth anyway, thank you very much. Buckley's famed town square was known across the state for its cobblestoned road and historical landmarks. Even still, seedy bars and failed business ventures filled the edges of the square, the same people roaming them for years. Then, later, their children and their children's children after that.

If you headed out of town south toward Myrtle Beach, you'd ride past Buckley High School, then over some railroad tracks and into the old mill village, a part of Buckley no God-fearing townsperson would talk about and many claimed should've never been drawn into the Buckley city limits at all.

That was Buckley—historical tours and meth labs, Confederate legacy and Friday night lights.

From the time we arrived, my older brother, Ryan, and I kept a map on his bedroom wall charting all the places we wanted to go—places so far away, so different from Buckley. I was always picking stupid ones like Albuquerque and Ann Arbor and Austin. They sounded unique to me. Interesting.

His dreams ran bigger. Florence. Berlin. Cairo. I'd listen as he talked, painting enchanted pictures in my head of places as distant as the imaginary worlds in his books. I hung on to Ryan's words when there was nothing else worth hanging on to. Buckley was a fence holding us in, a cage clipping our wings. Everything that mattered was outside, waiting on us.

Until I met Adrienne.

At Buckley Middle School, Adrienne had everything and she *was* everything. She'd hold court with her best friend, Claire, on the swings during lunch and tell Claire all the secrets everyone had fed her that day. Who was making out with whom. What party everyone was and wasn't invited to. Who had on a heinous skirt.

I was fascinated with the pair of them. Adrienne looked so different from everyone else in Buckley. I later found out her father had been a purebred southern bachelor and betrayed his heritage by going to law school at Northwestern and marrying the future Mrs. Maynard, a beautiful dark-haired advertising exec of some kind. That explained Adrienne's perfect tan skin, her shiny black hair. But the one thing that made her uniquely Adrienne was her hypnotizing dark brown eyes, the way they flashed when you had pleased her, offering the most specific kind of acceptance and love. Claire was the perfect unassuming best friend for Adrienne—small for her age, white-bread innocence, and all-American cute.

One day in class, Adrienne was talking about Elona Mabry, a slightly overweight classmate of ours who tended to overpraise Adrienne whenever she was within fifteen feet of her. I had no trouble identifying Elona's type—a specifically sad kind of wannabe in the middle school world. "It's that thing she does with her eyeliner," Adrienne was saying during fifth period. "It totally looks like she puts it on in a dark room while being groped. And that huge, clearly fake Coach purse she carries around, and she can never find *anything* in it. Like, what do you even think she's looking for in there? It's like—it's like—"

"Like a raccoon robbing a trash can," I said from my assigned desk catty-corner to her. I didn't stop to think about what I was saying. The words ripping Elona to shreds automatically strung themselves together.

Adrienne snapped her fingers, pointing at me. "Yes." Then she laughed, tilting her pretty head back until everyone was looking. Claire sat behind her, covering her mouth with a hand, giggling as if in spite of herself. Adrienne went on, "That's exactly what it is. You're Olivia, right? I've been meaning to tell you how much I love your hair. What do you do to it?" I twisted a strand of hair around my finger. I could practically feel others tuning in to what was happening, looking at me like they looked at her. Adrienne liked me; Adrienne thought I was funny. My smile was radiant. Later, I'd tell her about where I was going. The places on the map. She told me she'd seen some of them, from her parents' pictures or in person.

Adrienne was in Buckley, but she was so above it.

There's something about certain people that always draws me in. They make me feel more daring, more alive, more vibrant. They light a match and spark a fire, and the blaze is too enticing to be scary.

Adrienne was a fireworks show to my total eclipse.

Before I met Adrienne, Buckley was a colorless day, a roadblock on the map, a punishment to be endured. Everything about it was so boring, so lifeless and ordinary.

With her, everything developed an edge. And I loved it.

We sat on the swings day in and day out and observed our peers. Mocked them. Grew sharper than them, smarter. In my report cards, the teachers never used the words, but I could read between the lines and Mom could, too. *Bully. Mean girl.*

"Jealous." Adrienne would laugh.

I laughed, too. Life was easy when you were looking down on everyone else.

Three years later, Ryan packed up our map and put it in his trunk. He took it with him where he was going: Ann Arbor. Turns out, wings grow back. He flew out of Buckley.

He left me behind. I'd forgotten I was supposed to care.

And then he was gone for good.

2

Even though it's September, no one's bothered to take down the Fourth of July banners hanging from the lampposts. Most of the buildings around the town square are closing down, but Corley's Ice Cream is still open, and Buckley cheerleaders get half off on Tuesdays. Claire and I sit at the wrought-iron table out front. She has her fingers wrapped around a strawberry milk shake, slurping loudly. I lean back on the chair's legs and watch a white Jeep drive through the square, heading out from south Buckley toward the nicer houses in Buckton, the rich neighborhood near the Woodhaven Country Club.

It's all the normal conversation of the day: Coxie's pot habit and the shit Daniel Smith pulled in third-period biology today to finally drive Mr. Nickles to walk out in the middle of class. But as it does lately, everything else is eating away at the edge of my consciousness. Until I can't take it anymore.

"Do you think I'm doing this wrong?" I ask Claire. She is still the yin to Adrienne's and my yang after all these years, the light to our dark. She is still petite, but the cute developed into stunning somewhere along the way.

She pulls her straw away from her mouth, her perfectly shaped blond eyebrows furrowing. "What?" A green cloth banner blows in the wind behind her, saying GO EAGLES, the tattered ends whipping against the post.

I've already started, so I go ahead and spill the rest out. "Mr. Doolittle says everyone processes grief differently. When I go to his office, he keeps repeating it like it's his damn mantra. He says my non-reaction is the most obvious kind of reaction. That when I'm upset, I act even more callous to upset everyone else. So, it's like, when I'm hurting others by being cold, I'm really hurting myself. Am I cold?" I take the straw wrapper up from under my cup and wind it around my fingers. Every week, Mr. Doolittle tells me something else that creates another crack in my carefully constructed wall, gets too close to touching on something I don't want to think about.

"Hey," Claire says, and I look up at her, serious blue eyes trained on me. Claire has the kind of face that you believe, which makes her an excellent liar. "You're not cold. You're—you're different from before. You're doing the best you can."

I nod. I feel different. I feel . . . less. It's when I start letting myself feel too much that everything gets all fucked up. I like having a non-reaction. I like living how I did before Ryan died—ice cream with Claire, post–football games with Ethan. They're traditions. They hold things together. They remind me to hold it together.

I go through the motions. But it's hollow. Every second is hollow.

It's funny, but I don't think I'd understand the contrast without Adrienne. If I hadn't ingrained a picture of that mischievous and exuberant face she'd give me sometimes when she felt love for me in her particular way. If I didn't have to see every day the apathetic, disinterested one she gives me now. Sometimes, that hurts more than grief.

"Adrienne acts like she doesn't get me anymore," I finally confess to Claire, turning over the words in my head as I see Adrienne's face. "Like what I'm feeling is so beneath her. That I'm no fun. But I don't want—I don't know *how* to be fun."

"Adrienne misses the way things were. You know how she is," Claire explains away, not quite meeting my eye.

The way things were. I try not to think about it too much. I know what's right and what's wrong, who's good and bad, and I know if you sin against enough people, ultimately the universe will find you. I *always* knew better. That's probably what made it worse. I should've known even before he died. I should've known it was coming.

Ethan warned me, accidentally probably. He once said to me: "This isn't who you are. These things you do. They're Adrienne."

They weren't, but I could never admit that to him. Or that I thrived on top, on the way people looked when they were afraid. That drama gave me a kick of adrenaline. That sometimes I loved him more just because it pissed Adrienne off.

Those aren't things a good person thinks. Not things you think if you're the *right* kind of person.

"Ethan wants me to talk about it," I say now. "He's kind of like Mr. Doolittle that way. He thinks grief is a glass barrier I must break through and he'll be on the other side with warm fuzzies and hugs. I know he talks about it with his mom."

"Isn't she a psychologist for dangerous criminals?" Claire returns, sounding a little amused.

I snort. "Yeah. Hit the nail on the head, huh?"

"He loves you."

"I know." It's easy to hear the resignation in my voice. I finish off the rest of my ice cream and throw the empty cup into a trash can. I pick up Mom's keys from the table. "Anyway, I'm going over to Adrienne's house. She wants to choreograph a new routine for the pep rally next week, and I told her I'd help. She says I've been avoiding her."

I have. But I can't tell her why. I can't even fully explain it to myself yet. I only know I can't be who I was before my brother died.

I wave at Claire as I head out, purposely not allowing my gaze to wander down the street leading away from the town square. I still can't look at the white church.

Some sins can't be forgiven.

3

The countryside barrels by me as I take Mom's Bronco farther and farther into the outskirts of town. The Buckton neighborhood, built around the Woodhaven golf course, isn't exactly the stuff of network television perfection, but it's the nicest part of town. A place where little kids meet for playdates and dads golf on weekends. People who want Buckley to be something it isn't but were too sheltered to get the hell out of Dodge. It's a stark contrast to the other side of the town, where Buckley High School is. Over the railroad tracks where the mill-village kids roam, ratty backpacks thrown over their shoulders.

I come to the sign telling me I'm five miles from the next town over—a town with a movie theater and a Dillard's—and I take a left down a side road. Adrienne's parents are the type that decided they wanted to raise their family in the wide-open country, which seems sweet if you think about it but is actually totally ridiculous in practice. Mr. Maynard grew up in Atlanta, Mrs. Maynard in Chicago, and neither could shake the city from their system. Since Adrienne was old enough to stay home by herself, her parents have been leaving her alone—her dad traveling for work with her mom along for the ride. Adrienne's always hated staying in the big house on her own, so Claire and I crash there a lot to keep her company. And to get into trouble.

The closer I get to Adrienne's house, the more my stomach churns. Adrienne has always been hard to read, but lately she's been impossible. Deep down, I know she's worried, but at the same time, some sort of subtle anger bubbles under it all. Every conversation is clipped, uncomfortable. Like she wants me to snap, and I'm waiting for her to do the same right back.

Today, she asked me why I was so obsessed with things I can't control, and I told her I didn't really know.

Trees line the Maynards' long, winding driveway. I pull in up front, behind Ade's shiny red coupe. Outside it's eerily quiet, and the heat hits me like a wall as I get out of my car. I bound up the front steps and knock—I know neither of Ade's parents is home, and from here, I can hear music pounding against her upstairs window. I push open the front door and take the hardwood steps two at a time, hitting the landing leading to her room. I study the closed door for a minute, considering. She still hasn't answered my text that said I was on my way; she must be busy. But she wanted me to come. She'd yelled at me about not spending time with her.

I push open the door.

I should've trusted my instincts.

She's with a boy.

With a boy in a way that I do not want to see.

It takes a minute for me to stop looking and start seeing. It's not just any boy.

It's *my* boy.

Ethan Masters. All shaggy blond hair and long torso and silly grins just for me since the first day we met. My Ethan with Adrienne and her tan skin and her dark hair on the black sheets we'd slept on together so many times during innocent sleepovers. As I stand there and watch, every moment stretching as long as ten, one word keeps running through my head: *cold.*

Cold.

Adrienne. "Oh my God."

Cliché.

Ethan. "What the hell."

Obvious.

I turn and walk downstairs, carefully down every step, and then I sit on the couch.

Adrienne fumbles down the stairs after me in a Buckley High cheerleading T-shirt, sounding more like a herd of elephants than a 120-pound teenage girl, all doe eyes and shame. "Listen, O—"

I push a piece of hair back behind my ear. "Well, that should be an interesting beginning to our routine and will probably really get the boosters going, but maybe for your opening solo, you should dial back on the slut a little bit."

"O." We both turn as Ethan pokes his head around the staircase. Adrienne tells him, "Do not come out here," in a way I can't believe, like she has any right, and then it hits me so hard, I dig my fingernails into my palm if only to feel something concrete. I try not to look at him, because he is *my* Ethan. I never thought I'd get through losing Ryan, but Ethan had always been there. I never wanted him to know about Ryan's problems, but those few times Ethan found out, he stayed. He'd be with me. And sometimes—in those moments when our skin was touching, when he breathed in as I breathed out—that had been all I'd had.

And now he'd been with her.

"What is wrong with you?" I demand of Adrienne.

"I don't know," she tells me, and I almost believe it's genuine. "I'm lonely and I miss you and I'm trying to hold everything—"

"Spare me," I cut her off. "I'm going." I push myself up from the couch and look from Adrienne to the spot where Ethan disappeared and start to leave.

"You just came down and sat on the couch," she says behind me, the words coming out slowly like she's solving a puzzle for me. "You didn't storm out; you just sat. It's like . . . who are you even? Don't you care?"

I honestly don't know—I know that I should.

Care.

I want to.

So I slam the door, leaving nothing but the reverberations behind me.

4

TWO YEARS AGO

Adrienne was dark. She always had been. Not just her skin and hair and eyes. Not just her smooth voice, seducing everyone in her path. But her demeanor, the way she liked to set things aflame and watch them burn. And here's the thing: A trash can full of paper could keep us entertained when we were in middle school, but by high school, there was something much more interesting to set fire to: people's lives.

It was never personal, which I think was the worst of all of it. But I had fucked up. And I had fucked up bad.

It was a party at Coxie's—Claire's boyfriend. His parents were gone for the weekend, and his house on the outskirts of town ensured no adult would catch us. The music was too loud and the drinks too sweet, and what I remember more than anything else is feeling like I could destroy the world if I so chose. That power was a thrum of energy, a life force. It just so happened that Anna Talbert was too tall and too skinny and a JV cheerleader with very little promise. Which I had told her. Repeatedly.

Adrienne, Claire, and I were the only sophomores on the varsity cheer team that year, a fact that only bonded the three of us closer together as a trio. We were running with some of the senior girls, and things were looking up every day.

Never mind that my brother had gone over a week without answering a text from me. The obvious solution was to start shoving vodka down my throat, and the more I drank, the meaner I got. Anna had no idea why.

"God, Anna, I'd say you were a slut, but everyone knows a boy would never sleep with you."

Shot.

"Christ, Anna, are you still here? Has no one clearly told you to fuck off yet?"

Shot.

"Jesus, Anna, is there a world where you don't exist, because I'd like to live in it."

All this while Anna told me how pretty I looked, how goddamn funny I was. She brought me drink after drink, shot after shot. Adrienne laughed until she cried.

I handed Anna a bottle and told her to stay out of my way, permanently, if possible.

They told me she drank until the designated driver had to put her in the back of the car and take her to the hospital.

It all ended the next morning with me locked in Adrienne's bathroom, sobbing. A text from one of the senior girls had come through at six a.m. Anna Talbert in serious condition. Don't say shit. A few more followed, the last from Anna's cousin asking if we knew who'd given her so much vodka, if we'd keep her in our thoughts and prayers. I'd made it to the bathroom and thrown up, and now I was curled on the rug in front of the toilet, crying like I had never cried in my life. *I did this*.

I had fucked up so incredibly bad.

That's where Adrienne found me. She sat down in front of me, crossing her legs. "O . . ."

"I almost killed her," I managed to choke out.

"She almost killed herself," Adrienne told me calmly. "And they pumped her stomach. She's going to be fine."

"I was like Ryan. I was drunk and mean and everyone else be damned. Why couldn't I leave her alone?" I didn't get up to look at Adrienne, but her eyes found mine. "It's some kind of fucking gene that makes me a monster. And wait until she tells them I gave her the vodka. I don't know what they'll do to me." I wiped my nose with the back of my hand. "I deserve it. All of it. I'm dangerous."

"Get up," Adrienne told me.

I lost some of my conviction then, tuning out her voice. I stopped crying quite as hard. The thought crystallized in my mind. I was dangerous, and I needed to be away from here. Really, it was an escape.

Maybe this is my way out of Buckley.

Adrienne realized I wasn't getting up. She crawled down on the ground next to me, until our faces were right in front of each other, our noses inches apart. "She's not going to tell," she said to me.

I skipped a breath. "Why?"

She blew out a laugh that I felt on my cheeks. "Because I texted her first thing this morning and told her how concerned we both were about her. How we hadn't slept since we heard. I don't like it, but she's in now, O."

"In?"

"She's our friend. We love her like she loves us, so no more of that shit from last night, all right?"

I hadn't known up until that moment that we had an *in* or an *out*. But it seemed so obvious now. *In*. It should have felt better than it did.

It should've been more of a relief. I said, "Thank you," anyway.

Adrienne pushed a hand into my hair, holding it there tenderly. "You're not like him," she whispered to me. "You're my best friend and you're beautiful and hilarious and perfect, okay?"

I nodded.

"I love you," she said at last. She never said that. We weren't like the best friends who were always hugging, saying *love you*. That wasn't Adrienne. Coming from her, it was practically a confession.

"Love you, too, Ade," I said, my voice still the hangover of a cry.

She smiled. "That's why I'd never let anything bad happen to you."

5

It is gray outside.

I'd gotten fairly used to sleepless nights, used to the moment after the night had retreated and before the sun was really up yet. A bottle of Jack Daniel's stared at me sadly from my desk.

I'd found the bottles stacked away in my brother's closet right after he died, presumably for when he was home in Buckley and would need at least eight or nine drinks to survive each day. I hadn't wanted Mom to see them, which had to be the most futile part of Ryan's personality to hide. But I'd stashed them away, out of sight, and last night, I'd pulled this one out and set it on the desk.

I couldn't bring myself to take a drink.

Adrienne and Ethan had texted and called me until about two, when surely they had fallen asleep. With the pattern of the buzzes, I could only assume they were communicating with each other between texting me, while simultaneously laying the blame on each other.

I decided not to care.

One, though. One text—one small string of words—had caught my attention.

O, this is as bad as it gets. Tomorrow, we start trying to fix this again.

Adrienne doesn't ask; she tells.

The sad thing is, I like the idea. I like to think we could fix this and be best friends. Be best friends differently than we were before.

But she has to pay first. I don't want sorry.

I want blood.

I fall back into the thought like a safety blanket. The thought of revenge gives me life. Purpose.

That's what I was missing.

So I get up, and I get on with it. Tight jeans. Loose top. Red lips.

Let's do this.

She hasn't looked at me yet.

We're sitting there in fourth period, our first class of the day together. The first time we've been in the same room since yesterday and she's not looking at me.

It's the poetry section of the year. The one we all dread most.

The only concept worse than writing poems in English class is reading them out loud. I always see it in the teachers' eyes. They think they tell you to write a poem and you spill pain and heartbreak and blood all over a piece of college-ruled notebook paper because it's your only chance to get it out. Maybe they'll cry and you'll cry and it'll make a really great TV movie. You'll have conquered your emotional demons in the span of their fifty-minute class, all thanks to them. Written everything you're thinking, everything that's pulling you apart.

No one does that. Except me, I guess. Right now. My eyes boring into the back of Adrienne's head, I write it all down.

I start scratching out words on the paper, hoping to make it less honest, less raw, less *anything*. Mrs. Morrison calls for volunteers, then does that tut-tut thing teachers do when no one actually volunteers. "Don't make me pick someone," she singsongs.

Silence. The kind of silence that stretches into days. If she asks, I'll tell her I didn't write anything. She never said we'd have to read these out loud. *I can't. I won't.* But then Mrs. Morrison says, "Vera. Good."

I look up, my heart caught in my throat, right between my jaw and my esophagus. Vera Drake is this incredibly awkward girl, shy and quiet, someone who disappears outside of a classroom. I focus solely on her when she starts to talk—her short, uneven blond bob and wide-set eyes. Small wrists and nonexistent fashion sense. She stares at the floor when she speaks.

"Sapphire eyes, golden hair," she squawks, speaking slowly and taking deep breaths louder than is strictly necessary. "Your eyes look at me / but I'm not there. / Standing alone, locker-tall, / you're right and wrong, / above it all."

I die a million deaths for her with every word, squirming in my seat.

"Lovely, Vera," Mrs. Morrison lies. Even she is embarrassed. Vera rocks from her left foot to her right. "Why did you write that?" Like she needs to ask.

"You know that feeling," Vera explains, and oh my God, I wish she wouldn't, "where you're in the same room with somebody and you can't even remember to breathe?"

"I feel that way about pizza," comes a voice from the other side of the room, dark and confident; it fills up the empty space, turning the awkward silence into laughter.

"Miss Maynard," Mrs. Morrison chides as Vera crawls back to her seat, her eyes on the floor to shield off the humiliation. "Thank you for your opinion."

Adrienne smiles all bright and beautiful, flips her sheet of black hair over her shoulder. She has on her game face. I should've known: It's what she does. She doesn't let the guilt eat away at her like I do. I always do.

I scratch at my poem until the paper tears. It's all sex and grief, and sex and grief are the last things I want anyone else to think about me.

When I glance up again, Adrienne catches my eyes for the briefest of seconds before burying her face in her hair again with a fake shy smile. That shy smile she employs only when she's been caught humiliating someone who has no ammo to fight back with, like it was only an innocent joke among friends.

"I liked it," I say without thinking. If she doesn't think *I'll* fight back, she's dead wrong.

Everyone laughs again. Of course. They think I'm mocking Vera, too.

I glance back quickly, and Vera stares down at her desk, expertly avoiding eye contact with anyone. She stares so hard, I wonder if there is an alternate universe she can climb into somewhere down there. I wonder if she'll take me with her.

I'm not going to let Adrienne have this one.

"But really," I start to say, still looking at Vera. If I can convince her of my sincerity, I win today's game. *Olivia: 1. Adrienne: 0.*

"That is quite enough, Olivia," Mrs. Morrison cuts me off. "Unless you want me to talk to Dr. Rickards about your participation in homecoming week."

"But I did," I try to stress again. "Like it."

"Give it a rest, O," Adrienne says from across the room. Everyone's staring at me with these horrified looks on their faces, as if Adrienne didn't start it. Because it had been funny, until it wasn't. I lean my face into my palm, smearing red lipstick on my hand in the process. *Olivia: 0. Adrienne: 1.*

When the bell rings, I rip my poem up into eighteen different pieces. I catch Vera out of the corner of my eye as she's leaving. I can't help it. I grab on to her green jacket. "I meant what I said," I promise her.

She pulls away from me, a tear glistening in her eye. This is always the worst part. When they cry. I've always hated when they cry. I'd try telling myself it wasn't my fault, it was just for fun, they were too fucking sensitive and it was Buckley High, not real life, but I never meant to make them cry.

"Shit."

I throw the bits of my poem in the trash, watching them float down like paper rain. I think about how people are always saying how good guys finish last. I think about Adrienne tearing Vera down. Listening to it. Enjoying it.

I want to hurt her. I want to see her lose for once in her perfectly constructed life. I want her to come crawling back to me, to beg me for forgiveness. To beg me to *stop*.

I just want one moment to hold on to.

And I'll get it if it's the last thing I do.

6

Mr. Doolittle plops heavily into his wooden chair, letting a pile of papers topple onto the desk after him. He's an overweight man who's yet to admit it, shirt buttons straining where they stretch across his bulging stomach. He's pretty jolly for a high school guidance counselor. Like Santa on Prozac.

"So what do you want to talk about today, Olivia?" he asks me with a wide smile, adjusting his reading glasses.

Oh, just my latest personal tragedy. My best friend sleeping with my boyfriend. Pulling the trigger one last time to remind me who runs the show.

I shrug.

Mr. Doolittle shuffles through his notes, probably to some page marked Clayton, *comma* Olivia, *colon*: head case. That's how I'd label it anyway.

"I know it's been two months," he says. "It was a tragedy, but it's allowed us to spend some time together. I think we're really starting to make some progress, don't you?"

"Yeah." Mr. Doolittle sucks at this stuff. But I'll take it. The last thing I need is for them to put me in real therapy. I sit quietly, let my eyes wander. There are several pictures on his desk turned toward him.

Probably his kids. His wife got caught cheating with the chiropractor in town a couple years ago. Everyone knows.

"We're talking now, Olivia. This is great! This is forward momentum. Do you feel like you can tell me what's changed?" Mr. Doolittle says, watching me very seriously. I hate everything about the moment after those words fall to the ground. I can feel the walls closing in. *What's changed.*

Picture a girl.

She's sixteen, lean, long brown hair. Her clothes are affordable but cute because sometimes her best friend gives her hand-me-downs and every so often she scrounges up enough money to buy from the non-sales rack. Riding in a car, top down, wind picking up strands of her hair. She's talking to her friends about the next big party or some high school scandal or whatever, it doesn't matter, because she's blissfully unaware that anything could ever change. Nothing can change when you're sixteen and everyone loves to hate you because you have everything. You are everything.

Her brother dies and everything falls apart. She wonders whether any of it was ever real to begin with.

"Nothing's different," I say.

Mr. Doolittle leans forward, arranging his face into his idea of devastation. "Olivia."

A clock is ticking. People are moving. Nothing is different for them.

It's weird that time passes without Ryan here. I'm always trying to figure out how I can catch it, replay it. I have these pictures—these frozen moments of time—that I look through sometimes, and I keep thinking, *He's only gone for a minute, he'll be back.* When I flip through the pictures, everything's the same. Everything is like before. Ryan smiling at what he sees faraway in the distance, me smiling at him. Back then, everything was magical to us, a discovery waiting to happen.

Adrienne's there, too, and when she laughs, I laugh with her. If she thinks it's funny, it is. If she thinks it's a good idea, we'll do it. Adrienne makes the stars twinkle with her laugh; she gives dull Buckley days color, shimmer. She's unafraid.

And Ethan—when he looks at me, he sees me like no one else does. I am more than who I was before, at least to him. He loved who I was then.

"All the pieces are the same," I hear myself say. "But nothing fits into the right place anymore." I stare at the backs of the picture frames. Why can't I see them? Why does Mr. Doolittle have to separate me from his life and delve into mine? His wife cheated and I know, and my brother died and he knows. Both those secrets should belong to us, but don't. We don't know each other at all. He doesn't know what I did and I don't know if his wife wanted attention or fun or whatever. "I don't think I'm cold," I say, and I think of Claire.

He's watching me. "No, not today," he mutters, and I look up. He's still looking very serious, even moved.

"Anyway." I shake my head, try to pull myself out of it. Feeling sad is not the answer. I've tried it, but dwelling gets me nowhere. Thinking about Adrienne's lips all over Ethan and my brother six feet under gets me nowhere. I don't *need* grief. "I know it's all very upsetting for you, but since this is my problem, I'd rather you not cry."

"I'm sorry," he says. "I thought I saw the real you for a second, Miss Clayton, and it was good. Being vulnerable is hard."

Being vulnerable is bullshit.

"What do you do when it really hurts?" he asks me, still all sentimental and understanding. I crossed a line here. I crossed a line, and I have to get back on the other side where I can breathe.

And what kind of question is that anyway? It always really hurts. "Physical stuff," I tell him, crossing my arms over my stomach.

He makes a note. "Such as?"

Sex. With Ethan. Guess I can't do that anymore. "Running. Cheerleading."

"You're very good," he tells me with a smile. "I was at the game last Friday. You're extremely athletic." If things were like before, I would tell Adrienne this later and she would call him a perv. I would laugh.

"It's a hobby." I roll my shoulders, try to loosen up. I don't like the compliments. No one compliments me on anything except managing to exist in the Darwinist high school landscape.

"Have you considered any of the other activities I've suggested? Volunteer work? Chorus? Something for your college applications?"

"I cheer," I say automatically. That's always been enough.

Mr. Doolittle clears his throat, slides his glasses down his nose in dramatic fashion. "Miss Clayton, are you thinking about college at all right now?"

No.

"Yes," I snap.

"Your brother went to Michigan," he informs me. How could anyone suck at his job this much? I know my brother went to Michigan. It's where he died.

"Ryan hated it here." I glance out the window. A happy couple walks by outside, holding hands. She's a junior; he's a senior. Next year, he'll go to the community college in Central for two weeks before going to work at the cable company. She'll be pregnant at graduation, and they'll settle down in a trailer next to his mom's house. In ten years, they'll be divorced. "I hate it here." I turn to Mr. Doolittle. "No state schools. Nowhere *near* here."

"Olivia," he says cautiously.

I stare back without blinking. One of the buttons on his shirt has come loose.

"I'm sorry, but you couldn't get into a state school even if you wanted to."

Even though I know that, even though I knew it was stupid to say, it hurts. It stings like hell, and suddenly it hits me that I'm totally alone.

I've thought I was better than them for so long—better than that couple, these *people*, but I'm as pathetic as they are.

I'm alone because I've burned them all with a smile on my face, but I'm no different from them.

"I mean," Mr. Doolittle corrects himself quickly, trying to fix it, "not that you can't, but that you're behind." Slowly, he starts to build himself back up, expansive and jovial. "You're behind. You need to get your grades up this year and quite frankly, you need high SAT scores. Very high." He slides his glasses back on, looking at the Olivia Clayton head case file. "You *could* go out of state. You could. I'm going to make you a list," he announces.

Excitedly, he scribbles down some words onto a loose sheet of paper, folds it up, and holds it just out of my reach. "Some students who I think could help you prepare for the SAT if you could work out a small fee with them. All very smart, very accomplished."

Unlike me.

"You make a list of schools. You make that list, Olivia, and we'll figure it out. Start working with one of these students, and we'll get you in. You're not lost, Miss Clayton. Yes, yes, this is fantastic progress. Exactly the kind of project you need. Let me—"

I reach out and rip the paper from his hand, stuffing it haphazardly into my backpack without reading the names. A list. Like that would help. Like I can repair the damage I've done for three years here in three months. Out of state. What a joke.

I'm even stupider than I realized.

"Are we done yet?" I ask Mr. Doolittle, glancing at the clock. There are ten minutes left until the bell, but I'm exhausted.

He looks at me, smile still looming large. "If you promise to get started as soon as you leave. You're going to surprise yourself! I know you will."

I nod, getting up from my chair. "Thanks, Mr. D. Your shirt's unbuttoned," I say, pointing to the gap over his belly. Then, like I can't help it: "And too small. Seriously, give it up." With that, I flounce out of the room.

Olivia Clayton, biggest bitch in school. Well, second, as Adrienne would have reminded me. *Helpfully*.

Old habits die hard.

7

I sit on the sidewalk with my back against the redbrick wall, outside the gym, crumpling and uncrumpling the list of colleges I've written. It's ridiculous. Even Mr. Doolittle will laugh in my face.

I haven't even looked at the names of the people who will supposedly help me. No one can help me. I know that. So why do I keep hoping someone will fix this?

I glance up to see Claire walking over to me, legs clad in a pair of lime-green practice shorts. She watches me for a minute before squatting down. "Are you okay?"

I shrug.

"Did something happen?"

I look up at her, squinting. "Kind of. Not really. I don't want to talk about it."

"Okay," she says again, slowly. "Hey, listen, Ethan's been looking for you all day, and I know he's been smothering you lately, but he's really worried, you know? So I think you should talk to him, and I mean, he'll find you eventually—"

"He found me," I say, pointing over her shoulder. Ethan, already suited up in his football pants, is lurking behind her, watching me.

"Oh, hey, Ethan," Claire says, straightening back up and giving him one of her perky grins. "You're supposed to be buying those Snickers bars from me for the candy sale. You haven't forgotten, right?"

Ethan gives Claire a sad attempt at a smile. "No, Claire, of course not."

"All right." She spots Alex Cox—otherwise known as Coxie—who is still her boyfriend or whatever, standing in the doorway that leads to the boys' locker room. She grins, skipping off toward Coxie. Once she's out of earshot, Ethan turns to me.

"Hey."

I pull myself up so I'm standing in front of him. How exactly am I supposed to respond?

"Slept with my best friend lately?"

Well, that's always an option.

Ethan hangs his head, his blond hair glinting in the sunlight. I get almost no pleasure out of it. "Yeah, I guess I did."

I'll give him this. He has balls.

I cross my arms over my stomach, shake my head. There's nothing I can do, nothing I can change. If he sees me cry, then he'll know.

No one can know how much it hurts or how hard it is.

"Everything's messed up, O," Ethan says, squinting at me through the light. "But that doesn't mean—I don't want it to end like this."

I bite out a laugh. "Well, it did. What do you think this is, Ethan? I have a reputation to protect."

"What does your reputation have to do with anything?" he demands. "Just listen to yourself! You won't talk to me." He throws his hands up in defeat like he's in a play and the audience is supposed to feel sorry for him. Only this is my life, and I've seen enough.

"Adrienne?" I spit out. "She is my best friend, Ethan! And you *hate* her."

"I know. I don't even know why. . . ." And, oh my God, he's going to start crying. I see it bubbling up right there under those Caribbean-blue eyes of his.

"Don't you dare do that," I tell him. "If you do that, I will humiliate you." I go to leave, but Ethan grabs on to my shoulder hard and turns me back.

"Don't tell me what I'm not allowed to do," he says, slowly regaining control of that quivering bottom lip. Turning the tears into something else.

I smirk. "I won't anymore," I say. "I promise."

"Don't put all of this on me, O!" He touches the front of his practice jersey where he thinks his heart should be, but it's not anatomically correct. He never did very well with biology.

"I tried so hard," he says. "You won't even talk to me."

And the fact that he even thinks that he could try to blame me makes me angrier than I could ever put into words. "Are you kidding me?"

"You wanted this to happen," Ethan snaps at me, finally, before turning around and walking in the direction of the football field. Wiping his face on his sweaty T-shirt and then high-fiving his teammates as if this were any other day to him. As if I'd gotten what I deserved.

I used to wait for him sometimes, after practice; he'd hug me right after he got off the field, so tight I couldn't breathe. He'd be gross, drenched in sweat, and I would squeal about how much I hated it.

I didn't.

You never realize stuff like that until it's gone.

And then you have to live without it.

LAST YEAR

"Blood, sweat, and tears."

That was the football team's motto the year Ethan transferred in.

I remember because it was so stupid. Our football team had been 5–5 the year before. No blood or tears had been involved. The sweat was debatable.

Until one Friday during the new season. The lights were buzzing, the fans desperate in their green and white, we cheerleaders loud and sweaty in the late summer heat. On a third down in the second quarter, the new transfer fullback took a handoff from the quarterback. The pads slammed against each other as he drove through a hole in the line. He tried to take the ball straight up the middle and didn't get up after the whistle. They wheeled the stretcher out on the field and cut the guy's helmet off. As they were rolling him off the field, short-staffed thanks to an opponent's broken arm earlier, Dr. McCoy pointed at me, shouting, "Olivia, come here!" Alarmed, I ran over to the cart.

"Hold this on his head," Dr. McCoy told me, putting my hand on the white towel she pressed to the boy's temple. "Apply pressure."

I walked beside the stretcher as they wheeled him into the locker room.

"For Christ's sake, what a night," Dr. McCoy said as we stopped in the locker room. I wasn't looking at her—my eyes kept finding the boy's face, watching his eyelids attempt to flutter open. "This close to a compound fracture on Lattimer and now this."

"And we're down by ten," I added helpfully.

My hand had grown careless with the pressure, and a thin drop of blood escaped and fell down the side of the boy's face. I quickly wiped it away with a clean edge of the towel and pushed harder.

He was looking at me.

"Ethan!" Dr. McCoy said loudly, her voice relieved. "Are you okay? Do you know where you are?"

"Go Eagles," he replied, pushing himself up and pumping a fist.

"Don't do that too fast," Dr. McCoy said, putting her hand against the back of his head. He shook her off, and I kept the towel pressed against his cut, my arm brushing against his. He was still watching me. "I called for a backup EMT crew."

"I'm fine," he insisted.

Dr. McCoy stepped around the front of him, holding an index finger up. "Follow my finger," she instructed, moving it from the left side to the right. His eyes went along with her. "Okay. Where are your parents?"

"Mom's on her Divorcees' Retreat. She told me not to disturb her unless it was really important."

"This is really important," Dr. McCoy told him, then shined a light into his eyes.

Blue. They were so blue.

Ethan exhaled, like he wasn't so sure. "Not as important as hooking up with that dentist from Central."

Dr. McCoy tutted at that. "I'm going to run to Coach Bradford's office and use his phone to call her, okay? Olivia, will you watch Ethan?

And holler if he needs anything." She rushed off, leaving a roll of gauze trailing across the floor behind her.

"You sure you're all right?" I asked again. The stark paleness of his skin made his light blond hair look like an actual color in the locker room lights.

He gave me this half smile and laughed. Then winced. "Yeah. Did I get the first down?"

"And then some," I told him.

"Nice." He squinted his eyes as if he were having trouble making me out. "I know you." I raised an eyebrow, reminded myself this idiot might need brain surgery soon. "You're the most popular girl at this school."

I felt my face turn red, even though it was such a stupid thing to say. "I am not." Of course not. Adrienne was the most popular, and I knew my place. Solid number two.

Another drop of blood escaped. "You should be," he told me.

Then he passed out.

9

Practice. Yelling. Stunting.

Adrienne is in Renatta Youngblood's face, about as cheerful as a raging bull. She stretches her tan arm into the air, fist closed, elbow perfectly straight. "Is *this* straight?" she demands.

Renatta looks at her, shaking her head. "Yes, but—"

"But what?" Adrienne asks. "But you're from a secret fucking religion that doesn't believe in straight lines?"

"No, but—"

"No wonder everyone thinks you're such a dumb slut. Does it always work when a guy tells you he's lost his clothes and needs to borrow yours?"

There is an audible intake of breath and a chuckle from Anna Talbert before Adrienne steps away. Renatta tugs on the end of her braid as if to stop a retort, her eyes flashing dangerously against her brown skin as she stares at Adrienne's back.

"Do it *again*," Adrienne says, staring at the line of us.

"Adrienne," Claire calls out, a whine in her voice. She turns up her watch. "We're already fifteen minutes over. I have to pick up my sister."

"Fine." Adrienne crosses her arms. "Claire can leave."

Thirteen voices rise up in protest.

I feel Adrienne's eyes on me, but I refuse to return her gaze. "Olivia?" she calls.

I'm co-captain. It's my decision. I'm supposed to tell them to do it again. "Call it," I say, staring off at the football field.

"Fine!" she yells, looking upward as if only Jesus Himself could help her now. "You can all go. But when we suck, you'll all know why. Olivia—" she's calling out.

Before she can finish, I'm making my way across the grass to the locker room with the rest of the squad.

When I go inside, Renatta is at the locker next to mine, throwing shampoo bottles violently into her shower bag. I pull off my T-shirt as Adrienne comes in, brushing past me like I'm not there.

"What is her *problem*?" Renatta demands once she's out of earshot. "Is she not getting laid or something?"

I wince, but she doesn't notice.

"She's such a bitch. The way she talks to our faces, I can only imagine the shit she says behind our backs," Renatta spits out. I'm not surprised she's saying it. Everyone calls Adrienne a bitch all the time. But only when she's not around. The fear she instills in them is primal, and they're afraid for good reason. She knows more about most of these girls' lives than they know about themselves. Renatta calms, eyes me, the casual way my head is turned into this conversation. "Are you going to tell on me?" she demands.

I stare at her, letting her worry for a minute. She's earned it. She's not up there at the top with us. She doesn't have the right to run her mouth, and it doesn't hurt me in that moment to exercise a little power over her. I want to feel more important than somebody right now.

And that's what makes me such a shitty person. "No," I finally say.

Renatta visibly relaxes at my tone. "You really broke up with Ethan, then?" she asks.

My heart drops like a stone. Did she see us talking? If she did, she wouldn't guess what happened with Adrienne. It would still seem like I was the one in control. That's what's important. "Who said that?" I ask.

She inclines her head. Adrienne is leaning against one of the lockers in nothing but her underwear, laughing loudly at some joke, forcing everyone's attention back to her, same as always. Her eyes meet mine, a challenge in them, and then flit away until it's hard to be sure what I saw.

It was my secret. It was the horrible thing *she* did to *me*, and it was supposed to make her a miserable person who alienated her best friend for a boy she didn't care about. Instead, she's whispering my breakup to everyone in school, making me the loser. She doesn't feel bad at all.

I don't know why I thought it'd be different when my brother died. Why I thought she'd for one second care about me and what I needed. Not give and take secrets like presents exchanged in times of need.

I shake my head, turning back to Renatta. "Yeah. We did. I'm dating someone else." The lie rolls off my tongue, rebuilding the walls around me. If I'm desirable, it doesn't matter if Ethan and I broke up.

"Who?" she asks, her head tilted to the side.

I lean closer to her, my lips curling into a smile. I'm in a show and I'm fantastic. "It's a secret," I whisper.

She returns the look conspiratorially, throwing a towel over her shoulder. "Anyway, I really am sorry," Renatta says. "Whatever everyone says about you, Ethan's so nice. I thought he really liked you." There's almost a gleam in her eye, like *thank God Ethan finally wised up and saw the real Olivia*.

Like my brother's death left me exposed, freeing Ethan from a spell I'd cast.

Renatta follows the others into the shower. I'm left behind.

Adrienne was my best friend, I think. She brought me my homework when I was sick. I cried with her the day her dog died. We created a No

Boys Club in middle school, baked cookies on snow days, told each other every detail when we lost our virginity.

Smoked our first joint together, stole our first test, forwarded the first naked picture of one of our classmates.

I never should've let her. I never should've let her control me. I should've been a better person.

I have to do something.

I'm across the cold tiles of the locker room before I think about it, my feet slapping as I go. Instinctively, I twirl the code to Adrienne's locker—Claire and Adrienne and I all have one another's, in case of emergency. Her cell phone sits innocuously on top of a pile of her clothes—her flawless clothes, an expensive pair of bright pink-and-green-printed pants and a loose tank top her mom found in Chicago. An outfit so cheerful, I could only read it as meant to spite me. I grab the phone.

I type in her code and click open her texts. The very first one is from Ethan.

Has she forgiven you yet?

I almost laugh. That's what they think I am. That's what they both think I am.

I take a screenshot. Heart pounding outside of my rib cage, out of my body, into the floor, I hit forward. The phone prompts me to select contacts. I select the special group Adrienne has for cheerleaders. Send.

The sound of phones chirping in unison echoes over the walls. My fingers tremble. Nerves. Excitement. Adrenaline.

There must be more.

I scroll through, clicking and screenshotting conversations at random and forwarding to the cheer list. I try not to read them, because I can't stand to know what she's said about me—words jump out as I go: *slut, idiot, unhinged.* I know it's all horrible, every vicious word, and I want them to see it, too. I don't want her to be able to hide behind a lie anymore—she should be as exposed as I feel. Even thinking about her, the way she creeps under the radar of all her misdeeds, I feel sick to my stomach. *They have to know.*

I put the phone back meticulously, exactly how I found it, and slide the locker closed. My breath is the only sound in the room.

I gather my things and leave calmly. I did it. I made the first move. By myself. They'll all see I'm not her puppet—not anymore.

Outside, a light breeze plays over the trees around the school. The sound of a football coach's whistle floats up the hill from the stadium, cutting through the quiet. The leaves are changing color, the swift smell of cold making them shudder on their branches. They'll be falling soon.

I know what they call this kind of quiet.

The calm before the storm.

10

LAST MONTH

"Do we still love each other?"

Twilight was streaming in through a small crack in the blinds, barely lighting the room. Ethan was at the edge of the bed, sitting, his head buried in his hands. No shirt on, his beautiful, long torso bare in front of me.

The words stopped me, but not like they should have.

"You don't love me?" I asked.

"No," he said, turning his face. "No. Of course I do." But he sounded so tired.

His mom was out of town for the weekend. We'd holed up in his bedroom and done the things we did when we were alone. That was the right thing, I told myself. That's what we'd always done.

Except now it was different. Ethan wanted to go get ice cream, watch a movie, grab fries at the Rough House with Coxie and Claire. I wanted to lock ourselves inside and not leave the solitude even for a minute.

"Sometimes I wonder, though," he said.

I scooted over from where I was sitting cross-legged in one of his too-big T-shirts, and moved behind him. Wrapped my arms around his waist and rested my cheek against the warm skin of his back.

I closed my eyes and thought about nothing.

"Remember that night at the lake?" he asked me, and I heard the smile in his voice.

My fingers tensed up, my face moving away from his skin. "We were at the lake when we got the call about my brother."

He turned quickly to face me, his mouth an apology. "Not *that* night. I meant the night we—" He trailed off, the memory ruined.

It hit me in a second then which night he meant. That night eight months after first meeting in the locker room, with the lake water lapping and our hearts banging against each other. He had told me he loved me, and we kissed and we did all the things we'd never done before. And then we did something else—*this*. For the first time. And when he looked at me with those bright blue eyes, I felt like a good person. Like a person who deserved happiness.

It's so hard to remember that feeling.

There on the bed, I wanted to tell him it was okay. But everything in his eyes questioned who I was. He'd always questioned, but the answer had changed. I had been a girl pretending. Now I was just the remnant of a girl pretending.

You can't love something that was never whole to begin with.

I didn't know what else to do, so I kissed him.

11

I've never seen a car crash, but I've spent a lot of time imagining them. Brakes screeching, car slamming into a tree, the sound of metal against metal. Those bright spotlights. That acrid smell.

I imagine that's what school will be like tomorrow.

In my room, I open up the list of schools I made, all far away from here—pretty schools with sunny West Coast skies or crisp autumn leaves or snowcapped mountains in the distance. Then I dig into my bag and uncrumple the list of tutors. I run my fingers over the names, tracing the letters. Vera Drake. Justin Thomas. Whit DuRant.

Whit DuRant.

Adrienne hates him. The way she hates Michaela Verday with her class presidency or Meisha Allen winning every talent show with her perfect voice. Whit DuRant is Buckley's prized athletic possession—a state champion golfer with a GPA that has colleges drooling at his feet. He has an easy better-than-you attitude that he wears around school like an Olympic medal.

I think I hate him, too.

My phone buzzes from where I've locked it in my desk drawer. I am too nervous to open it. I know I've done something bad. When the cheerleaders read those texts, they'll know about Adrienne and Ethan and me and God-knows-what-else.

I sacrificed my own secret to expose her and, even though I know it was worth it, I'm not ready to face reality yet. I need her to see us on the same footing—to know I can be her equal and not her toy.

When she's down and out, she'll need me. And when everyone else knows what she's done to me, maybe they'll start to understand. Maybe I can escape all this hatred. Finally.

Something moves outside of my bedroom door. "Olivia." Mom peeks in, first her messy bun perched on top of her head, then her thin-framed glasses until she's half in, half out.

Story of my life.

"Are you okay?" she asks. She does that a lot lately—like she cares.

"I'm fine," I lie. How would she know the difference?

"I made you dinner," she says. "It's in the fridge."

I turn back to my computer, keying in the name of the first school on my list. Ryan smiles back at me from a picture on my desk. "Thanks."

I can't do this right now. I can't deal with trying to produce what she would consider an appropriate emotional response. Even the thought of it is exhausting, especially when I can practically see the cogs spinning as she tries to string the words together to speak to me, build a bridge over the chasm too deep to cross.

She can't decide to turn on her feelings now, like it's time for some special relationship. I'd filled that hole with cement a long time ago and done perfectly fine on my own since. And if I hadn't, well—it was still too late.

When I look back up, she's made it all the way into the room. On my computer screen, the cursor is spinning as a new page loads. My heart pumps a kick drum rhythm as I wait. "Can I help you?" I finally ask.

A pretty school building with brick walls comes up. Admissions facts. Just looking at the average GPA, my heart sinks.

"How are you doing?" Mom asks. She clips the words strangely on the end like she is translating into a language she knows only the technicalities of.

It pisses me off.

Using my toes, I swivel around in my chair. "Exactly how I was doing before Ryan died. So if you could revert to pre-dead-Ryan life, I would really appreciate it. I'm not going to have a breakdown or anything, I promise," I say, choosing my most hateful words carefully. I don't need a guidance counselor with a local university master's degree to tell me I'm deflecting.

She doesn't say anything. I can feel her growing colder by the minute, turning in on herself. I used to wonder how Mom could be so bad at talking to other people—watching her make stilted conversation with the PTA parents and the cheer moms or try to find a connection with our bright-faced, Buckley-bred teachers. I used to wonder how she could be that bad at talking to me, first like I was an adult when I was too young to know better, then like I was an acquaintance, after I was too old for it to matter. I remember a sign she used to keep over our kitchen sink in our apartment in Charlotte, before we moved to Buckley: ROUTINE ROUTINE ROUTINE, it reminded her. "You think it's funny to talk to me like that?" she asks.

"Deep down inside, I'm laughing so hard I can barely breathe." I swivel back around in my chair, adjust the picture of Ryan ever so slightly on my desk, and wait for her to leave. I know I should feel bad for what I said, but I don't.

"You're welcome for dinner," she tells me, and then slams the door so hard, the frames on the wall shake.

That level of anger is practically unprecedented in our relationship.

Ryan never got mad at me. Just disappointed.

He got disappointed that time in ninth grade when Adrienne and I gave Daniel Smith a pair of Sheila Reeves's underwear that we'd stolen from her house. I remember because it was the first time he looked at me differently. I'd spent my whole life living for Ryan's approval, and when we moved to Buckley, we'd become closer than ever, trapped together in the house on Main Street. Things had changed, though, when I'd met Adrienne. Ryan and I had stopped spending so much time together, the way older and younger siblings do. The truth was, somewhere along the way, Adrienne became as close to me as a sister. We had the same tainted blood running in our veins.

But Ryan never minded. *Liv* is what he used to call me. I can always hear him saying it with a laugh in his voice, showing me the world from an angle only he saw, pointing out some Buckley hypocrisy or quoting a cult movie. I couldn't ever be the type of person Ryan was, but I *had* Ryan and that was enough.

I can still see the way he looked at me with so much devotion, as his most loved family member, the little girl he protected. But I didn't see the look that day. I remember it, when his eyes met mine. I didn't see the little sister he adored reflected back, but someone else. He looked at me that day the way everyone else did: like I was dangerous, and he had to stop me. Or get away from me.

Mostly I remember because it was the day he got accepted into Michigan.

12

LAST YEAR

I jimmied the lock on Meghan Stanley's locker, trying to force it open. Meghan was Mrs. Baker's teacher's aide, and it was rumored she kept copies of old tests to create study guides. Everyone knew Mrs. Baker re-used test questions. I'd been instructed to "fetch," but I felt I'd been mis-informed as to the locker combination that Adrienne got off Meghan's boyfriend.

The stupid thing was, I'd never even use the test myself. After two and a half years with us in a school this small, the teachers knew who the smart kids were and who the dumb ones were. The Mrs. Bakers of the world expected me to be a prototypical cheerleading dumbass, so if I did too well on the test, they'd know I cheated—that all of us cheated. Adrienne was the brains of this operation, clearly. She schemed the schemes and she made the grades. The faculty knew what kind of person Adrienne was; they just couldn't catch her.

I never understood why she bothered. Cheating wasn't worth the has-sle for me; if I wanted to memorize the answers, I'd study. No one cared about my grades anyway.

"What are you doing?" I heard behind me.

I jumped around, face-to-face with Ethan Masters, star fullback. I gestured at the locker. "Getting tampons. For Meghan. I think she gave me the wrong combo." I smiled, pleased. I'd managed to totally put him off Meghan, and I didn't look like a petty thief anymore.

Ethan winced. "I think that falls on the side of too much information."

"I had a sign, announcing it." I shrugged. "So no suspicious guys would come up behind me, asking questions. Must've fallen down."

Ethan smiled, and I loved it. He moved in a little closer to me. "Can I tell you a secret?" he asked.

Of course. "What?" I returned coyly.

"Some of the guys on the team told me not to mess with you."

His words took me aback more than a little. Sure, I hadn't dated anybody seriously, but the guys seemed to like me. I was pretty, I was popular, and I looked great in our cheerleading uniforms. Why would they say that about me?

I didn't answer.

"They said you serve Adrienne Maynard."

I leaned back against the locker, folding my arms, pretending it didn't hurt. "They're just mad I wouldn't go out with them."

He shrugged. "I told them I'd talked to you before. And you weren't like her at all."

I blinked, momentarily stunned. "I'm not," I heard myself say.

"I can tell." He nodded at me and then turned as if he were going to walk away.

"Why were you asking about me?"

He looked back, grinning. "You can probably guess that."

I chewed my bottom lip, watching him go. Left the scene, test forgotten.

That's the part Adrienne knows. She still brings that up.

13

Anna Talbert is waiting in my parking spot at eight a.m. We've been at a tense truce since the party two years ago. She hates me—I know she does and I don't blame her—but she stays in line for Adrienne. She smiles at me and compliments my clothes and invites me to parties for Adrienne.

I hate everything Anna Talbert reminds me of, and it's not even her fault.

"Where have you been?" she demands, marching over to me in oversized knee-high boots. "I've sent you, like, a thousand texts."

I stare at her silently.

"Haven't you seen?" she demands, dropping the edge in her voice.

"What?"

"The texts!" Anna says. "People are about to fucking mutiny."

I twirl a piece of hair around my finger, maintaining my calm. "Where's Adrienne?" I adjust my sunglasses and stare up at Anna. I watch her hate me and watch her tread carefully around me.

"Over in the old building bathroom."

I spin on my heel to walk off through the parking lot. "Everyone's saying she hooked up with Ethan!" Anna yells behind me. Even though I don't turn, I know she's smiling.

Buckley High has two buildings, connected by a breezeway. The senior parking lot runs the length of the old building with the gym hanging out in the back. The newer building gets its name by virtue of being built in the eighties. People cluster together on the connecting sidewalks before school starts and between classes, kicking the ancient vending machines and trying to text on the low. The whole place is essentially held together with Central High's unused budget and misplaced pride.

I tear into the old building from the parking lot.

Elona Mabry corners me in the hallway, clutching her cell phone in her hand until her knuckles turn white. "Tell her I quit. Tell her I can't believe she knew that about Daniel and told Anna *and* tried to blame everything on Michaela. Tell her—"

I put my hand up to silence her. "You think you're the only one with problems?" I ask her, looking up and down the hall. "This isn't about you. And don't take this personally, but honestly, you should be grateful that you're done with him." After the words come out of my mouth, I realize they were likely not as helpful as I intended.

"Do you *know* what she said about you?" Elona asks me then. "Do you know how pathetic she thinks you are?"

I stare at her, stone-faced. No matter how pathetic Adrienne currently thinks I am, she finds the rest of them infinitely more so, and I can't drop that persona now.

Elona pulls her notebooks to her chest, eyes slitted at me. As she walks away, I hear a defiant *bitch*.

I glance over my shoulder nervously, then push my way into the bathroom.

Adrienne is in the corner, typing frantically away at her phone. Her dark hair cascades into her face, blocking her eyes from sight. But she looks up when I come in, and everything about her look is defeated.

I should feel good. Finally, a victory.

"Olivia. Thank God you're here," she say, and then she crosses the room and throws her arms around me, like she's not even Adrienne anymore. She pulls back quickly. She knows she shouldn't be showing me a sign of weakness. "Everyone's saying they're going to quit the squad and they're hating me out loud and I totally *don't care*, but I—" She stops mid-sentence, looking at a new message on her phone screen. She covers her mouth with her hand, then pushes her palm over the rest of her face. "Who would do that? Fuck around with my phone? The whole school has seen me sexting with Daniel Smith, and it was only because I wanted good gossip."

"He's disgusting," I say, because she wants sympathy and I won't give it.

She looks up at me, at the harsh words. "You hate me." She shakes her head.

I do. I want to tell her how I *won* this time. But "How could you do that to me? How could you sleep with Ethan?" is what comes out instead.

My still stoic face is reflected back at me as tears well up in her eyes. "O, I'm sorry. It didn't mean anything. But w-why is it always that *I* slept with Ethan?" She pushes the tears away from her bottom eyelash. "*I* did it, like I forced him or something. We slept with each other. *I* didn't cheat on Renatta, and I didn't force anyone to buy me alcohol, and I'm not a slut. He did it, too, O. Ethan did it, too. All these people are so pissed at me, but they made their own choices and did things themselves. They want to blame *me*. *You* want to blame me. I'm not some evil mastermind. I'm not anything except who I am, and I made a mistake, so stop looking at me like you're so much better than me!" She's yelling, and I blink, slow. "You're all I think about, all I'm ever worrying about. I didn't know what to do, and I was watching you withering away. He's pushing you and I pulled you and no one can get to you. What was I supposed to do?"

I don't say anything.

She steps so close to me, I have no choice but to stare straight at her. "It's me and you against the world, O. That's always what it is, right?"

It almost feels physically painful for us to be this close because the thing is, I *do* want it to be us against the world again. I want it so badly that I can taste it, visceral and alive. I miss everything we used to be in that moment, in the before—the two of us, young and wild and not caring about anything. And even when it hurt, something about it still felt good.

It was easier then, when I was so lost in where Adrienne ended and I began. I never had to think about if what I did was right or wrong, because if we were doing it together nothing ever felt out of place. Some people spend their whole lives waiting for someone to love them, the good and bad, and I wanted that someone to be Adrienne, from the moment she set eyes on me. Maybe I was always waiting for her approval, waiting for her smile. But I wasn't waiting anymore.

I finally beat her. Wasn't that enough?

Because I still feel it—in the months she's been cold and we've drifted apart. I still miss her so much. I miss *me* so much. I miss us.

"Right," I agree. And her shoulders slump as she breathes out, the relief palpable on her face.

"I need help," she tells me as her phone buzzes again. "I need someone who can do damage control like you can. You're literally the only person in this school I can trust right now."

I think of Claire but don't mention it. I feel as if my brain has rebelled and I've turned on autopilot. Instead, I say, "Okay."

She breathes in a shaky breath. "I knew. I knew you were mad, but not that mad, right? Everything is hard right now, but we'll find our way back. Now we have to deal with this." She pushes down her hair and looks at herself in the mirror, fixing her makeup. I hear the way she keeps using the word *we*. As if we are two parts of something whole.

"Maybe you should say the texts weren't you," I suggest, trying to fit back in the place I'm supposed to belong.

She glares up at me. "Don't be an idiot, O. That would never work."

Idiot. It hits me like a brick all over again.

Things don't change, not on Adrienne's watch. Of course I'm just an idiot to her. Still.

Meredith Rogers bangs through the bathroom door right then, screaming, "Fuck you, Adrienne Maynard," and Adrienne goes straight into flattering mode, all "Chill, Meredith," and not even completely knowing why, I chime in, "Calm down, pull yourself together," and instantly it's two on one.

As Adrienne soothes Meredith, all cool crisis-situation charm, she whispers to me, "Damage control, O? Can you call a team meeting?"

I nod like the good girl I am, backing out of the door, not knowing *why* exactly, even in that moment. I'm walking down the hall with my arms crossed over my chest, wondering if I can do it—really just pretend all this never happened. Rewind back into what it was like before Ryan was dead and when Ethan was mine. Find that girl again. Be that girl again.

At least that girl felt control over something.

Alone, I exit the old building and cross the sidewalk to the new.

Inside it's chaos.

A large group of students is gathered around a locker. It's Claire's—one of the prime lockers in school. The janitor scrubs away at the door of the locker—uselessly, from the bit of paint I see—and Dr. Rickards is screaming at him to "Go faster, dammit" and trying to clear students away from the scene. The janitor ducks the cloth for a moment, and that's when I'm able to make out the word on the locker.

The locker says DYKE.

14

People rush in from both sides of the hall. In a panic, I open a classroom door to escape. A trash can is just inside the door, so I kick it over. "Shit!" I bang my fist against the hard wall, my other hand still clasped around my cell phone. I instantly realize I've made a huge mistake because that was outlandishly painful. "What. Is. Wrong. With. You?" I demand of myself, turning around and hurling the phone across the room like I'm trying out for a spot with the Atlanta Braves. It hits a glass beaker sitting on the counter. The beaker falls to the ground and shatters, and my phone bounces sadly away from the crash.

I take ragged breaths in and out, bathing in the destruction. Nothing has ever hurt as bad as my hand does right now and felt as good at the same time. Until it hits me, in the silence, that someone is watching me.

I look up. Whit DuRant is sitting in a desk across the room by the window, his pencil hovering loosely over a paper. We stare at each other. I push a piece of hair behind my ear with my good hand. "What?" I ask.

Turning away from him, I walk to the broken beaker, bend down, and carefully collect the remnants of glass in my hand. I carry them over to the trash can, picking it up and letting the glass pieces fall into it.

I go back over and kneel next to the counter again to swipe up the last few shards of glass, watching Whit scribble away through the desks. That is a dumb move. One of the pieces slices into my ring finger, creating a crimson smile across the skin. *"Shit."* I drop the glass, my eyes watering. My knuckle is already throbbing, and blood oozes from the cut. I slide my monogrammed ring—the one that matches Adrienne's—off my finger. The blood leaves a streak all down my hand.

"Well, that was something," Whit tells his paper, as if my tantrum was so dull, he just now noticed it. When I stand to face him, he stops, glancing at me right as a tear spills down my cheek. He jumps up from his desk, coming toward me. "Jesus!" he says when he catches sight of my bleeding finger, his face breaking out into genuine worry. "You need to go to the nurse."

"Fuck the nurse," I say, defiant through tears. "Fuck this whole place. How can I be so goddamn reckless? I had her. I had Adrienne!"

I smack the ring down on a table. "But *some*how I got sucked right back in, and it's *Claire* they're going after. How do they even *know*? I am so stupid." I look right at him. "Who forwards texts without reading them? I'm actually as stupid as you all think I am."

Whit's eyes search mine for a second. Finally, he says, "I have some Band-Aids in my bag. Hang on." He turns away and goes to his book bag, lying against the desk. I squeeze the forearm of my injured hand as hard as I can, as if that will help. Like a Boy Scout, he returns to me with the Band-Aids.

I hold out my hand to him.

"You need to clean this," he says, wincing as he turns my palm faceup in his own hand. "It's bleeding a lot, but I don't think it's as bad as it looks." He unexpectedly reaches around me, tearing a paper towel from a roll on the lab counter and wiping off the blood as best he can. His callused fingers smooth the Band-Aid over my cut, and then he trails a finger over my skinned knuckle. I try not to make any sound and instead focus on the sight of his thick brown hair swept to the side like he's some sort of junior senator. When I look down at my finger, the Band-Aid is soaking up the blood, growing darker as it stems the flow. He was as gentle as possible, but it still hurts. It hurts like hell.

"You sent out those texts," he tells me as he finishes. It isn't a question. "About all the cheerleaders."

My blood goes cold. Under the haze of pain, I realize everything I just told him. "What do you know about it?"

He shrugs. "Only what everyone else does. Ethan Masters?"

I pull my hand back. "Don't say that name to me."

He shrugs again.

"Don't say anything about this," I command, using my most authoritative voice.

Something blazes into place behind his eyes. A challenge. "Why not?"

"Because you know what's good for you."

He snorts. "Are you going to thank me?"

A moment or a second or an hour passes where he's looking at me, all expectant.

"I changed my mind. Do whatever you want. No one cares what you say." Then I turn and walk out.

15

LAST YEAR

I dipped a fry in ketchup and held it up over the cardboard carton, watching as the ketchup dripped like blood spatter back onto the table. In my peripheral vision, Savannah Harrison was drinking a water bottle full of toilet water.

I'm the one who replaced her old water bottle.

Claire wasn't eating. She was running her fingers over the screen of her phone, texting God-knows-who. She finally looked up from her screen. "Are you okay?"

I bit off the end of my fry, watching Savannah drink. "Do you think there's, like, karma for every bad thing you do?" I looked away because it was too disgusting. "Ethan thinks there is."

Claire set down her phone in one of her Serious Claire Moves. "He did not say that."

I sighed. "He must have been talking to his mom again. He thinks I latch on to Adrienne because of some kind of psychological trauma. Like, I let her control me to fill a gap in my life."

"He doesn't know Adrienne," Claire replied. "If anyone's psychologically traumatized, it's her."

"He *hates* her," I said. "Like for no reason. And he'll tell me I'm not her and to stop acting like her. He's such a jerk about it."

"Does he say that about me?" Claire asked, her eyes a little wider.

"Of course not." I got up from the table, sliding past Savannah as I did. With my right hand, I knocked the bottle to the floor, letting the contents spill everywhere.

"Bitch," she called out behind me.

I closed my eyes, absorbing the blow.

16

Claire is in her car.

Her tiny little Oldsmobile, a laughable hunk of junk her grandfather handed off to her when she turned fifteen, is parked on the far end of the senior lot, doors locked. I knock on the window and she lets me in. Glancing around, I toss my bag onto the floorboard and slide into the seat beside her. "This should get them talking," she mutters. Her eyes are bloodshot, a bottle of cheap vodka resting between her thighs.

"I don't care what they think," I say. It's almost true. I get a better look at her then. "Are you drunk?"

"A dyke actually. Haven't you seen?" She wraps both hands around the bottle and tilts her head back to gulp the clear liquid. I cringe as a droplet escapes her mouth. Her cheeks are blotchy. Tears follow the vodka down.

"Claire," I demand, ripping the bottle out of her hands. "Stop."

"Ellie won't even talk to me anymore. She ignores me while we work every day like she never cared about me at all. Because of Coxie." She puts a hand up to her cheek. "Who would do this?" She turns to me. "Did Ethan really sleep with Adrienne?"

I take a heavy sip of the drink as a yes.

"What's wrong with her?" she asks, letting the question sit in the silence. It's so easy to let her say that—what's wrong with Adrienne—because it's the right question.

But what's wrong with us if we're her best friends?

"What's wrong with us?" she asks then, as if she read my mind.

I lean my head against the window. *Just tell her.* "I don't know."

"What did she say to you?"

I think about that for a minute. "That she's sorry."

"Did you forgive her?" Claire asks. She drinks again.

I shrug.

"She probably is sorry. That's what she told me. That you two didn't mean anything by those texts you sent about Ellie. Not that anyone even knew it was Ellie, so thanks for that. At least I get to weather this storm alone."

I swallow. *We two*. Wait, I forwarded texts from Adrienne to me? Shit.

"She said she could make it go away." Claire twists her fingers up in her hair. "That's like her, isn't it? To create the problem, fix it, and then wait for thanks."

"I'm so sorry, Claire," I say then, though I'm not even honestly sure what the texts said. It was so incredibly idiotic to send those screenshots without reading them all. Adrienne would've never done anything that stupid.

Claire looks over at me, and I see the accusation there. "At least she offered to fix it."

"Claire, I—"

She shrugs. "I mean, it's fine. It was an accident, right? Coxie will do what I tell him to." She finishes this sadly, leaning against the window. "Would you mind leaving me be, O? I'm really sorry; I need to be alone right now. I need to think."

I want to point out that she won't do much thinking once she's fucked up. To remind her she weighs ninety pounds and is a notorious lightweight. To tell her that I can fix it, too.

But I'm not sure how.

I grab the door handle and then stop. "Just please don't—"

"I'm not going to drive," she answers automatically.

I get out.

17

LAST YEAR

Adrienne threw her head back laughing, the moonlight glinting off her dark hair. I always loved the sound of her laughter, like a reassurance that I had done or said the right thing. Crickets called in the distance as we sat on the stone bleachers, the stairs leading down into the empty football field. The lights were out, the stars shining as they can only do in the middle of nowhere. I grabbed up the bottle of vodka that Adrienne had talked our twenty-four-year-old cheer coach into buying for us. Coach Evans would be fired for it later that year. She went to the admin about some hazing Adrienne was doing to the JV girls, and Adrienne got her fired.

But for now, it was the three of us—Claire, Adrienne, and me—in the darkness, with waves of alcohol and freedom rolling off us.

"Fine, fine," Adrienne said, letting me have the bottle. "It's yours. Truth or dare."

I licked my lips. "What should I do, Claire?"

Claire grinned conspiratorially. "Truth."

"Truth," I said.

Adrienne's eyes flashed as wind blew her black hair around her face. "Were you really scared to have sex with Connor from Central? Is that why you backed out?"

I turned red. She'd been so cool about it at the time. All *I totally get it* and *if you're not ready, you're not ready*, after she'd spent over a month hooking me up with him once she'd noticed me drooling over all his social media accounts. But then we'd met in real life, and he was so dull and small-town simple, and there was no way I was going to have sex with him, no matter how much Ade insisted it was time for me to get it over with.

I'd thought she was cool with it. I should've known better.

"He sucked," I told her defiantly.

She laughed in a mean way. "Who cares? He was hot. I didn't tell you to marry him! God, since when are you so fucking puritanical, O?"

I looked down, fiddling with the cap of the vodka. "That's not how I wanted it, okay?"

She grinned. "O-kay, then. Shit answer. Drink!"

I did, alcohol coursing like anger through my veins.

"My turn!" Claire called, reaching across me and holding the bottle aloft triumphantly, cutting through the tension. She stood up on the bleacher in front of us, letting the alcohol fall into her mouth until we were both laughing again. She stopped and finally called out, "Truth!"

I looked over at Adrienne to see her watching me, ready to judge whatever my question would be. I wanted her to like it.

"Do you really never get tired of Coxie?" I asked. Coxie and Claire had been dating since they were toddlers, basically. Claire was sassy and athletic and adorable. Coxie was bleach blond and simple and usually high. Accordingly, he orbited around her like she was the earth and he the moon.

Claire stared at me thoughtfully. I could see her eyes shifting between Adrienne and me, and then she said, "I never get tired of Coxie." It was a *total* shit answer until she said, "But it helps that I'm not in love with him."

Adrienne and I looked at Claire and then at each other. I was the first one to speak. "What the hell, Claire?"

She shrugged and sat down on the other side of Adrienne with a sneaky smile.

"So you like someone else, then?" Adrienne said.

Claire smiled bigger. Of course Adrienne was right. Of course she knew what Claire was trying to tell us before I'd been able to figure it out.

"I just . . . ," Claire started. Then said, "You can't tell anybody, all right? I'm serious."

Adrienne put her hand out in front of us. "Just the three of us, right? Get in here."

I put my hand on top of hers, and Claire's hand went over mine. Adrienne squeezed. "Promise," I said.

"Okay," Claire said, staring down at our intertwined hands. "Her name's Ellie." I felt Adrienne's hand clench harder. "She works with me at the Rough House." Then she looked up at the two of us, waiting to hear what we'd say. I wanted to ask her a hundred questions. If she liked girls and if she always knew, and how had she hooked up with Coxie if she liked girls, and if she would tell people.

"Do you think she likes you back?" Adrienne asked the perfect question instead of all the idiotic things on the tip of my tongue.

Claire laughed, taking a swig of vodka. "She kissed me when we finished cleaning up last week. Back behind the building. You two better not tell anybody, because she wants it on the down low, too. But how could she not like me, right?" Her voice went kind of high, as if masking nerves.

"Right," Adrienne agreed. "Oh my God, this is such a relief! I thought you were going to marry Coxie."

I leaned over Adrienne, taking her cue. "Tell us everything."

I'd never seen Claire look so happy.

18

The bleachers are hard and hot. Cement bleachers—another reminder of a bygone Buckley era—burn up the backs of my legs.

I decide I don't care.

I braved the quad during lunch, but it was a hellscape of cheerleaders who counted me as an Adrienne substitute for their hatred, people asking whether Claire Barber was really into girls, and Ethan watching me steadily. Before, it would've been so easy to smooth over the cheerleaders, to talk to them about context, about not believing everything you read, about how *this is totally someone else's fault anyway so go attack them.*

But I realized I can't do it anymore. I don't want to do any of it.

So I'm going to read every message instead.

I scroll through them in my phone. Every goddamn message Adrienne had typed up, all perfect, perfect Adrienne messages. She tears people down perfectly. She builds people up perfectly. She tells the best jokes and quotes the best movies and insults you in the most unexpected way.

You want to tell her your secrets.

I scroll through our conversation about Claire.

Adrienne: She MIA again??

Me: El must do it *right.* Maybe we should hook up with girls?

Adrienne: Ha-ha. She was so much more fun when she was pretending to be straight

Me: Limited shelf life. They fight all the time. I call them Coxie probs

Adrienne: Omg, I just snorted. Call me xo

It's a singular feeling to realize how much you can hate yourself. There it is in writing—me mocking my best friend's relationship problems with glee. We were the only two people in the world Claire told about Ellie, and it was another joke to us. We didn't deserve her trust.

It was such an old conversation, I don't even know how it had gotten to the top of Adrienne's recent messages.

There are two more from me. One that's some embarrassing story about hooking up with Ethan—I only told Adrienne because she was mad at me and I wanted her to let it go. And then another about how useless the cheerleaders were. It's all framed very nicely to capture what a terrible person I am.

I click onto the screenshot I was saving for last. Adrienne and Ethan. I'd read the most recent texts only yesterday.

Adrienne: O's simple. I just need to tell her the right thing and this fight between us will be over in a day. I can't help you

Ethan: I can't believe you

Adrienne: You don't get it. She loves me. She tolerates you. And now there's no reason to do that anymore

Ethan: That's what you wanted, isn't it? For her to catch us

Adrienne: Like you didn't fucking want it too

Ethan: I wanted her to stop hurting. Now we've ruined everything.

Adrienne: Ethan

Adrienne: Just meet me after practice tomorrow. Let's talk.

I drop my phone finally, letting it all burn through me. Feeling the betrayal as fresh as before, I can't believe I let myself fall for her all over again. I was willing to let it go earlier, to admit to myself that this revenge idea was all a mistake, to start rebuilding. But this isn't friendship. And I can't let her have me back.

I have to end this. I have to get away from it all.

How?

I lie back, staring up at the sun until everything in my line of vision blurs. Closing my eyes, bright spots are left dancing on my eyelids. I keep them closed for a while.

My eyes clear out after a few minutes, and when I can see again, I reach into my pocket and extract the list of names. I turned the whole school upside down and blew everything to shit for Adrienne without her knowing anything, and I'm still a simpleton who can be pulled back in with a perfectly practiced string of words.

Not this time.

Something drops next to my head, making me blink away from the paper.

"Here."

I glance up. Whit DuRant is standing beside me, glaring down, a baseball cap pulled over his eyes. I sit up and look back down to see he's dropped my monogrammed ring onto the bleachers. There's a bit of dried blood on the *O*.

"What is that?" I ask, even though it's obvious.

He sighs as if looking at me were too much of a burden for him. "If you don't want people to know that you lost your mind and destroyed school property, don't leave your monogrammed ring in the midst of all the destruction. Are you an idiot?"

Yes.

I feel anger and hurt mingling on my face, and I can't turn them off. Remorse fills his eyes and he tries again. "Look, I didn't mean—"

"I must be," I cut him off. "An idiot."

"I wasn't saying that," he replies.

"You did."

"Never mind." He shrugs. "I thought you might want it back. Not that I care." With that, he turns away, walking across the rest of the aisle and back up the stone staircase.

"Wait a minute!" I call after him, leaping up and swiping the ring. I jog to catch up with him near the top of the stadium. He's on his way back out to campus. I match him stride for stride.

"You're on the list," I tell him, brandishing the paper forward. It's right there: *Whit DuRant*. Salvation.

He tears the paper from my hand and stops, looking it over. "What list?"

I point at his name, right there in pencil. "The list of people who can tutor me for the SAT."

"What?" he asks, his eyes narrowing at the marks. A car drives by us in the back parking lot, slowing suspiciously as it passes before speeding off. "No," he says, thrusting the paper back at me. "Absolutely not."

He starts walking away again, turning from the school to the baseball field in the distance. Behind the field is the school's dilapidated putting green. That must be where he's going. "Mr. Doolittle said you'd help." I hurry after him.

"No," he repeats. "Ask Vera. Ask Steve. Ask anybody, I don't care."

"Why not?" I demand.

He gives me nothing in return, continuing doggedly ahead.

"What, you don't have time? You don't like me? I'm too dumb, too pretty, too scandalous? What is it? You think you're better than me?"

He stops again, his eyes shifting to mine. "Yes."

"Yes?" I ask, circling in front of him so he can't get past me. "Yes, what?"

"I think I'm better than you."

The bottom falls out, the last of my pride crumpling somewhere at his feet. "You don't know anything about me."

His gaze is intense, holding mine. This boy, *this boy*, who just has impressive hair and a killer golf swing, some boy who doesn't matter at all, says he's better than me. Where does he get off? What does he know about it? "I know that in less than twenty-four hours' time, you fucked over the people you claim to be your two best friends."

I deflate. He watches me for a moment more, defeated girl with defeated eyes, and walks around me. "She fucked me first," I say.

But it doesn't matter. He doesn't care.

No one does. Because what I did was worse.

19

LAST YEAR

We sat around a table at the Rough House, the five of us, sipping soda out of straws. It was a perfect spring day, a breeze slicing through the beginning of the summer heat. A communal tub of fries sat in the middle of the table.

"So, I've been thinking . . . ," Ethan began, and Coxie groaned.

"That again?" He sighed.

Ethan shook his head. "We need to start thinking about senior trip."

"We don't do those in Buckley," Adrienne told him. "We're not like your fancy Charleston schools, Masters."

"Sounds like a party," Coxie said, contemplating a fry. "I'm in."

"Not like a traditional senior trip," Ethan went on. "I thought—and don't laugh—something like a backpacking trip through Europe."

At that, Coxie burst out laughing, slapping his hand against the table through guffaws. The girl at the counter stared. "With whose money?" Coxie demanded.

"Not all of us have moms who are criminal psychologists," Adrienne said, grinning at Ethan with a nasty edge.

Ethan's face fell, his eyes going to the table as he shrugged. "Honey"—I touched Ethan's arm lightly—"most of us can't really afford something like that."

"Give her credit," Coxie said, pointing at me. "She didn't laugh."

Ethan lifted his eyes up to the spot where my hand rested against his arm, then up to my face. "What if you could?" he asked in a way that had *graduation present* written all over it.

I bit into a fry, relishing the thought, leaning back on the chair's two legs. But the whole time I could feel Adrienne watching me. Expecting me to say yes to what Ethan wanted, to prove that I couldn't think for myself. Backpacking through Europe was everything I dreamed about, but I couldn't stand the thought of her judgment. The thought that I couldn't live up to her carefully crafted image of me. "I don't know—don't you think Europe is kind of obvious?" I asked.

"Obvious?"

"Everything about him is obvious," Adrienne snapped, getting up from the table, leaving me wondering if I'd miscalculated and said the wrong thing. She slammed her just-vacated chair back in as Ethan rolled his eyes, and she walked over to the jukebox near the pool tables. Over Ethan's shoulder, I saw her flipping through songs.

"I don't know," I finally told him. "Wouldn't it be cool to do somewhere like South America? Somewhere where we weren't doing what everyone expected?"

"Somewhere you could be dead," Coxie interrupted, slurping his soda through a straw.

"South America," Ethan repeated. He grinned at me. "We'll have to see what my mom thinks about that."

"What do *you* think?" With Adrienne out of earshot, I could save my opportunity here—to go to Europe or South America or, shit, just across the county line.

He leaned forward. "I'd go anywhere with you." He kissed me. Hard.

I pulled away, my stomach churning uncomfortably even as my heart fluttered. Ethan tugged me one way, Adrienne another. I hated them fighting, but I hated even more the idea of them not. Adrienne insisting I was a bright star shining in the night with her, Ethan looking at me as if he kept expecting the sun to rise. No one had ever wanted me the way the two of them did. Looking back, I realize it finally made me feel important.

Adrienne leaned against the jukebox, still flipping through nineties hits. Automatically, I rose and went to her. Nothing hurt like Adrienne dismissing you.

"What's up?" I asked, sidling in beside her. I put on a big fake frown. "Ethan got you down?"

"What's the deal with him, O? Why does he think he's better than the rest of us because he's not from Buckley?" She didn't look at me as she spoke. I felt the slight like a burn on every inch of my skin. This was what Adrienne did to lesser people, people who were nothing to her. I was supposed to be above that in her eyes.

I leaned forward a little. "He doesn't always get it."

She looked up at me finally, glaring. "He *never* gets it. He controls you, and it's like you live for him. We're your friends. Tell him to realize that."

Each cold word had me reeling. "He realizes it. Plus, you didn't even hear him. He said he'd go to South America if that's what I wanted to do."

She watched him over my shoulder. When I followed her gaze, he caught my eye and gave me an ironic wave.

Adrienne slapped her hand against the jukebox, stealing my attention back. "I knew this would happen!"

"What?" I asked, thinking I could calm her down. Actually believing for a second that I could fix this.

"You. I knew as soon as you had a serious boyfriend, you'd be all wrapped up in your relationship." She said the last word contemptuously, drawing out the syllables. "This hero worship is so typically you. You see someone who can get you what you want, whatever you think you're lacking, and refuse to see everything else. Like you can't even *listen* to the suggestion that your brother's an alcoholic even though we all know he is, because he's *Ryan*, and you're *Liv*, and that's how it is."

She wouldn't look at me, and she'd used those words to cut me down to size like she was always doing to everyone else. In that moment, she turned on me. I bit my tongue, bit back tears.

"Look around, O," she said, moving in for the kill. "Claire and I are your best friends. We're the only people who won't let you down. And if there's anyone you should go to South America with"—she finally picked a song, pressing the play button hard—"it should be me."

She was probably right.

20

It's Friday—otherwise known as the day after. Claire cut school and won't answer my calls. Mr. Doolittle has had her locker door completely removed and taken all of her stuff out of it. It's particularly sick that it's her they went after when she tends to mostly stand around Adrienne and me while we scheme, but I guess it was too easy to pass up.

The wounds are still fresh and my phone buzzes constantly. People double-checking stories and making accusations and asking questions. I start responding to them all: I don't know, was that before or after my brother died? and never get a response.

The longer this goes on, the clearer it becomes how poorly conceived the whole plan was. Everything in Buckley has a life cycle. The way the math works is this—Adrienne has to convince exactly half the people she shit-talked that it was all a big misunderstanding. That keeps her in the loop on fresh gossip, party invites, etc. And eventually, since Buckley is such a small town and there are so few people, everyone else will see her enough that they will come around to her again. Because Adrienne is only ever exactly as irresistible as she chooses to be.

She's already started recon. I saw her switching desks to sit next to Elona Mabry during English today. They were laughing.

I decide to avoid her for as long as possible while I think about what to do next.

Mom packs my lunch every day—she's never trusted the school district to adequately care for my nutritional needs—and we usually all eat out on the quad at the best table. Me and Ethan and Claire and Coxie and Adrienne and whoever else we're feeling generous toward that day. Today, I pretend Mom forgot my lunch and go stand inside in the long lunch line, biting my cuticles as I wait. My eyes travel around the caf, searching out the ever-present drama in Buckley's midst.

Cate Roberts is sitting with Meghan Stanley's crew. She used to hang out with Meisha Allen and her people, but now that she's a cheerleader, I guess she's got better things to do. She was always kind of a bitch anyway, and judging by the way she's eyeing Meisha's ex, a catfight of epic proportions could break out at any second.

I can't solve an algebra problem to save my life, but looking at all these people, I don't need instructions or a manual to figure them out. It's all right there, written on their faces. Whether they're hurt or scared or superior. I have such an eye for it, Adrienne used to tell me to watch people for her. She wanted to know what they were up to. I'd know without having to ask.

With Ethan, though, I didn't see anything. Not in his face or his gestures or any other part of him. Maybe I didn't want to.

"What do you want?" the old cafeteria lady asks me.

I frown at the options. "Mac and cheese." She plops a scoop onto a cracked ceramic plate and hands it over the glass. I smile or grimace or whatever, slide down the line, and pay my bit. As I turn around and hold my tray in front of me, I survey the scene. I can pretty much sit wherever I want and no one will question me, even if they hate me. Comes with power in this school. But there's no one I want interrogating me about Ethan or Adrienne or whatever other trouble I've gotten myself into.

Most of the cafeteria's filled with long tables, but up near the front, where it smells really awful, are a couple small circular ones. Sitting alone at the one closest to the cash register is Vera Drake. I watch her for half a minute before going over to her table and plopping down in a seat.

"You mind if I join?" I ask, cracking open my Diet Coke top. She looks up from her salad and stares. Hard. Says nothing. It's really weird. People around us start staring, too. I dig into my macaroni and cheese like I don't care.

When I glance up, I catch Whit DuRant watching me from the next table over. He averts his eyes. I try to think of something to say to him, but I can't come up with anything.

"You know him?" I ask, gesturing with my fork at Whit.

Vera follows the line of my fork, then turns back to me. Her eyes are wide, as if she's not quite sure who I'm talking to. "Whit," she finally says.

"Yeah." I stab a piece of macaroni.

"He's fine," she mumbles. Fine—what a completely apt word to describe such a nonentity. Polished and smart and boring and *fine*. Still, that's not exactly what I was asking.

"Do you think he'd, like, do something bad to me? If he had the chance?"

Vera's wide eyes go wider, but she doesn't say anything. I didn't really want her to anyway.

Anna Talbert walks by. She stops and leans down toward the table. "Paying penance, O?" she asks nastily.

"I didn't do anything."

She laughs, tossing her hair over her shoulder as she turns away. "Right," she calls as she walks off.

I sigh and reach out for my Diet Coke, catching a glimpse of Vera's notebook. It's covered in bright, colorful pictures, masterfully collaged together. "Is that Venice?" I ask, pointing to one.

She reaches out and pulls the notebook to her protectively. "I like the pictures," she tells me.

"I know." I stretch out over the table, tugging the notebook back over to my side of the table. "I just want to look. My brother and I used to talk about going to Venice." I scan the pictures, touching them with my fingers. "These are great. Do you collect them?" Without thinking about it, I flip the notebook open.

Right to a picture of Ethan.

It's from the first newspaper of the semester. He's at football practice, taking a break, laughing with the guys, the camera catching his eye. It's a moment of pure happiness. The thought that he can feel that happy and alive anywhere and anytime after what he did to me turns my stomach. "Oh." Slowly, I close the notebook and slide it back over to Vera.

After a moment, she blurts out, "I'm sorry."

She's looking at me as if I may jump across the table at her at any second. I almost laugh, it's so ridiculous. "Your problem's not with me, Vera. You'll want to take it up with Adrienne." I don't know why it's suddenly so easy to say out loud. Something has snapped, I realize, sitting here with Vera, and I just don't care who I'm pretending to be anymore. It's been building for a while, I guess, but I'm ready to let that girl go. Maybe it's because before, I at least had reasons to go through the motions. Not anymore. Before, I was a picture of control—over my life and my boyfriend and this whole fucking embarrassment of a school. But what part of that was real? What of that was *me*—the me I always thought I'd be? The me my brother and Claire loved and maybe even, at some point, Ethan.

Why had I given in to this narrative?

"Hey, Vera. Are you okay?"

I jump at the voice and swing around to find Whit DuRant right there behind me, towering over my shoulder like a cartoon hero.

She nods, and I truly begin to believe I am the Big Bad Wolf.

Whit checks his watch. "Do you have a little bit of time so we can talk about our assignment for biology?" he asks her.

"No problem," Vera squeaks. She pulls her notebook to her chest and picks up her tray, walking away toward the trash can.

"What are you doing?" Whit asks me once she's out of earshot.

"Sitting." I gesture around the table. "It's a free country, isn't it?"

"Leave her alone. I'm sure slumming it is hilarious to you, but come on—"

"I was being nice." I watch Vera's back. "Has she always been in love with Ethan?"

"Yeah, it's—" He shrugs off the question. "She's a nice girl. She means well, and the last thing she needs is you messing with her."

I cross my arms over my chest defensively. "I wasn't." He looks after Vera, away from me. He's turned to leave when I blurt out: "Why haven't you told anyone?"

He stops, back turned to me. Motions for Vera to wait for him by the door. Turns back. "Are you a masochist?" he asks.

"Is that synonymous with loser?"

"You're one of the most popular people in school," he informs me. "For reasons I can't even begin to fathom."

"And you could ruin it," I say, biting into a cold piece of macaroni. "So do it."

He shakes his head. "Then you'll think I care."

"You could at least hold it over me or something." I chew. Swallow. "That's what Adrienne would do." I glance up, and he catches my eye and holds my gaze for a minute before looking away.

"I can't imagine a bigger waste of time than holding something over you."

"There probably isn't one." I drain my Diet Coke. It's all methodical. Easy.

I could probably choke down a nail if I put my mind to it.

Without another word, Whit turns on his heel and goes to catch Vera at the door. I watch him with disinterest, the door swinging shut behind them as they go. He hates me. Well, not me, I guess. More like a symbol of everything he thinks is wrong with this place—a living, breathing reminder that sometimes, nastiness is rewarded.

To him, I'm not a person.

Fair enough. I still haven't figured out how to be one.

21

The Rough House smells like pizza, beer, and crushed dreams.

I figure Claire has to be here. It's the only free Friday we have during football season, so she was supposed to pick up a shift. My eyes scan the room for her, but I find only Ellie behind the bar. I approach with caution to ask if she's seen Claire.

Mr. Peters, who owns the Rough House, sits at the end of the bar, sipping on a drink. This is generally where you will find him, as he is *technically,* per letter of the law, not allowed to leave Ellie alone at the bar. She's eighteen, so she can serve the beers, as long as she is not pouring or popping tops. The kind of contrived law that backwoods folks love and love to gossip about. Everyone and their mom knows Ellie tends bar at the Rough House when she's not cutting classes at Central High. That's why half of the customers come out.

The other half come out because they haven't found Jesus yet.

Ellie's wiping down the bar, her long brown hair sticking out on all sides from her fishtail braid. I stop in front of her with a soft hey. Her wiping slows precipitously as she looks up at me.

"What's up, Olivia?"

There's a reason the guys at the Rough House love Ellie. She is one of those effortlessly cool girls you see in movies, the kind of person you want desperately to emulate, even knowing you would fall pathetically short. She's like a Cali surf goddess dropped into Buckley, South Carolina, and I'm jealous of her for it.

I was jealous she became Claire's new best friend when they started working together. Until I found out they were dating. Or in love. Or whatever you are when you're best friends who like to make out back in the Rough House alley.

Then again, maybe I was even more jealous then. Claire was supposed to be my best friend first, and I never liked sharing.

"Have you seen Claire?" I ask.

She tosses her rag out of sight. "Nope." Cool indifference drops from her voice, and she glances at Mr. Peters sitting with a regular at the bar. "She missed her shift."

"She wasn't at school." I sit down at the bar stool to make it clear I am not leaving.

"Mr. Peters, are you good?" Ellie calls down to the other side of the bar. He raises his beer in reply. I grimace at the pair of them, the complete depression dripping from the ceiling and covering them whole. The Rough House—alcoholics by day, fake IDs by night. Satisfied that the men are preoccupied, Ellie leans down in front of me, elbows on the bar, face in hands. "What's going on over there? Everyone at school today was saying people were sending all sorts of outrageous texts yesterday. Somebody had, like, screenshots that were supposedly from Adrienne's phone."

Central had always been Buckley's big brother, but it was an incestuous relationship. Central had more—a mall and a community college and even a couple of hipster-y restaurants. But gossip flowed back and forth between us. Gossip and relationships and vitriol. Everyone at Central High would know Buckley High's despair.

"So you heard, then? Did Claire say anything to you?" I ask. She knows more than she's letting on, but she wants me to say it. She wants this on us—me and Adrienne—but she also knows she hurt Claire first.

It's easier to blame her than myself. If the guilt works, I can't tell. Ellie shrugs.

"No one knows that it was you. If you were worried."

"Don't try to scare me," Ellie says. "I don't have time for that."

I tilt my bar stool back. "That's so not the point."

Ellie glances down at her fingernails for a minute, flicking at a piece of dead skin on her cuticle. "Everyone at Central is saying they heard Adrienne was with Ethan Masters now. That you saw them hooking up but didn't care, because you'd pretty much gone off the deep end anyway. What's that about?" She looks back up at me, flipping her hair over her shoulder.

My throat feels dry. "If you heard it, it must be true."

Ellie holds up her hands in defense. "Just telling you. It's better to know what's being said. Anyway, you know what I did." She glances at Mr. Peters. "After *we* broke up."

I don't know what she did. Claire won't tell me. When Ellie gets mentioned, all we hear about is how well her volleyball season is going and how she must be *so* busy and how she can't wait to go to lunch with her sometime because *oh my God they're still best friends and that's it—just like all the straight girls*. "What did you do?" I ask, feeling contempt for pretty, perfect Ellie.

"I started dating Thomas Cruz. He's accepted a baseball scholarship to Florida and has an absolutely phenomenal body."

"That's a bitch move."

Ellie points at me. "Coxie is a bitch move. She *never even* broke up with him, O. Even you have to think that's fucked."

"She wasn't sleeping with Coxie," I return.

"Only because she doesn't want to, with him or any other boy," Ellie snaps at me. "Like that makes it okay. What if *I* had been dating a guy at the same time we were together? Bet it wouldn't have been 'no big deal' then. Anyone would have ended it and moved on."

I watch her, silent.

"But whatever, I don't want to talk about it—that wasn't my point. I'm just saying, if you don't want to hear about Adrienne and Ethan, change the conversation. That's the only way you won't look pathetic. Hook up with someone else. Date someone better than Ethan."

"I don't want to date anyone. It's exhausting," I say, thinking of the energy-zapping moments spent trying to keep our relationship alive day by day. Trying not to let him slip away because I was unstable and ridiculous and didn't know how to love him all the way.

"It's all perception. And sex, of course. You think Thomas isn't temporary? We all need a rebound sometimes, O." Ellie looks away from me, picking up her rag and turning to the soda machine. "You can go now. Tell Claire she better be at work tomorrow if she doesn't want to get her ass fired." And then she turns on the loud spray cleaner.

As I leave, I think about what she said.

Perception is everything.

22

The weekend gives me some time to think. Claire sends me a text that she's all right and asks to cancel our usual Claire-Ade-O Sunday lunch at the Rough House. It's fine with me, as it's more time I can spend out of Adrienne's orbit, where it's harder for her to manipulate me.

I formulate a plan.

I've learned a lot about getting my way over the years.

I think it's a talent I picked up when I was young. Probably had something to do with Mom—getting my way with her was nearly impossible. So I started figuring out how to get it from other people.

That's why it's important that I corner Mr. Doolittle in the hall right after second period on Monday. If I find him in his office, it might take too long. It's important he does it now.

He takes his mid-morning break between second and third period to go to the teachers' lounge and get coffee and a chocolate-chip bagel, which is one of those things that shouldn't exist.

I bombard him when he steps out of his office, like I was just about to come in. "Mr. Doolittle, thank God!"

"Olivia?" His face goes all concerned. "What's wrong? Do you need to come in?"

"No." I shake my head. "Want to walk and talk?"

"All right."

So we walk down the hall. "I've been so, so down this last week." This is a nasty, cheap trick that I feel totally gross for using, but hell, I might as well give them what they want. "I really need something new to throw myself into, and I think—well, I *know*—it's got to be this SAT prep, but I've talked to everyone you mentioned and they're so busy but Whit—"

"Whit DuRant?"

I nod enthusiastically. Then bite my lip just right. "At first, he said he had some free time since golf season isn't until spring, but I'm having a really hard time with him. He's so—hostile, I guess."

Mr. Doolittle stops walking. "Whit DuRant is *hostile*?" He sounds incredulous.

"It's complicated. He's holding this grudge against me, and I totally understand—I totally deserve it. But I really feel like I *need* his help for, like, my journey that we're always talking about, and I thought if *you'd* talk to him, maybe everything would be okay." I look down. "It's just that I know he has this really negative image of me, and I want to change it. I *have* to change it. I know it's stupid."

Mr. Doolittle looks like a textbook picture of helpful concern. "This is really important to you?"

I nod.

"Let me talk to Mr. DuRant."

"Before the end of the day?" I ask.

"Before I even go back to my office," he assures me in front of the door of the teachers' lounge. "I'll get him out of class."

"Oh my God, thank you." I act like I consider hugging him, but he steps away in fear of sexual harassment charges, no doubt.

"It's no problem, Miss Clayton. Whatever I can do to help you." People who want to help make it so easy to use them.

He closes the door to the teachers' lounge in my face. I walk past Adrienne in the hall. And I smile.

Give 'em what they want.

It's raining.

Rain means cheer practice is inside. Adrienne is being especially kind to the girls, cutting through the tension with a smile. She's getting T-shirts made for the team. Come look at the design, tell me what you think. Omigod, so cute. I can't believe they buy it.

I can't believe I used to. I can't believe I'm going so far as to avoid her because I'm afraid she might change my mind.

I'm stretching my arm against one of the walls, standing as far from Adrienne as possible, when I hear my name being shouted across the gym. "Olivia. Clayton!"

I look up. Whit DuRant stands in the doorway of the boys' locker room, looking as murderous as is humanly possible while wearing a bright green polo. The rest of the cheerleaders stare at me. I don't talk to Whit DuRant.

Until now.

I go across the gym to where he is, flash him a smile. "What's up?" I ask nonchalantly.

He is not amused. "I need to talk to you."

"So talk."

He glances at the cheer team. "Somewhere else."

I shove past him into the boys' locker room and lean against the wall of the entrance. He turns around, letting the door swing closed behind him. The girls will love this. I snicker.

"What did you say to Mr. Doolittle?" Whit demands.

I shrug. "That you wouldn't help me."

He tugs at his hair. "I'm too busy to help you. Why should I have to help you?"

I throw my hand out to him, so he can see that the answer is so obvious. "It's, like, your civic duty for being born tall and talented and smart and rich."

"Is this some kind of game to you?" His hair is practically standing on end. It's kind of funny, actually.

"No." I step closer to him. "Getting out of this shithole town is not a *game* to me."

"Why do you need me, then? If it matters so much, do it on your own. I don't want to help you. I don't like you."

"I'll do a trade-off for it."

"A trade-off?" He laughs like he has never heard anything more ridiculous in his entire life. "What do you think you have that I would want?"

I look at him Very Seriously, like when I used to lie to teachers to get out of tests. "I'll be your girlfriend."

"I'm sorry," he says, his voice so saturated in sarcasm, I can see the excess oozing from his pores. "There must be smoke somewhere in the building because I clearly just blacked out. *What* did you say?"

I scoff. "You heard me."

"Why would I go out with you? What the hell, don't you *have* a boyfriend?"

"No. And I don't want a boyfriend." I glance at the closed door to the gym, imagining Adrienne behind it, burning with curiosity. "But you could have sex."

I swear, he backs *into* the door. "Sex?"

"With me."

"With *you*?"

I nod.

"Have you lost your mind? Why would I want anyone to think I was having sex with you, much less actually do it?"

I fight to keep my face as stoic as possible. Like there has been a time in the history of my life when I have ever felt so totally and completely rejected. Even when I saw Ethan with Adrienne, I didn't feel quite so unwanted. "What, like you have so much going for you." I let my eyes linger over his body. Which would admittedly be a perfectly good body if he knew what to do with it. Then back to the eyes. "Sexually or otherwise."

"Then why are you asking?"

I shrug. I can't tell him *because I thought it would work.*

"Seriously," he says. "What's in this for you?"

Another shrug.

His eyes are hooded, annoyed. "I'll tutor you. That's it."

"Fine," I say.

"Fine. Don't tell anyone we're dating."

Shrug.

We stand there in silence for a few moments, toe-to-toe. Finally, he says, "Don't you have practice?"

"Yeah." I turn. "Better go."

The door swings shut behind me, opening and closing. He stands there, wondering.

I know he's curious. Whatever he might say, I can feel him watching my back.

Whit DuRant. The town golden boy with scholarship offers from colleges coast to coast. He has something that Adrienne can't get, something that Ethan will never touch. He has respect. He has potential. He has everyone's attention.

He's perfect.

23

Whit finds me on Tuesday morning to set up our first session the next day. He still seems supremely annoyed, so I let him go for the day. There's still plenty of time.

I notice Adrienne watching me from across the hall as Whit walks off. She's finally caught me out here alone in the hallway, where I can't answer her with one-letter texts or run away into a crowd of people. She's on me in a matter of seconds, her eyes digging into mine. "That's the second time I've seen you talking to Whit DuRant in two days, which is two times more than I've ever seen you talking to him before. What gives?"

I've got absolutely nothing yet.

"He's going to tutor me. SATs." I can't really meet her eye, and I'm not sure why.

"Since when do you give a shit about the SATs?"

Since I want to get the hell away from you, I don't say.

"God, do you think it would kill him to not be an asshole, though?" she asks, staring at the place where Whit was standing. "Are you going to mess with him?"

I shrug.

Adrienne leans back against a locker, crossing her arms. "Yeah." She shakes her head. "It's something you would've done before."

"I don't bite the hand that feeds," I say.

Her eyes flash. "You going to let him feed you?"

I roll my eyes. *Escape.* "I don't have time for this, Ade. I have class."

"Of course," she says as I start to walk away. But she grabs on to my arm before I go. "We're good, right? Me and you? I feel like you're still avoiding me, but you wouldn't lie about us being good."

I see people watching us as they walk by. Laughing behind their hands, and I know it's directed at me. At Olivia Clayton, standing there with the girl who screwed my boyfriend last week. Who wrote how simple it would be to get me back in a text that I forwarded to the entire school. One thought runs through my mind:

I will ruin her.

"We're good."

24

Wednesday afternoon, I take the road headed toward Central. The road toward Adrienne's. My free hand is out the window. The hot September air plays over my fingers, making waves in the wind.

I take a turn down a winding side road. In moments, the golf course comes into view. Rolling hills of too-green grass give way to a large clubhouse. I slow and turn up the driveway to this place where I don't belong.

To my right, a man knocks his ball into a sand trap and throws his club. How bourgeois of him.

I park and grab my ratty old backpack from the car, swinging it over my shoulder. Traipse up the stairs and into the magnificent lobby, full of polished wooden panels and polo-shirted girls.

"Can I help you?" the girl at the front desk asks.

"Deck," I tell her, shrugging my bag higher onto my shoulder.

With a big fake smile, she points to a door at the far end of the lobby.

"Thanks!" I yell behind me, heading in the direction she indicated. If only a funeral dirge were playing. There goes the last of your pride, Olivia.

Whit is sitting at the table nearest the course. I navigate through rows of wrought-iron tables shadowed by brightly colored umbrellas and fall dramatically into the seat across from him, letting my bag plop onto the ground. "Hey," I say.

He turns his head from the green to look at me. "You're on time."

"Well spotted," I say, icy, reaching into my bag to pull out my prep book. "Make me smart." I toss the book onto the table. He slides it toward him, opening it up in the middle to read. I reach across and pull it back. "Over here." I point at the spot next to me.

He sighs as if the world were against him but begins the loud process of scraping his chair across the deck to sit next to me. He leans over my shoulder. The proximity makes me feel totally uncomfortable and useless, and I have no idea why. Whatever I thought I was doing, it backfired.

"Can I get you a drink?" someone whisper-asks behind me, causing me to jump around in surprise.

It's Vera from English. When she sees me, she turns the color of her red polo. I go into Bitch Olivia mode. "Pardon?" I say, even though I heard her.

"You want something?" Whit asks for her. "You can put it on my parents' tab."

I frown at him. "Lemonade, I guess. If you have it." Vera scampers off as quickly as possible. Whit turns back to the book. "What highly confused person made her a waitress?" I ask him. "She can barely make eye contact in one-on-one conversations."

"She doesn't usually waitress," Whit says. "They must be short-staffed." He isn't looking at me—not at all. "And the problem is you, not her."

"What does that mean?"

"You. Even the way you ordered lemonade is like you're so superior. She's terrified of you and you enjoy it."

"You're not," I say.

"Why would I be?" he replies, flipping over a page and scribbling on it. Watching him, I almost want to do something bad to him, to go after him like Adrienne and I used to do, feel the angry fire burning through my veins. Something alive hits me that moment in a way it hasn't in months.

Not since Ryan died.

I know it's totally irrational. Something about him accusing me of being a bad person makes me want to be a bad person. "You're not invincible, you know," I warn him. "And if you're not careful, you're going to find out exactly how not invincible you are." If it sounds over the top, then that's the point. We've really messed shit up for people with more solid social standing than Whit DuRant. I have to keep reminding myself that he is helping me.

His eyes slide up from the book. "Are you threatening me?"

"I'm warning you. You're on Adrienne's radar now that you're helping me." I cross my arms. "Some people would consider it helpful advice."

He looks at me incredulously. "If I'm on Adrienne Maynard's radar, it's because you put me there with your bullshit. Is this always your thing? Putting people into your orbit of idiocy and then acting like you're helping them by warning them?"

My defenses go up. "I'm not like her." I lose a little bit of my fire then, diminish slightly. "She's gone to war with me, but I need this so I can escape. I want to get *out* of this orbit, okay?"

"Then why did you say that?" he asks, his stance still casual.

"I don't know." I push my hair behind my ear. "I know you're helping me. I was trying to look out for you. Maybe this situation would be easier if you pretend for five minutes that I'm an actual person."

He shakes his head, watching me. Sighs. "Why else would I be doing this?"

"Here." Vera sets a glass of lemonade between us.

"Thanks," I say to her fleeing back.

"Verbal reasoning," Whit says loudly, pointing to the page. I scoot a little closer to him.

About an hour later, I'm taking my last watered-down sip, pointing at the book with my straw. "I don't even know what any of those words mean. Like the words in the sentence."

"You can use context clues there, though. Like, okay, you know what *severance* means."

I shrug.

"Don't you?" he asks, looking at me.

"Kind of."

He tosses his pencil up and it cartwheels through the air. The abruptness of the motion startles me. "*Try*, Olivia. Just try."

"I am trying," I tell him, my temperature rising again. "I'm trying, and it's so obvious you think I'm stupid—"

His face changes, softens slightly. "I never said that. Look—" He grabs his pencil back up, leaning in closer. "If we're going to do this, we're going to do it, you know? You're going to get that score on the SAT and do whatever it is you're trying to do. Or prove what you're trying to prove. This isn't going to be some failed experiment, okay? I don't fail."

He doesn't fail. There is a fervent expression in his eyes, as if success were a religion and he worshipped at the altar. I'm not sure if it's inspiring or concerning.

I stare at the paper in front of me. *It's funny*, I think. I'm not used to someone expecting anything intelligent to come out of my mouth. Telling me I need to try. Ryan was the one always attempting to pull me kicking and screaming through the completely dull construct of the public school system. Since he left, Mom had made it clear slightly below average did not bother her, but of course not much did. "Yeah, fine, I know what *severance* means."

"That's what I thought," he says, scratching awkwardly at the piece of paper like he can use his pencil to dispel the tension in the air.

"Yeah, motherfucker, nailed it!" some obnoxious guy screams from the last hole. We both look up, startled, as the guy slides his putter against his side like it's a sword.

The boy on the course high-fives his partner and congratulates himself again.

"Dick," Whit mutters, and I giggle.

"Who is that?" I ask, surveying the boy and his bright orange pants with interest.

"I have no idea. We need to get back to this."

"Whit!" the boy shouts, pointing his putter toward the deck. "Did you see that?" And he's bounding over, up the deck stairs in his muddy golf shoes, stopping in front of our table. His eyebrows go up in clear amusement. "Who is this?"

"Olivia," I say, smiling in greeting. Ethan always said I looked the most innocent when I smiled.

"Aren't you friends with Adrienne Maynard?" he asks me. "I remember you from the JV cheerleading squad."

I try to place him. "Something like that," I say.

The boy has this mischievous grin on his face, like he's seen something naughty and can't wait to tell. "What are you two doing?"

"SAT prep." I point at Whit, and then look pointedly at him, because this is *so nothing but tutoring*, just like he wants. He ignores me.

"Tutoring," the other boy says. "Right. *That* makes sense." He shakes his head. "What'd you hit?" he asks Whit.

Whit shrugs. "I don't know. I think it was seventy-something. I'm working on this new mid-range shot."

"That isn't going to get you a starting spot. Not even close."

"I've got this season to worry about first," Whit replies, pretending this whole conversation isn't bothering him and doing the worst acting job of anyone I've ever seen.

"You want to beat my record?"

"I don't know, Cason. Do I?"

There it is. Cason DuRant, Whit's older brother. He graduated from Buckley two years ago and now golfs for Duke. I can't believe I didn't recognize him before—he and Whit are nearly mirror images of each other, Whit a bit taller, Cason with auburn hair. And yet, it works so much better for Cason. He was always known in school as being good-looking, popular, charming, and smart. He was Whit with a cherry on top, always dating some pretty girl and running some mischief at school. Nothing that ever got him in trouble, of course, but enough to make him important.

Something his brother is not.

Cason laughs. One loud *ha!* before slapping Whit on the shoulder. Then he's studying me again, that amused look on his face. "Aren't you one of the girls that was always causing trouble with the underclassmen?"

I am both ashamed and proud, the emotions combating each other in my stomach. I was powerful; everyone knew who I was. It was so comforting, but what I did to get there—it wasn't worth it. I think.

Whit is looking at me, all *see, you're a bad person.* "Trouble is relative, I guess." I swish my straw around my empty glass.

"Whit never gets into any trouble," Cason goes on, taunting his brother. "I'd like to keep his robe white and all, if you catch my drift."

Whit turns noticeably red. "It's just tutoring," he says.

Cason laughs again, kind of obnoxious. "Like I don't know that. If you managed something *that* interesting, everyone would die of shock." Again, his eyes go to me, all over me on *interesting,* and as easy as I can take the attention, I wish I weren't here. As far as sibling rivalry goes, this is a little much even for me.

Whit turns to his brother, his shoulders back and proud. "Kiss my ass."

"I'll let you get to your . . . ah, tutoring." Cason acts like he's going to walk away before he turns back. "Feel free to come by our house."

Whit's jaw is clenched tight. "Shut the fuck up."

Cason laughs, leaps down the deck steps, and strides off.

I stare after him, the fading light catching his auburn hair. He stops at the deck bar to flirt with the girl there. She scolds him with a laugh and leans forward, buying whatever he is selling. Then, with a quick glance around, hands him a beer. I look away.

Whit is watching me watching Cason with this look on his face like he's tasting something horrible. When my eyes catch his, he looks down at the workbook. "What?" I say.

Whit glances up at me. "What what?"

"That was really weird." I shrug. "You should have told him we were dating. That would knock the smirk off his face, you know."

"Hilarious," Whit replies, scribbling in the book like it insulted his mom and his dog, too. "I don't care what he thinks."

"He doesn't think someone like me would be caught dead with you," I offer helpfully.

Whit rolls his eyes. "He thinks I can only get girls from the Central High Fellowship of Christian Athletes because I'm 'nice.' "

"And clean."

He doesn't reply, but now it seems the notebook has insulted his golf game, too. I take a sip from the melted ice at the bottom of my cup.

"What does that mean anyway?" I ask.

"What?" He punctuates the word with a period.

I twirl the straw in my drink. "Like, I couldn't be in the Fellowship of Christian Athletes?"

He snorts.

"Oh, screw you. The whole point of all that Christianity stuff is forgiveness and absolution." I lean over the table, my chest almost flush against the wrought iron. "Don't you want to absolve me?"

His eyes are close enough that I can pick out green flecks in the brown. For a second, he has no answer. No defense. He's just an innocent boy in my game.

"I'm not *dirty*," I insist, almost to myself.

"I never said that," he finally replies.

Then either ten seconds or ten minutes pass with us just staring at each other. Suddenly I realize someone is *seeing* the two of us. When I turn my head, Vera is there, her expression pure confusion. I fall back in my chair.

Whit sees her, too. "People know what kind of person I am, and I'm fine with that."

I've decided he pisses me off. "Boring."

"Can we just study?" he shoots back.

I lean back over beside him. "So what would Cason think?"

Whit stops and looks me over, eyes tracing my body from head to toe. He meets my eyes again. "Nothing. Cason wouldn't think anything."

He's a bad liar.

25

I drive through the town square to get back from the country club. A few cars are parked out front of the Rough House, but otherwise, it's dead. I pull into a parking spot at the Bellvue, a local tourist trap that is half hotel, half restaurant. Lean my head against the steering wheel and stare at the Episcopal church. It isn't in the square exactly—just visible around the corner. It's huge and white with stained-glass windows from the 1700s. There's a rumor that Sherman was totally determined to burn it during the Civil War, but some townspeople banded together to stop him.

We've never been a religious family, the first thing to make us official pariahs when we moved to town. But Ryan never missed a service at the church. I think it was the windows more than the sermon that spoke to him, though. I always thought this church was the only thing he liked about Buckley. He said no one appreciated anything beautiful here.

Sometimes I think I'm woven into the fabric of Buckley now, along with everyone else who can't leave. Towns like Buckley are a magnet. No one can stay away. They move to the next town over or across the country, and Buckley keeps pulling them back. Surnames last forever, and the graveyard is already full. There's no escape.

It's suffocating.

I drive the rest of the way home.

The light is on in Ryan's bedroom. I haven't seen it on since the funeral. When I go in the house, his door is slightly ajar, noise coming from inside.

I nudge the door with my shoulder, making my way in. There's not much to it; Ryan moved most of his things with him to Michigan and always took summer classes so he'd never have to come back to Buckley. The university returned his stuff in garbage bags, but we kept them all lined up in the garage, one by one. All that he left behind in this room were a couple of old movie posters, a bed, and his bookshelf.

His bookshelf. God, he loved his books so much.

That's where Mom is, a trash bag on one side of her and a box on the other. She has a book open in her hands, her eyes skimming the page. The last time we were both in here together was the night after the call. I wanted to sleep in his bed, and she wouldn't let me. I remember crying, telling her she sucked at grieving anyway, and her calmly watching me bawl myself to sleep on the couch.

She said she couldn't give me that one thing I wanted because she knew best and it was a dangerous way to mourn.

"He liked that one," I tell her, walking closer to peer at the book over her shoulder. Ryan wrote in the margins and highlighted in different colors. Some of it doesn't even make sense, just scribbles and pictures. I feel the ice in my veins melting. I reach out to touch the words.

"Do you want it?" Mom asks.

I nod, pulling the book out of her hands and into my chest. "What are you doing with them?" She takes the next volume off the shelf.

"Donating them to Goodwill," she tells me stiffly. The words take me aback, but I try to remind myself. He's dead. He doesn't need them anymore.

"You're keeping some?"

She nods but tosses two more into the box for donation. She hasn't been particularly sentimental since I was five—and we never talk about that time, like so much else. I could count on one hand the things she still kept that belonged to my father: a set of University of Maryland pint glasses and an academic journal with an article he had written and a funny card I'd found tucked into the top of her dresser.

Ryan told me once he thought the reminders were too painful. But she always told Ryan more than she ever told me.

I thought this—Ryan's death—might send her into a spiral. I kept waiting for it to hit, anticipating. I think some sick part of me even wanted it. But that wasn't who she was anymore. I had started filtering so many of my thoughts about my mom through what other people said. Her clients and Aunt Kate and even some of the more enlightened Buckley residents. Smart. Tough. Mom adapted and survived; that was how she rolled.

Sometimes I hate her for it.

"I could help," I say, pulling my memento tighter to me. If I hadn't walked in when I did, I'm sure it would be in the box with the others. *Adapt and survive.*

"Oh, Liv, I don't—" Then she breaks off and sighs when she pulls an empty mini-bottle from the shelf. It spilled at some point, the book next to it soaked in brown and wrinkled. He must've hidden it when he was visiting from Michigan one time. He never drank that much before he left. At least, not that I knew about. Without a comment, Mom tosses the ruined book and empty bottle into the garbage bag. I hear it clank.

I don't know what makes me ask: "Did Dad like to drink?"

She pauses, looks up at me because I never ask about Dad. He had been a forbidden topic for so long. With practiced calm, she wipes the back of her arm over her forehead. "Only socially. At parties. A beer when he went out with all the other academics." A barely-there smile finds its way to her face but falls away just as fast. "Not like your brother." She turns back to the shelf.

"It was a phase," I tell her.

"We'll never know," she replies, not looking back at me, not believing me.

"It was a phase," I insist. It was college. Everyone drank. Everyone hid alcohol all over their room and guzzled wine by the bottle.

Ryan would've been back to Ryan as soon as school was over. He would've.

Mom turns back to me. "Are you okay? You seem upset." *And getting more so by the second*, I think. I'm watching my brother fade away, and everyone knows Adrienne completely betrayed me; I feel stuck in this same spiral of petty bullshit and games.

I'm going to get out.

"Why would someone who says they're your friend be horrible to you?" I ask Mom. I haven't spoken to her this much in three years, and she knows it. I don't even know *why* I'm saying it except I don't know who else to say it to.

She turns around, all the way around, and faces me. Adjusts the glasses on her face. "What did she do?" Mom asks. Mom expects Adrienne to be terrible—she's told me as much before. She expects Adrienne to dress up as a slutty nurse for Halloween, to write nasty texts about everyone and steal boyfriends and be everything she expects people like Adrienne to be. She once called her a big fish in a small pond, and I couldn't help but think she was talking about me at the same time.

At the end of the day, what she really knows about me and Adrienne is less than nothing.

I make eye contact. "It wasn't her. It was me."

I don't think she can face me then, face the fact that I am failing to adapt. *Ask me*, I want to say. *Ask me what I did*. "I know things are bad right now. I know we're both . . . processing. Go easy on yourself," she replies stiffly. She doesn't want to know. She can't face who I really am. In truth, she's never wanted to know. I turned into a monster somewhere along the way, and she let me be one.

That was why I'd missed Ryan so much when he left. At least if I was horrible, he cared.

I stare at the emptying bookshelf, feeling like now, every last thing he touched will be gone.

Including the good parts of me.

26

TWO AND A HALF MONTHS AGO

Ethan's dad blew out of town with his "other woman" two years ago and never looked back. That was when he and his mom lived in Charleston, before they moved to Buckley. All his dad left for compensation was an open invite to his lake house. We stayed there more or less all summer, feeling cool and superior and independent until Claire's mom figured out we were lying about spending the night at each other's houses and tried to make Adrienne's mom and my mom care enough to stop us.

The subterfuge got exhausting, but not enough to stop going. That weekend, it was me and Ethan and Adrienne and that guy she was hooking up with from Chesterfield, all sitting around, trying to bounce quarters into Solo cups filled with beer. Ethan had his hand over the small of my back—he was always just barely touching me like that, as if afraid where I might go.

It was then that my phone started ringing, buzzing against my back pocket. I pulled it out, shrugged off Ethan, and wandered into the small hallway before I answered.

"Hello?" I whispered, glancing over my shoulder, not wanting anyone to hear my conversation.

"Olivia?" he said, like he was surprised I was the one who had answered the phone.

"Ryan, what are you doing?" I asked, trying not to sound desperate. Loud music blared in the background, some indie song I'd never heard before.

"Listening to Mike at Night." He was slurring. "Thought of you." Someone laughed in the background. There was a smile in Ryan's voice. Even though he was so obviously drunk off his ass, I was relieved. It was my brother and he was listening to Mike at Night and smiling, and it was like he was right there with me for a minute. And then: "Mom's a bitch, isn't she?"

I looked around again as if someone wanted to sneak up behind me and dig into all my horrible family secrets. "Ryan, come on," I said, hardly convincing.

"No, she is. Remember after Aunt Kate moved out, and Mom'd lock herself in her room to work and forget we hadn't eaten? You were, like, five, and all I could make were cheese sandwiches. All you ate in 2004 were cheese sandwiches." I remembered. I remembered Ryan covering for Mom every time Aunt Kate called to check in. *Yes, we're fine*. She wasn't fine.

"She always apologized," I said. Mom was the one who finally told Aunt Kate we weren't fine. Aunt Kate lived with us for four years after Dad died, and Mom finally snapped when Kate moved out and left the three of us alone. I barely remembered the six months Ryan and I had lived with Kate, but I did remember the day we moved back in with Mom. I remembered the image of the woman she had been before we left, at her computer, making phone calls and signing documents, coffee mugs sticking to every surface of the bedroom, her thrumming with energy and barely contained emotions. I remembered the taste of gourmet Monterey Jack on Gouda on cheddar. And I remembered when she'd snap out of it, hold on to me as bone-crushingly tight as she could in her bed and sob into my back for hours, and I knew she loved me so much.

That wasn't the woman we moved back in with. She sat us down in our new apartment five miles from Aunt Kate's house, glasses on her face, hair in that messy bun she still wears, and told us she'd had a breakdown. She talked to us like adults. She had a routine now—we ate breakfast at seven thirty, went to school, she picked us up on time, and dinner was at six. Routine, routine, routine. She never again held me the way she used to. "And she always bought *really* good cheese," I said softly to Ryan.

Ryan was silent for a minute. I heard the sound of Adrienne and Chesterfield laughing through the door, but I was somewhere else. "I'm sorry I let you down, Liv. When I started—you know—and you had Adrienne and didn't need me . . . and Mom. If it were different, I'd come get you. You'd come live with me. You aren't happy there."

I pressed my forehead up against the wall as if it would help me think and then fell back with a sigh.

"I'm not happy anywhere," he said. "We should go."

I didn't know what to say. "Go where?"

"Mike at Night."

"Yeah," I said, encouraging him.

"I bet it wouldn't be that great. Once all the mystery is gone, nothing's that great anymore. It's all bullshit. I hate this place."

"We could go somewhere else."

"Fuck it, Olivia. There's nowhere to go that doesn't suck, doesn't drain the life right out of you. You don't get it. Sometimes I think Mom had it right, when she gave up on reality. Just let yourself feel fucking everything."

"Ryan, listen to yourself," I said, my voice near a shout, forgetting myself for a moment, my privacy. Ethan poked his head into the hallway.

"You okay?" he asked, and I panicked.

"Stop talking like that," I said to Ryan, trying to keep my voice firm. "I can't deal with this right now. I'm with my friends, okay?"

There was silence on the other end of the line for a moment and then: "You're not who you used to be, Liv. You're so . . . selfish. You like it there, don't you? With them. Those *people*. Those people we promised each other we'd never become."

"Ryan, shut up!" I yelled, near tears. Ethan tried to creep up on me, to touch me, and I pushed him away. "I had to adapt. I'm the one who has to live here and figure out a way to be happy, and you can't tell me I'm wrong for that."

"If you're happy with them, I don't know who you are." His voice was growing angrier and angrier. "I don't know who you are anyway. You're just some generic mean girl, aren't you? That's what everyone says."

"That's not who I am!" My own anger built up. Usually when he was drunk, I tried to talk him down, keep him calm. See what was good.

But he couldn't say things like that to me.

"Fuck this, Liv. Fuck all of it."

"Fuck you!" I said, and hung up the phone. Then I turned on my heel. "Go away, Ethan. I'm trying to have a conversation and fix things, and you're lurking."

"Why can't I help?" he asked me.

"Because it's none of your fucking business," I said, stepping around him and back into the kitchen. Adrienne looked up when I came in, her dark eyes glinting.

"What'd he do?" she whispered to me a little while later, when Ethan was talking to Chesterfield about the Panthers' upcoming season.

I shook my head.

"Well, he must have done something," she insisted.

I glanced at Ethan, caught his hesitant smile. "It's, like, not intentional. It's that whole psychiatry thing."

Adrienne sneered at him, like him being alive was intentionally pissing her off. "Who was it anyway?"

"Ryan."

"Ryan is a dick," Adrienne told me. "The sooner you realize that, the happier you'll be."

My phone sat there, silent. I wondered what he was doing. I wondered if he'd even remember any of this tomorrow. "He's my brother. I can't abandon him."

"You can't fix him, either," she snapped.

I felt the tears brimming in my eyes again. It wasn't *fair* of her to make me cry when no one was supposed to be able to hurt me. No one but my best friend who always seemed to be looking for a way.

"What is your deal, Adrienne?" I asked. "I am going through some serious shit with my brother, and I can't get so much as a sympathetic nod from you. Look at me!" I snapped, serious and hurt and confused. My voice was hard, sharp edges, punctured syllables. "It's not fair. That's not who you're supposed to be. You're supposed to be the one who makes things better."

She pushed her lips together. "You can't fix everything, O. Sometimes it's easier to give it up or you'll end up as miserable as they are." She lifted a hand, pushing a piece of hair back behind my ear like she was comforting a child. "Look at everything you have. You've got the best friends who would do anything for you, you've got the stars shining on the lake on a Friday night, and you're the kind of person everyone our age wants to be. Ryan needs to figure his own shit out. It's sink or swim right now, and we're *living*, bitch!" She thrust her drink up into the air and took a swig, laughing all the while.

For a beat, I couldn't look away from her. Disbelief covered every edge of my vision. It was that simple for her.

Just don't care.

"Fine," I said quietly. "Fine."

27

I cram some books into my locker, crushing balled-up papers in the process. For the first time in two days, I glance at the pictures on my locker door. Then I start taking them down.

A voice floats in from the other side of my open locker door, a conversation not meant for me. "Have you talked to Adrienne?" It's a voice I would recognize anywhere—the sound of our morning announcements. Michaela Verday—class president, local overachiever, and cheerleader hater. I lean into my locker so I can keep listening.

"No," someone—I think it's Meghan Stanley—replies. "It's—she isn't going to like it."

"Well," Michaela continues as if she were guiding a wayward soul to the Promised Land, "you have to change stunt groups. You can't keep working with Claire. What if she, like, gets off on it or something?"

I slam my locker shut and stare straight at Michaela. She doesn't turn away as she says, "I wouldn't be surprised if she's not the only cheerleader who enjoys mounting other girls."

That's it.

I throw my book bag down on the ground in front of a locker and shove Michaela.

She startles, gasping, then regains her balance. "Are you out of your *effing* mind?" she demands.

I get in her face. "Wanna find out?" I say, a fist clinched at my side.

"Olivia, what are you doing?" I whip around to find Claire next to me, looking between Michaela and me.

"I—said something I shouldn't have," Michaela tells Claire, gently backing away from me. "I'm worried about you. Those texts!" The more she talks, the more people slow down to listen. I have to stop her.

"Don't push me, Michaela," I say.

She laughs as if I bore her. "Don't be so dramatic. Everyone's worried about Claire. A lot of people aren't quite as *accepting* of alternative life-styles as I am."

Claire grabs my arm to stop me from lunging at Michaela.

"Claire, hey, what's going on?" With that greeting, Alex Cox steps out of the crowd and to the other side of Michaela and me, facing Claire. I think they call this an escalating situation.

Coxie—the boy Claire lost her virginity to in ninth grade. The boy who thinks they've been destined to be together since middle school and spent half his life trying to prove it to her. She's never loved Coxie, but they have always been "a couple." Even when Claire was with Ellie.

I can tell that whatever their last conversation was, Claire isn't eager to continue it. "Claire?" he asks more sharply.

I shake my head. "It's just Michaela being a bitch. Lay off," I order. Because I don't like the tone of his voice or anything else about his bleached-blond head right now. I slowly start to back away from Michaela.

He glances at the crowd, which seems to be holding its collective breath in anticipation. "Why?" Like he's that clueless.

Michaela's giggle behind me matches everything about her: her white hair and cool stance and inferiority complex. I swear to myself I won't re-engage. "Like you don't know, Alex," Michaela says. "We were talking about Claire and her issues twenty minutes ago."

"Shut *up*, Michaela," Coxie commands, desperation creeping into his voice.

"It's fine. I don't care what either of you say about me. If you want to go out with her, Alex, go ahead," Claire says to Coxie. "It's not like Adrienne hasn't seen you together."

A swift nonverbal exchange between Michaela and Coxie seems to say it all. Suddenly things make sense—Michaela wants Claire out of the Coxie equation, and the solution fell right out of the sky into her lap.

Claire blows out a tired breath and looks down at the floor.

"Claire." Coxie sounds defeated. He grabs Claire's wrists and I barely hear him. "It's not like that, and I'm not mad, I promise. It's what everyone was saying—I thought you'd been using me as, like, some kind of cover-up, but I know that's not true now."

Claire looks up at him, angry. "Get off," she tells him. "I'm so sick of having to explain myself to you."

He doesn't stop. "Please listen."

"She said get off her," I repeat.

He turns on me then. "You stay out of this, Olivia. You're always determined to draw so much goddamned attention to yourself. This is your fault." He gestures around him at the people watching. This is more my fault than he'll ever know.

And that really pisses me off.

"She doesn't want you, so get off her," I snap at him.

He's a good half foot taller than me, and his letting go of Claire and rounding on me makes me a lot more nervous than getting into it with Michaela, but I want them to leave her alone. I want everyone to leave Claire alone, and if I have to make a spectacle of myself to get that, I will.

He gestures wildly. "Well, if she didn't hang out with those girls at work and act like a—"

I grab on to the front of his shirt and yank him toward me. "I dare you to finish that sentence."

I can feel the angry rhythm of his heart; his eyes are alight with murderous energy. God help me, I wish Adrienne were here.

"Hey." A calm voice breaks through the silence, extracting my hand from Coxie's shirt. Coxie and I both glance up at the same time, and I imagine the baffled look on his face closely mirrors my own. "Maybe you should chill out, Olivia."

Whit's looking right at me with his big brown eyes. I didn't see him arrive, but now I see him with painful clarity. So close, I can make out the green-gold streaks in his eyes again, lit by the dingy overhead lights.

"What's it to you, DuRant?" Coxie asks, but I can already tell that he regrets the whole confrontation. None of it does much for my heart rate, though. I can't stop staring at Whit, inexplicably coming to my rescue.

Whit glances back at me and makes a decision. "I don't like it when people get that close to touching my girlfriend." Like it's the most normal thing in the world for him to say. There's this jolt right in my midsection, a change in the atmosphere. A shift in the power.

Claire studies the two of us carefully—even she can't believe it. Coxie's eyes flit between Whit and me as if he's not quite sure that can be correct.

"She just needs to . . ." Coxie trails off, looking lost. Even though I hate him, his feelings have been used far more than he knows, and he's always been just dumb enough not to notice. But he has no right. "Whatever," Coxie finally finishes, leaving the way he came. Not really like he's going anywhere at all. I sigh in relief.

I glance back at Whit, watching me. Then Claire and everyone else, watching the two of us. I gesture at him kind of helplessly. "Claire, you okay if I go?"

Her eyebrows knit together, but she nods anyway. The crowd

around us begins to disperse. Whit leans down, picks up my bag, and throws it over his shoulder. I smile weakly.

Totally normal.

We walk past a line of lockers in silence. Out to our assigned parking spots, where my mom's beat-up Bronco sits in my space next to Whit's Jeep. He hands me my bag. "That was—" I scratch the back of my neck. "Thanks."

He sighs. "I have no idea why I did that except if that guy hit you, I was going to feel like shit." He checks the time on his cell phone like he already can't wait to be away from me.

"Thanks," I say, but this time it comes out cold.

He leans his hand back into his car. "So that's done."

"Yeah." I'd feel a lot better about this if he didn't seem to be so repulsed by our nearness.

"Okay," he says.

"Okay."

We stare at each other. We've reached the end of our scripted lines here, but neither of us knows the next stage direction.

I'm turning to leave when he says, "That's what's bothering you, right? Why you're so scared of me? You thought I would tell someone you'd sent out those texts and Claire would find out? You actually feel bad about hurting her." I keep noticing all these little things he does—shaking his arm so that gold watch on his wrist slides around, running his hand over his three o'clock shadow. "You didn't mean for her to get outed like that."

"Yeah. I guess."

He shrugs. "That makes you not totally deplorable."

I stare up at him. "I might be."

"Look, I have to go. I'm meeting a couple of guys from Central to play in a half hour. Why don't we meet up at your house in a little? You're the one on Main Street, right? Is that okay?"

I nod.

He shakes his head, moving along toward his Jeep. "Later?"

I nod again and watch him drive off, the sound of the engine rumbling behind him. I look down at my hands.

They're still shaking.

28

I text Adrienne that I can't make it to cheer practice without offering any details. I never used to miss cheer practice before, never would have unless Adrienne told me to. I'd started skipping sometimes after Ryan, and she'd pretended to understand at first.

But I've read that psychopaths can only fake empathy for so long.

She texts me back:

This is starting to look really bad to the girls, O. They're counting on us.

That at least makes me laugh. Then:

Why is everyone in school saying you're dating Whit DuRant?

I don't answer.

Mom has left to go to the grocery store by the time Whit comes over. It's not totally surprising he knows where my house is—Buckley is small enough that everybody knows where everybody lives. But I'm surprised all the same. I thought remembering information like where Olivia Clayton lives would be beneath him.

He's standing there at the front door, all awkward in his golf shorts and flip-flops, looking the least comfortable I've ever seen him. Not that I can really blame him. I let him in and close the door behind him.

"So, this is your house," Whit says, hands in his pockets, glancing around the family room.

I feel self-conscious. I know he's always seen me as the girl with all the friends and the popularity and the perfect relationship I didn't deserve. But now he's in my crappy house, surrounded by pictures of my dead brother and my unsmiling mom, and I'm this girl, too.

"Don't tell anybody my house is such a piece of shit." I figure it doesn't look so bad from the outside, maybe kind of charming and small, but on the inside, it's dark and messy. Neither Mom nor I have been particularly invested in housework in the past two months.

His eyes meet mine, a little confused. "I won't. I mean, it's not."

I nod in the direction of the hallway. "Come on. My bedroom is back here," I say, and he does this typical boy face of "oh really." So I talk over it.

"When I first moved here, I wouldn't let Adrienne and Claire come over." I glance back at him. "I was so embarrassed that it was, like, the three of us in this tiny house. That's Ryan's room." I point. A question crosses his face. So I say, "He's the dead one." I walk into my room, wait for him to enter behind me, and close the door.

I guess I feel like maybe if I let him see these little things about me, he'll understand me. As though maybe I can get him to think I'm not so bad. I don't know why.

I'm so tired of everyone thinking they know me.

"I heard you were taking that really hard," Whit says, and then has the decency to look embarrassed. "I mean, not that—I don't know. It's none of my business." He pauses. "I'm sorry," he says.

I look at him seriously. "That's a pretty stock response, DuRant." His face goes from zero to horrified in sixty seconds. That's when I flash him a smile. "It's fine."

"Oh." He breathes. "Jesus. I see why people are scared of you."

"Are they? Scared of me?" I ask, honestly curious.

"Seems like it." He looks at me, interested.

"Still?" I don't want to sound like it's important to me, but in a way, it is. What my perception is out amongst the commoners.

"Most people think you're pretty screwed up. Still pretty scary, but in a more unhinged, less scary way."

I nod. "I kind of am."

"But really," Whit says, no hint of sarcasm in his words at all. "That sucks."

I nod. Hold my hand out in front of me. "So this is it. The place every Buckley High guy has imagined, after he realizes he can't get with Adrienne." I move my hand from side to side as if presenting the grand finale.

Now he looks terrified, clearly wondering whether or not I'm joking. As his eyes travel around the room, a little snicker escapes him. "It is pretty funny, though," he says.

"What is?" I ask, pushing my hair behind my ear self-consciously.

Whit looks from me to my bed and back. I wait to read all his dirtiest, most horrible thoughts on his face.

Except I can't read him at all.

"You have," he says, grinning, "a teddy bear." Then he laughs, turning his face away from me. "I'm in Olivia Clayton's room, and she has a teddy bear."

A slow grin spreads across my face. "What?" I ask.

"You're supposed to be some sort of untouchable badass. You have a *teddy bear*."

I pick up the teddy bear and hug it to my chest. "I'm a person." I snuggle my chin against the soft fabric. "Not untouchable." I'm unstable, I think. I'm totally unstable and ridiculous and not untouchable or badass at all.

Whit stops, looking at me, still inscrutable.

I hold out the bear to him. "His name's Mister Cotton Muffin. Don't laugh."

He does anyway, but he takes the bear out of my hand. "Very nice."

"Don't tease me," I say.

"Well." He gives the bear back to me. "I am your boyfriend." At that, he looks even more embarrassed. "Did you want me to do that? I'm sorry."

"I *told* you to do that," I remind him. "I thought it was fucking great." I try to be as cool as I used to feel. *That* was the Olivia people loved.

And he does love it a little, I can tell. He's kind of pleased.

"So we just roll with it?" he asks.

I shrug. "Works for me."

"Don't you think—I don't know. That it's a bad idea? If someone finds out?"

"Why would they find out?" I say. "I'm not going to tell anybody. Are you?"

"No, of course not," he replies. Perish the thought. "But there has to be a time limit, don't you think? You know, we'll work on your SAT stuff and we can do the whole 'dating' thing, I think a month. Does that work for you?"

I consider that I don't really have a choice. After a moment, I nod. "Works for me," I say again.

"Okay," he replies. Then, in this totally awkward way, "Can I ask you something? Do you really think I'm obvious? People know what I'm going to do and who I'm going to be before I do it? Like my brother thinks?"

I frown, picking through our past conversations in my mind. Then I remember him and Cason that day at the golf course and realize I have to capitalize on this opportunity—this insecurity. "Maybe," I say after a minute.

"I can't believe I said that." He won't meet my eyes. He stretches his arms up over his head, exposing the tiniest bit of skin where his T-shirt rides up. *This is the moment*, I think. If there's going to be any moment where I can bring him to my side. He wants them all to believe he can be something different. He doesn't want to care what anyone thinks, but he does.

His brother most of all.

"You surprised *me*," I tell him.

He almost smiles.

29

"What are you doing?"

I jump at the sound of Ethan's voice, deep with an unexpected edge. He's wearing a Buckley football T-shirt with cutoff sleeves. He's an intimidating figure even without his pads, his muscles defined under the loose fabric of a T-shirt. I lean against the chain-link fence that circles the edge of the locker room and kick up a foot against the links, my cheerleading skirt hitching up my thigh. My heart syncs up with the marching band's incessant beat, their drums banging in post-win elation.

"Just thinking," I reply, my voice cold.

"About?" He leans next to me on the fence. At the edge of his hair, blood leaks under a bandage.

"What did you do to yourself?" I ask.

"Oh." He shifts. "I got a cut from my helmet the first game of the season, and it keeps opening back up." He points at the blood. "Haven't you noticed before? At other games?"

I shake my head. "Bleak," I say. There's probably a metaphor in there somewhere. "I was actually thinking about the first time we met. Cliché, huh?" He doesn't say anything for a minute, and as if I can't stand a second of silence, I keep talking. "You blame me for what happened."

"O . . ."

"I never thought a guy would actually choose me over Adrienne. Especially not one who was new and interesting. But you did, and we were happy." I glance at him. "Weren't we? Before? But you blamed me for changing when my brother died." I bite the top of my fingernail off and spit it over the fence. "Why am I even saying this?"

I push away from the fence, ready for a dramatic exit, and Ethan grabs my forearm. "What?" I ask.

"Whit DuRant."

I almost laugh. Finally. What's the point of getting all up in his face and letting him sweat on me if he doesn't crack?

I blink. "What about him?"

"You don't even know him," Ethan says.

"Dating people I do know hasn't worked out well for me so far," I say.

"You didn't bother to know me." Ethan shakes his head, then shrugs it off. "I've heard you and Adrienne making fun of Whit DuRant. Calling him a tool and shit."

I shrug. "I like him. He's not . . . like us." It's true. "No drama. I'll try to keep the pornographic texts to a minimum."

Ethan buries his face in his hands. "Look, I didn't mean for any of that to get out."

"How convenient." I look down at my foot. "Are you still hooking up with her?"

When he doesn't meet my eyes, I let out a laugh. "Pretty low."

"You don't get it," he starts to say, but apparently he doesn't either because he goes silent. I take that as my cue to walk away. I've seen Whit walking out of the stands.

"I'll see you later," I say, trailing the chain-link fence out to the parking lot. As I get closer, Whit walks up to me and grabs my hand, nodding to acknowledge Ethan. We cross the asphalt, and Ethan fades into the background.

"What did he want?" Whit asks after we've gained some distance.

"I don't know." Our feet pound away over the parking lines. "Thanks for the ride."

"No problem. You *are* my girlfriend. Where are we going?"

"Cheerleader initiation."

"What's that?" he asks.

I grimace. "You'll see."

30

The sound of silence is deafening in Whit's Jeep as we drive out of the parking lot. He turns on the radio and flips it from rap to country, tapping his fingers against the steering wheel.

"We're not very convincing," I say.

He glances at me. "Am I doing something wrong? I'm going places with you—that's what couples do."

I shift in my seat, uncomfortable with my own need for conversation. We don't know the first thing about each other. "If we're going to do this for a month, we're going to have to talk."

"When we're alone?" *Ouch*.

I sigh and lean my cheek into my hand, my elbow at the edge of the window. "No."

"So where is this 'initiation'?"

"You know that playground at the Y?"

"Yeah."

"There."

"Great," he says, turning on his blinker. "Trespassing."

Adrienne has been all over me the past two days. I can hear her voice replaying in my head right now.

Whit. DuRant. Whit DuRant. Is that what all this SAT bullshit is about?

I had lied through my teeth. Said the tutoring had been going on for a few weeks, and I was so embarrassed I'd had to ask someone for help. The thing with Whit had just happened, and honestly, it was really a relief she had slept with my boyfriend so now I was free to follow my heart.

Well, not that last part.

The truth was, I'd almost enjoyed watching it slowly eat away at her. Whit was out of nowhere, completely out of character. She'd never seen it coming. And that—well, it felt like armor. Like my strategy for a coming war had paid off.

Adrienne thought this was the last breeze of a storm she had weathered and survived, bruised but alive.

I knew different. The blowback from the texts would die down; it would have to so everyone would leave Claire alone. But then, I'd end this. She'd find out how not simple I was.

"Should I go around back?" Whit asks, breaking the silence.

"Yeah," I return. We pull into the parking lot of the Y. It's an old brick building one street over from Main. Whit turns into the driveway that circles around to the playground in the back, hidden from the road. Cars are already parked up and down the edge of the fence, hard to make out under the cover of night.

"Listen," I say to Whit as he puts the Jeep in park. "I'm not exactly sure what this is going to be like. Every class does their own thing for initiation. I don't know what Adrienne has cooked up."

Whit takes that in with what I consider to be an appropriate amount of concern. "What did you have to do?"

"Naked lap at the community pool." I shrug. "Grade school hazing at best."

"Maybe for you," he mutters, and gets out before I can reply.

"Cool, I was hoping you'd do that judging thing every time we're together," I call as I slam my door, walking behind him toward the fence. He jumps it before me, grabbing my hips when I'm halfway to help me down, for once keeping his mouth shut. The sound of screaming reverberates across the playground, echoed by our classmates' laughter. We make our way past the empty swings toward the noise. Past the slides and jungle gym, over to the sidewalk that runs adjacent to the Y building. That's where everyone is, where Adrienne must have planned something totally absurd.

I see the freshman cheerleaders lined up on the sidewalk, all on their knees in nothing but their underwear, each one dripping with water and shivering, blindfolds covering their eyes. Anna has a water hose and a grin.

"There you are!" Adrienne calls out when she spots me, bounding over. She throws a sideways glare at Whit before putting one arm around me. In her free hand, she has a squirt bottle of ketchup. The other cheerleaders and the boys they've brought along are laughing. Renatta has a bottle of mustard, and grocery bags line the ground behind her.

"You almost missed all the fun," Adrienne tells me, her mouth next to my ear, reeking of alcohol—bad enough to make me wonder if she had been drinking *during* the game. Her eyes are bright and glassy. "Do it," she says, gesturing at the girls, pulling me down alongside her. I catch her before she doubles over. "Call the next cheer."

"Do 'Who Rocks the House'!" Daniel Smith yells. Claire's next to him, weary but dutifully holding a bottle of chocolate syrup, too. Of course there are football players here, if only to add to the humiliation. But Ethan didn't show—he wouldn't like this at all.

I take a deep breath. "V-for-Victory. One, two, three, V-V!" I yell, and the girls pick up my words. As they cheer, Adrienne and Renatta cover them with condiments and yell "LOUDER!" right in their faces. Adrienne insists one of the girls isn't enunciating and squirts ketchup into her open mouth. When she sputters, Adrienne laughs even harder.

I glance at Whit, who looks supremely annoyed. Everyone is yelling taunts at the blindfolded girls.

"We'll never get victory with these sluts!"

"Do you pad your bra or what, Kim?!"

I'm playing right into every cliché he ever dreamed up right now.

Fuck it, he doesn't know how to have fun. I grab the syrup out of Claire's hand and pour it down the line of girls, then squirt some at Claire with a flourish. She wrestles it back as other girls grab more condiments to throw on the freshmen. The lights around the parking lot are dim, buzzing, but good enough to show off the variety of colors all over each girl. No matter what we throw on them, they never stop cheering.

Adrienne steps in front of a tiny redheaded girl. "Hey, isn't this the one with the crush on Daniel?" she asks, glancing back at him. The girl misses a line of the cheer, her head moving back and forth, nervously trying to take in the unseen scene. Adrienne crouches down in front of her, smiling. "What would you let Daniel do to you? He wants to know."

"I—I—" the girl stutters. My heart pounds against my rib cage. Too far. She has to take everything too far.

"Anything?" Adrienne asks. And then, "Say 'anything.' "

"A-anything," the girl replies. People start to quiet down, slow down, listening. Every word has a sinister edge to it now.

"Excuse me?" Adrienne says, standing back up with her hands on her hips. "I thought you were a cheerleader? Show him how loud you'd scream."

"Anything!" the girl yells obediently.

"Hear that, Daniel?" Adrienne asks, turning to him. Laughing out loud, he hands her a plastic bottle filled with something greenish that catches the light. "Daniel brought you a special present from his family's farm. It's goat piss. Would you like that?" Whit has a coughing fit next to me. I don't dare look at him.

It's pickle juice. Oldest trick in the book. Not that the girl knows that. "Y-yes."

Adrienne upturns the bottle all over the girl's head, and she can't help but scream in disgust. Everyone laughs even harder, but it's not fun anymore. Nothing about it is fun. "Hand me that peanut butter," Adrienne yells at Anna.

"I'm allergic to peanut butter!" one of the freshmen yells, panicked.

"We'll see about that," Adrienne says as Anna places the jar in her hand.

Without thinking about it, I run forward and put myself between Adrienne and the girl. "*Enough*," I say.

Adrienne rolls her eyes. "What are you doing, O?"

"You heard her," I say, my voice steady. "She's allergic."

Adrienne pulls out a clump of peanut butter with her finger. "It's not like she's going to die."

"How do you know that?" I challenge.

"Oh, so this is what you're going to do now, huh? That's hilarious. Come on!" she says. All of a sudden she's trying to lunge past me, but I grab her shoulders and shove her back. The plastic jar falls to the ground; everyone goes silent. Adrienne stares at me.

I bend down and pick up the jar, chucking it across the playground. Close enough to lean near Adrienne's ear, I whisper, "What the fuck is wrong with you?" I turn on my heel and walk past Whit. "We're leaving," I tell him.

"Jesus, I was kidding!" Adrienne says, laughing still. Then her laugh catches for a minute. "She's not that good in bed, you know!" she yells for everyone to hear. I stop in my tracks. "I mean, you probably already do know. But that's what Ethan said. He prefers me a lot, he said."

In my head, I beg him not to, but Whit turns around anyway.

"You think you have a lot of power, don't you? Screaming at cheerleaders, threatening them with sexual assault and deathly allergic reactions. Do you think you're important to anyone who matters? Do you think anyone out here isn't waiting to watch you self-destruct? They all saw the texts. You're living on borrowed time. And getting with Ethan Masters? Everyone knows a desperate move when they see one." There it is—everything I've always thought about us, about me and Adrienne, in those angry words. I've been waiting so long for someone to finally say them.

He said them to Adrienne.

That's *terrifying*. Everyone knows that's terrifying, but he isn't scared.

Adrienne's face darkens. "Nice try." She flips her hair over her shoulder. "Watch your back, golfer boy."

Whit waves a careless hand, turns, and continues the walk to his car. "Come on," he says as he brushes past me.

Back in the Jeep, I lean back against the seat with a sigh. "You shouldn't have done that."

"I don't like her," he says.

I twist my head to the side. "The feeling's mutual."

He looks over, as if weighing his words for a moment. "I'm not sure I like you, Olivia."

He was on my side for a minute. Defending me. I thought—"Oh."

The car starts under his hands. "I'm not trying to be a jackass. . . ."

"Well, you're failing at it," I say, pushing a loose strand of hair out of my eye. "Is it the uniform? Or just everything about me?"

He doesn't bother to deny it. "How can you let that shit happen? Those girls are fourteen and we're out there, staring at them in their underwear. It's sick."

"It's like a bathing suit," I brush him off.

"That shit with Daniel Smith was wrong. And disgusting."

"You were there, too. You didn't stop it."

"Exactly," he replies quickly. "I'm not some superhero or something. I don't know what to say. I'd rather not put myself in those situations."

"So don't. But just because you're not there doesn't mean it's not happening. That's what's so great about you, Whit—you think you can live above it all. At least you could do something to stop it."

He turns to look at me, incredulous. "You mean stop you?" He shakes his head, eyes back toward the road. "And everything you do—it's so fake. Like, there's not even a real version of you." He puts on a blinker to turn onto the street.

"What would you know about what's real? Trust me, you wouldn't want to know the real me." I glance at him out of the corner of my eye, tell myself not to cry. "You'd hate her even more than the fake me."

"I don't hate you," he says. I can hear in his voice how much he regrets starting this conversation. "You're just—is it worth it?" There's a genuine question in there. I'm reminded of how he looked at me that first day, when he bandaged my hand. He wants to know something about me, about what I think.

I shake my head. "You don't understand, Whit. I have to be *this* to be somebody. It's how I made my mark—it's the only power I have. The only way to not be another nobody in Buckley.

"And at some point along the way, I realized I was really damn good at being this person. I was close to being the best. Don't you like being the best? At golf? It's not like there's so much more value in that than what I do."

I've now managed to really offend him. "You've got to be kidding me," he scoffs. "At least I have something to be proud of."

"But to them—to Buckley—you aren't worth their time or their thoughts. They hate you." *We* hate you, I don't say. I don't want to be a part of that—a part of Buckley. "You think you're better than everyone else."

"Well, fuck them."

I almost laugh. "They respect me," I keep on. I like the idea that he hates them as much as I do. Them and their tiny box of a world. So I keep talking. "I guess the truth is I always thought this whole thing—Buckley and this version of me—was temporary. I thought I could do whatever I wanted because I would leave here someday. Because this isn't the real world. I was only pretending to be this person."

"Pretending?" he repeats, shifting his fingers across the leather of the steering wheel. "But you're miserable."

The words hit me very hard in that moment. It's not that I don't know it, but to hear it verbalized is powerful. I laugh, but I'm stifling a cry. "I *am* miserable." Whit stares straight ahead as if purposely not looking at me, his face as clear as he can keep it. "God, I am so miserable," I say it again out loud, giving in to it. I have to admit it's over. The nights laughing at others' misfortune and the days of whispering with my best friends and the simple act of not allowing myself to feel so damn much. The way it was—all of it—is over. I watch as Buckley flies past. The one-story homes and broken-down little shops and the road that goes on forever, out of Buckley.

"I have to stop her," I say, the words becoming true as I hear them. "Adrienne. I can't let her keep doing this. I can't be a part of this bullshit anymore."

"So don't," Whit says, as if it were the most obvious thing in the world.

"Don't you get it?" I demand of him. "It's like I said; even if you're not there, it's still happening. We have to stop her. From hurting those girls and everyone else."

"And you," Whit supplies, glancing over at me. "Right?"

Me. It's such a simple concept. I have to save *myself.* "You're still going to help me?" I ask, surprised.

His eyes close for half a minute when we stop at a red light. Finally, he says, "Yes."

I nod. "Why?" I can't help but ask.

He doesn't look at me. "Because you're so fucking sad, I don't know what else to do."

We drive in silence for a moment. The radio clock says it's nearly eleven. Instinctively, I reach out and flip the radio over to AM.

"What are you doing?" Whit asks me.

Tongue between my teeth, I adjust the station. "Do me a favor?"

He cuts his eyes at me.

I go for my best do-something face. "Please."

Sighing, he leans back in his seat. "What?"

"Drive out of town." I run my thumb over the radio. "I'm not sure what channel picks it up. We always had one of those knobs we just twirled."

"Out of town?" he repeats.

"Out to the highway. It's not that far." It occurs to me as I say it that I may not get my way from him. I'm not used to that. "I'll get you gas money," I offer in a last-ditch attempt.

"I don't want it," he tells me, putting on his blinker to turn toward the highway. "Just stop asking me for favors."

I keep all my possible replies to myself, enjoying the feel of the night air through the open window, the bright-lit sky.

"Out near Brown Creek, there's this little dirt road. Out to a big field. You see?" I point ahead to where an overgrown willow shades the path. "Your Jeep should be fine."

Whit makes the turn, his car creeping over the ground. We're pitched into darkness as the trees blot out the sky. "The trees break up over there. We'll get it then."

"Get what?" he asks.

"It's just—" I bite my lip. "Can you just drive?"

"Fine."

As the trees begin to clear, I continue my ministrations with the radio. The signal begins to come in, clearer and clearer until I hear the music. "Stop!" I tell him.

Whit puts on the brakes, shifts into park. "What?" he asks again.

I shush him, listening as the man in the radio speaks. "... a new band from Brooklyn, lead singer Marks says their sound is a mix of new pop and alternative. Here's Cronix with 'Lose That.'" A frenzied beat starts up, a violin cranking up in the background. It's instantly both fun and terrible, and all the tension releases from my stomach as I listen. I can practically hear it leave my body.

Whit, sensing *something* is going on here, turns the radio up a little. The song is unpolished, untamed, all made up of sounds that shouldn't work together, all the trademarks of a debut band. It's cathartic and primal and even when it's bad, it's interesting.

It ends on a sour guitar note and the DJ is back, introducing whatever's coming next.

"Was that, like, your favorite band or something?" Whit asks me.

I shake my head. "It's Mike at Night," I say as explanation.

He tries to stop himself from asking, but apparently the need to know is too strong. "What?"

"It's a radio show from Chicago. It's all these upstart bands that we've never heard of and never will." Just talking about it makes the whole world make sense again. This hasn't changed. "It's, like ... it's, like, we can drive out here into the middle of nowhere and this whole other world opens up to us. Get it?"

The next song starts in, a slower one, mournful and strange.

"Ryan and I figured out we could get the signal a few years ago. It was an epiphany. We used to drive out and listen to it for hours. Before he moved. Dissect the songs and be a part of something, you know? A discovery. It's stupid." It used to bug Adrienne that I would waste Friday nights listening to shitty bands in a field with my brother. She never got it—never understood that no matter how different Ryan and I became, that time together meant everything. To Adrienne, all it meant was that my devotion to her was incomplete.

Whit doesn't say anything. The longer he's silent, the more stupid it seems, the more I think of Adrienne making fun of Mike at Night. The beats of the song start pulling at all these imaginary strings in my heart that are long sore and better left hidden. "We can go. I—I wanted to see if we could still pick it up."

"That's it?" he asks, turning toward me. "You made me come all the way out here, and you don't even want to listen to it?" He sounds kind of pissed, but in a forced way. There's something comforting about his impatience—like he's making it okay if we stay for a while longer.

"Can we stay?"

He sighs.

I lean back against my seat, close my eyes, and listen. In town, Adrienne is plotting the next move of her reign of terror. Somewhere in the distance, the creek flows over the rocks. Somewhere far away, Mike at Night picks his next song.

I'm there and I'm here and I've never felt so lost in between.

31

The only people at the Rough House when I walk in are some regulars posted up at the bar, drinking their pathetic lives away. Ellie is behind the bar, leaning against the soda fountain.

Claire bounces over from waiting a table, her white sneakers squeaking against the floor. "Hi!" She's all smiles and sunshine, far from the girl trapped in the confines of Buckley High, even if the smile's not quite in her eyes. That's Claire—she'll grin at everyone even if they're waiting to tear her apart.

"How's tricks?" I ask.

Claire sets her mouth thoughtfully, looking around the dark restaurant. "You tell me." She smacks my arm. "Grab a table. I'll take my break. Want a soda?"

I nod.

Claire heads for the bar, and I slide into a corner booth. From my spot, I watch her smile at Ellie, bob her head up and down, asking a question. Ellie's face is guarded, carefully hiding emotions. But then, Ellie is always guarded. Some of the regulars watch them talk. I know they've heard—people never stop talking around Buckley. All I can think is that Claire's everyone's favorite topic of conversation, and Ellie remains hidden in plain sight behind her long brown hair.

Claire comes back toward the table, balancing two sodas in one hand, and slides into the seat opposite me. I can't help letting my eyes flit back over to Ellie. It doesn't go unnoticed.

"She's mad at me," Claire says, staring down into the depths of her Coke. "Because apparently everyone is going to find out about her because of me and it's *all my fault* for already ruining her life and starting drama. She won't even, like, exist in the same space as me."

I don't know what to say, so I do what I do best—I don't say anything at all.

Claire rolls her eyes, reaching into her pocket and extracting a mini-bottle of vodka. She goes to put it in her drink, and without thinking, I stiffen. Her hand stills over her Coke.

"Oh my God, I'm so sorry, Olivia. I wasn't even—" She hides the bottle so quickly, she almost knocks the saltshaker off the table. "I didn't mean—"

"It's fine," I say, fighting to keep my voice even. The image of Mom pulling the empty mini-bottle from its hiding place in Ryan's bookcase hits me so suddenly, such a punch in the gut, that I don't know how to react. The last time I saw him, he couldn't do anything without a drink in his hand. "But . . . are you okay?"

She shrugs, looking guilty. "People have expectations, you know? I'm Claire and that's what they expect. Happy and content and that Claire Barber smile. If I act differently, it will just be worse." She pauses for a minute. "But I guess I don't know how to be what they want right now."

I push the saltshaker over.

"I'm not an alcoholic or anything," she says defensively.

I shake my head. "I'm not delicate. If you want to drink, whatever. It's none of my business."

"I don't need to," she says, taking a sip from her Coke. "Obviously. Have you talked to Adrienne since initiation? She was kind of pissed."

I shake my head again. It's Sunday. Our day. The three of us always meet at the Rough House for lunch, to chat through the weekend's events. Who hooked up on Friday and whose mom was drunk at the football game and if we should go to that party one of Michaela's friends is having next weekend. I tried to get out of it again, but Claire begged me. I'm not sure what I'm going to say to Adrienne, but this has to be the last time, and it's only for Claire's sake.

Claire is waiting for me to force some words out, to explain who that girl was on Friday night, but it's so hard to think of any, much less say them. Everything out of my mouth is a lie. And if it's not, it'll fuck things up that much worse.

I don't know what makes me more pathetic: being this selfish or knowing how selfish I am and not doing anything to change it. "I was with Whit," I say easily. "Some things are just going to be different now, you know."

"Do I?" she asks. "Nobody knows about you and Whit."

"I'm sorry I didn't tell you," I say. I hate lying to Claire about this. It seems worse after everything, another betrayal in a box I'm trying to dump out, not reload. But this one's for the greater good. "It just kind of happened. With everything going on with Ryan and then the texts. Whit was there."

Claire processes that for a moment and then her face clears, as if it had never bothered her at all. "It's fine, of course. It was . . . kind of shocking, is all."

"I'm too dumb for him, right? That's what everyone's saying."

She blushes. "Shut up." Then she shrugs, as if to throw that shameful thought away. She holds up her phone for me to see. "Anyway, I was bored and looking through all of his accounts. You two are really discreet. How long has this been going on?"

I open my mouth, a lie already forming there when someone interrupts me.

"Well, hey there, Miss Claire." Both of our heads snap up at the same time. It's Mr. Simmons, a Rough House regular who runs on 70 percent beer at all times. He leans against the end of our table in a NASCAR baseball cap and a flannel shirt, a putrid smell emanating from him. He is every ugly part of Buckley. Mom would die.

Claire smiles brightly, not the least bit stymied. "Hey, Mr. Simmons! Is Ellie treating you right up there?"

"Ellie always treats me right." He smiles, revealing a missing molar in the back of his mouth. Word has it that Mr. Simmons served a stint in Vietnam but got a bad reputation hiding from the action. Doesn't really seem fair to me for him to get blamed for a time when he was probably just a scared kid. But that's how it goes, I guess. You get the reputation you get. "This your girlfriend?" Mr. Simmons asks, leering at me. "That's the word around town."

Claire's smile falters, but she doesn't turn away. "This is my friend Olivia. And I—I have a boyfriend. You know Alex Cox." Her voice grows softer and softer, weighed down under the eyes of Mr. Simmons and everyone watching at the bar. Ellie stands, wiping the same glass down over and over again, her knuckles tight. I want her to do something, even though I know how unfair that is.

"That better be right, Claire. A girl like you's too pretty to be actin' like that." He laughs because it's funny, *just so funny*. I want to tell him to go away, but I don't know what Claire wants me to do. She's shaking her head at me like she's worried I'll make it worse. It's a fairly accurate assessment. I can't resist escalating things, and if I get her fired, she'll never forgive me.

Mr. Simmons stumbles spectacularly then, straight into our table, accidentally sending Claire's Coke all over her. "I'm sorry," he starts saying, and then Ellie calls, "*Shit*, Mr. Simmons!" coming out from behind the bar with a towel.

She throws the towel at Claire when she gets to the table, with a "Here." Claire dabs at the stain, watching Mr. Simmons wearily. But Ellie is staring. "Go back to the kitchen and change. I've got an extra shirt in my bag."

Claire's eyes shift to Ellie with a look that can be described only as *want* before she shakes her head and takes off back past the bar, through the door into the kitchen. Ellie escorts Mr. Simmons out using a variety of swear words, then comes back to the table, pulling another towel out of her apron to clean up the rest of the spilled drink.

"Awesome job looking out for her, O. Really A-plus effort you're putting in over here," she says without looking at me.

"Fuck off, El," I say, so she won't know exactly how much her words affect me. "She can take care of herself." I pull out my phone so I don't have to talk to her, not really sure what to do with it. She walks away, still muttering under her breath.

Then I remember. Whit's social media. Right.

I pull up one of the pages. I don't follow him, so I at least make that small step toward actual coupledom. I should probably comment on a couple of pictures, too, for the sake of reality.

God. Fuck this.

I scroll through his pictures, staring. Whit golfing. Whit at a banquet. Whit's ugly guy feet stretching off the edge of a boat on a perfect day. Whit and his family.

I stop at that one, looking closer. His mom's got her hair curled up, pretty. His dad looks like he's just finished laughing, and Cason looks like he knows he's better than me.

His life is so different from mine. So full of privilege and great expectations. He's traveling and being asked to come to schools because of everything he's already done.

I've done nothing.

There's a comment at the bottom of the picture.

Case in One: @whitrant how does it feel to constantly be upstaged by that good-looking man on your right

WHITrant: @caseinone you'd have to ask dad

WHITrant: @caseinone mom just mentioned she liked me better

I giggle without meaning to, accidentally thinking of Ryan, of the way he teased me. It's a good thought. A way I haven't thought about Ryan in a long time.

"He honestly is kind of cute, isn't he?"

I jump at Adrienne's voice, turning to find her standing over my shoulder. I close out the screen on my phone.

"You're late," I say.

"Where's Claire?" she asks, standing next to the table with sunglasses pushed up over her head. I glance in the direction of the bar. Still no Claire and Ellie's disappeared now, too.

I shake my head at Adrienne. *Long story*.

"Where have you been?" she asks, falling in the seat across from me. Her voice is starting to border on the edge of desperate when she asks. "I called you yesterday and this morning."

I think about Friday night and my mission crystallizes. I have to stop her. "I didn't see a missed call from you," I say.

"God, at least don't lie to me, O. Is it Whit? That whole thing on Friday night?" she asks. "To be honest, I was kind of drunk."

"Right," I say. Then, "It's fine. He's over it."

She opens up a menu, not looking at me. "I'm actually kind of impressed. That was a smooth move."

"Smooth move?" I repeat.

"Whit," she says, paging through the menu. We've eaten at the Rough House half a million times, and the menu has never changed. "I'll admit, I never even thought of all the potential there. He really makes you seem kind of exciting, O. On the cutting edge."

I curl my fingers around the lip of the table. She's messing with me, and I can feel it building up inside me. This might finally be the moment. The one where I draw the line in the sand so she can see it clearly. When I finally tell her it's over.

She drops the menu and looks straight at me. "I mean, that's what you wanted, right? That's this new leaf you're trying to turn over. Whit DuRant and Olivia Clayton. So much goddamn potential."

I shake my head, looking anywhere but at her. "Don't do this right now."

"Oh, what, like hang you out to dry? Like you keep doing to me?" she asks. "Suddenly you're dating Whit DuRant and siccing him on me over freshman cheerleaders?"

"You were drunk," I say. I don't want drama. "It's fine. We're both over it."

"Fine." She slams down her hands on the menu. "I am, too. We'll all be best friends tomorrow. Like I said. I'm impressed that you managed to pull it off. That's all." She says it like a compliment. Like I should be grateful to her that she noticed Whit was a good *find*. That I found someone with *potential*.

"I can't do this," I say, sliding out of the booth. "I'm done."

"O . . . ," she calls as I turn to go. "O, get back here!"

"Tell Claire I said bye."

"Olivia, sit back down!" I hear her calling behind me as the door closes.

32

I'm changing out of my workout clothes in the locker room on Monday when Anna finds me and says Adrienne has asked to see me. After yesterday, I had managed to avoid her for most of the school day, tailing Whit around like a lost puppy and then working through our cheerleading routines at practice like it was my reason for living, but she'd finally figured out a way to get to me. Time to face the music.

I pause for a moment outside of the office, bracing myself. Our cheerleading coach, the one they hired after Coach Evans, does exactly enough to keep us from getting drunk at away games and get her cheerleading stipend for the year and nothing more. She leaves choreography, organization, and punishment up to her captains. Adrienne has full access to the locker room office. When I go in, she's leaning back in the desk chair, feet propped up on the desk, office phone pressed to her ear. "Mm-hmm," she says, surveying her nails. "We're very concerned, too, Coach. We just wanted to keep you abreast of the situation."

Anna giggles from next to the door, manicured hand over mouth.

"Thank you. I'll be in touch." Adrienne smiles broadly at the phone, dropping it onto her chest. "Olivia! Glad you could make it."

"What are you doing?" I ask, looking from her to Anna. Something isn't right.

"Hang on!" Anna says, leaning over the desk and pointing at the cell phone lying there. "He just got a text from *his mom*." She swipes the phone, reading the screen with a giggle.

"Whose phone is that?" I ask.

"What does it matter?" Adrienne says, leaning farther back in her chair like some sort of evil mastermind. "You don't really have boundaries with phones, do you?"

I swallow. "What are you talking about?"

Adrienne kicks her feet off the desk, leaning forward onto it instead. "Just calling up a few of Whit DuRant's recruiters to let them know about his small—"

"But alarming," Anna cuts in.

"Exactly," Adrienne agrees. "His small but alarming drug problem." She tilts her head to the side. "He very unfortunately failed a drug test today."

My whole stomach drops. I suck in a quick breath. "What is wrong with you?"

Adrienne tosses her head back and laughs. Without thinking about it, I lunge at Anna and try to pull Whit's phone out of her hand. Quicker than anything I would have expected from her, she bends back my wrist. "Nuh-uh," she says, dangling the phone over my head.

"Fuck you, Anna," I spit out as her grip tightens. "Adrienne thinks you're a joke."

She shoves me away from her. She thinks she's thrown me off, but I push her hard into the bookcase with both hands and grab the phone. As she rubs her shoulder, she looks at Adrienne, as if she should punish me. "Trying to kill me again, O?" she asks.

I turn away, flipping the phone in my hands. It looks undamaged.

Adrienne is smirking at the two of us from her throne. "Leave, Anna. Close the door."

Anna walks behind me, jabbing her elbow into my back before she slams the door closed behind her. Adrienne pushes up from the desk, dramatically using both hands. Walks slowly around it, head tilted inquisitively to the side. "What's wrong with me?" she asks. "What's wrong with you, O?"

I hold up Whit's phone. "This is a new low. Jealous? Thinking maybe you could get his number and sleep with my new boyfriend, too?"

"Yeah. Like you were so upset about Ethan," she replies coldly. "Took you *so* long to get over that. Whit deserved it. No one talks to me like that."

I cross my arms, force a laugh so I seem in control. "So that's what this is about?"

"This?" She points from the phone to her. "This is nothing. This is about you. I know what you did."

My hearts skips a few key beats. I clutch the phone tighter. "What?"

"What?" She throws the word back in my face. "You forwarded my texts, my private conversations, to the entire cheerleading squad. You humiliated me and you outed Claire and you walk around here like you're some wounded puppy, like the world has wronged you. People die, Olivia; grow the hell up. People die and boys cheat and you're not wounded, so stop acting like it." She points an accusatory finger at me. "You're a snake."

I stare straight at her because that's exactly what she doesn't want. I almost hiss. What a joke. Every part of this: ridiculous, hypocritical, inevitable.

"I hate you!" she screams at me, picking up a paperweight and chucking it at the wall next to me. My hand curls up reflexively into a fist. I flinch in spite of myself, half with fear, half with pain.

"How'd you even know?" I say, trying to keep my voice calm. If I don't, I will shatter, and I don't shatter. I'm Olivia fucking Clayton. I'm better than that.

"Anna saw you."

"You're going to tell," I say, resigned. It seems about right. The moment I decide to quit her, she fires me. It leaves me with nothing. Down two best friends, one older brother, and a boyfriend. That would be the end of Olivia fucking Clayton.

A part of me feels ready for it.

"I'm not going to tell," Adrienne practically snarls.

My eyes narrow.

"You want that, don't you? Me to tell Claire so you can feel even worse for yourself and make everything all about you again? I'm not going to tell."

"Stop messing with me, Adrienne."

"I didn't tell anyone about your brother, did I?"

Every part of my body constricts. My chest, my stomach, everything. "That's not funny."

"I'm so not laughing." She shoves the chair violently into the wall behind her, and I wince at the crash. "You think that stupid text is all I've got, O?" she demands. "I have *years*. Years of supposed friendship where you ran over anybody in your way. I've got Anna *fucking* Talbert, who will do whatever I say. I've got texts for days. And you're the kind of person who's too fucking stupid to not send out a goddamn text message implicating yourself. God, you are *useless*."

She rounds the desk until she's right in front of me and shoves me against the wall. When she goes to do it again, I grab on to her forearms to stop her.

"It fucking hurts, doesn't it?" she says to me.

My heart pounds in my chest. "What do you want?"

"I want Whit DuRant's head on a spike. I want medieval shit, O."

I try to keep my cool, but my hands are shaking. "Fine. Do whatever you want." I take a deep breath. "I won't stop you."

She smiles at me then, the most disconcerting thing she's done. "I want more from you. First, say you're sorry."

Tears fill my eyes. This isn't what I wanted. "I'm sorry."

"You're on my side now, O. I own you."

I nod, running my hands through my hair. It's a specific kind of hopelessness. "Let me break up with him. He'll leave us alone, go back to living his life in anonymity or whatever. I won't talk to him, I swear."

"Where would the fun be in that?" she asks me. She's standing right in front of me, this girl I've always known, dangerous as ever.

I kept a wild animal in my house, and now she's turned on me.

"Can't you leave him out of this?"

"You put him in this. You can't back out now. You had that chance. I wanted to talk yesterday, but you didn't have time for it. The time for talking is over."

"Adrienne." I hear the desperation in my own voice.

"You're my best friend. You're going to be my fucking best friend. You've sulked long enough. You wanted my attention, right? You got it. This is it. This is how we bounce back.

"And if you don't, I'll destroy you, O."

I close my eyes, fading. Waiting for every last good part of me to leave.

I feel her fingers on my chin, tipping my face up. "Look at me." I do. "Remember what we used to do for those biology tests?" She smiles. "I have a cheat sheet for Mrs. Baker's *super* tricky test on Friday just in case Whit doesn't have time to study." She steps back from me, and I let out a shaky breath. Completely calm, she reaches into her bag on the desk, pulling out some stapled-together papers and holding them out to me. "I'm sure the two of you have better things to do anyway, right?"

I grab the test out of her hand and say nothing.

"I'm not going to tell, okay? I wouldn't do that." She opens the door to dismiss me, checking out the empty locker room. Seeing it's clear, she gives me one last almost-tender look. "We're best friends."

33

I fall into my chair at the library table opposite Whit, dropping his phone on top of his pile of books. He came in early today so we could meet and study before class. Thanks to the emotion I've identified as guilt, I can't make eye contact with him right now.

"Where did you get this?" he asks me, instantly suspicious. "I was looking for it everywhere last night."

"From Adrienne. You need to keep an eye on your shit if you're going to hang around me." I blow my hair out of my face. "She called some of those coaches. On the office phone. You should—you need to get Dr. Rickards to call them. Tell them someone was playing a prank."

"What?"

I push back my hair. "She's a bitch, okay?"

His mouth is wide open, eyes going from me to his phone like he can't figure out which one just bit him. "This is your fault."

"Excuse me?" I demand.

"Fuck," he says, as naturally as if all this time it'd been a polite word made for a nice boy like him. "Fuck fuckfuckfuckfuck. None of this would've fucking happened if I hadn't agreed to fucking help you. Do you know how important those coaches are? Do you know how little time they have for Adrienne *fucking* Maynard?"

I actually don't. But I expect he is asking rhetorically.

"Don't yell at me," I tell him.

"Yell at you? This is so not about you, Olivia!"

"I got your phone back for you." I cross my arms. "Can't we just study?"

"Can you not see I'm freaking out?" he demands, and he totally is. He looks almost unkempt then, like his anger's mussing up his hair. His voice is too loud in the library, his eyes darting around as if some solution were going to pop out of the shelves, and I think, *I can help, I can do this*, and I lean forward and kiss him like I would anybody I was dating.

Perception is reality.

It stops him in the moment, all mouth on mouth over the table. The moment is real between us, tangible, so true I can almost savor it. When I pull away, his eyes are on my mouth. After a moment of silence, he tells me, "We can't do this."

My heart drops.

"Look, I can help you with your SAT prep if that's what you need but this whole"—he glances around, leaning in close, close enough so I can see individual lashes over his eyes—"dating thing, or not really dating, that's more than I can deal with."

I shake my head. "It's not." His breath smells like spearmint gum. "It's just a long con. Think about it."

"There's nothing in this for me."

I bristle. "Some people wouldn't consider me 'nothing,' you know."

He stares at me.

"Look how easily you lied to Coxie."

"It wasn't so bad," he admits slowly.

"It's never that bad," I tell him, and it won't be. Even if I have to do some double-crossing of my own. He can't get out of this now. If he does, Adrienne will tell Claire what I did and everything will be ruined.

Adrienne's patience is always a ticking time bomb—if Whit is what she wants, I need Whit. If I can dangle a bigger prize in front of her, I can distract her from telling Claire and ruining my last functional relationship.

Our faces are barely apart, our eyes lined up perfectly. A moment passes. Then another. He ducks away, staring ahead. "I've got to call it off. You don't get it."

"You can't." I grab the side of his face and make him look at me again. Desperation saturates my voice. He has to hear me say it. "I need you. I *need* you, okay?"

He can't resist it. He's like a moth I'm watching fly right into the flame. "Okay."

He'll save me if it's the last thing he does.

The dark thought crosses my mind before I can stop it.

Some people are so pathetic.

I come in from practice on Thursday night, beat down. It's been a long week of dealing with Whit's barely concealed judgment of everything I do and avoiding Adrienne when he's around while attempting to placate her when he's not. It's like I'm being torn in more directions than ever, more lost than I was before things fell apart with Ethan.

Claire dropped me off at my house after practice, concern etched in her eyebrows. "Are you okay?" she asked, which was a ridiculous question for *her* to be asking *me*.

"Why wouldn't I be?" I returned, already reaching for the handle of her car.

"Your brother died and then your best friend slept with your boyfriend, for starters."

I fell back against her passenger seat with a laugh. "Oh. That."

"It's okay for things not to be normal right now, is all I'm saying." She pushed her hair back behind her ears, checking herself in the mirror. "If you need to, like, retreat or whatever."

I stared out the window, thinking of the test Adrienne had shoved in my hand Monday. "I think I'm feeling more like myself than I have in a while," I said, the thought breaking me a little. Then I turned back to her, smiling, because she was one good fucking thing that I still had. "But what about you? Things are better this week, right? Less bullshit."

She held up her hand for a minute, and I thought she was going to tell me to leave it all alone but then, instead, she said, "Yes, it's all been properly swept under the rug. Coxie broke up with me and got back together with me this week. My parents are satisfied it was all a misunderstanding. Ellie can bang Thomas Cruz to her heart's content and continue to let her eyes glaze right over me." She stared straight ahead out the windshield. "Everything can go back to normal."

I ran my fingers through my hair, unsure how to answer. I saw the normal that she so clearly didn't want stretched out in front of her. I felt that so much with Claire, sensed the bone-deep ache that was always haunting me. I wanted her to say it out loud, that Buckley was nothing. I wanted her to run away with me, but Buckley wasn't nothing to Claire.

There's so much more in the world that's not here, Claire. Let's go find it.

But that was more belief than I could find in myself right now. With the test in my bag and Adrienne's delicate fingers wrapped around my neck.

So I got out and watched her drive away.

I trudge into the kitchen now, feeling defeat in every curve of my body. Mom is working at the kitchen table, as she does quite often, some papers gathered around her. She looks up when I come in, her face quizzical. "Bad week?"

I throw my cheer bag on the ground in response. "What's for dinner?" I ask, making my way to the fridge and pulling it open like a meal will smack me in the face. I figure I'll take whatever is available to my room and study my SAT booklet for the rest of the night. Whit was expecting me to have some test questions done tomorrow because he is the most demanding sucker on the planet.

I flinch at the thought, hating myself for letting it exist.

"There's nothing," Mom says, while I'm living out my own personal hell. "Why don't we go out? Want a burger? I'm craving a burger. We stay in too much, don't you think? Let's go."

I turn around, shocked, as the fridge closes behind me, and she has hopped up from the computer like her work couldn't matter less to her. She's picking up her keys, basically ready to leave right then, and I am staring at her, shell-shocked.

No, I want to say. *I do not want to go get a burger with you.* There's so clearly some therapist or parenting book behind this, that I can do nothing but balk. But she's standing there in front of me, eye to eye, with an almost hopeful look on her face, and there's nothing but dread and comparative questions in my future.

"Fine," I say. "Let's go."

And that's how we end up at Ellington's, the greasy café right on the outskirts of town, heading toward Central. Ellington's is small enough to be called cramped, and all of the furniture is from no earlier than 1977, but people drive a hundred miles for an Ellington burger. On a weekend, the wait is typically over an hour, and people mostly just skulk outside around picnic tables, taking pictures with the five-foot-tall multicolor ceramic cow.

Tonight, though, as if a higher power is on our side, Mom and I sit down at Ellington's in fifteen minutes. "Oh, the Chipper Burger," she reads off the menu. "That's new."

" 'Hit a home run with the Chipper Burger!' " I quote.

Mom smiles, flipping the one-page menu over.

It's nice. It's weird, but it's nice because I'm too busy thinking about how weird it is to think of anything else. And I actually appreciate that. I appreciate she did that for me.

Then I spot Daniel Smith and some of his friends at the table across from us, and my heart sinks. It's not that I care about Daniel, or whatever, but school seemed so far away for half a minute. There's no escaping your demons in Buckley.

"What's wrong, Olivia?" Mom asks, and my head snaps back to her. She has put down her menu and is watching me intently.

I shake my head, not really meeting her eye. "Just saw someone I know from school," I tell her. I hope Daniel doesn't see me back.

"Not just now," Mom says. "This whole week. It's been worse, hasn't it?"

I never thought she noticed. I shrug.

"We don't have to talk about it," she says. "But we can, if you want to. How's Ethan?"

I suck in a breath. Right. That. "Ethan and I broke up. *I* broke up with Ethan," I say. Half the town must know that. Hell, probably more. But she doesn't, because I haven't told her.

"Oh, Olivia," she starts to say, and I shrug her off again.

"I met someone else," I say. I'd never planned to tell her the Whit lie, but it was the easiest defense. The moment is mercifully interrupted by our bubble-gum-chewing waitress arriving to take our order. I get the Chipper Burger.

I stare off past the waitress as Mom orders. The café splits into an open kitchen toward the back with a narrow hallway leading to the bathroom. Some guys are getting out from the last table in the back, chatting and laughing easily with each other. As our waitress goes to take her leave, I realize I know one of the boys.

Oh, shit.

I glance over at Daniel's table wildly, and he averts his eyes so that I know he was looking. Whit and his brother are getting closer, and I am panicking because this was not how anything was supposed to go ever. The absolute last thing I could afford to do was act like a total freak in front of Daniel and have it get back to Adrienne.

I hop out of my booth with forced enthusiasm. "Whit!" I call, right as he reaches our table and I am staring at him and he is staring at me so I wrap my arms tightly around his neck.

"Liv," he says, and the nickname rolls so easily off his lips, the same one Mom and Ryan always used. I've always been O to everyone at school. Ade and O and a world of trouble.

"So weird," I say, hearing the frantic note in my own voice. "I was just talking about you. Mom, this is Whit DuRant, my boyfriend."

Mom's eyes go wide at the sight of Whit in his khaki shorts and button-down white shirt. He extends a hand that she takes. "Nice to meet you, Mrs. Clayton," Whit says, not really missing a beat. But now Cason is looking at him as if he's completely lost his mind.

"And his brother, Cason," I introduce quickly. "He goes to Duke."

Cason's face clears completely as he smiles at Mom, and then he turns, grinning, to me. "So good to see you again, Olivia! I'm so glad tutoring is going so well for you."

Whit smiles wider at me than is strictly necessary.

"Whit's been tutoring you as well?" Mom asks. God, please let me disappear right here.

"Just helping me get ready for the SATs," I say. "He's number two in our class. Has a bunch of scholarship offers."

"To golf," Whit says modestly.

"Twenty-five percent scholarship to golf. The other seventy-five percent is all coming from academics," Cason says, a note of pride in his voice. Whit looks away, rolling his eyes.

"It's so nice to meet you both," Mom says and I can tell she means it.

"Well . . . ," Whit starts, glancing between Cason and me, "we better get going. Cason is just home for the weekend, but we had to get some Ellington's."

"Of course," I say, not really sure where to put my hands. It's not like I hadn't dated Ethan forever, not that I don't know how this goes. But everything had been so natural, so predetermined. There is no Whit and me as a couple, no *us*, so I don't know how to be. So I do the first damn thing that pops into my mind. I grab the front of his shirt and pull him down to pop a kiss on his lips. "Text me later," I say.

His face is still dangerously close to mine, colored in surprise. "Of course," he says, so low only I can hear him. Then he pulls away, and he and Cason are off. I slide back into the booth across from Mom.

"Whit DuRant?" she asks. "And you've been doing extra work for the SAT?"

I nod.

"Why didn't you tell me?"

I sigh deeply. "That whole coping thing where I don't like to talk about it," I say.

She looks behind, at where Whit was standing. "He seems very nice."

"He does, doesn't he?" I don't want this. I don't want her to be here to see any of this, to be drawn into this bullshit. I want to keep it simple, in and out. "It's not serious, though. He's kind of full of himself."

Mom's, like, half smiling about it. Which seems like the exact opposite reaction she should have when I imply I'm screwing around with some boy. "What?" I demand.

"I was always that way with boys when I was younger, too," she says. "Kept it all very casual to keep from admitting when I had feelings for someone."

I roll my eyes. "This isn't like that."

"It's fine if it is," she says, like she's making some sort of damn progress with me. Like I am a task she can conquer.

"He wanted to slum it to get his brother's attention and that's what this is. I'm just another science project for him," I snap.

She purses her lips, that look wiped off her face. "Olivia, I'm sure it's not—"

I stand up from the table. I can't listen to her tell me how alike we are when we have nothing in common at all. "Drop it," I answer. "I need to go outside. Adrienne wants me to call her." I head for the exit, hating the feel of her eyes on me as I go.

34

When I go to see Mr. Doolittle on Friday morning, something bursts out of me before I can stop it. "What do you think about relationships?" I ask him.

His shock at this breakthrough is evident. "I—I think they can be very complicated."

I nod like that's remotely illuminating. "No shit."

The victory fades away as fast. "Miss Clayton."

I see Ethan in my mind then. The way he waited for me after class with a crooked smile. "I think—it's funny, isn't it? How one day this person is your best friend that you do everything with and the next he's some stranger you don't even wave at in the hall. It goes from everything to nothing in the blink of an eye. Like with your wife. Is that right?"

He bristles.

"And then, you can just, like, *create* relationships out of thin air, you know? It goes from stranger to sex like that." I stare off.

"Excuse me?" Mr. Doolittle asks.

I look back at him. "Sex," I say, letting the word hang in the air. Shocking in Buckley, where everyone's a virgin until they're pregnant.

"I don't think that's the right way to look at it," he says gently.

I don't want to be gentle. "I mean, it's one of the basic building blocks of life. Nothing wrong with it, right?"

He treads carefully. "Well . . ."

"There's nothing wrong with *me*. I mean, for wanting it, so I don't get why someone would just say no. Colleges don't look at your sex transcript, do they?"

He is sweating. "Of course not."

"Whit's helping me," I say. "With SAT prep. Thanks."

"It's natural," he continues, face all red, "when dealing with loss, to seek other types of comfort."

"Sex."

He dies on the spot. "Yes. For one."

"You're saying it's not healthy?"

"I'm saying—" To my surprise, he actually chills out for a moment, sitting up a little straighter, fixing his tie. "That it may be more important to make an emotional connection than a physical one. That may be what you're missing."

I'm not missing anything. Except sex. "He still doesn't like me, which doesn't seem very fair."

"Mr. DuRant?"

I nod.

"Olivia, Mr. DuRant means well, whether or not he lets on. But you should be careful with him."

"He might hurt me?" I ask, amused and almost touched by his concern.

"You might hurt him."

An hour after Mr. Doolittle says this to me, I'm standing at Whit's locker about to plant a stolen answer key.

I stand there and Mr. Doolittle's words dig right under my skin. He's no different from Adrienne. He thinks I might *hurt* Whit. In spite of everything, in spite of everything I've lost, I am still a weapon, not a person. A danger to real people—a bomb that could blow up at any moment, and everyone is a potential target. I can't imagine what I'd have to do for my feelings to count. I can't imagine ever being wounded enough for anyone here to care.

I can't be dragged through it all again. I can't be reviled anymore. It hurts too damn much. I'll have to find another way to stop Adrienne.

This is the only way out.

Whit doesn't care about me. He doesn't need me. He hates me.

I have to.

I fold the answer key up and slide it in through the grille of the locker. It slips out of my fingers and falls on top of his books.

I glance around the empty hallway. Wipe my face clean. Don't let it hurt.

Adapt and survive.

35

"You'd think the shock would wear off eventually," Whit tells me as we walk together between classes, and people stare at us walking by.

I glance at him, feeling guilty. "You should hold my hand or something," I tell him. "Or look like you enjoy my company even slightly."

He shrugs.

I decide not to feel guilty. I stop at my locker.

"I have bad news." Whit leans against the side of my locker, watching me. I cram some C papers inside, and Whit grimaces, as if the sight of it actually causes him pain.

I cock my head to the side. "What, Masters jackets are going to be orange from now on and it's not your color?"

His eyes practically roll out of his head. "Very funny. Like I'll win a Masters." Wow. "No," he goes on, "my parents heard I had a girlfriend."

"Well dressed *and* a girlfriend? You'd think they'd be pleased." He doesn't laugh. "Did Cason tell them?"

"No, they already knew somehow. They were grilling me about it last night," he says. "My parents know everything."

"That's so weird. My mom doesn't want to know anything." I slam my locker. "Who cares, anyway? Aren't they, like, adults? They should be used to the idea."

"They want to meet you."

I stare at him for a second. "What? Why?"

Whit puts his head down, getting closer to me in the process, his words so soft that only I can hear them. "Because our country club is having this stupid charity ball tomorrow night, and my parents think I have a girlfriend, and since you're the girlfriend they think I have, you have to go with me."

"No."

"It's part of the deal," he insists. "It won't work otherwise."

"I'm not meeting your parents. Then it's like—it's like—"

"Real." He nods and starts walking toward his own locker. "But I met your mom, right? Turnabout is fair play."

Right, I guess he did do that. And totally had my back. I can count on one hand the number of people who have my back.

"Hang on," I say, reaching my arm out and grabbing his. Several people run straight into me.

He turns back. "What?"

"I think Adrienne put something in your locker. I heard her talking to Elona Mabry yesterday and I—I just realized."

Whit puts his arm on mine and pushes us over to stand next to the wall. "Okay. What did she say?"

I swallow. "Mrs. Baker's test. Something about that." I am no longer entirely sure who I am stabbing in the back, but I can't do it. I can't watch him fall directly into her trap. I run my fingers through my hair. "We can probably get rid of it if we go now. I could go."

He watches me closely, his gaze going through me. I can almost see the decision click into place behind his eyes. "I'm not going to let you take the fall for that. If we get caught, I can get out of it easier than you can. C'mon," he says, and holds out his hand for me to take. I do. "Let's go."

We get to his locker, and he opens it up and then looks at me expectantly. "There's nothing in here."

"Whit."

We both turn at her voice. Mrs. Baker, our chemistry teacher, walks over to his locker. My hand is on his arm and Mrs. Baker's eyes are on my hand on his arm and she's holding the folded-up test and looking over her black-rimmed glasses.

He shifts my hand on his arm in a way that makes me let go. "What's going on?" he asks Mrs. Baker.

"Can I speak to you?" She gives me a disdainful look. "Alone?"

It's fine. Mrs. Baker has never liked me. I gave her hell in freshman chemistry, and when she looks at me, I can tell she's remembering the mean girls in her own high school. She must've been the bottom of the social ladder back in the day. She was totally a person who hated high school. Now that she's been here a few years, though, everyone thinks she's cool.

I cross my arms over my stomach. "Sorry, I wasn't trying to be a *problem*," I say.

Whit keeps his voice calm. "What is it?" he asks her.

Mrs. Baker kind of half glares at me, like my continued existence is a personal insult, and holds up the answer key to her test. Her neat handwriting fills up the lines on the page. "Where did this come from?"

Whit squints his eyes. "I don't know." He side-eyes me. "Why are you asking me?"

"It was found in your locker." She looks at me again like she knows I put it there.

"Who put it there?" he asks, right on cue. It's totally what I would have said.

"I'm hoping you can tell me," says Mrs. Baker, and I swear her eyes flit to me again as if she can see straight into my soul. "So I don't have to tell anyone else."

"Who told you it was in there?" I demand, my anti-authority reflexes taking over. "And what right do you have to go through his locker? What are you, like, his girlfriend? That's illegal."

Mrs. Baker brushes me off. "Check your amendments, Miss Clayton.

They don't count at school." To Whit, whom she clearly likes much better than me—if she's heard the gossip that we're dating, she must hate me even more—she says, "Elona Mabry said she saw you going through my papers when I left class yesterday. She said you took something."

"I did not."

Mrs. Baker shakes her head. "C'mon, Whit. Let's go talk to Dr. Rickards about this."

He follows after her, shooting one last angry glance behind him as he goes.

I'm at one of the cement tables in the quad behind the new building, trying to concentrate on this SAT booklet, my mind everywhere else. I jiggle my leg. Whit still got caught, so Adrienne can't change her mind.

I glance up, looking for Whit at the thought. Nothing.

I turn back to the question.

IN LINE 5, "SURVEYING" MOST NEARLY MEANS:

I'm such an idiot. If I had just spent any time caring about any of this in the past four years. If I—

"I know you probably think this is going to change my mind, but I'm not going to let her intimidate me, okay? *We're* not going to do that."

I look up from my booklet, surprised. Whit throws his coat and backpack down angrily and falls into the chair across from me. "But first tell me one thing," he says.

I nod.

"Tell me you had nothing to do with it. That you want nothing more to do with Adrienne and her bullshit. Promise me that. Knowing you two, this could be a setup; I know that. It totally could be. But I believe you hate her and I believe that you don't want Claire to know what you did, so please." He looks down. "Just please tell me, okay?"

His eyes have this pleading look in them. He really wants this to be true, and I do, too. We're in this together and we can beat Adrienne. I run my fingers over the SAT question, watching him watch me. He's going to introduce me to his parents. He could tell, through it all, that I was miserable. He wants to help me.

No one thinks I'm worthy of help.

"Okay." I nod. "Yes." I can undo this. I can make everything I said to him in the car true.

"I'm not going to be a prick anymore about the other stuff. What's in the past is in the past. If she doesn't like that we're together, we're going to give her the"—his eyes flit around to be sure no one is listening—"best fake relationship anyone has ever seen."

I smile. "Yeah. Definitely." I play with the edges of my SAT booklet for a moment before I ask, "But what happened? With the test and Mrs. Baker?"

Whit shrugs nonchalantly, even though I can tell it's bothering him. "Not that bad. Mrs. Baker loves me, so she helped out. I even think she believed me, but we didn't have much ground to stand on."

"I can talk to Elona, if you want," I tell him. "Assuming Adrienne's behind it—"

"Oh, she is," Whit assures me.

"Yeah. Well, I can pull some strings. It's what I do."

"So I got detention and a zero on the test, but she'll let me do some extra credit. Adrienne's not quite as smooth as she thinks she is."

"What about your college coaches?" I ask.

He doesn't meet my eye. "Adrienne can't hurt me, all right? I promise." He's so determined to prove to me that Adrienne is nothing. I can't let her ruin him. Or me. I'll have to play her game, but I can be on the right side of it this time.

"So we're in this thing?" he asks me. "Together?"

I nod. "Together."

36

The night of the Woodhaven Country Club Charity Ball, Whit picks me up right on time. My mom is so nice to him, it almost physically hurts me—I halfway wish I would have changed at the Gas 'n' Go and driven to his house like I planned to at first. Later, when we pull up at the country club, he tells me his parents aren't there yet, so he walks me over to the patio off the ballroom. People sit at the tables, sipping cocktails and laughing. Whit pulls my chair out for me, catching me by surprise.

I look at the people all around us with their nice clothes and expensive drinks. "Do I look okay?" I ask him.

He takes me in. My brown hair braided to the side, my bare shoulders, navy dress that flares out a little at the bottom. "Yeah. Of course," he says, totally ruining the moment.

I put my face into my hand. "Of course," I mutter.

"Well, you're just asking to ask," he tells me. "You already know you look great."

I didn't, actually. I lean back and relax. "So I talked to Elona," I tell him, shuffling my feet against the cobblestone patio.

He tenses. "What'd she say?"

I gaze up at the clear night sky, purposely avoiding his eyes. "Adrienne put her up to it, obviously. She said she'll tell Dr. Rickards she didn't really see anything, if you want."

"Yeah, that should do a lot of good now that they found the cheat sheet on me," he bites off. He sighs. "Mrs. Baker was telling me all about how much recruiters would hate me disregarding the honor code, and that she'd tutor me if I need help." He snorts. "Do you even know who took the test out of her room? I know Adrienne doesn't do her own dirty work."

"Anyone could've done it," I say dismissively. It's so easy for me to lie. I've been doing it for years. Stare straight at them, don't blink, act like it doesn't matter.

I almost wonder whether I enjoy it. Lying to both Adrienne and Whit makes me feel like my old self again. It makes me forget Ryan for a while.

That doesn't last, though. When I shut my mouth, I have to remember all over again.

"Luckily, the coach from Duke has known my family forever. He's diagnosed me with 'senioritis.' Like that automatically makes me some kind of idiot."

"Well, that's where you're going anyway, right?" I say as much to reassure myself as him.

He looks across the table at me.

"Like Cason," I conclude.

"Yeah," he says after a minute. He glances at his phone. "Just like Cason." He stands up. "Let's go. My parents are here."

I follow him.

The inside of Woodhaven Country Club is all glossy wood. High-vaulted, polished wooden beams make up the ceiling. The hardwood floor's shine shows our reflections. I keep catching sight of myself and losing it a second later.

"Can you not do that thing with your hair when you see them?" Whit whispers to me as we walk around the room.

I stare at him blankly.

"The hair-flippy thing," he explains.

"Why?" I shake my head. Braided like this, my hair's not moving that much, anyway. "Do I look smarter when my hair is still?"

"You look less dangerous." Well, that explains everything.

"Less like I'm having sex with you?" I suggest.

His eyes travel around the room, scandalized. Someone might have heard. "Please don't say anything like that when you meet my parents," he says, as if I had no common sense. "They already think I'm on a tragic downhill trajectory."

I cross my arms, stuck somewhere between annoyance and guilt. "I won't."

All around there are clean people in clean clothes. Which is good. It's normal. It doesn't feel like Buckley.

Whit isn't Buckley.

He's waving at people and throwing out greetings as we walk by: "Mrs. Clark." "What'd you shoot yesterday, Tripp?" and "Hope you're feeling better, Everett." And all the while, I'm a step behind, nodding politely and giving each of them some kind of half smile as we go.

If I'm going to meet his parents, I have to be this girl who's acceptable. Worse than that, I have this growing suspicion that I want to please these people. That, if they see me as someone who could be dating Whit DuRant, then they'll see me as acceptable. They'll see me as *someone*.

Something cold and rough hits my fingers and squeezes. With a jolt, I realize Whit has grabbed my hand. *Right.* Because we're supposed to be dating.

But I have this dry, sinking feeling in my stomach and a thudding coming from my ribs. I finally recognize it.

He's making me nervous.

"Are you always this, like, put together?" I finally ask.

"What?"

"I don't know," I admit. "It's—you're so natural at this stuff. Impressing people and being friendly and all that. Why are you always so over it at school?"

He quirks an eyebrow at me and glances around to make sure no one else is listening. "I thought you said I was kind of a dick?"

"You are. There. But here you're, like, the king of country club bullshit."

"I'm supposed to be," he says. "It's how you act. Oh," he continues, his eyes at a point over my shoulder, "there they are."

The bottom falls out of the little calm I have left.

"Come on," he says.

I can't tell if he's dreading this as much as I am, but soon we've crossed the room and I can't think about it anymore. "Mom, Dad, this is my girlfriend, Olivia. Clayton."

Smiling feels like it might actually make my face crack in two, but I do it anyway and hold out my hand to shake like I'm supposed to do. "It's nice to meet you."

Whit's mom has a thinner face than him; crinkly, kind green eyes; and auburn hair. His dad has Whit's strong jawline. He's tall but rounder.

"Nice to meet you, Olivia," Mrs. DuRant says. Her voice is as cautious as the look in her eyes.

Dangerous. Right.

"Wouldn't believe it until I saw it with my own eyes," Mr. DuRant chimes in. "Did you get here all right, son?" Mr. DuRant grabs his arm.

"Yes, sir," Whit says.

"Your brother's wandered off, of course," Mrs. DuRant says, giving Whit a conspiratorial smile. "If you two have been looking for him. Have you met Cason yet, Olivia?"

"Briefly," I say.

"He's home from Duke this weekend," she says proudly.

"Probably tired from all of that damage control he's been doing for you," Mr. DuRant says to Whit in a way that's simultaneously light and menacing.

"I thought Marilee would be here tonight." Mrs. DuRant switches gears again, touching her face thoughtfully.

"Mom," Whit chides, causing me to turn to him. Who the hell is Marilee?

"Do you come to Woodhaven often?" Mrs. DuRant asks me.

"Just with Whit," I say, feeling smaller by the second, willing myself to get sucked into a black hole under the floor. I glance out over the room, trying to hide the fact I'm looking for a way out, and I see it.

I see them.

Adrienne and Ethan. Ethan in a light blue button-down that I got him for his birthday last year and Adrienne in black. The color of her fucking soul. Why is he here with her?

Whit's dad is laughing at a joke he's just told, so I keep the smile pasted on my face. I wonder if it's obviously fake, one of those plastic smiles that scares people. "We'll see you two later," Mr. DuRant finally says, putting a hand on Whit's shoulder and waving to catch someone as he walks by.

Mrs. DuRant's smile is anemic. "You two look lovely," she says coolly before she exits, and I wish for both of our sakes that I was more impressive. I'm standing there, torn between not watching Adrienne and Ethan and not watching Mrs. DuRant leave, nervous and wrong and totally at odds. There's no one here I can actually compete with because I don't belong at all.

I never will.

"Are you okay?" Whit asks me, but his eyes give him away as he steals a glance at Adrienne and Ethan.

I won't look. My broken heart is beating too hard. It's one thing for her to show up here to screw with my head, but it's a whole other thing to see her here with Ethan. I'll never get used to that sight.

"I'm fine," I say.

I'm not.

I smile at Whit—a fake smile that gives me away crack by crack. His thumb scrapes over the back of my hand. Back and forth.

Cold comfort. All this nervousness tumbling around is making it worse.

"Let's go find my brother," Whit whispers in my ear.

I feel like I might cry. "Where is he?" I hear my voice break, giving me away. Doesn't he hate his brother?

He sounds worried, softer. "Liv."

"Are people looking at me?" I answer. Then I shake my head. Flip my hair. Why can't I disappear?

"Yeah." He stops, turns me toward him, and puts his hands on my shoulders. "You look amazing, that's why. Ethan can't stand it." He leans toward me intimately. "Now stop. You're freaking me out." He kisses the top of my hair, and even though I know it's for show, my heart goes twice as ballistic.

"Where is he? Your brother?"

Whit gets a wry smile. "You'll see."

37

The more time I spend with Cason, the more I realize he is a lot like Whit in all the obvious ways. The self-deprecating smile. The defined jawline. The apparent knack for dipping his tie in whiskey.

"Whit, take your tie off!" I yell. When he turns to face me, I reach up and take his tie out of the loop, grabbing on to an end and pulling it out of his collar. And out of nowhere, he leans forward and kisses me. He tastes like Jack Daniel's—I hate that taste.

His brother cheers and he pulls back, flushed. He has this guilty look on his face, like he did something he wasn't supposed to.

An hour ago, Whit led me through the country club kitchen, across the cement surrounding the pool, out to the pool house, where a bunch of Woodhaven employees in colored polos were pouring out shots on a pool table, splashing dark liquor onto the green felt. Laughter bounced off the walls. Cason had his arms wrapped around two girls, grinning, smooth in every way that Whit was not.

Cason might be a pain in the ass, but he knew how to have fun. And fun was the one thing we both desperately needed.

"Girls who drive the beer carts," Whit whispered to me, the look in his eyes somewhere between distaste and admiration. "Everyone loves Cason." *Almost everyone*, I amended in my head.

Cason had started in immediately on Whit's troubled past two weeks. "It's a good thing Coach Holt's seen you play before. What'd the other coaches say?" Cason asked, his expression serious. I didn't want to hear it. I was so disgustingly responsible.

"Clemson said they'd hold my scholarship for the time being. Florida was annoyed. Said they wanted a commitment by next week or they were gonna offer my scholarship to someone else."

"Screw 'em!" Cason laughed. "DuRants are Blue Devils."

Whit rolled his eyes.

Cason clapped Whit on the shoulder. "But for now, let's drink, little brother."

So now we are standing around the pool table, pouring shots into our mouths like the whiskey is water, and I'm laughing with one of the beer cart girls, named Sheila, who apparently has math class with me.

Whit's kissing me was another part of the act, then. Of course.

We're still staring at each other when I ask him, "Who's Marilee?"

Whit rolls his eyes, leaning down to pour himself another shot. "A girl I used to date." The whiskey fills up the shot glass, slipping down the sides. I already made him promise we would find someone to drive us home before I took a shot. I don't like shots anymore but tonight—tonight it seemed all right. "A girl I broke up with. Her mom and my mom are best friends." He tosses the shot back before turning toward me again. "My mom thinks she walks on water." He laughs to himself about it.

"And that's funny?"

"Marilee is a very religious girl," he tells me. "It was a joke."

Oh, shit. "So that's why she was looking at me like that."

"Like what?"

I don't get to reply, because that's when the door opens.

Adrienne leans back against the door to allow Ethan to follow her in and throws the room a dazzling smile. "We heard this was where we could find the real party!" she announces, instantly taking over. "O, you could've texted me." Ethan at least has the shame to put his head down when he walks in.

"Didn't want it to be awkward," I mutter, glancing at Whit.

Adrienne walks right up to the table, takes a full shot glass out of Cason's hand, and downs it. "Cason DuRant," she says, wiping her lips with the back of her hand. Whit's whole face goes dark watching her.

Cason's eyebrow goes up. "You were JV cheerleading captain my senior year."

She smiles. "You remember." She sets her shot glass down. "So what are we doing?"

"Celebrating my little brother's new relationship," Cason answers unhelpfully.

Adrienne's eyes travel between Whit and me, her grin taking on new life. "You know," she tells Cason, "Ethan here got replaced by your darling little brother, not that he's mad about it or anything. No one could believe it. They're the talk of the town. You." She snaps her fingers in Sheila's face. "Pour me a shot."

Whit takes a measured sip of his drink, his eyes glassy. "You hate that, don't you?" he asks Adrienne.

"Stop it, you two," I interject between them.

Adrienne giggles. "And now we know the real Whit, don't we? Smoking pot, cheating on tests, and dating slutty cheerleaders." Then she shoves me like it's all some big joke.

You could hear a pin drop in the room.

"Shut up, Adrienne," Ethan mutters. I glance at Whit to see his fist clenched at his side. He doesn't take the bait, though. He's silent.

"I could tell you stories about O that would make your blood curdle, couldn't I, sweetie?" She turns to me. "But *best friends* keep each other's secrets, even if they've been bad, bad girls to their cute little boyfriends."

My heart is pounding. I can't even feel anger through the panic. She could tell Whit anything. *Not now, please.*

"Funny how it all happened, huh?" she goes on. "O dumping Ethan for Whit and now Whit in all this trouble. Bad influences, right? Remember, Whit, study time has to come before sexy time."

"Hilarious," Whit finally says.

"Let's play a drinking game," Cason cuts in nervously.

Sheila shoves a shot glass into Adrienne's hand. Adrienne holds it up to her mouth, licking her lips and eyeing the room as if it were all one big juicy snack for her. "Never have I ever . . ." She looks straight at Whit. "Been a low-rent version of my brother." She laughs.

Whit's jaw stiffens. Cason sends Adrienne a hard look before turning to Whit and squeezing his shoulder. "She's joking. Lighten up." Whit takes the shot like the good little boy he is. For once, I wish he'd stop.

I want so badly to say something, but I'm afraid of what her reply might be. I can't show my hand.

"Your turn, Ethan." Adrienne laughs as she speaks, and a thousand unsaid words hang in my throat. She's having the time of her life.

"I'm not playing," he tells her.

"Why? Because of them?" She gestures at Whit and me.

Ethan shakes his head. Calm, cool. "Leave it alone." But his voice is all nervous edges.

"Oh, come on!" Adrienne claps her hands together, her hair spilling over onto her shoulders. Joy has overtaken her, lighting her up. She finds her joy where she makes other people hurt. "Let's call it what it is. This whole thing is to make you jealous."

The light leaves and the dark shines through.

Ethan's eyes meet mine. I've known him long enough to know his expression is *sorry*, but he brought her here. He knew what would happen, and I'm tired of his innocent game. I try again: "Listen, Ade—"

"I'll go," Whit says over me, pouring another shot a little haphazardly. I watch him, clear and bright, everything beyond him just a little hazy, pieces of colors blending together. He and Adrienne lock eyes.

"Never have I ever slept with my best friend's boyfriend and then tried to make her feel like shit about it."

Adrienne laughs as she takes a drink, a dark brown Jack Daniel's tear running down her neck, wet and long. Adrienne turns to me. "You hear your boy, O? You gonna let him talk to me like that? Tell him whose fault it is all this happened."

I shove Whit out of the way and get face-to-face with Adrienne. "Don't talk to her like that, Whit," I say, directly in front of her.

"Thank you," she says, taking her time to enunciate each word.

"I'm leaving. I need to be alone, okay? Please don't follow me," I tell her.

"Fine," she says through a fake-saccharine smile.

I flee the room; Whit is on my heels.

I sail down a long maroon hallway and take a hard left, finding myself in another immaculately clean hallway. I keep going until I spot a closet door and jerk it open, sliding inside and slamming the door in Whit's apologetic face.

No sound comes from the other side of the door for a moment. Outside, I imagine him having one of those fabled silent debates with himself.

Then the door opens, and I fall into him, mouth first, attempting to knock him over with nothing but the sheer force of my lips on his. As I pull him into the closet, I reach around him to grab the doorknob and slam it shut.

I tug at his hair as my tongue slides into his mouth, really believing for a moment I can taste him from the inside out. Believing that this thing might be real. I breathe every part of him into me. A mop tips over onto the floor and crashes somewhere far away.

I press myself against him, moving ever closer, shoving him against the hard metal of the closet shelving, trying to do what I'm good at. Being a slutty cheerleader.

He's letting me, I think. *Because I am so damn good at this.*

I yank at his button-down shirt with both hands, pulling it loose from his slacks, my fingernails sliding under to rake the skin on his lower abdomen. He tilts his head at just the right angle then, to bring our mouths closer together, as if that were even possible. He likes me right now. He likes me a lot.

I fumble my dress out of the way and straddle one of his long legs with mine, and I can feel him. His words can lie to me all day long, but his body can't—he wants this as much as I do. I move my hips, hard, just to check, and grab the back of his head again. This is the moment I love. Right before he grabs me back and we're panting and he's trying to bring every part of me closer to him and there's nothing but damp skin and adrenaline.

Oh. My. God. This is so good.

It's like I always knew. From that moment in the classroom, I knew I had to get something from him. I had to be something to him. I decide to do it then—I reach down and start loosening the buckle of his belt, unbuttoning his pants.

He pushes me back.

Panting, he asks, "What"—pant, pant—"are you doing?"

My mind's just run a marathon without my body. I glance quickly around the room, taking in the dim outlines of metal shelves and cleaning supplies, the faint Clorox smell. "Doing what feels good." The words come out easy. Soft. I wrap the collar of his shirt in my fist, clutching it tight to pull him back into me. "Kiss me."

Instead, he removes my hand, pulling farther away, and stands there in front of me all disheveled with his belt unbuckled. "No." It hangs there between us. "I'm not doing this, Olivia."

He's so high and fucking mighty—he was *just* doing it. I start to turn to leave, and he grabs my arm. "You aren't even going to ask why?" he says.

Because I don't care. I repeat silently: *I don't care, I don't care, I don't care.*

"Fine. I'll tell you anyway. Because you don't want to have sex with me."

I roll my eyes. "Yes, I did. That's what I was trying—"

"You can't just use sex to forget all your problems. I'm not going to be a part of it." He runs his hand through his hair, attempting to swoop it back into place.

"Oh, what? Now you're going to tell me you won't have sex with me so you can feel important and noble or something?" I spit the words out. Strands of hair stick out from my braid and my dress is all mussed up. The air is heavy and close, and I can only make out bits and pieces of Whit through the darkness. "I hate you." I grab something off the shelf behind me and throw it against the floor. It's a plastic bottle so it doesn't break, but I can hear the angry echo of liquid sloshing around inside. "You just don't want to sleep with a slut."

And then my fucking voice cracks. Suddenly I'm no longer a danger to be near and his forehead is touching mine and we're close, as if he'd never put any distance between us in the first place. His Adam's apple bobs up and down several times before he finally starts speaking. "I want you to be okay, but this—this isn't," he says. We're breathing the same air, skin touching, living in this same moment in time where nothing is ever okay. "And I want—this isn't what *you* want."

"Don't tell me what to do," I say. "You're not my boyfriend."

"I'm your fake one."

"You're drunk. Leave me alone."

He sighs, shakes his head sadly, and walks out of the closet.

I lean back against the door, and the rest of the world leans on top of me.

TWO AND A HALF MONTHS AGO

"I'm sorry," Ethan whispered next to my ear. I was leaning up against the wooden column of the house's back porch, the wind rolling up tiny waves on the lake behind the house. My arms pulled tight around me, my head against the cool wood. I looked at him.

"I don't want you to be sad," he explained.

I studied him a moment before turning back to the water. "I know."

"Why don't you want me to know about Ryan? When we met, he was all you talked about."

I shrugged. "I guess that's why."

"Why don't you *talk* to me?" he asked, and I heard every desperate edge in his voice. The sharp scribble of words written in the air between us.

I didn't say anything, which seemed to prove his point. There was a faint noise in the background, a chorus picking up in volume. "Crickets," I finally said.

He snorted. Behind me, he scooted closer, leaned down, and rested his chin on my shoulder. "Crickets," he repeated, and the word reverberated into my shoulder, down my back. "I love you."

I shifted my head from leaning into the wood to leaning into the side of his face. Slowly, I turned my entire body until we were kissing and it wasn't just kissing. It was like an argument with our mouths but so much better. It hurt in the best way.

"Promise," I demanded between kisses. "*Promise* you won't hurt me."

"Yes," he said, kissing me and kissing me and meaning it, I knew.

"You won't change." I pushed him into the back wall of the house, his skull knocking against the siding.

"No," he swore, wincing into my mouth.

"Please." I was almost crying.

He stopped, looked right at me, a fire blazing behind his eyes. "I promise you, Olivia."

I kissed him again. Never did notice the phone ringing.

39

I'm at the Rough House, like usual. One slice of supreme pizza larger than my head on a bright orange plate. Identical plate across from me.

Claire leans against the table into her palms. "You know why she's not here, don't you?" She taps her fingernails against the table. "What's going on?" she says.

I take a pepper off my pizza and a little cheese hangs off it. It burns my mouth when I bite. "She doesn't like Whit, I guess." I swirl my finger around the top of my paper cup. "She's always jealous of the guys I date."

Claire steals a glance at the bar. Ellie isn't there. "Adrienne is jealous of anything that isn't her. In elementary school, she was jealous when the teacher told us the earth revolved around the sun instead of her. She was jealous when she heard that she needed oxygen to live." Claire's eyes flit to the door to be sure Adrienne really isn't coming. "She said she didn't need anything. I'm sure she heard it from her mom." It did sound like something Mrs. Maynard would say. She'd press her overripe lips together and arch her perfect eyebrows, look at you with those too-dark eyes like Adrienne's, and tell you she didn't need oxygen or anything else.

Which is bullshit, given that she needs Mr. Maynard's money like a fish needs water.

"Why don't you do the things we do?" I ask Claire. My pizza is already getting cold. Her face is all inquisitive, scrunched up and cute.

"What things?"

"You know," I tell her, because she does. She sees us every day, plotting, acting. Playing the evil queens of our kingdom, keeping the villagers down. "We like it. We like being the most feared girls at Buckley High."

Claire shifts uncomfortably. "Why are you saying this? What happened last night, really?"

"I don't think anyone will ever actually be able to love me. I thought Ethan might, but maybe I have this inherent badness inside of me. You aren't like that. You're a good person."

Claire is quiet for a moment, staring at the table. "I'm kind of tired of your shit, actually," she tells it, her voice quiet.

I am speechless. Claire is the sympathetic one in this game we play. She's the one who grabs us from the edge when we go too far.

She just pushed me over.

"I am *exactly* like you and Adrienne. If I wasn't, why would everyone at school keep trying to hurt me? Why would I be your best friend? Why would I be so in love with Ellie?" she asks me, the words falling a little bit desperately. "I love people who treat other people like shit, so now I'm getting a taste of it, aren't I? Nothing less than I deserve."

"Claire—"

"You know Maggie Rogers? She used to play basketball and she transferred schools last year?" she asks me.

I nod.

"I kissed her in ninth grade. Like, I just did it because I wanted to, and I've always gotten whatever I want, right? And I made her promise not to tell anyone." She jiggles her foot nervously, even though we're the only ones here, looking like she either wants to burst wide open or shrivel up on the spot. It never even occurred to me there had been other girls she'd wanted to be with besides Ellie. And I realize in that moment that I never completely understood who Claire was: I thought Claire just liked Ellie in particular because she was so cool and smart and beautiful. I've been so ignorant of my own best friend.

"The next day, she asked me what it meant." Claire's face goes from totally heartbroken to expressionless as she says it. "I told her it meant she was a dyke. I hate that word. I *hate* that word. And of course it wasn't that. It wasn't that at all. It's that she wasn't *good enough* for me. She wasn't cool like you or Adrienne, and it's not like I'm in love with you or Adrienne, but what would you have thought? Not if I was with a girl. But if I was with *Maggie*. I couldn't be with someone like her. I'm Claire Barber, you know? I'm the best cheerleader on the team." She has this look of disgust on her face, at herself.

"Yeah, that was wrong, but that doesn't make you a bad person."

"Well, then all of your shit doesn't make you a bad person, either. You're not *inherently bad*. If you were inherently bad, you wouldn't even know that what you were doing was wrong. You wouldn't *want* to make it better."

"Then I'd be like Adrienne," I say, without realizing the words are out in the open.

Claire's eyes are wide. "I'm going to pretend you didn't just say that." Like speaking against Adrienne is a crime against humanity.

"Why not?" I ask her. Why do we continue doing this to ourselves?

"Adrienne is your best friend," Claire replies, whispering despite the fact no one else is in the restaurant. "And whatever else Adrienne is, you know she loves us like nobody else."

"She has a bad way of showing it sometimes," I say.

"So do you," Claire replies. I think back to the texts. Back to everything else. I don't know how to defend myself.

"I'm sorry," I say then.

"I know."

The bell over the front door chimes, and Claire jumps up. Whit's flip-flops make sticky sounds against the Rough House floor as he enters. His eyes travel around the room and land on me. So I stuff a piece of pizza in my mouth, only realizing a second later that he can't talk to me from over there.

"I'll talk to you later," Claire whispers to me, and then kind of disappears. Whit slowly approaches the table, and I chew like a dumbass, hoping I'm not blushing from the memory of last night's tongue assault. I swallow cold cheese. "Hey."

He looks more embarrassed than I feel, so I guess that's good. I get the feeling he wants to ask to sit, so I say it first.

"Sit."

He does.

"It's like Buckley High mythology that you guys are here every Sunday. So it's true," he tells me.

I rest my head on my hands. "In the flesh." I am cool. I am in control. I scoop tomato sauce onto my finger and suck on it. "Adrienne didn't show, though." I glance up at him. "Were you looking for me?"

He shrugs like he doesn't know what he was doing. "Sort of."

"Sort of?"

"Yes."

"Wanting to pick up where we left off?" I point behind the bar. "This place has a really nice broom closet that I think is ripe for a christening."

He pretty much dies on the spot.

I laugh. "I'm kidding." Even though my insides feel totally jellylike and I am still mostly mortified beyond belief because Whit DuRant of all people didn't want me. Still.

I study him. "Are you really as much of a church boy as you seem like you are? It isn't all a big act? Isn't that what you people do?"

His eyebrows arch up into his bangs. "You people?"

I toss my hair, putting my shoulders back, and try to imitate his haughty posture. " 'I'm Whit DuRant and I'm a fantastic golfer and I'm a super good guy who never thinks about sex or watches porn on my mom's computer. I'm your parents' dream come true.' " My hair falls back. "Is that for real?"

"No. I mean"—he glances around—"I don't watch porn on my mom's computer."

I cross my legs. That's not what I was asking.

"Look, I came to apologize, not to get cross-examined, all right?" he says.

"Apologize?" My interest is piqued. "For what?"

"Last night," he says. "I shouldn't have—" He blows out a breath and rubs his swooshy bangs nervously to the side and, oh my God, he really is this guy. "Well, you were right. I shouldn't try to tell you what to do or how you feel. That sucks."

I shake my head. "You were right," I tell him, and I hear something like relief in my own voice. I guess I'm just glad I don't have to make up another excuse or tell another joke about it. "I was upset about Ethan and Adrienne, and you were there, and—"

"Don't worry about it," he says.

"Sometimes it's just nice when someone's there." I lean into my hands, thinking of all the things I should apologize for. This probably doesn't even make the top ten. "I'm sorry that spending time with me has Adrienne after you. It's not fair."

Neither of us says anything for a couple of moments, and it's awkward, and it's not. Because I maybe wanted him last night and he maybe wanted me back for a few minutes, and both my yes and his no were a little bit of a lie.

He did let me.

"Have you been doing those practice math problems I sent you?"

he asks me then. The return to a semblance of normal conversation is beautiful.

I think about it, nodding. "Yeah, my answers are matching up most of the time."

"Awesome," he says, giving me a smile made brittle by nerves. "Don't take this personally, but you seem . . . smart?"

I push my hair back again and pretend everything is totally casual. "No, I'm not. You don't have to say that just because . . . whatever. I know I'm dumb." I point to the now-very-cold pizza on the plate across from me. "You should eat that," I tell him.

He digs in for a bite. "You are smart," he tells me through a mouthful of pizza. He wipes at his mouth with a napkin. "You think I'm, like, bullshitting you for the hell of it?"

He's probably not. I roll my eyes at the suggestion anyway.

"I'm just saying . . ." He shrugs and finally starts to relax. It's almost like I'm seeing the real him for a minute. For the first time. "You shouldn't be in this much trouble with your grades. I don't get it."

"It's school," I tell him. "It's useless." And then, for some reason: "I think I do it to annoy my mom actually. The not caring about it."

"Why?" he asks, mouth full.

"Ugh." I throw a napkin at him. "I guess it was, like, an attention thing when I was younger. My mom's single and doesn't have a ton of time with work and everything else, and she's really quiet. Don't say anything," I tell him, because he was about to. He doesn't. "But, you know, school used to be important to her, and Ryan was already great at it, so I just decided to not."

"To not?" Whit asks with an empty mouth.

"To not do school. School was so boring, you know? Mom didn't really care, and it was something I could do to be like Adrienne—like, she had the best grades so I couldn't get better grades than her, but if I could have the worst grades, that was sort of the same? And back then all I wanted was to be like Adrienne. She was the light of middle school life."

"She was something," Whit says darkly.

"Some of us choose to live in shadows, I guess."

His eyes almost cross, looking at me like I've said the most bizarre thing he's ever heard. And it is pretty bizarre, when I think about it. I think of all the people I've lived my life for: Adrienne and Ethan and Ryan. All of it's kind of sad. Like there's nothing that ties together the pieces of Olivia except my connections to other people. Like when you start snipping away at all the tethers of my relationships, there is nothing left that exists when they're cut.

At least if I am some horrible bitch, there's something left to define me.

"Yeah and the rest of us spend all our time trying to climb out of someone else's shadow," Whit finally says, once he's digested the pizza and my words. I like that he doesn't want to have a conversation about my feelings of futility.

"Cason," I guess.

He turns his pizza around and bites into the crust, chewing and swallowing before he answers. "It's, like, everything I do, he's already done it, you know? Whit won a state championship; Cason won two. Whit graduates salutatorian; Cason was valedictorian. Whit has a girlfriend? Cason has three!"

I giggle. He's joking, but I know he's serious. "No one thinks that. Come on, you're, like, the best at everything."

"Everything I do, Cason's already done." He drops his pizza. "It's not a big deal or anything."

"That's stupid."

"Well. Sometimes people are stupid. I don't know. You like him; you like him better than me."

"What?" I ask. "Where did you get that idea from?"

He shrugs. He acts like he's going to pick up his pizza again but, instead, grabs at all the toppings. And for a second, I see him. All of him. All the insecurity under that haughty exterior.

"I like you, Whit," I say. "I know that probably doesn't mean much coming from me, but I appreciate what you're doing for me. You're a lot nicer than I thought you were. Nicer than your brother. Plus a little funnier."

He gives me a half smile. "Thanks."

I pick up my pizza again. "It's nothing," I say, and take another bite.

40

Parking lots are a very big deal in small southern high schools. Everything goes down in the parking lot—gossip and fights and sex. Last year, the Central High football team all parked in a line between our school and cars to egg everyone's car during last period and salute our team as they walked out of classes. Ethan went back to my house with his nose snapped in the wrong direction, courtesy of Central's defensive line.

Everything is pretty normal as Whit and I come out of the school building on Tuesday. Cliques gather around trucks, girls swinging their feet off the beds. Couples face each other, performing their ten-minute good-byes before unbearable hours apart.

It's all normal. Everything's normal and I'm normal and my relationship is normal. In a few moments, we could be one of those couples.

We start walking toward Whit's Jeep. "Hang on," Whit tells me as we walk out of the school building. He swings his bag around and unzips it, pulling out a baseball hat with a golf logo and propping it up on his side-swept hair.

"Seriously?" I ask as we start walking again.

He adjusts his hat. "Pretty sexy, huh?"

I snicker.

I lean into the side of his Jeep, tilting my head up to look at his face. "Are you going to practice? Or just seduce another girl before Mommy gets home?" I almost blush. I've promised myself I will never kiss him again because I'm probably going to ruin his life in some way or the other.

But he just grins to himself as I reach up and steal his hat away, setting it at a jaunty angle on top of my hair. The sun beats across his face, casting shadows around his defined jawline, his high cheekbones. He has a five o'clock shadow, and I'm about to reach out and touch his face for reasons that may come to light only after years of therapy—when my name rings out across the parking lot.

"Olivia!"

Adrienne flies toward me in a flurry of black hair, shoving Whit out of the way. She grabs on to my arm and hauls me back across the parking lot like I'm her favorite rag doll, here to be thrown to the ground whenever she's in a bad mood.

"What do you want?" I ask, pretending her grip on my wrist isn't killing me.

"Are you even on this planet right now?" Adrienne returns, her voice dripping with disdain. "Whit on the mind?" She says it like his name is the dirtiest, most disgusting word she's ever had to roll off her tongue. I can't push her away, not when one false move will send this whole carefully constructed house of cards tumbling. "It's Michaela."

Those are the right words to send all my alarm bells ringing. Adrienne may be on the other side of the battlefield, but I'm happy to call a truce and take up arms against Michaela Verday and her too-proper-to-wear-eyeliner face.

"What did she do?" I ask. I see her up ahead in a group of newspaper staff girls. She sips on a drink from the gas station up the street, taking her mouth off the straw long enough to giggle, probably leaving a ring of her terrible nude lip gloss behind.

"Somehow she got ahold of a picture of Claire and Ellie. I guess they were making out behind the Rough House last weekend or something? She texted the picture to Coxie and he sent it to me." She hands me her phone, a picture message pulled up. Honestly, it's kind of hard to tell it's Claire and Ellie in the picture unless you know what you're looking at. Their heads are close together in a sort of intimate way, back behind the Rough House. The message below reads, "She says more where that came from."

"Has anyone else seen this?" I demand. Even if I'm against Adrienne, I can have this. *This* is worth ruining someone over.

Adrienne puts a hand on her hip. "Not yet. But . . . matter of time, right? Michaela's hated us since we cut her from the JV squad. Loser."

Instead of blacking out in rage like I should, my blood goes totally ice-cold and I feel like I could do anything. I recognize the feeling, the one I shouldn't allow myself to have. It's like before—before Ryan died. It was so easy. I feel alive, the path laid out for me, Michaela's bright green vest a light at the end of the tunnel. Without pausing, I stride forward and smash directly into her, upending the drink in her hand all over her designer vest. Adrienne barks out laughter next to my ear, the noise colliding with Michaela's horrified scream.

The very bottom tips of her blond hair drip dark soda. "What the hell is wrong with you?" she demands, her too-girlie voice lilting and falling.

"Coxie doesn't want you. Leave Claire alone before I end you," I say. I'm barely taller than her, but I can feel everyone else take a step back, intimidated.

"If you think I'm not reporting you for this . . . ," Michaela says, seething.

"Report me," I snap.

Finally, Michaela's face falls, contorting into something like remorse. "I *have* stopped messing with Claire. I felt bad, okay? I shouldn't have said what I said to her. But it's not like everybody doesn't already know—"

I cut her off. "It's none of your business what everyone does and doesn't know."

Michaela throws up her hands, wet and sticky with soda. I don't know why she's trying to reason with me right now. "Fine," she whines. "Get out of my face, both of you. I didn't do anything!"

"You're completely pathetic," I tell her. "You and your fake voice and padded bra. Going around claiming you're a virgin when everyone knows you went down on Daniel Smith at a party last year in the basement like some kind of huge slut."

"I can't believe you just said that," Michaela snaps back at me, standing up straight. "I can't believe a good person like Whit can even stand to be in the same room as you, much less date you. Even a guy as dumb as Ethan should have known better. Girls like you are what's wrong with this school, you know that, Olivia Clayton? And no one buys you crying over your brother because you're heartless and no one feels bad your boyfriend slept with your best friend because *you're* the one who's pathetic." I glance behind me, ostensibly at Adrienne, but my eyes search out Whit by his car. I can tell he's watching me, but his face is completely passive, shut down the way he's so good at. *Why can't I hide my emotions like you, Whit?*

I don't want to think about him.

"If it was such a betrayal, why are you still hanging out with her?" Michaela points out to me. I turn back around to face her. "You're an idiot. Everyone's glad you're hurt, and they can't wait until Whit wises up."

My pulse speeds up, my hands shaking nervously.

"Do you know what I'll do to you?" I say, holding on to my anger like a comfort blanket. Michaela just delivered the knockout blow. But I can't let her win this. Anyone but her.

Adrienne puts a hand on my shoulder. "She gets it." She turns to

Michaela, in control. The peacekeeper—this is a show we've put on a thousand times before. "If you delete the picture, we'll let it go." I really glance at Adrienne behind me this time, turn back to a confused Michaela momentarily, then shake my head, walking away.

"Let it go," I say to myself, adrenaline pumping through me. I could've burned the world down, and she wouldn't let me.

Adrienne sidles up next to me, pushing her shoulder into mine. I'm about to tell her to back off when she slips a knife case into my hand. "Hunting knife. Swiped it from the bed of Coxie's truck earlier. It has a nice karmic justice." She smiles at me, and I give her a weak one in return. But when she loops her arm through mine, I allow it.

I have to look out for Claire. That part feels good.

When we walk back, Whit is waiting not so patiently for me by his car. "What was that?" he asks me. I don't answer. He gives Adrienne the kind of look he usually reserves for, like, dirt or something before turning back to me. "You want to ride with me and hang out while I practice? We can go to my place after."

My forehead wrinkles up, almost in shock. I'd forgotten who I was supposed to be for a second, and now I can't believe he asked me that. That he's staring at me, waiting, like he meant it. I'm going to say yes, I know it, when Adrienne nudges me. "We have to do something," she says.

Whit averts his eyes. "Fine," he finally says. He probably wasn't serious anyway. Just putting on a show for Adrienne. "We can study at my place when I'm done. I'll leave the front door unlocked for you, okay, Liv?"

I nod. "We'll see you later," Adrienne singsongs, wagging her fingers at Whit as he turns around and gets in his car.

"Stop it," I say as his Jeep roars to life. He pulls out of the spot and I stare after him. With him gone, I start wondering. What would it be like if I was with him? What would we have talked about?

Why did I let Adrienne, of all people, make that choice for me?

This friendship with Adrienne. It's supposed to be fake.

But when someone goes after Claire, after our *best friend*, we have to do something to stop it. Because it's the only thing that feels right, and it's bigger than Adrienne. "C'mon," Adrienne says.

I do.

We slink around, foxes in a metal forest. Michaela's car is this cute little convertible, a hand-me-down from her older sister. We sit down on the curb behind her car, and Adrienne is giggling, but I've lost all my edge.

"Go ahead," Adrienne tells me.

I pop out the knife and stare at the sharp three-inch blade in my hand. It's nicked in places but impeccably cleaned. Dangerous.

I plunge it into Michaela's tire and watch the air bleed out.

LAST YEAR

"Adrienne!" I called. I yanked open her front door in a rush and stopped short in the foyer.

"Olivia." Adrienne's mom was there, perfect in a light pink dress. She pushed back a piece of black hair that hadn't fallen out of place. "I'm glad you're here. Our flight is in less than two hours, and I don't have time for her to be childish."

"Sure," I said, because Mrs. Maynard scared me.

"Tell her," Mrs. Maynard said, coming straight up to me and holding her hands together in a pleading gesture. "Tell her I'll be back in three days. I'm sorry she can't come, I am. But he'll be fine. He always is." Then she turned away, the warmth leaving her eyes as quickly as she could extinguish it. "Honey!" She grabbed up her rolling suitcase. "Honey, we need to go now!"

"I'm right here," Mr. Maynard called, and he rolled his own suitcase into the foyer. "Oh, good, you're here, Olivia."

I nodded.

"Adrienne," Mrs. Maynard called up the stairs, "we love you!"

"We'll call you when we get to the airport!" Mr. Maynard yelled.

"Thanks, Olivia," Mrs. Maynard said to me. Commanding me to

stay and clean up this problem. She squeezed my arm affectionately. Then they were both gone, rolling away like they always did.

"Adrienne!" I screamed again, stomping up the stairs of the house I knew as well as my own. "Ade!" I banged on her door.

She opened it.

She had done her best to look like she hadn't been crying. She had scrubbed away the eyeliner that had run down her face, splashed water in her eyes. "What bullshit did they tell you?" she demanded.

"They had to go," I said. It was weak.

"He's going to die," she told me, her voice flat. "Grandpa. She thinks I don't know, but I do. She says I can't just quit my life. I hate her."

"Ade," I said.

"Ade," she repeated. "She wants me to have less feelings. Like she does."

"So fuck her," I said.

"Just fuck her?" Adrienne repeated with a laugh.

"Yeah," I said, gaining steam. "Fuck her. C'mon, let's go. Who needs her?"

So we did. We ate an entire chocolate cake. Broke the lock on her parents' liquor cabinet and drank shots of tequila until we could barely see straight. We got out a paint set from her mom's hobby room and destroyed the foyer wall and then a white couch. I don't think her mom was ever mad about any of it. She just replaced it all.

We went skinny-dipping in her pool and then wrapped ourselves in towels, leaning against each other as we doubled over laughing.

After, we both stretched out on the back of her car, drying as we watched the stars. Adrienne had found Mike at Night on satellite radio for us to listen to, even though she thought it was stupid. It ruined the point of Mike at Night and the magic of Brown Creek, but I never would've told her that. The night buzzed all around us. I felt so small like that, every bright pinprick of light painted against the sky. It made the world seem vast in a way that thrilled me.

Adrienne didn't need words. She knew. She reached over and grabbed my hand, lacing our fingers together tight.

"It's always going to be like this," she said. "Me and you against the world."

I squeezed her hand back.

42

I spend the rest of the afternoon at practice, buzzing from the high of revenge, the symphony of Michaela's slashed tire on repeat in my head—I can't believe she talked to me that way. I can't believe she thought I'd roll over and die. My adrenaline is still pumping when I pull into Whit's driveway. He'd left the front door unlocked, so I slam into his house, flying through the hallway until I find his room, then go through the open door, smiling.

I clap my hands together. "What's up?"

Whit glances at me and turns away, and like that, the temperature in the room drops to subzero.

"How was practice?" I try again.

"Fine," he tells his homework. "I'm going to be really busy tonight. I have to work on this paper."

"Oh. Of course. I thought—" I stop, feeling stupid. I thought he had invited me over to study. "My mom probably made supper anyway."

He doesn't answer.

Everything feels so surreal all of a sudden. Like I'm standing next to Mom, and Ryan's casket is closed, and I'm screaming until my throat is raw, but no one hears me.

Then I'm back in Whit's room standing quietly, the afternoon's angry adrenaline dissipating, leaving emptiness in its wake.

Pay attention to me.

I pick up a golf ball from his shelf and hurl it at his desk. It bounces off the wall, hits the trash can, and rolls across the carpet.

I freeze in horror as he jumps up from his seat. That was so Adrienne. It was so, so Adrienne.

I can feel it, deep in my bones . . . some part of me still *wants* to be like her. Even now.

To be worse than her.

"Oh my God, Whit," I blurt out. "I'm so sorry."

"Jesus!" he snaps. "What are you doing?"

"I didn't—I'm not . . . This is your fault. Stop treating me like this."

Whit rolls his eyes, dropping back down in his desk chair. "What am I treating you like?"

"Like my mere presence pisses you off," I reply.

"What was that shit with Adrienne back there, huh? Why did you act like that?" he asks me, eyeing me critically over his homework. I've commanded his attention over cosines, so this is a big moment.

"I didn't even think you cared. You asked if I wanted to go to practice with you."

He looks at me like he can't believe I believed that. "I didn't want to make a scene in front of Adrienne. Did you want me to?"

I cross my arms. "Of course not."

He's shaking his head at me. "And then you *went* with her. I was offering you a way out of the situation, and you went with her anyway." I can practically see the frustration rolling off him in waves, taste the betrayal in the air. "And then I couldn't stop thinking about it at practice, and now I've been sitting here, still thinking about it, and I—" He rubs his eyes with the palms of both hands. "I don't understand."

"I have everything under control," I lie. "Why are you worried about it anyway?" I kick my shoes off and fall on his bed, curling my feet up under me in the process. Like he'll forget he doesn't want me here.

"Because I don't see why you have to antagonize Michaela Verday or why you'd ever side with Adrienne and let her humiliate you like that. What you did today was messed up." He looks away, tapping his eraser annoyingly against his desk.

I scoff. "Are you kidding me? Do you know she has pictures of Claire with—her friend? That she was basically threatening to show them to the entire school for kicks? Like Claire needs any more shit on her plate." I'm getting angry again, just thinking about it.

He snorts and doesn't look up from his homework. *God, I hate him.*

"You think that's funny?" I ask. I am really and truly ready to get up and walk out of this forever if he doesn't understand the lengths I will go to stop people from hurting Claire.

"Who told you that?" he says.

I stare straight ahead, not answering. He knows who told me what Michaela planned to do. He always knows.

He nods. "That's what I thought."

My heart is pounding. "She has the text from Coxie. I saw it. 'More to come,'" I say with finger quotes.

He swivels around in his chair to face me. "And Adrienne never has access to Coxie's phone? You guys hang out with him all the time. She took my phone once already."

"She wouldn't do that." I defend her for some reason. Claire is the one thing that is still sacred to both of us—if not, she would've already told Claire what I did. I've seen Adrienne defend her over and over again.

"Would you have?" he asks me, his eyes on my soul right then. Judging, always judging me. "If you thought you could manipulate Adrienne?"

"No," I insist. "Claire's not a game. She's one of us."

His eyebrows arch. "What about before—" He stops before he says *your brother died.* "Before everything?"

I swallow through my dry throat, not wanting to say the words. Not wanting to lie to him. "I don't know," I finally manage, letting myself revel in the bit of self-hatred he brings to the surface. It's a comfortable feeling, one I know all too well. Like a reflex, I begin to spin the narrative. "But Michaela has every reason to do it. She hates us, even Claire, *and* she wants Coxie." I say it with so much authority, I almost believe myself.

Whit turns back to his desk, scribbling on his paper again. "Did it ever occur to you that maybe Claire doesn't need you to defend her? Or here's something novel for you to chew on—Michaela has more important things to worry about than Coxie."

"What?" I say when I can't take it anymore.

"You don't want to know," he tells his calculus.

I get up and walk across the room. Rip the pencil out of his hand. "What?" I repeat.

He sighs and looks up at me. "What do you know about Michaela's life?"

I don't meet his eyes. "Nothing. And I'd like to keep it that way."

"Well, I hate to burst your secure little bubble, but Michaela's mom is really sick. Like sick enough that Michaela can't go away to school next year after she's busted her ass at Buckley to do every extracurricular under the sun, so she doesn't really need you shitting all over her life to add to it." He shakes his head, turning away from me. "I don't even want to know what you did, so don't tell me."

All my defenses go up as though I've seen an incoming army. "How do you know that? About Michaela?"

"You always act like everyone thinks you're some bitch because they don't know you and they don't know what you've been through. But you don't know Michaela, either." He says all this calmly, like the world's still spinning in the right direction, when I feel like the poles just switched under me.

"I don't want to. She's always been horrible to me. She's always been jealous of me."

"My aunt has been her mom's best friend since high school." He takes his pencil back. "I don't think she wants anyone at school to know about it, so don't tell everyone. If you can help it."

I drop my head. "What do you want me to do?" I ask him. "Not be me?"

"Not this you. When you're like this—all I can think of is the Olivia Clayton I thought I knew before I knew you."

I stare at my toes. "Who was she?" I don't think I actually want the answer.

"I don't know." He shrugs. "Someone who *wanted* everyone to be afraid of her. And jealous of her."

"I just want approval or love or something. I guess I'm desperate." I think about it. "I'm always angry," I offer. He doesn't say anything.

I stare around at the walls listlessly. I'm getting that postapocalyptic feeling that hits me sometimes when I don't know where to go or what to do. "I'm going to go," I say.

"What? You don't have to go." He actually stands up to stop me. He looks all serious, but that's Whit's go-to face anyway. I can't really tell what he's thinking.

I glance at his door. "What you said, about who I was before? I'm still her. I still wanted to believe what Adrienne said. I'm still doing her dirty work."

"You're not," he says, as if it were that simple.

I am. I blink up at him. "You make me think that's true. That's why sometimes I don't like being around you." I swallow around this big lump in my throat. "You make me feel—you make me *feel.*"

"So that means sometimes you do like being around me." He smiles.

I shake my head. "It's complicated. It shouldn't be. You're just tutoring me."

"And dating you."

"Kind of."

"But not really."

My teeth dig into my lower lip.

"It sounds messed up, and it is, but I think sometimes I still say the shit I say and do the shit I do because it's what it was like. Before."

"Before your brother died?" he asks, looking so serious and smelling like pencil lead, and I feel the raw nerves in every part of my body and want something in my life to be tangible so badly.

"I really freak sometimes . . . because I can't exactly remember what he looked like. I can't see him anymore."

"That's scary," Whit agrees, instead of telling me it's silly or I'm wrong for worrying. My heart feels lighter. It *is* scary. Finally, someone agrees with me.

"See, like you," I continue, because I'm finally talking about something real, "when I close my eyes, I see you perfectly." And I do it just to prove my point. I reach my hand out until I'm touching his cheek, which should be weird, but right now, it's not. "Your cheek that kinda goes up when you smile." I run my hands over his mouth. "Your lips, sort of thin but long, and I can even remember how you press them together when you're concentrating really hard." My thumb catches against his chin. "And my favorite part. Your jaw. It's so strong and you. I could recognize you from anywhere." I open my eyes. He's staring at my floating fingertips. I dish out a sad smile. "I knew Ryan for seventeen years; I've only known you for a month. It's not fair. I should remember."

"You do." His voice sounds strangled as it comes out. The way he's taking in my face, I can tell he's trying to memorize the details so he can spit them out the way I have. "It's just stored away right now. You'll remember."

I shake my head, breaking out of my reverie. "I know it doesn't make sense. But it's like if I'm closer to her, that girl I was before, I'll see him again. Maybe. Or I can pretend he's not gone. I even thought—even after Ethan—I thought I could go back. I thought I could do it all over again. It's like this whole thing is just catching up to me. But I want you—everyone—to see me as someone better. I know that now." I sigh.

He stares at me, his Adam's apple bobbing up and down as he swallows.

"So you think you have time to study?" I ask, shaking it off.

He looks down sheepishly. "I think I can make some."

43

Mr. Doolittle can't get a word out of me the next morning. Even he is staring at the clock by the end of our session. Still, nothing will deter him from trying to get me to admit what happened to Michaela's car. "Miss Verday said it was a heated argument."

I shrug, staring out the window. "I don't remember."

"Do you think all this anger has to do with your brother?"

I should tell him to ask Whit. I've already discussed this. "No." I sigh.

"If you don't want to talk about it, Olivia, just go. I can't help you if you don't want it."

I look at him, stunned. Is he giving up on me after this month? He flips through some papers, looking haggard. I almost argue with him. At the very least, this isn't what the school district pays for. But I don't.

Instead, I get up and leave his pathetically small office, heading out into the small waiting room that connects all the administrative offices. I don't make eye contact with anyone as I walk toward the exit with my head down, getting away as quickly as possible before Dr. Rickards or someone else who might give a shit can see me. I only glance back as the doors swing shut behind me, leaving one last chilling image.

Adrienne. Crying.

* * *

The thing about rumors is they all start somewhere.

That's the key. You make an innocuous comment to someone and plant a seed. *Did you see how close they were sitting at lunch? Hasn't Daniel been looking tired lately? They got here at the same time?* The seed takes root, grows. That's when you can escalate the story. With Adrienne, the rule of thumb was, tell only one person. If you go around telling everyone, eventually the rumor will catch up to you. If it spreads itself, it's not your fault. They'll never track you down.

Eventually, the lie is so big, it must be true.

This rumor is going to blow the top off the entire building.

Anna is the first one to ask me, eyes full of mirth. "Where's Whit?" She puts her hand on her hip and tilts her head to the side. She loves taunting me like this, but I'm not in the mood for games right now.

"Unlike some people, I don't have to put a tracking device on my boyfriend," I reply.

She laughs. "Maybe you should," and walks away like it's nothing.

My heart races.

It throws me when I can't figure out what she means. Whit wouldn't blow me off, would he? He could be dating that girl from Central again. That's something he should've told me, though. We're supposed to be in this together.

I can't help but feel like I did about Ethan, even though this is nothing like that. It can't be. But the feeling is the same: the fear of betrayal. The gnawing in my stomach.

It's Anna, I reassure myself. *She's lying.*

But I've been whispered about plenty of times before, and I know when it's happening.

I'm down at the water fountain, taking a sip and trying to listen to the conversation some sophomores are having next to me, when Claire grabs my arm. I jerk up.

"Can I talk to you for a minute?" Claire asks, glancing around nervously.

"Yeah. Sure."

"In here," she says, pointing at Coach Bradford's classroom to our right.

I nod.

In the room, a solar system hangs from the ceiling, brightly colored planets dangling on fishing line. Some of those glow-in-the-dark stars light up the back wall, creating a dim light in the darkness of the room. "What's up?" I ask Claire.

She flexes her fingers, pulling against them as if desperate for a way out. "I heard something," she says, and Claire saying it makes it so much worse. Claire doesn't gossip for fun, especially not now.

"What?" I say, gripping my bag tighter, thinking—knowing this is about Whit. It's about what Anna said.

"It's about Whit." She can hardly look at me.

He's cheating.

No, not cheating. He's in a relationship—a real one. Maybe with someone he cares about. He's in love or something.

Claire can't talk, so I do. "Spit it out. What's going on? Don't make me be the last to find out whatever it is."

She shakes her head. "I can't believe it."

"Claire, it's not a big—"

"There's a rumor going around that he's sleeping with Mrs. Baker."

"What?" I almost laugh—really? That's the best they can come up with?

She nods. "I mean, I heard it from everybody. I heard it from nobodies."

I scoff, like *Claire, you're so much smarter than this*. "You don't believe that. I mean, that is the stupidest thing I've ever heard."

"There are pictures. People have seen them."

I cough. "Excuse me?"

"Everyone says they're in the process of putting her on leave so they can investigate. Mrs. Baker, I mean."

I stop. Then start. Then stop again. "Wh—*how*?"

Claire looks confused, and who could blame her? I don't know what's going on, either. Finally, without a word, I nod at her and turn away.

I walk quickly through the halls, head down, thinking. *Adrienne.* This is Adrienne. Her crying was all part of a show. Everything is always part of a show.

But what has she done? How has she made this happen? It's not true. *Is it?*

Adrienne is out on the football field during her free period. I watch her in silence as I walk down the stone steps of the stadium. Adrienne's dark hair flies around her head as she swings down to the ground, thrusting out her hip and putting out two straight arms. She's a study in beauty and sensuality when she moves. She finishes a turn and makes a note on her clipboard.

Then she glances up. She shields her eyes with her arm and waves when she sees it's me. Like it's nothing.

That's when I pound down the rest of the stairs. "What the fuck is wrong with you?" I demand of her, hitting the grass on the football field and throwing my bag down.

She smiles her Cheshire cat smile. "What are you talking about?" I know I should expect it by now, but I can't believe it. I can't believe after everything—everything I've been through, all the hurt she's caused me—ruining something good for me is making her smile.

But that's why I did it to begin with, right? To make her angry. She sees it as a game. One she's winning.

"Whit is sleeping with Mrs. Baker? How did you even cook that up? That's sick." Mrs. Baker, who looks at me with such disdain, such superiority. With my boyfriend. *Not my boyfriend.*

"Actually," Adrienne says, consulting her clipboard, "it's pretty common. Happened at Columbia earlier this year. Some women just need attention, and you've met Mrs. Baker. She'd love a little piece like Whit." She snorts. "I actually posted some picture online of them having some sort of tutoring session. It's amazing how things look from the right angle. And don't even get me started on the special treatment he received when they found the test in his locker. She probably gave it to him so he could hook up with her instead of studying."

"Fuck," I say, running my hand through my hair. "Fuck!"

She stands there, smirking at me as rage builds up in my chest, and then I run at her, shoving her to the ground. I surprise myself more than her, I think, as she rolls me over and sits on top of me, cutting off my air with a knee. I choke.

"Listen here, O," Adrienne says, grinning. The itchy grass rubs against my bare skin, where my shirt rode up my back when I fell. "There's not enough to go on now to really stir up any shit. Which means there's only one person who can make this work. You." She nudges me again, and I am gasping, dying, can barely hear her over the rush of blood in my ears. She notices and lets up a little, but I still can't move. "You're going to say that you saw them together. That you know something is going on. That'll really screw with them. They're already *so worried* and this allegation is *very serious*. Are you listening?"

I want to escape. I nod.

"It's fucking brilliant. It'll be just like old times. Like it's supposed to be, you know?"

She sits back on my legs and I choke. "I won't do it. It's not worth it. I'd rather Claire hate me than for me to hate myself." My voice is hoarse, ragged. I think back to everything. Ryan dead. Ethan gone. This idea that I could somehow escape seems so ludicrous now. So I laugh, too.

She knees me in the ribs. "Shut up!" she demands.

"I'm not like you!" I shout back, even though I have barely anything left to shout with. "Some things are more important to me than my reputation."

She stares at me, and I can almost see the cogs turning in her head. And the smile. It creeps back on slowly, innocently. "What about your mom? What about Ryan?"

For all her weight on my lungs, I have never felt true breathlessness before. Now it's not just that I can't breathe—oxygen no longer exists.

Adrienne's face creeps closer to mine, her hair spilling all down on top of me. "You want her to know? You could've stopped him."

"Shut up," I whisper.

"I didn't *want* to do this," she assures me. "We're friends, O. We're friends." There is desperation in her voice, a total disconnect with reality. "I've always tried to protect you."

"Don't tell Mom," I say. What if it's the thing that irreparably breaks her? What if she finally, permanently can never look me in the eye again? "I'll do whatever you want. Just don't tell her."

"Okay." She punctuates the word with a nod, like we've settled a particularly difficult negotiation. The smile has melted off her face, replaced by something else. She rolls off me and reaches down a hand to help me up. Like this is fine. I ignore her hand and pull myself up. I am in extreme pain, holding my ribs. I'll be bruised when I look myself over tonight, and then I'll poke the sore spots until they go numb. "I'm sorry it has to be like this," she says, solemn. "I'm really sorry, O."

She's not sorry. I have to do it anyway.

I'll take the voice mail to the grave with me.

44

TWO AND A HALF MONTHS AGO

"Olivia, open the damn door." I could tell in Adrienne's voice that she didn't mean it. She did that sometimes, using that harsh tone to bring us back to reality. Claire affectionately called it Adrienne's mom voice. I called it something else.

But I opened the door.

It was the day after. *The first day after Ryan*, I couldn't help but think morbidly. Mom had called me frantic at four a.m. on Sunday and we had left everything exactly where it was (including Adrienne's latest conquest) and driven back to Buckley in the gray light before dawn. Nothing and everything had happened that day, the way it does when people die. I remember lying on the couch after a sleepless night, still sure that Mom was the most horrible person alive when I finally looked at my phone again.

Ryan's friends had started messaging me the day before, the questions and consolations lighting up my inbox. I scanned through them, feeling a righteous anger at everyone's nerve at intruding upon my personal pain, until I saw it.

Missed Call. Ryan. One voice mail.

It's likely I stopped breathing, but I don't remember. Suddenly, it was six the next night, and Adrienne was standing in my bedroom.

I fell back down onto my bed where I'd been all day, holding my pillow between my arms. My room was tiny, nothing like the sprawl of Adrienne's, so she sat down on the old chair at my desk and leaned her forearms against her knees, staring at me.

"What are you doing, O?"

I wasn't sure I could speak and, worse, I wasn't sure if I knew what I was doing at all.

"It's going to be all right, you know," she told me. "I'm not sure how, but I know it will. You're the toughest person I know." She held out her hand to me, and I laced my fingers through hers and she squeezed. "I love you," she said then, and a tear fell as she blinked. "I do."

"Thanks," I said.

"Why don't you get up?" she asked. "I think your mom would like to see you."

"I can't."

"Why not?"

"Because I can't look at her."

She was going to do the unthinkable. Take my mom's side. She began, "Olivia, she didn't mean—"

"I could've stopped him."

Adrienne's hand fell out of mine. "What?"

I sat up then, something about the depth of self-loathing propelling me forward. I played the message for her on speakerphone because that hurt a little worse. Her eyes didn't leave the phone as it played.

"Delete it," she said when it ended.

"No."

"Delete it, O," she was telling me then. Commanding from on high. "I'm not going to let you keep that around so you can hate yourself."

I guess that's when it really started to unravel. The thought that she could *let me* do anything. Of her trying to control my emotions after my brother died, trying to tell me how she wanted me to react.

And the sad thing was, I think she might have been trying to help.

"I should've answered," I said.

"Give me that," she replied, going for my phone. I pulled it out of her reach, shoving her away in the process. She lunged on top of me, and I rolled over as she tried to reach around me. "O! Stop!"

But she was the one who had to stop because I wasn't moving. When she finally backed off, I stared up at her, feeling disgust. "It's mine," I said. "You can't have it."

"Fine," she said, standing up to look down at me. "But do not tell your mother. She will hate you forever if she ever hears that."

I watched her, quiet. Looked down at my phone and pressed the save button to make sure nothing would happen to the voice mail.

"I need to call Ethan," I said at last. "He's been trying to get to me all day."

Her eyes narrowed. "Right. Ethan." She got up and went back to the door. She turned the knob, then looked back at me one last time. "Don't tell your mom, O."

45

It's an hour later, and I'm still sitting on the bleachers, Adrienne long gone. I turn it over and over in my mind, and then I do something I haven't done in almost three months. It's morbid to keep the message, but I can't let it go.

It's all that's left of him.

I dial into my phone, my fingers twitching anxiously. "You have one saved voice message," the robotic female voice says in my ear. "To listen, press three."

Three.

The line is quiet for a moment, the wind or an air-conditioner singing in the background. Then his voice crackles in. He's been crying. "Olivia. I'm sorry," he breathes into the other end of the receiver, still alive in every moment, every inhalation and exhalation. "For everything. Everything now and everything then. It's all so fucked up.

"Olivia, where are you? Why aren't you answering?" His voice fades in and out. It still hurts too much to cry as I listen. His voice is a knife in the heart, cutting it into pieces, leaving me broken. Listening, it hits me over and over again that this moment was real. The words are real, still. "I love you, and I miss you." I squeeze my eyes together furiously. *Stop*, I plead. *Take it back.*

"End of saved messages," the woman on the other side says. I keep the phone pressed to my ear until she starts giving me instructions again, wondering what's wrong with me. Everything, I want to tell her. If only I'd answered—if anyone had known—

I will never tell Mom. I can't. If she found out . . . if my brother drove off the road on purpose. . . . If she knew I could've stopped him.

I don't know if I'm protecting her or myself.

Or both of us.

46

It's cold in the sitting area outside of Dr. Rickards's office. I figure I should be numb to anything at this point, but the goose bumps all over my skin disagree.

Dr. Rickards comes out of his office. "Olivia. Please."

I stand up, at once feeling nothing and feeling too much. I shake my hands out, flexing my fingers, tight then loose. Tight, then loose, then follow Dr. Rickards into his office.

Mr. Doolittle is there and so is the school nurse, Mrs. Ansley, which I don't even begin to understand. They sit on either side of an empty chair like guards, armored with compassion and kindness and bullshit. I take the seat between them. Dr. Rickards takes his, and everything is a funeral procession with Mrs. Baker in the coffin.

I'm going to explode.

"I expect you know why we've asked to speak to you, Miss Clayton," Dr. Rickards says, all regal and sad.

"Is it a cheerleading scholarship?" I can't help but spit out. Mr. Doolittle looks at me like *that was some cold shit.*

"Olivia, is this the time to be making people more uncomfortable?" Mrs. Ansley asks.

"She's hurt. It's her defense mechanism," Mr. Doolittle explains. He should wear a sign that says WORST GUIDANCE COUNSELOR EVER.

Dr. Rickards clears his throat because he has a PhD and apparently a little bit of sense. "Olivia, you know we have some questions about Mrs. Baker. And the"—he coughs—"nature of her relationship with a friend of yours."

"Whit," I reply, stone-faced.

"Yes," Dr. Rickards agrees. "But this conversation is not to leave this room. *If* any of these allegations are true, he is considered a victim in all this."

"Of course," I answer. I can hear the horrible staccato beat of my heart. They have to be able to hear it, too.

"Now." Dr. Rickards leans over his desk to be closer to me. "Is there anything you can tell us about Mrs. Baker and Mr. DuRant? Anything that struck you as strange or you felt was off? We've brought Mrs. Ansley in if you'd feel more comfortable talking to a female about this."

I shake my head. "No. It's okay." I look into my lap, hoping they'll see the cracks in my façade. *I'm lying I'm lying I'm lying.* I pick at my cuticles.

"I know it's natural not to want to get anyone in trouble," Mr. Doolittle nudges me on. "But this is a matter of utmost importance."

It's all clear for a moment now. I have this idea of who I want to be. This independent, driven person. Someone who takes control of her life, irons out the moral flaws, and doesn't feel quite so much hatred for herself all the damn time. And it's right there, at the tip of my fingers. It's studying after school in the library with Whit and telling Claire everything I did and telling her I would never do it again and deciding right in that moment between heartbeats to let it all go, this façade of control. To stop trying to maintain the narrative of Olivia Clayton.

But I blink and I see Ryan and Mom and Adrienne and I *can't* let that go. The words build up behind my lips with an unbearable pressure, words I know I can't say because I know I won't be able to take them back, but I have to—"IsawWhitwithher." Exhale.

They all stare at me in this stunned silence like none of it was true until this minute, and my hand flies over my mouth, trapping my gasp. I can't believe I did this. This was the wrong thing to do.

I have to take it back.

I can't take it back.

"What do you mean?" Mrs. Ansley asks carefully.

In elementary school, before I moved here to Buckley, I almost drowned once. Ryan always said I overreacted, but I'd jumped into the deep end because Leanna Reigart dared me, and she always had the best parties and everyone else could swim in the deep end. I could do anything if I wanted; I knew that. So I jumped, but then for a split second under the water I knew I'd overestimated myself. There was nowhere to go, no breath to breathe, and the light was reflecting from every direction, and I was drowning. The more energy I exerted, the less chance I could survive. Only then, somehow, I wasn't drowning anymore. I made it up for air. I saved myself.

That's when I learned you can never rely on anyone else to save you.

"Nothing explicit," I manage through the constriction in my lungs. "But it wasn't right."

The room is deadly silent. I'm swimming but I don't know if I'm headed up or down yet. I put my hand up to my cheek, but I can't feel it there. It was so astoundingly easy to slip back into this person, but I can't help but feel like I'm watching this girl I know so well, in her chair, talking to Dr. Rickards. I'm watching her from far away and I know every trick she knows and I know every secret she does, but I'm not her. I can't be her.

She was supposed to be dead.

Just once, I was supposed to be the right kind of person.

But it's *so hard.*

"It was—" She looks up, this girl who is someone I want to forget, making eye contact with each of them, but quickly because she's scared she's doing it wrong. She knows this is the part where most people would fuck it up. Go for broke. Say Whit and Mrs. Baker were banging on her desk. *I was horrified; didn't know who to tell. I love him so much and it hurts so bad* and tears all over. Tears everywhere.

She knows better.

"Intimate." Stare at the hand touching her cheek. "She was touching his face, and they were looking at each other, and I felt wrong. I felt wrong that I'd seen it."

Right then, I feel myself crash into the cement at the bottom of the pool. "Is that it?" I ask them, wiping everything clean. Waiting for O to fade away again. "Can I go?"

They're, like, completely stunned. Finally, Mr. Doolittle speaks. "That's it? You didn't hear them saying anything? Just saw"—he kind of glances at his hand then stops himself—"her touching him."

"Whit won't talk to me about it." I give them half a shrug, voice flat. "I really thought he was different," I say, and Mr. Doolittle just about cries. It's too easy. I don't have to actually say I saw anything at all, and they believe me.

"We can talk about this tomorrow," he tells me, face all heartbroken like he's the one who let me down.

"You can go, Miss Clayton," Dr. Rickards tells me. "Nothing leaves this room. Understood?" I nod, picking up my bag. I'm watching myself and I am myself and I'm dead and I'm alive. I turn, slowly walking out, waiting for the door to close behind me before dumping my bag on the floor and sprinting out of the office, down the hall, outside into the fresh air. I bend over, hand on my knees, and retch. Past the steps, I vomit onto the grass.

Who am I?

If I were Ryan, I would have a drink.

47

There are not that many feet between my car and Whit's house. I know that. I also know that each one will feel like a mile.

Logically I know that. And logically, I know, the longer I sit out here, the stranger I look. So I take each step—every excruciating one—to his front door, and my reflection stares back at me, some pretty, broken girl who thinks that's an excuse to—

I don't know. To live, I guess.

I ring the doorbell. I don't have to anymore, but it seems like I should. That I would be invited in, trusted just to come in the front door and kick my shoes off, feels like a foreign idea.

I'll always be as dangerous as everyone thought I was.

It takes a minute for him to open it. When he does, he's rumpled, all ankle socks and old T-shirt, squinting across the threshold at me. He runs his hand through his hair, surveying. He holds the door open, finally, after a minute, like it only just occurred to him. "Hey."

I go in. *There had been a choice*, I'm thinking, trying to rationalize: Adrienne could tell him what I'd already done and he'd never speak to me; or I could do something worse and he'd be totally fucked but at least he'd be fucked with me.

He closes the door behind me, like he always does, and he's there like he always is, calm and steady. Except he's not—there's an urgency in his eyes, a stiffness in his lips. "Can we study?" I ask.

He shakes his head, like he'd forgotten I was there, like he had to remember. "Yeah. Okay." Then, without waiting for me, he turns around and takes off into his room, using strides so long, I jog to stay close to him.

I don't know why. I can't help it.

He falls into his desk chair. "What did you say to them?" he asks without looking at me.

I stop in the doorframe. He can't see my face. He won't know I'm a liar. I mean, he knows I'm a liar, but not to him. We're on the same side, or at least, we're supposed to be.

"I told them it's bullshit. What do you think?"

"I—I don't know what this means, Liv. I don't know what they'll do."

Something isn't right. About his voice. About him. "We can't study."

He shakes his head, then buries his face in his hands.

I try to stop myself, but it's too late. I've crossed the room, and my arms are wrapped around his chest from behind and my face is buried in his hair, and there are two separate Olivias; I feel it again. I'm here in the room with him, and the other one is somewhere else, far away. Some part of me stabilizes then, slides back into place. There is more to me than my lies. I can be someone else—I am with him. As long as I remember that he trusts me to be the right kind of person, I can keep going. And this Olivia—not the one who was in Dr. Rickards's office—he doesn't push her away. He lets her touch him and breathe him in and he doesn't hate her.

He doesn't hate *me* and I won't let him.

"Do you ever think," I say into his hair, "that there's just something wrong with some people? That they're fundamentally fucked up?"

He tenses. "Not really."

My hand grips his shirt. "I'm so sorry," I mutter into his hair.

"Just don't leave," he says. So I don't.

48

Everything is cleaned out of Mrs. Baker's classroom when we get to school Thursday morning. All that bare space makes it feel haunted, gives me chills all over my skin. I keep having this horrible flashback to the picture on her desk, this tiny blond girl smiling at the camera, and feeling so sick to my stomach I can hardly walk down the hallway. Whit asks me what's wrong, and I have to physically find a way to separate myself from the person who did this. Good Olivia and bad. I've done bad things before, but never anything like this.

Never.

The words are all over school, buzzing louder than before. In the gym, the caf, the teachers' lounge, I'm sure. When I walk down the hall with Whit, random guys offer to high-five him, laughing their asses off, and Whit turns redder and redder, barely able to look anyone in the eye. When we finally manage to find a table off by itself in the quad to study, he slumps his head into his hands, and I'm scared he might cry or do something really embarrassing.

"Maybe if I'm with you, nobody will think it's a big deal. You know, more normal."

He doesn't look up. "My parents are going to find out. Dr. Rickards told me this morning that he has to bring them in today before it becomes a full-scale investigation, even though I told him it was complete bullshit. Apparently, someone has screenshots of texts Mrs. Baker and I supposedly sent each other, and they're completely fake. I even told him he could have my phone. So the principal is going to tell my parents I had *imaginary sex* with my teacher. Mrs. Baker's mom goes to church with us."

The part of me that's Whit's Girlfriend and wants him to be happy reaches out to touch him. Everything else about me holds me back. Touching him right now feels over the line. "You told Dr. Rickards absolutely everything, right? It's just a rumor. It will *go away*. They always do."

Whit doesn't say anything for a second. Then he opens up my SAT booklet. "Have you been studying your prefixes?"

"Sort of."

"You want to do these?" he asks me.

"Do you?" I tug on the pencil he has in his hand until his palm falls open. We're barely touching, fingertips on the pencil rather than skin to skin. Some sophomores are watching us from the other side of the quad, in that we-totally-aren't-watching-you kind of way. Whit looks ashamed.

"I know it's stupid, but I hate everyone staring at me. I hate everyone talking about me. I hate that because of some grudge Adrienne Maynard has against me, Mrs. Baker is in huge trouble. God, I just feel so out of control of my own life and I don't understand it. I want to take it back."

"I know you said you weren't going to let Adrienne scare you or anything. But—" The words are hard to choke out, especially when he's saying things out loud that consume my every thought. *Take it back.* "This is a new low. If you want to walk away—"

"Then I look even guiltier and she knows she won," he says, his voice hoarse. I guess, in his competitive mind, it makes sense. Like if he weathers this storm, we win somehow.

I should tell him we'll never win.

I don't.

"She's just some girl," he's saying. "She's some broken girl, and I'm—we're so much better than that, Liv." I can't believe he said that. *We.* We're better than her.

I want to be that. I feel how much I want it in every fiber of my soul, and I am more heartbroken than I've ever been and happier than I have a right to be.

Let's take it back.

I glance at the staring sophomores, who are joined by some cheer girls. "Stand up," I tell Whit.

"We've got—"

"Just do it."

He stands up, the brick wall of the quad behind him. I climb up on top of the stone bench, stepping over to the one he was sitting on, and jump off the seat, landing with a small hop in front of him. I grab the front of his shirt and pull him toward me, kissing him with everything I have.

He pushes me back with both of his hands. "Olivia."

"Look," I whisper, my mouth right next to his. We turn our heads at the same time to see the sophomores staring. He tilts his head back down and kisses me. Hard.

A teacher has to separate us.

49

Whit and I are sitting together in the front office supposedly because PDA is against the rules, but I'm guessing because the two of us have turned Buckley High into a public relations nightmare in the past two days. We're sitting quietly shoulder to shoulder when his brother comes in. He's supposed to be at school; I can only assume that he just plain took off from Durham sometime this morning. The secretary demands his identity, but he ignores her.

He's Cason DuRant, so he can do things like that.

"Whit, I need to talk to you. We need to go," Cason says.

I stand up.

Cason kind of winces. "Olivia . . ."

"She goes," Whit says firmly.

Cason nods, his jaw clenched tight. We head toward the exit of the school, everyone watching us go. Some people *ooh* under their breath. I even hear someone say, "Don't be jealous, Cason!"

In the parking lot, we cram into Cason's sports car. I slide into the back, drumming a beat on Whit's seat in front of me. Cason cranks up the car and speeds out of the parking lot, absolutely obliterating the posted speed limit.

"You don't think I slept with a teacher," Whit says.

Cason's eyes meet mine in the rearview mirror. "No, I don't." He doesn't say anything for a moment. "But that's not the problem. Olivia, check my bag."

I slide out a newspaper from his book bag and am leaning forward to pass it up to Whit when the picture on the front stops me. It is a haggard picture of Mrs. Baker, out of some old yearbook, I'm pretty sure. They caught her halfway into a smile, and she looks kind of crazed. Like she's coming after your horny teenage son. The headline reads LOCAL TEACHER ACCUSED OF RELATIONSHIP WITH STUDENT. Before I can read any further, Whit grabs the paper out of my hand.

"What the fuck?" he demands of Cason.

"At least no one knows it's you," I say.

"Everyone knows it's him," Cason tells me. "Local paper assholes. As if that's not enough, just read the last sentence of the article."

Slowly, Whit reads, "'Little is known about the student involved, except for that he is a well-known athlete at Buckley High.'" He closes the paper. "Dammit." A moment. "Fuck. My life is over."

"So you had imaginary sex with a teacher," I finally say. "Your life isn't over." *Hers is,* some faraway version of me thinks.

Whit whips around toward me. "You don't understand. No one cares what you do, Olivia. Everyone expects shit like this from you, but I'm supposed to be someone with character, okay? You don't get it."

"Whit," Cason says. "Chill out, bro."

I try not to be hurt. "Yeah, don't go wasting all that good character on me."

"Don't tell me it doesn't matter. Just don't."

No one says anything else as we drive toward the DuRants' house. The silence has expanded through the car and engulfed us all when Whit's phone begins ringing. He looks at the screen and then toward Cason.

"What?" Cason asks, his jaw tense.

"It's the coach."

Cason slams on the brakes so hard, I hit the headrest in front of me. "Take it," he says. "Get out."

Whit steps out of the car, slamming the door behind him. We can almost hear him through the door, but not quite. He walks forward on the sidewalk, head tilted away from us.

"What is going on with this?" Cason asks me, his eyes still on Whit.

I rub at the back of my neck, uncomfortable. "You know as much as I do."

He turns on me, and there's something I've never seen before. Cason is the older, easygoing, cool brother, but every bit of his face is Whit in this moment. Serious and haggard and worried. Always so worried something he did is wrong. "Whit has never been like this in his life. Suddenly he's with you and everything is falling apart for him. There's only one conclusion I can draw."

"It's me," I reply.

"It's you."

Whit walks farther away from the car, running his hand through his hair. I can barely stand the sight of him. I want to argue with Cason but I have nothing to say. No words are on my side. I want to brush it off or tell him it's no big deal, but I can't look at Whit and think that. It matters to him.

So it matters to me.

"I think you need to leave him alone. I can tell he cares about you a lot." Cason sighs. "But Whit's never met someone like you before, Olivia. Every moment of every day isn't important to you like it is to him. He loves that you don't care, but he can't handle it."

Whit has taken his phone away from his ear and is staring at it like the plastic personally hurt his feelings. His whole body looks near collapse—the whole tall, solid pillar of him, defeated. "It's not that simple," I find myself saying. "I can't just let him go like that."

Whit walks back to the car and gets in.

We don't say anything the rest of the way.

50

Whit's dad sits alone at the kitchen table with a cup of coffee. It's like their family has been blown up by a nuclear explosion, and I don't know how to hide the fact that I dropped the bomb.

The thought of Mrs. Baker makes my entire body itch as if the wrong person were wearing my skin.

The three of us amble into the clean white room, all wearing our guilt like a badge. No one says anything for a minute.

"Your mom asked me to come home." Mr. DuRant folds his fingers together, watching them as if they're the only things in the room. This must be killing him on so many levels. Parents hate thinking about their kids having sex, period. They like to pretend their kid is different—they'll be the one who makes the right choices. Or, at the very least, they'll love their parents enough to pretend.

But if your son's banging his teacher? Then everyone knows.

"We're going to handle this," Mr. DuRant continues. "We're not going to let these rumors stand. It would be ridiculous for us to hide in the shadows over something that isn't true."

"It doesn't matter what we do," Whit says, resigned, like he's plotted out every battle and lost each one.

"Olivia, I'm glad to see you have the good sense not to believe such nonsense," Mr. DuRant says, turning to me. "To think that they would print gossip in the paper. Journalism is a dead art form." He's saying the right things, he sounds angry enough, but I don't really believe him. I don't think he believes himself. He knows Whit didn't do it, but there's that voice in his head that won't stop whispering:

What if he did?

Mr. DuRant drains his coffee. "I have to get back to work. And probably call a lawyer." As he walks by Whit, he puts a hand on his shoulder. "We'll figure this out, son." And then he's gone.

"My own dad thinks I'm sleeping with a teacher. Great." Whit shakes his head. He's mad at everyone and everything. I don't think there's anything either of us could say to fix the situation. But even if there is a perfect response, it's definitely not—

"Quit being a dick, Whit," which is what Cason decides to say then.

Whit takes a swing at him. He misses, on purpose I think, and then Cason shoves him into the counter. "Chill out!" Cason says, but Whit has already pushed around him and taken off toward his bedroom. Cason shakes his head as I try to follow him. "He doesn't want help," he warns me.

I go anyway.

I nudge open the closed door. For some reason, Whit is just standing there, staring absently at his wall. I close the door and walk up behind him, silent even though I know he knows I'm there. The wall is covered in letters bearing college letterheads—recruitment letters. *Mr. DuRant, we are pleased to offer you* and *we think the academics are a great fit,* a full wall of pride and choice.

"It's not like it changes everything you've accomplished," I say.

"You know, I got three more offers than Cason," he tells the wall.

"So what?"

"So what?" He turns around to look at me, incredulous. "So what? That's everything. That's what I am."

"Oh, for fuck's sake. Get out of my way." I climb on top of his desk and start ripping the letters off the wall. I throw them to the ground, one leaf of creamy stationery after another.

"What are you doing?" he demands.

"Getting. Rid. Of. These." I punctuate each word with another letter torn off the wall. "It doesn't matter, Whit. None of this does."

"Stop it!" he demands and then his arms are around my waist, pulling me away from the wall, and I'm still trying to rip at the letters like they're the punishment, not the prize. "Stop, Liv." The whole weight of the day is in his voice. "Please stop."

Just like that, the whole moment comes to a standstill. He lets go of me. I turn away from the wall to face him, sitting down on top of his desk. "They're not you," I say after a moment. "You're Whit. You're not Cason's little brother and you're not the guy who slept with his teacher and you're not some golf recruit with a bunch of pros and cons. You're Whit and that's all I want you to be, okay? If it matters at all."

He kisses me, and just like that, everything begins.

Our lips are barely touching for a breath, and then I have my hand around the back of his head, gripping him as hard as I can and pulling him into me. His arms wrap around me, and I tense in surprise for a moment, but then I love it, relaxing into it. I love the feel of us so close together, and him kissing me and me kissing him. His hand slides up the bare small of my back under my shirt, pulling me up toward him until we move to collapse on the bed. My mouth tracks along his collarbone, searching for sensitive spots. We're kissing and it's everything it should be and, in this weird moment where all that matters is we're kissing, I am so completely happy.

Except he's Whit. Except he's sad because of me, angry because of me. Because everything wrong with his life right now, I did.

I pull back. "We shouldn't do this. I told you this wouldn't get fucked up."

His fingers float in the space between us, and I push his bangs to the side, unable to stop myself. "This *is* fucked up," he says, almost to himself.

This is what I want. I can feel how badly I want this.

But I can't do this to him.

He bends his head down, so close to mine, defeat in every line of his body. "I'm sorry," he tells me.

"Don't be," I say before I can stop myself.

"That was—exactly what I promised I'd never do," he says, blowing out a shaky breath. His veneer keeps cracking right before my eyes, all that insecurity he keeps buried right under the surface. I can't stop myself.

I want him so badly.

So, hit with the sudden realization that this might be my only chance, I go for it. I kiss him again, soft and slow, and let it linger. This is the scariest thing. This is what I'm afraid to give up.

"Don't keep that promise," I whisper, inches from his mouth.

Glance up. His eyes are dark with lust.

I shove him down onto the bed and climb on top and just let my hormones lead the way. If we stopped, everything would be ruined, so I don't give us time to think. I tug at the front of his jeans, sliding my fingers over the stretch of skin above the waistband, pulling at the silver button. He grabs the bottom of my shirt and pulls it over my head, slinging it away a little too dramatically when it's off, and I roll over next to him, laughing. He slides on top of me, grinning. "This is trouble."

He draws his fingers across my stomach, down to the rough fabric of my jeans, and I arch my back, throwing his shirt, too. All the while, we keep smiling at each other. I'd forgotten that this was supposed to be fun.

I push both of my hands into his hair, holding him from either side so we're looking right at each other. "Take your pants off."

His eyes flash with clarity, and even though I'm joking, these serious tingles start over my body. When his fingers slide up my thigh, my heart really gets going in that honest way you can't make stop. My breath is hitching and my legs feel shaky and the safe part's over for good.

Every inch, every moment, every heartbeat is changed now.

This is trouble.

51

Yesterday, I was the girl who made up a lie to ruin our class's golden boy and coolest teacher. I hate that girl.

Today, I am totally sure that boy loves me, and I'm going to forget that girl.

Whit will never know. No one will ever prove anything, and I'm done fighting with Adrienne. I'm Whit's Liv and that's all I need to be.

I get to school early the next morning—Mom had to drop me off since she had a client meeting. Whit and I are supposed to meet up to go over some SAT words before class. I'm coming up on the library when I see Michaela in a blush-pink sweater with mascara running down her face. One of her minions is trying to comfort her, but Michaela is inconsolable, clutching a copy of the school paper to her chest. And then she spots me looking at her.

"No." She points a finger at me like I'm a misbehaving dog. "Leave me alone. I didn't do anything."

Shocked, I stop. "What?"

"I didn't do it, okay?" And at this, her voice cracks and she lets one little tear escape, giving way to another and another until she's not

Michaela anymore. Just a girl in a quiet hallway whose mom is dying, whose world is so much more than here.

"What is it?" I ask, snatching the paper out of her hand, dreading and certain it's going to be about Whit.

But it's not. The *Buckley Bugle* isn't much—two seventeen-by-eleven-inch pages printed front and back and folded down the middle. The cover story looks normal, something about vegetarian options in the cafeteria. When I flip it open, a loose leaf of paper floats out and falls to the ground.

It has a color picture of Claire and Ellie printed on it, from the same night as the picture Adrienne told me Coxie had sent to her. But this time Claire is *definitely* kissing Ellie.

The caption says "Yeah, Coxie, she's totally straight." Because this is all about him.

When I look up, Michaela's still crying.

My heart is pounding. "Where did this come from?"

"I don't know," the minion says. "We left all two hundred copies in here after seventh period yesterday"—she indicates the library—"and we dropped them all off in homerooms this morning. They were fine yesterday!" She sounds frantic.

"They're out?"

"Everyone has them," Michaela manages to say. "I'm going to lose my editor job. It means everything to me." I believe her.

I stuff the paper back in the minion's hand and go back down the hall, a ringing in my ears. This is it. Adrienne can't sink any lower. Nothing I have done or will ever do can match this. This is Claire. This is *us*, our secret, our hands wrapped together on a cold football field. The one line we weren't supposed to cross. Claire was supposed to be off-limits.

The exceptions have to stop. Screw the bullshit rationalizing. There's no more greater good to be gained, only the destruction left in our path.

I have to tell Claire. I have to tell Claire everything. I have to tell everyone everything. I'm afraid they might be together, but I go after the person I know best. I look for Adrienne.

I look at her locker first. She's not there. Not in the quad commanding the center table. Not even at her desk in first period, hiding. It's usually a relief not to see her, but today her absence can't mean anything good.

It's bad. I know it. I bump into someone holding the paper. The person next to them has it, too. And next to them, and next to them.

A boy with sloppy blond hair nudges me when I walk by. "So is Claire a dyke or what?"

I punch him in the face.

I get sent to the principal's office.

My hand swells and, my God, it hurts. This hand has seen some serious damage lately—it's still healing where I cut my finger. I sit in the uncomfortable wooden chair outside the office, focusing on the pain. I spread my fingers apart and try to make a fist out of them. It almost brings tears to my eyes. There's no way I'll be able to hold a pom-pom tonight.

Whatever.

I roll my shoulders, the fabric of my cheer top going up and down. Up and down.

I'm counting to a thousand when Mom comes in. She is prim and petite in business casual. Her hair is down around her shoulders, out of its usual bun. She had to turn around on the way to Atlanta. She must've had to cancel. She'll hate that.

She stands directly in front of me, my eyes reflected in her own. Her hand waits for mine. "Let me see it."

I gingerly lay my purpling hand in hers. She surveys it with a critical gaze. "What did you do to him?"

"Black eye," I mutter back. If I'm lucky. Punching people looks way cooler on TV.

Mom turns to the secretary. "Why doesn't she have any ice?" she asks, venom in her words.

The secretary gets up to get me ice. At least I know where I get it from.

We sit silently next to each other. Time goes by. When the secretary comes back, Mom holds the ice against my hand. It's too cold to feel at first, then so cold it hurts, and after a while my hand is finally, blissfully too numb to feel anything. I watch people pass by the window. Normal, non-dangerous people.

Dr. Rickards comes out of his office and gestures the two of us inside. For a public school principal, he cuts quite a figure. Tall and regal with slightly graying brown hair.

We sit down across from his mahogany desk. His big bookshelf towers over us, there so we know how important and educated he is. Mom would school him.

He cuts right to the chase. "We're worried about your daughter, Mrs. Clayton."

"I understand," she replies. Of course she does. I'm a walking fucking time bomb as far as they're concerned. Light the fuse and watch it explode—all I'll leave is pretty colors and cheerleading uniform debris.

Dr. Rickards gestures at me as he talks. "Olivia says the boy was making a derogatory comment."

"I think it's called hate speech," I tell him.

"Either way," Dr. Rickards goes on, "we can't tolerate violence in response."

"Understandable," Mom says. "Olivia's had a very hard time since her brother's death." Her voice is cold, like Ryan's just another fact.

"I understand," Dr. Rickards says like he actually does. "And obviously we've tried addressing that by having her work with Mr. Doolittle. But the fact of the matter is, Olivia has a history of bullying even before this particular incident." He folds his fingers together. "We're very intolerant of bullying here at Buckley."

Mom glances at me like she already knows everything he could say about me.

I hang my head. *She hates me, she hates me, she hates me.*

"We have reason to believe Olivia may have put out school newspapers with inappropriate and quite hateful content included."

"What?" I barely manage to spit out.

"Olivia." Mom puts her cold hand on me, holding me down.

"We found more copies of the—*ahem*—flyers in your locker, Miss Clayton. And the havoc you've wreaked with your actions this year—"

"It was Adrienne!" I shout over him. "Michaela." I shoot out of my seat, frantic. "Ask Michaela; she saw me when I found out! *M-my* locker? Why would I punch him if I did it?" I demand.

Mom stands up next to me. "Olivia, sit down," she says, so clearly embarrassed it hurts. Unshed tears well up in my eyes. Mom turns to the principal. "You're telling me someone snuck into the library, stuffed two hundred newspapers, and distributed them to the student body, but they couldn't possibly have broken into Olivia's locker? So besides that unlikely coincidence, exactly what proof is there that Olivia had anything to do with this? Why doesn't your school have cameras to monitor this kind of thing?"

Dr. Rickards shifts uncomfortably. "I understand that based on the circumstances, there's no proof. But I can't have this nonsense going on anymore. The student body is on edge." He looks down. I can spot that sign of weakness a mile away—Mom has the upper hand here. "Based on today's events, I think it best we suspend Olivia for three days, starting today." Pause. "And I think it's best, with the circumstances, if Olivia is no longer a member of the cheerleading squad."

I curl up the fingers of my numb fist. "You can't do that," I hear myself say.

"Olivia," Mom begins.

"Don't talk to me," I bite back at her. She won't fight for me.

"I think it might be best if you look into getting your daughter a therapist outside of school, Miss Clayton."

"Dr. Rickards, it's not that I don't agree with you on some points, but do you really think this punishment fits the crime?" Mom asks evenly. "For defending her friend?"

"We don't have the facts," Dr. Rickards says. He might as well say he knows I did it. That it's exactly the kind of thing I'd do.

"I believe my daughter," Mom tells him. "Let's go, Olivia." She stands up, putting her arm around me. "You'll be getting a call from me once I've gone over some things. Thank you for your time." And she shakes his hand and whisks me out. She guides me through the halls, click-clacks through the parking lot in her sensible heels, and sits me down in the passenger's seat of her car. Closing the door and walking around the car, she sits down beside me.

A moment passes. Then two. Finally, I manage to get out: "Thanks."

"You wouldn't do that," she says, though it sounds more like she's trying to convince herself.

I shake my head. "No. Things have been better lately. With Whit. I think I was wrong about him," I say. Then I remember that Whit doesn't even know the real me. If he knew what I'd done, he'd know I was just as bad as Adrienne. I really am pathetic. "Maybe. I don't know."

"I miss him, too, you know."

I didn't, actually.

"And I'm trying. But this self-destructiveness. Olivia, this is what killed your brother," she tells me. I shiver.

I've wondered, more than once, if she's the one who broke him and when that happened. When Dad died or when she lost it or when she got it back and shut down. I wonder if I did it when I became enamored with Adrienne. I wonder if it was Buckley or Michigan or the whole damn world and if I'd answered the phone, none of this would have happened. "If he'd just stayed—"

"He hated it here," she tells me.

I know. *I know*. "So do I."

After a moment, she says, "It's funny," like it's not at all. "When we moved here, I looked so hard for the perfect place. We had to move, you know? Kate was finally able to go live in Europe like she'd wanted to, and God knows she deserved a respite from me. I had been stable for four years, and part of that was that I was working less. Then the recession hit and I couldn't afford to keep our house on my salary and, even after ten years, there were too many memories everywhere. Of your dad," she clarifies. "But Buckley had it all—good school, small town. I thought you'd be part of the community. I thought if I did a bad job as a single parent, there'd be so many people around for you to look up to. I thought it would be a welcome break for all of us—a little solace after all that and normalcy for you and Ryan. We needed something different." She shakes her head. "Maybe I idealized what a small town would be like. I know Ryan never liked it, and I've always had trouble fitting in, but, Olivia, I always thought you were the happiest of all of us with all this. Ethan and Adrienne and cheerleading and popularity."

I sit back in my seat, not sure what to say, feeling all over again like she doesn't know me at all. But Mom doesn't tell me these kinds of things—these honest things—she doesn't tell me anything. She is closed off and quiet. I think of one of my SAT words. Impenetrable.

I know she won't allow herself to feel too much, but I just want her to feel *something*. "You know what happened when Ryan died? I figured out what's wrong with me. I realized Ryan was the only real relationship I've had in my entire life. He's the only person who knew everything about me and loved me unconditionally." I lean my head against the window, the honesty making my throat raw. "Maybe I'd be better off if I just accepted that Buckley is it for me and go curl up in the graveyard with him."

I stare out at the trucks in the parking lot, out beyond that to all the dull colors that paint this town, and imagine fading completely into them.

Mom cranks the engine on that note and doesn't speak for the whole drive home. When we pull into the driveway, and I finally glance at her, she's crying.

Silently.

52

I'm staring at a practice test Whit printed out for me, tracing my pencil over his handwriting, incapable of concentrating. I have to do something else—something that doesn't involve geometry. I have to figure out how to make things right.

I jump out of my window because Mom won't let me leave the house. Apparently I'm suspended *and* grounded. Ryan's old bicycle is in the backyard. I brush some sticks and leaves off it and wiggle it free of the chain-link fence.

It's a long bicycle ride. And it's cold, too. The wind whips my hair and my sweatpants.

I hear the sounds from the stadium a half mile out. The band playing, fans screaming. Girls cheering.

Bright lights. Everyone in town.

I don't go into the stadium; hell, I don't think I'm even allowed. Instead, I go around the back of the school. I lean my bike up against the brick wall outside the locker room and slide down it, letting the bricks dig into my back.

I'll wait. I'll wait right here for Claire to come out, and I'll tell her everything.

Even if she won't answer my text messages. Even if Adrienne got to her first.

After about ten minutes, I start shivering. The thin fabric of my shirt catches on the jagged edges of the wall and pulls at the loose threads. I get out my cell phone and dial. I hope Adrienne hasn't gotten to him, too.

Whit picks up on the last ring. "Hello?"

I can barely hear him over the sounds of the game. The announcer's voice rings out first through the receiver and then echoes over campus where I sit. "Come by the locker room!" I yell into the mouthpiece. "Please," I add.

"Liv?" he answers.

"Locker room!" I yell, and hang up the phone.

A little while later, I see him, walking through the darkness, squinting into the distance. When he sees me, blending into the wall, he speeds up. "Olivia, what's going on?" he asks, approaching me, squatting down in front of me. His hand reaches toward me, but he stops himself.

"I didn't do it," I tell him. "Sit." I gesture next to me, He twists around and sits. Our knees are touching.

"I know you didn't do it," he says. "You kind of saved me, honestly. Coach told me I couldn't miss the game because it's the damn honor-your-state-championship-golf-team night, like anyone cares. I barely convinced my parents not to come, but Coach said it looked worse if I didn't show up." He huddles his shoulders up as a blast of wind hits us. "Anyway, I was just trying to hide next to the ticket booth until the buzzer sounded, but this is better. We're a couple of social pariahs, huh?"

I sigh, relieved. Nothing has changed between us. "I have to tell Claire."

Whit doesn't say anything for a minute. The silence builds ominously the more it lingers. "It might be a little too late for that."

"What do you know about it?" I ask him, knowing I sound like a dick.

"I know in the court of public opinion, you've already been crucified."

I stick out my bottom lip. "I don't care. It's just Adrienne. Claire will understand." Then a sigh escapes me. "You know the stupid thing about it? I keep trying to figure out how she could've done it—how *I* would've done it. Like, do you think she saw them making out and just had to get a picture? Just in case she ever needed it?"

Whit snorts. "Probably."

"The thing is," I say, and I still can't believe I'm shocked at the idea, "I always knew she did that to *everyone else*. Gathered up real and imagined intel for safekeeping. But it never occurred to me she did it to us. Claire and me."

Whit watches me like that is the least surprising thing he's ever heard, but he has the decency not to say so.

"So okay, she sent the pictures to Michaela from Coxie's phone. Played me like a drum with that little frame job. Then the distribution." You almost had to admire the lengths she went to. "We used to prop open one of the windows in the library sometimes to sneak in if we wanted to fuck with someone's locker, so it would have been easy for her to print out two hundred color copies and stuff them in the papers after cheer practice. I just wonder if she did it by herself. Maybe Anna?"

Whit is still staring at me, confusion mingled with disgust. "Why would she go to that much trouble?"

I laugh, even though it's not funny. "It's all about maximum drama. You, of all people, should understand not half assing things."

He's sizing me up. Thinking. "Would you have done that last year?" he asks. "Helped her with some grand plan to humiliate someone?"

"She probably would've made me do it alone," I say, and I shouldn't be bitter, but I am.

Whit leans his head back against the wall, looking tired. Everything about him looks tired.

"Only twelve more days," I say.

"Huh?"

"You only have to pretend you like me for twelve more days. Hang in there, DuRant." I nudge his shoulder.

"You rode a bicycle here? Really?"

I shiver. He puts an arm around me, and I lay my head against his shoulder. I can't believe he'd touch me after what I told him. "I'll take you home," he tells me.

His side is so warm. "Who says chivalry is dead?"

He snickers.

"How was your day?" I ask. "Did you talk to any of the coaches?"

"We don't have to talk about it," he says, and I can tell he doesn't want to. "It sucks. Like, they can't officially yank my scholarship if I slept with a teacher—which I didn't—but they can use any bullshit character issue excuse they find. Florida said they aren't even interested anymore."

I can't meet his eyes. All the pain I caused everyone is pressing in on me.

"Everyone thinks you snapped because of me. They think that's why you did it." He shakes his head. "How were you ever friends with her? My life, yours, Claire's? Nothing is sacred to her. I want to talk to Mrs. Baker and tell her how sorry I am about what's happening, but I can't. It would make things worse for her. What's wrong with Adrienne, Liv?"

There are no words available to me for a second. He's so easily accepted that there's this line between who I am now and who I was. He *believes* me. "I—I don't know." I wipe away a tear.

"Were you okay? After yesterday?" I have no idea what he's talking about for a minute, and then I realize.

"Yeah," I say. "I was. I mean, it was fun. Not that—it's just, what you said. About how I should know this isn't real. I just don't want you to think that I think—"

"I know you don't," he says quickly. "It was just a thing." He shrugs, smiles. "It was weird."

"Thanks a lot," I answer, trying not to let it sting.

"I don't mean—you know what I mean. For me. It was weird for me. Because, you know . . ."

I turn to him, a realization hanging in the back of my brain. "No," I say. "What?"

He is definitely embarrassed. "Do I really have to say it?" He groans.

Oh my God. "Were you a virgin, Whit?" I ask, incredulous.

He won't meet my eye.

"Why didn't you tell me that?" I demand. "I thought you had that girlfriend before?"

He snorts. "Marilee? Yeah, right. Don't overreact," he says. "It's not a big deal."

"It is—" I begin to say, but am interrupted by the final buzzer going off. My head whips around in the direction of the stadium, where people are beginning to exit, and I feel queasy. Now it's not just Whit, now I have to face Claire, and who knows what Adrienne's said to her. I slide back up the wall, pushing my palms against the bricks until it's painful. Whit gets up beside me.

"You should've said something," I tell him.

"I know," he says. "But I didn't want you to think I was some church boy. Like you do. I'm going to go, okay? So you can talk to Claire."

I nod, the gnawing in the pit of my stomach growing.

So he leaves me alone with the darkness and loneliness, and it's a lot colder without his arm around me.

The cheerleaders start filing in past me, not saying anything. One by one, I learn and relearn the meaning of *if looks could kill.* They've always hated me, but it's okay now that Adrienne has spoken from on high.

I see Claire off in the distance, overshadowed by the massive form of Coxie, who almost shields her completely. I leave the wall, sliding my tennis shoes loudly over the sidewalk. Claire shrugs Coxie off at the boys' locker room and starts my way. She sees me and stops.

I take one step forward. "Adrienne—"

She puts one hand up. One tiny, pale, bony hand with five fingers, all making a sign to stop. Stop what, I can't even begin to make out—stop talking, stop living, stop breathing, stop being so goddamn wrong about everything.

Just *stop*.

"Leave me alone," she says after sixteen whole seconds pass by.

I bite my lip. Hard.

"Move," she says.

"You're not—not listening."

"I'm gay, okay. Gay gaygaygaygay! Are you fucking happy now?" she yells, and if people weren't staring before, they sure are now. "You can stop finding new and creative ways to humiliate me. Can you *please* leave me alone now, because thanks to you, no one else will."

And for some reason, I'm yelling, "It's not like that. I want to—" and she shoves me right out of the way and goes into the locker room.

Fuck.

"Claire!" I call. Tears cloud my vision.

There's a buzz in my ears, but underneath it is the sound of someone clapping, getting louder until it drowns out the ringing in my head. I look up.

Adrienne leans against the wall, shoulders pressed casually into the brick. Smiling. Applauding. I am on her in the time it takes to cross the twenty feet between us. She laughs harder.

"What is wrong with you?" I hiss at her. I didn't want her to see me cry—I don't. But what else can I do?

"You keep asking me that but, like, O, you truly suck at this," she snaps back. She can't hide her anger through all the fake laughter and giggles and bullshit. You can't hide that much ugliness, no matter how pretty you are. "This is why I run the show."

"I did everything you said. I lied to Dr. Rickards. I hurt everyone I cared about and I still stood by you."

"Fuck that. The deal. You were faking."

I want to break something. "What the fuck difference does it make? Everyone who smiles at you is faking. Open your eyes, Adrienne! They're all faking. They hate us."

"Wrong. They hate *you*." She brushes her fingers through her black hair slowly. Satisfied.

"Why are you doing this?" I ask.

She's still not looking at me. Twisting her hair, scuffing her shoes. Trying so hard to look untouchable, unruffled. "Because I can," she finally says. "Because you used to run around hiding in my shadow when bad things happened like you had nothing to do with them and getting all this love from Claire and Ethan. You almost killed Anna Talbert and, somehow, it was *my* fault."

"So that's what you want? Claire and Ethan?" I ask. "Love? Open your eyes. They don't love *you* because I'm not around. That's not how it works. Do you want me to say I'm sorry, that I always knew the shit we were doing was wrong?"

She shakes her head. "It's always that, isn't it? What about what you did to me?"

"*You?*" I demand.

"Ethan. You picked him."

My mouth drops. "What?"

"After Ryan died." She swipes her hand under her eyes, smudging her eyeliner. "I was there for you, I was the one you told about Ryan's voice mail, and you went running straight to Ethan. Like Ethan was more important than me. Like he knew you better than I did." I know she's a false prophet, and yet I'm hanging on to every word, ready to follow her to the holy land. This can't be real. This has to be another play. "You were my best friend, O, remember? Some asshole guy counted for more than that? You were supposed to be my best friend, and you picked Ethan."

"Are you joking?" She can't think that was about her.

"I had to take him," she says defiantly. "I was supposed to be the one you needed." An actual tear rolls down her cheek. "Only then you just went right to Whit without a second thought. After everything I've done for you."

I have to get away from this and her before she sucks me right back into her whirlwind. "Do you hear yourself?" I ask, trying to keep my voice even. I've seen Adrienne go over the edge before, but this is new. This is more than I was ever prepared for.

"I can't do this anymore." She yanks at her black hair, just like when she was younger. Her mom had her in therapy for two years to stop her. Even seeing the motion instinctively pulls me forward. Without thinking, I touch her hand, and she recoils so hard she hits the wall. "Don't touch me!" she shouts.

I speak to her slowly, as if approaching a dangerous wounded animal. "Ade, after Ryan died, I was using Ethan. I was using whatever I had. I was hanging on by a thread.

"Then you did that to me," I tell her. "And even after I caught you with Ethan, I wanted revenge, yeah, but I didn't want to lose you. Only I've realized, after it all, that I've never been anything to you. No more than another person you can control, and you've proved it again. You told Claire after you promised you wouldn't. It was another lie."

Finally, finally she meets my eyes. Her face clears until she's back to laughing and everything goes dark again. "Don't you see? I kept my promise. I didn't tell Claire anything about the texts or your brother. I wanted to end this at the Rough House weeks ago, but it's all a game to you. You're so fucked up, O."

My heart is pounding, hitting harder and harder against my rib cage, demanding penance. There's nothing I can say. I twist away toward the parking lot. Adrienne latches on to my wrist. The damaged one. "You're worse than me, Olivia. You're the worst of all. I tried to help you, but you didn't want it."

I go to open my mouth, but she cuts me off again.

"And you know what's worse than what you did to Claire? What you did to Whit. At least Claire was an accident."

"You made me," I say.

Everything about her is hard and soft; black and white; cold and hot. She's everything familiar to me and everything that keeps ruining me. "Again with this I-made-you shit! You know why you did it? Because Whit has everything you want. He has a good life and a good future and you're stuck. People like you, O"—she shakes her head—"people like you are just a stepping-stone to people like Whit and me, on our way out of this town. You can't stand it. And that is why you do what you do. You want us all to be on your level. You say you want to change, but I know you. You still want to be who you were before. I just happened to be the one you turned on this time, and I wasn't willing to roll over dead.

"But go ahead, if you think you're so different now, admit what *you* did. He loves his new Liv, right? Tell him what you did to him so I can see him forgive you."

It's there in her eyes. So sincere. She really believes it. Somehow there's a scale in her head, and it's tipped in her favor. I'm everything wrong and mean and ugly.

I think she might be right.

For a whole minute, I don't breathe. When I can move again, I take off away from her, out to the parking lot. Whit waits by a trash can, his hands in his pockets. He's another reminder of how wrong I am. I reach out and kick the trash can over, spill out garbage onto the paved sidewalk. I thought I had this under control. I actually thought it was *possible* for me to have this under control.

It didn't make any difference, I realize. None of it made a difference.

"Olivia?" Whit says cautiously.

I look back at him. It's as if everything were moving in slow motion. The trees behind the school blowing, leaves ruffling against one another; the hair whipping at my cold, cold face.

"Olivia," he tries again.

Blood pulses through my body, white-hot, melting every good feeling in its path. I pick up a rock and hurl it at the school. It falls short. I've done nothing. I'm just one useless, irrelevant person who keeps falling apart.

I turn back to Whit and hold out my hand. "Let me drive your car."

"Liv—" Again. Again, my name turning into something else in his mouth. That girl I'm not, because I'm Olivia Clayton, I'm *O*, who ruins everything I touch. I rip the keys out of his hand and walk around the car. No amount of destruction, no pain I can cause someone will ever be enough.

"Olivia!" Whit is calling louder now, but I slam the door in his face. He races around the car and jumps into the passenger's seat as I tear off through the Buckley parking lot.

"Calm down," I hear Whit say through my haze. "Slow down. I like this car. I like my face. I'd like to keep them both intact."

I guess he's trying to be funny. I don't know.

The moon and stars are so bright tonight that everything is alive with an eerie glow. Shadows jump from behind trees; ghosts of dead brothers dart through the night as I speed past. I always thought if I pushed hard enough, I could put my foot straight through the floorboard.

I can't. But the car sure does go fast.

"Are you going to talk to me? Say anything at all?" Whit asks.

I can't tell him because I can't talk. I'm too hot. It's too hot. We pass the Woodhaven Country Club, pass the shady bar on the outskirts of town. Over a quiet country road, silence stretching between us all the while.

"Olivia, where are we?" he finally asks. He keeps saying it again and again. My name, like if he calls it enough, I'll come back.

I slam on the brakes at the front of her driveway. Whit throws his hand out against the dash to keep from flying headfirst into it. I whip the Jeep into the long driveway, lined with trees. Just give me one chain saw, and they'd be gone by the end of the night.

Unfortunately, all I have are golf clubs.

The lights are all on, but nobody's home. The neighbors are supposed to check on Adrienne when her parents aren't home. They make sure the lights are on and the car is parked in the driveway. So they're always on and Adrienne's car never leaves.

"Whatever you're going to do, don't," Whit tells me. I can barely hear the words through the cliché.

I rip a driver from the backseat and step back out into the cold. This time, I'm numb to it.

Holding the driver like a bat, I swing it at the windshield of Adrienne's car, the glass shattering with a crack, the reverberations echoing up the shaft and into my forearms. I feel Whit's hand on my back, trying to stop me. I run away and swing, hitting the car again, and I hear him repeating the same things behind me. My name so many times that it loses its meaning. Olivia. Olivia. Olivia, stop. Olivia!

With one final swing at the driver-side window, the head of the club goes flying off into the front yard and I start sobbing. Whit catches up to me and holds my arms back.

"Stop saying that!" I scream at him through my tears. Whit tries to touch me, and I push him off again and again. Trying to remind him he doesn't want me, either. Not really.

"What should I do?" he asks, the picture of desperation.

"Forget me." I sit there, on the pavement, among all the glass. "Which looks more broken?" I ask, knowing how dramatic I sound. Sometimes when you get your voice back, you have to say the most ridiculous thing that comes into your head.

"Let me take you home." He crunches across the broken glass toward me and reaches his hand out.

I stare up at him. "Would you take it all back if you could?" My face is still wet, and the chill finally begins to hit me. Shivers run up and down my spine.

He crouches down in front of me. He runs his calloused thumb across my cheek. A smear of blood comes away on the pad of his finger. "I can't," he says.

That's not what I wanted to hear.

I grab the back of his head and pull him toward me. Toward a kiss.

He pulls back and his eyes do that searching thing, from one side of my face to the other. I don't know why I did it except he's right here and he's so nice and so cruel all at the same time.

"It's dumb that people actually believe we're dating, isn't it? You could never love someone like me." The look in his eyes is so far away and so confused. I did this to him.

"We have to go, Liv," Whit says, and I feel the whole weight of the day come crashing down on me. Heavy enough to pull me down to the bottom of the ocean if I let it.

"I don't want to." I say it like a child. "Not now."

"We can drive around first. We'll go listen to Mike at Night for a while. Okay?"

He's so sincere and patient with me. Like I am a problem he can solve. Something cataclysmic hits me then, shakes the ground beneath my feet. I imagine this scene from someone else's perspective. Him holding a hand out to me, me on the ground, surrounded by broken glass. Adrienne's house in the background, looming over us like she's here, even now stealing every last thing from me. Me letting her.

Everything is so fragile. I see it now—the car and Ryan's life and Whit looking at me like that. Asking me to go with him. Any moment might be the last time his brow furrows as he stares at me—the girl he can't figure out and won't walk away from.

So I nod and let him pull me up.

53

Ellie is furiously wiping off the counter when I come in on Sunday. Some small part of me is hoping tradition might be a powerful-enough force for Claire to show up. The bell jingles above my head, a bright sound in the dark bar. "Leave," she tells me, her eyes blazing. "Claire's not here, and if she was, I wouldn't let you near her."

I don't. I keep walking. She's just Ellie. Whatever. "You're so full of shit, you know that?" I sit at the counter in front of her, even though she's watching me with murder in her eyes. If anyone could kill you with a look, it'd be Ellie.

She leans into her hands. "Me?" She glances around at the empty bar. "You have a lot of nerve to even show up here right now." Then she looks me over. "What happened to your face?"

I reach up and feel it. There's a long cut in my neck that will probably scar. "I busted out Adrienne's car windows with my fake boyfriend's golf club."

"Adrienne is going to fuck you up," she says, no longer murderous, just matter-of-fact. "And she's going to have the whole school backing her up now. Using Claire like a pawn in the middle of whatever medieval shit the two of you are up to? You crossed a line."

I could argue with her, try to tell her the truth, but what's the point now? "Were you ever mad at Claire? For being friends with Adrienne?"

Ellie shrugs. She's already over being mad at me. "Adrienne's a bitch. It's not like it's a secret to anyone who meets her. So I don't feel bad for anyone who gets involved with her."

"What about you?"

"I'm a straightforward bitch. There's a difference." Ellie swings her hair over her shoulder. "When it looks like I'm about to fuck you up on the volleyball court, I'm about to fuck you up on the volleyball court."

It strikes me, maybe for the first time, that Ellie is no cooler, no less insecure than I am. She just plays it off better. I thought I could do that. But everyone knew. Everyone saw through me.

"What about me?" I ask her.

"You're a secondary bitch. Not even the one people bother to get pissed about." She smiles then: The chance to hurt me is all she wants. Even though she's calmed down, I've hurt Claire. I can't avoid her wrath. "You know, people probably have I-hate-Adrienne-Maynard clubs, but you're just some second-stringer. You do the dirty work. How does it feel?"

"Like maybe it's not so surprising I'd finally take my turn."

"Maybe not." She thinks for a second, wiping away at the glass mugs with an already dirty rag. "Really, Adrienne's done you a favor, I guess, because congratu-fucking-lations. You're public enemy number one and all alone. Finally, right?"

"I don't care what anyone in this town thinks of me," I hear myself saying, willing it to be true. "I'm going to own the SATs and leave all of this behind."

She nods. "Right, Liv. And I'm going to the moon."

"I don't need anyone, Adrienne least of all," I promise her. "Like

Claire doesn't need you to fight her battles. Like she can't count on you."

"But she can count on you?" Even though Ellie never gives away much, her eyes show a tiny break in her façade. It's enough.

I leave.

Don't look back.

54

SIX MONTHS AGO

"Claire!" I called, stepping through the Rough House door and onto the barely cleaned floor. "C'mon, I've been outside for fifteen minutes. Adrienne is going to freak!"

"Of course she is!" someone answered. I looked toward the back of the bar where Ellie had one arm propped up against it, her other hand on her hip. "Claire, quick, run off and do whatever Adrienne wants."

Claire was standing against the back wall of the bar, both arms crossed over her chest. "Don't talk to me that way," she said, her voice sharp edges.

"O, thank God you've come to call and take Claire away from all this. I know she can't wait to get back to her perfectly constructed Buckley social life."

I stepped farther into the bar. This was beyond none of my business. "Ellie, lay the hell off her, okay?"

Claire put up hands toward both of us. "I don't need you fighting my battle for me here. Either of you."

Ellie dropped her arm, looking at Claire. "I'm sorry if I don't want you to go when Adrienne calls and hang all over Coxie. I mean, am I being ridiculous here?"

"No," Claire said, stepping toward her. "No, I know."

"So, you're going to break up with him? Tonight?"

I can tell this isn't going to end soon. "Claire." I said it again, more of a desperate plea. Adrienne was texting me nonstop.

"Goddamn, Olivia, can I live for a second?" she demanded, turning on me. "Can you, like, wait outside for a minute? I'll be right out."

I sighed and went back outside. It was three minutes later, per my cell phone clock, that Claire finally came out. I was ready to roll like it never happened at all, and she was smiling as she walked out like she was, too. But then her face changed when she saw me standing there so eager. "Just once," she said to me, "just once, can the two of you try not to control my life?"

"I was only . . ." I trailed off, looking down at my phone. Adrienne had sent me, like, three different sets of question marks.

"What's she going to do, O? What's she going to do if I completely fuck off from the party to go hang out with Ellie? Is she not going to be friends with me anymore? Why the *fuck* are you so scared of Adrienne?"

I took a deep breath, not used to Claire talking to me like this. Not used to her being anything but the peacemaker. "I don't want her to hate me," I said after a minute, not looking her in the eye.

Claire sighed, putting her face in her hands and then pulling back to look at me. "No one hates you."

I laughed a bit at that. "Everyone hates me. My own mother hates me."

"C'mon," Claire said, starting to walk toward Mom's car. "We can just tell her it's my fault we're late. And you know I don't hate you. Adrienne definitely doesn't hate you—that would be impossible. She thinks you're two parts of one soul or something ridiculous like that." She opened the passenger's door and slid in. I walked around to the other side, thinking about that, about how specific and strange it sounded.

I got into the car. "Nah, it's the three of us."

Claire snorted. "Olivia, c'mon. It's you two and me. I'm the spectator to whatever the two of you are doing. It's kind of a relief sometimes, you know?"

I cranked up the car. "Why?"

"Because sometimes the two of you scare me."

55

If I got hangovers, I'd imagine this was one. This empty, painful feeling that increases with every second I'm left alone in my head. Any moment, I think. Any moment everything that I have left will come toppling down. Whit will know about Mrs. Baker. About all the terrible things I've done. I'm just waiting for payback from destroying her car.

And then I will actually, without a doubt, have nothing.

The bell rings, signaling lunch hour. I trudge down the hall to my locker, flipping through flash cards as I walk. I had time to color-code one thousand words over my three days of suspension, finding myself constantly texting my best handiwork to Whit. He started using all the words in ridiculous sentences to answer me. Sometimes, studying with him doesn't suck. Sometimes, I wish I'd done it for the past four years and wasn't cramming it all in now.

But here we are.

Without looking up, I put my hand up to my locker. It's sticky.

I jerk up immediately, pulling my hand away. Gross.

I twirl the combo on the lock anyway, unhitching it from the handle. I pull at it but it doesn't give. I drop my bag; I know Adrienne's done something to it, I do, but whatever it is, I can deal with it.

It opens to a rain of falling bottles.

They fall around me, a cacophony of glass against tile. Liquor bottle after liquor bottle showers down around me as I push myself up against the locker door in an attempt to stem the onslaught. I see them fall in slow motion, each bottle tumbling into the other, each clatter deafening.

Until, just like that, it ends. The last bottle rolls across the hall and swivels to a stop. It felt like more, but now I see there are only five full-size bottles littering the floor.

Laughter surrounds me, enveloping me in its embrace like an old friend. The laughter of a pleased crowd, so familiar to me, only this time, it's *me* they're laughing at. I bend down to pick up two bottles, not knowing what I'm going to do with them, just so I don't have to look up.

Because I'm crying. *Ugh*. I knew I wouldn't get away with smashing her car up, so what's the matter with me?

I paw at my face.

"You ready?" I hear someone whisper behind me. A peppy voice. I turn my head up, deciding I am about to rip some JV cheerleader a new one. As soon as my face hits the light, something hits my face—something wet and bitter. I choke as the liquid hits my open mouth, sputtering.

Then I get hit again. And again.

The liquor burns my eyes, soaks my hair to my scalp, drips down everything. All I know to do is crouch down in front of my locker and cover my face.

But no one helps me.

Not one person.

I want to crawl into the floor, melt there into the pool of liquor, and stop existing. At least for that one moment, just stop altogether.

These horrible racking sobs are filling my ears, and they're coming from me. There's a name on the tip of my tongue, not mine: It's *Ryan*, over and over again. That's what this is. This is his ghost, him and his

Jack Daniel's he loved so much and his car and that tree, all the things I imagine every night. *Oh my God, this isn't real.*

It can't be.

"Somebody go get Whit DuRant or a teacher or something," a voice says in the distance. One voice of sympathy through the laughter.

"Why should we? Would she help if it were one of us?" Footsteps retreat all around me.

"Olivia," says someone closer. A warm touch on my arm. "Get up. Let's go."

56

LAST YEAR

Mom said "get out" to Ryan, and my whole life realigned. If Ryan was the problem child, then what did that make me?

Ethan had just gone home, his face uneasy as he left me alone in my room with the sounds of fighting coming from the den. I'd wanted him to leave—didn't want him to know that Ryan, the boy I'd spent my life worshipping, was so broken. I lay in my dark bedroom, my too-short dress tangled up around my legs, hair mussed from sex. I'd close my eyes and it'd all go—

"Ryan, for God's sake, we had this dinner planned for a month and now you can barely stand up. Can't you think—imagine—what this is doing to me?"

"Of course it is," he replied, his words coming together as if one. "Of course it's all about you and pretending *you* have everything under control."

Mom's voice got low. That's when I went closer to the door to listen. "This isn't about me, Ryan. This is about you. What do you think seeing you like this does to your sister?"

I heard him laugh. "Oh, because you care about her so much." I almost smiled. "She was smart and happy and bright, and you brought her to this shithole and look what it's done to her."

"*Ryan,*" Mom said.

"Look what she's become. Another fucking—"

"Get out."

She hadn't screamed. She hadn't even sounded angry by then. She just said it.

I leaned against the wall of my room, my hand on my chest, momentarily stunned. And then I pulled open my door, running into the middle of them—between Mom, all hard-faced and serious, and red-eyed Ryan, confused and sloppy.

"I'll go with you," I said automatically. I don't know what made me do it. Why I thought I could change his mind, convince him to see me for who I was. For who he'd always known.

I was heartbroken and I wanted him to love me again.

Ryan kind of stared at me, mystified for a moment, and then he shrugged one shoulder and turned toward the door.

When I went to follow him, Mom grabbed my arm. "Olivia, don't!" she commanded. Her fingers squeezed into my forearm. "You're not helping this way. This enables him." For a second, I got a clear view of the desperation behind her eyes. "You can let me handle this."

I was incapable. Because of course I was.

I yanked my arm out of her grip and tore off after Ryan, running out the door behind him. He was leaning against his SUV outside. I went to him. "Where are the keys?" I asked.

Mom stood in the front door, the light shining on her from behind, casting her face in shadow. "Please, you drive, Olivia," she said, holding up Ryan's key ring. I leapt back up the stairs, taking the keys from between her fingers. I ignored the way she was looking at me, the hurt on her face, and pounded back down the stairs.

"Get in," I told Ryan.

When we drove away, she stared off after us, but I don't think she could see us anymore.

That night, Ryan and I ended up on the high school football field, stars strewn against the Buckley sky above us, itchy grass rubbing against our bare legs. Ryan found a bottle of Jack Daniel's in his trunk. He'd take a swig, hand it to me, and wait patiently while I did the same. "The stars are brighter here than anywhere else," he told me as I pulled the bottle out of his hand.

I've always hated the taste of Jack Daniel's.

Finally, after another excruciating swallow of dark liquor, I asked, "Why do you do this?"

He stopped, the bottle halfway to his mouth, and let it fall to his side. "You sound like her."

"Don't say that." There wasn't going to be an answer, I saw. I don't think even *he* knew why.

With some effort, he twisted his head to the side, looking at me through glassy eyes. "Remember how I used to tell you all those stories when we were younger? About all these places around the world? Back when Mom was practically a robot, and then after we moved here, how it'd be our escape from this nothing town? How everything would be so different once we were on our own?"

I nodded. I'd been clinging to that hope my entire life. That I'd go someplace where the Rough House wasn't the highlight of a Friday night and where people weren't defined by what side of the railroad tracks they lived on. Where I could atone for my sins. Where I'd finally feel totally and completely loved and whole.

Anywhere else.

He laughed, hollow. "It's all bullshit, Liv. I thought I'd be happy if I could just get out of Buckley. Out of my head. But now I'm more trapped than ever." He stopped, breathed. Brought the bottle back to his lips and sucked down another gulp. "So that's why I do it."

I closed my eyes, took a deep breath, and said it: "Do you hate me, Ry?"

He shifted his head to face me then, and I followed so that our eyes lined up to each other, our same dark hair side to side. "Of course not, Liv," he said very carefully, as if trying to make sure I knew this wasn't coming from the Jack Daniel's. "You're still my favorite person in the world."

A chill swept through the air, and I wrapped my arms around myself. "Then don't go back," I said. Especially if I was never getting out.

But he did. That's the thing about us Claytons.

We never know when to quit.

57

The world is covered in alcohol—it's in the smell and the sights and the feel. I'm drowning in it right outside my locker, waiting to cease existing.

Someone's hand hoists me up from the floor in front of my locker, marching me down the hall. A guy's hand. I can't open my eyes. They sting so badly, I want to claw them out of my head. He leads me through a doorway, slamming it and turning the lock behind him. Then I feel cool water brushing across my face. I cringe away from it, but he brings me back in closer.

"Are you okay?"

I open my eyes.

Do you know what color Jack Daniel's is?

It's like if you mixed honey and soda and bile and just a little of whatever makes it swish up against the glass, that's the color of Jack Daniel's. Or, right now, the color of the wet paper towel in Ethan's hand. He looks like he has witnessed the first truly tragic thing in his life.

I shake my head, afraid if I talk, the taste will be worse. I pull more paper towels out of the dispenser, wiping at my mouth, scouring my tongue with the rough material. It's like trying to stop a flood with a piece of gum. I drop the paper towel and lean against the bathroom stall. Ethan stares, his dark blue eyes thoughtful.

"Where's Whit?" I ask because it's the first thing that pops into my head.

He winces like that actually stung. "I don't know. He's *your* boyfriend," he says, his voice with a chilly edge.

I push my sopping-wet hair back out of my face. I'm not thinking about him. I'm not thinking about Whit.

Ryan. Ryan. Ryan.

"Did you know she was going to do this?" I ask, still trying to choke back my feelings. Swallow them. Stomp them into the ground.

"Of course not. Do you think I would let her do that to you after your brother—" He stops and shakes his head. "It's so fucked up." He pulls at the ends of his hair. "Everything is fucked up."

"I didn't put that photo in the papers. Of Claire. She did," I say. "Not that you care; you're so wrapped around her finger."

"What do you want from me, O?" Ethan asks. "To tell you you're a hundred times more important to me than she's ever been? You already know that."

I glare at him. "Fuck you for saying that to me." I smell like a distillery. "Look at me. She throws Ryan in my face like he's the king of hearts in a poker game. You do it, too. You slept with her and told me it was my fault."

His face changes. Anger flares to life on his usually calm façade. "What else was I supposed to do?"

"Are you kidding me?"

He doesn't say anything for a moment. Swallows, his Adam's apple bobbing up and down, in thought. Making a decision. And then: "I didn't know how else to get your attention."

I laugh out loud. "That's the excuse now? You wanted attention. Well, bravo, you sure got it."

"I don't know, O. I was so desperate for you to talk to me, and you wouldn't, and I thought Adrienne would help." He runs a hand through his hair with a sigh. "It's all I've wanted for weeks. For you to look over and see me with her and finally tell DuRant to go fuck off and for it to fix this chasm between us. I thought the one thing you wouldn't be able to stand was seeing me with Adrienne and eventually you would want me back. Even if it was just to stop it."

I open my mouth. Then close it. Then open it again.

He laughs, a mean laugh that doesn't suit him, looks down at his feet. "And it finally hit me. If you don't care about me being with her, then you don't care about me at all." Accusation drips from his words; hurt, too.

"But, Ethan, it wasn't over until that last moment. The one where I had to see you like that." I resist the urge to chew on my lip, not even sure if I'm lying or not. When was it over? "I bet the whole thing was her idea, huh?"

"Adrienne may have done a lot of things, but driving a wedge between us was not one of them. That was all you."

"I was heartbroken." I clutch at my ruined shirt. If I think back, I can actually feel my heart shattering again. None of what I remember about that day is Ryan. It's Adrienne on a boat dock, every laugh line in her bright face. Ethan belly-flopping into the murky waters outside, arms outstretched to his side like a cross between a skydiver and a skimmer bug. Coxie nuzzling into Claire's neck, eyes alight with adoration.

My whole life was a beautiful lie built upon this one person who I didn't realize held me together. And then the unraveling, for months after; I was unraveling like a frayed ribbon.

"I wanted to help," Ethan says, his voice raw, his expression honest. "But you were dying in front of me, and you didn't care about anything I had to offer. Nothing but sex." The way he says it, I wonder if he's the first teenage boy to ever make sex sound like a swear word.

"Is that what you're doing to DuRant, too—using him?" he asks me like it's an accusation.

If Whit and I were real, he'd be right, I guess.

"You don't know anything about us," I say. Because otherwise, he'd be laughing in my face right now. He'd laugh knowing how much more I've used Whit than I ever used him. He'd laugh about the karmic retribution of it all—me wanting someone so badly who would never want me back once he knew the whole story.

It's all a great big tragedy, and it's nothing less than what I deserve.

"You don't understand how it feels to lose everything that's important to you," I say.

"You don't understand what it's like to be fighting for someone who doesn't see you. You hadn't lost *me*."

Tears are bubbling right beneath the surface again. I loved him so much then, when he never thought of me as second-best. But it wasn't the same as Adrienne, as her fucked-up love I thought I had to earn. Ethan gave without question. And I took every bit I could get my hands on. "I wish things had been different," I say honestly. "But you did what you did. It's still not right."

He pulls at the fraying edges of the paper towel he's still holding. "You didn't want it to be different. You wanted to blame someone. I'm glad I at least gave you that."

I go silent. Stare hard at him. There's nothing else to say, and I know that. Even though he was the catalyst for this whole mess, he's not important anymore. He's a pawn in Adrienne's game now, same as the rest of us. Just a boy caught in the middle who once loved me, probably more than I loved him. So I let him have this.

He's right anyway.

Ethan watches me as I wash my hair out in the sink and redo my makeup, trying to pull myself back together.

"C'mon," he says after, bending over to pick up my still-wet book bag. "I'll walk you to the office."

I bend my head down and follow him out of the bathroom.

Some of the varsity cheerleaders are in the hall, decorating a bulletin board, along with Michaela Verday and a couple of student council members. A lot of them are teacher and office aides for this hour. They line our path to the office, and I really don't want to walk past them looking like this.

"Stop," I tell Ethan, grabbing his arm. He does.

"You can't avoid them forever."

At the sound of voices, a couple of girls' heads turn. Adrienne's cat-like eyes catch mine and she smiles wickedly, hollers at one of the other girls to toss her a glitter stick.

The look on her face makes me sick. Everything always goes her way, falls into place however she imagines it.

"I know," I say. "But just." I take his arm and turn him to face me. Set my jaw. I think about it. Stare at the contours of his face. Whit's sharp in all the places Ethan is soft—jawline, eyes, nose. Ethan over-compensates with a severe haircut, bulking up on protein shakes and hours lost in the weight room. I remember he used to win me over constantly, make me feel good about myself.

But he never challenged me.

Adrienne is watching us, I know. She hates that Ethan wants me more than her. She always has. Before I'd ever seen him, she'd announced he was beautiful, one day early in our junior year. She hates remembering that, as much as she hates that she can't change his mind about me.

It's the one game she can't win.

I lean my head forward and kiss him. It's less of a kiss and more of a touch between two mouths, one that has recently been doused in whiskey, until he gets over the initial surprise and presses against me a little harder. I make it last as long as I can, until I feel him realize this is me he's kissing. At which point he stops, rocking back on his heels.

"What are you trying to do?"

I glance back to make sure Adrienne was watching. When our eyes meet, she turns away to hide her fury. I push my lips together and walk in the opposite direction of the office, knowing everyone else in the hall is watching.

Maybe it worked, but as far as ideas go, even I know that one was pretty terrible.

58

I race out of the front entrance to the school and hear Whit call my name as the door closes behind me.

I stop and turn around to see him pushing through the door after me. "What happened to you?" he asks.

"Don't tell me you haven't heard. Surely my popularity hasn't taken that big of a hit at this school." I lean against a column holding up the breezeway that leads to the parking lot.

"Yeah, I heard. I've been looking for you. I had to go get a hall pass from Mr. Doolittle because your BFF, Adrienne, told on me." He scratches the back of his neck, and his watch jingles.

The thought of him putting in that much effort kind of warms me. And I'm staring up into his gold-streaked eyes, and I open my mouth and offer, for the hell of it, "Let's go somewhere."

"What?" he asks as if I just suggested we fly to the moon, as if the rules are so goddamn important he can't move to break them.

"Do I look that bad?"

"Well"—he pauses—"kind of, but you did just get showered in Jack Daniel's. And Dr. Rickards was looking for you. And we can't just leave and go somewhere in the middle of class. Aren't you upset, Liv?"

I shrug. I don't know how much he's been told, how much he's figured out, but it's already more than I want him to know. I don't want to think about him knowing this.

Not about Ryan.

I lunge forward and grab on to his arm. "Come on, Whit. This past week has been shit for both of us. Let's go somewhere." His eyes are still shifting around like he's standing in the middle of a crime scene. I don't let go of him. "Aren't you—aren't you tired of this stuff? Everything?"

"Where do you want to go?" he finally asks.

"You decide," I tell him, smiling ever so slightly. I want to kiss him, get the taste of Ethan off my mouth. Get the taste of the day off my mouth. But I can't do that—just kiss him.

Not again.

His eyes rove down my body. "Come on. I have a change of clothes in my car."

According to the T-shirt I have on, I am a South Carolina golf state champion. It smells like dryer sheets and the moment right before it rains and Whit. Mostly like Whit.

"Where are we going?" I ask.

"Somewhere," he promises, his eyelids fluttering as he watches the road. It doesn't look like he's shaved in a couple of days. Stubble is creeping up along his jawline.

We head in the direction of Adrienne's house, and I start getting nervous so I twist my hands together to stop them from doing anything weird. I think Whit's watching me for a minute, but when I turn to look at him, his eyes are on the road again.

He pulls onto a gravel road that goes through a tunnel made of trees, the sun spilling through the small cracks it can find in the branches. Whit pulls his car up alongside the trees and gets out. I throw on the sweatshirt he's loaned me and follow. I sidle up alongside him. "Well, this is special," I say, because the world would end if I didn't make a sarcastic comment.

"Never said it was," he tells me. Then I spot the golf ball in his hand.

"No." Whit pulls me forward by my fingers with his one empty hand, but I stop stubbornly and cross my arms. "Whit, no. No golf. I'm serious."

"Can you just trust me?" He rolls his eyes. "I know I'm corny as hell; you don't have to tell me."

I tap my finger on my chin for a second. "You're insulting yourself now. Nice."

His eyebrow goes up. "Well, you did look pretty tired. Figured I'd do it for you."

"Fine." I start walking again, swinging my fingertips back and forth past his. There's an ache under my skin and all over it. The pain is steady and thrumming, and I think if his hand just grabbed mine again, it would be gone.

It doesn't make sense to feel so much longing for something that's right in front of you.

"Where are we?" I finally ask.

"Oh." Whit shakes his head. "It's this pseudo driving range our club owns." He points at the copse of trees in the distance. "The course is over there."

Pseudo is definitely the word for it. Sloping grass, not mowed carefully like the course. Oak trees towering over us, cutting out a cove to drive balls from. To the far left, a little piece of the course's lake. "It's . . ." I touch the bark on the closest tree. "Nice."

He shrugs with one shoulder, looking self-conscious. The cove might not look like much, but I can see that it means something to him. "It's kind of a place to de-stress, you know? I can hit the ball like it doesn't matter. See how far I can drive it." He laughs at a private joke. "Cason and I used to do that when we were kids. See who could drive it farther. Me," he answers the unasked question. "It's my short game that sucks. I'm too volatile or something to concentrate on those shots."

I shove him. "Shut up."

He smiles. It's fake. Cold comfort for the girl who got doused in Jack Daniel's. "I used to get so pissed at my dad. He'd tell me no one would ever recruit me if I didn't stop acting like such an asshole when I played a bad game. It got in my head. I'd get worse and worse."

"That sucks that he said that," I say.

"He was right. That's what golf is—if you fuck up your world on the twelfth hole, you start over on thirteen. You have to play every hole and every shot and every day like it's the first one ever. It's just . . . exhausting sometimes."

"So why do it, then? If it makes you feel bad? It's all about keeping up with your brother, right?" I say, parroting his words back to him.

He thinks about that for a second and shakes his head. "I love it."

"You tell yourself you love it. To please everyone else."

His expression changes. He comes forward, takes my wrist, and pulls me toward him. "Come here," he says, as if he were leading a child into something magical. He positions me in the center of the cove, out over the stretching range. His skin is warm where it meets my wrists. The wind blows my damp hair, drying out the last of the terrible day. "Close your eyes," he commands. As my eyelids flutter closed, I watch him disappear. Face eager. Nervous. "Now . . ." He blows out an errant breath, and the warmth of it caresses my forehead. "Listen."

I do. To the sound of the leaves rustling, to the wind shifting. The sweet smell of honeysuckle permeates the air, tinged with the sharpness of freshly cut grass. When I open my eyes, the ground is so green and the sky is so blue and Whit watches and watches and—

With him there, it's so beautiful it hurts.

Hurts so much, my throat burns with the pain. Tears threaten again. "I'm going to Clemson," he tells me, and I stop looking at the sky and look at him. "They all want me to go to Duke, like Cason, but I don't want to. I'm going to Clemson."

I lunge forward and hug him, wrapping my arms as tightly around him as I can. And even though I am so, so happy for him, I know part of me is trying to hold him down. Keep him here with me. Keep him from flying away. I'm seeing all the things he loves, and I want to—need to—know: "This is what makes you happy?"

It's an embarrassing question; I can hear that once I've said it. "I guess," he says, like it's stupid.

"It's okay, you know. To say if something makes you happy."

"What makes you happy, then?" he asks. It's a challenge. He knows I'd never admit anything.

I sink my teeth into my lip. He's right. After a long silence, he smiles and leans forward until his forehead is against the top of my hair and we're staring each other right in the eyes. "Let me go get a club. I'm going to show you how to do it the right way." Then he grins with all his teeth and lets me go.

I have to admit it to myself.

He makes me happy.

59

I peek from Whit's garage into his kitchen, giggling. His hand grazes the skin of my hip under my T-shirt. I turn around to meet him, our mouths inches apart. "Coast's clear," I say with a smile.

We stand there, grinning at each other for half a second, and then he lunges forward and kisses me. After all the shit that happened today, it feels like we were both waiting for this moment to forget it all and kiss again. We know it's wrong and we know we should both be worried about a million other things, but neither of us wants that. We just want each other and peace for half a minute.

We stumble through the side door into the kitchen, still kissing. It's the really good kind of kissing. Kisses that look sloppy and terrible but feel amazing deep in your stomach, the kind where you can laugh between every kiss, where you can smile mouth to mouth, where there's nothing more you want than for every minute to last longer than the one before. This is what it feels like to be alive. Like kissing and traveling all over the white tile kitchen and past golf awards and family portraits, all the way back up into the beige hallway wall.

Whit stops against the wall, breathing hard. He laughs and I laugh, and then without a word, we start kissing again. My hair still smells like

Jack. This morning Adrienne was throwing my brother's death in my face. I can't believe I'm allowed this good an ending for a day like today.

I wonder then if I'm allowed to stop hurting. Then we're still kissing and I stop wondering. In his room, I back into his desk, sacred altar of homework that it is, and a bunch of papers fall to the floor. "Oh, shit." I start laughing again.

Whit stares at me, then stares at the papers, then me, like he's about to have a nervous breakdown.

"Oh hell, Whit." I slide off the desk to pick them up. I catch sight of something then. A photo, its colors bright against the papers. It's a picture, one I posted online the night of the charity ball so everyone would see the two of us together. Whit's looking at me, laughing, and I'm smiling at the camera, my hand resting against the front of his shirt. There's a sticky note on it: "I was 'researching' Olivia on my phone. You two looked so great that night, I had to print this off. Love you, Mom."

It's so real. His laugh and my smile and the way we're touching. The note his mom wrote.

This isn't real.

"Stop," Whit almost-growls then as if he were sexy enough to pull that off. I pick up and straighten a newspaper article on him and his recruitment that came out before the scandal, sticking the picture under it so he can't see, slowly setting the stack of papers back on his desk. How could I have let myself forget what this is? Soon it will be over, and I'll have nothing left to prove he ever kissed me this way. Nothing but the memory of this moment when he wanted me this badly. In two days, there will be no Whit and Olivia.

That's how it's supposed to be. That version of me—the girl in that picture, this girl he's looking at so kindly right now—isn't real.

He tries to kiss me again.

"I kissed Ethan."

He stops halfway between us, the emotions on his face blurring like he's an Etch-A-Sketch I just shook up. His face doesn't change; it just stops. Stops smiling or thinking or caring. "You did what?"

I stare at him, hard and clear. "I kissed him."

"Okay." I wait for his expression to change, to shift in some way. For some hurt to cross those stoic features of his. It doesn't. Whit's a professional at holding in his feelings; that's what he's supposed to do. If he fucks up his world on the twelfth, he has to go to thirteen and start over. It's that simple.

I want to ask him if what I just said even affects him at all because some part of me can't help myself, but I don't because there's no right answer.

"So you're getting back together," he says, like he's informing me.

"No," I reply. I can honestly say the thought hadn't even crossed my mind. Maybe back then, I wanted to, but not anymore.

"It's just, like, something I had to do," I say. *I had to remind Adrienne, to prove I was better than her. That Ethan could never love her.*

He answers clearly. "Yeah."

I put my hand on the desk behind me, holding myself up. "So we don't have to—"

"Let's just do it," he says.

I forget to breathe for a second. Then I say, "Yeah, let's," like that will fix everything, and he closes his mouth and kisses me and we just do it.

Just like that.

The truth is, I don't know what I wanted. Him to tell me I had broken his heart, that it was all real for him. Or him to tell me that I was a terrible person and to get out of his life right now.

I like kissing him. I like the feel of his calloused hands against my skin. So I guess that's why I did it. Because I wanted to. Because I thought it would change his mind, bring him back to me.

It isn't supposed to go like this, I think before, and during, and after.

This smart boy with real emotions is not supposed to be okay to *just do it* after I kiss Ethan—he was supposed to stop me, to say *this isn't what I wanted at all.* He's supposed to *feel* something, make me feel something. Who is he, I wonder, looking up at his face, if he's not that boy?

How can he not care?

I wonder if I finally broke him.

Or if maybe I'm the broken one.

60

I have to talk to somebody. Someone who knows I'm a person with feelings, breakable and complicated and not just some damaged cliché on skinny legs.

I can't rely on myself.

I sit in the car in Claire's driveway and listen to my radio. One of Ryan's favorite songs is on. He used to lie by his stereo, right next to the speaker, and listen. He'd call me over and demand I lie down in front of it, too, and listen. Listen to the lyrics. Imagine putting that much emotion together, line by line, word by word, enough to lay your entire soul bare. Leave yourself defenseless. Nothing exposes you like words.

Ryan was always full of bullshit like that.

A knock on my window startles me. It's Claire, barefoot, in a pair of athletic shorts, her blond hair piled up on top of her head. I jump out of the car. "Hi," I say.

Claire crosses her arms over her stomach. "I'm not allowed to have girls over. On account of my unnaturalness." She sniffs.

"Does it help that I just had sex with a boy?" I ask.

She shrugs, crossing her tiny goose bump–covered legs at the ankle. "How long are you planning on sitting out here?"

"Can I come in?" I ask.

She stares off at the neighbor's house.

"Please?" I try.

She starts up the sidewalk, up the porch stairs, and back into her house. The door stands open behind her, a halfhearted invitation.

I sigh and take it.

Claire's house is the kind of picture you'd imagine in a Christmas card. Wood-paneled walls and carpet that squishes up through your toes and one of those huge fireplaces Hallmark scours the country for. When I thought of the word *home*, Claire's house was always what came to mind.

She sits on the couch, hugging a pillow to her chest. "What do you want?" she says into the pillow. I stand there, awkward, in the center of the room.

"I got suspended because I punched someone in the face for talking about you," I say. It's the most convincing argument I have. "Why would I do that if I made those papers?"

Claire's still staring at a spot on the wall across from her. I don't know if she doesn't believe me or she just doesn't want to hear it.

I decide to beg. "You're my best friend and my life is pretty shit right now and yours is too and everything sucks and I don't know what to do if I can't talk to you. I don't."

"You know what's funny?" she asks. She glances at me to see if I'm listening, and then it's back to the wall before I can meet her eyes. "The same people who call me names behind my back and whisper how I'm going to hell and stuff, they're the ones who rushed to defend my honor or whatever. To throw whiskey in your face. They're mean, Liv. They're just mean."

I shift, try to find a place to fit in among the cozy furniture and family portraits. "And here I was thinking that was vigilante justice."

She snickers.

"I didn't make those flyers. But"—I swallow—"the texts. You probably already know. Adrienne probably told you."

She's staring at me, eyes all wide like saucers, and I can't believe of all the promises Adrienne's ever broken in her life, this wasn't one of them. I don't want to say this, and I have to.

"I was pissed at her after she slept with Ethan so I thought I'd forward a bunch of her texts, but I had no idea what they said. I wanted to do something to hurt her because I was hurt. But I'm sorry. I'm so, so, so sorry, and I deserve however you want to treat me." I'm crying, like it's my problem. I'm the most selfish, terrible person, but knowing that doesn't make the tears stop. "Fuck."

"What?" Claire asks. "Slow down."

"Maybe it doesn't matter. I didn't do it to you, but I'm one of them. I'm just like them. I never try to change anything. I get pissed at what Adrienne does when it's convenient for me. I've spent all this time trying to convince myself—trying to convince everyone else and especially Whit—that I'm somehow better than her. But I'm not and he knows it. I'm disposable—and worse, I'm only getting revenge on them because it's not fair that I have to stay in Buckley forever."

Claire stares at me. "Why?"

"Why what?"

"Why do you have to stay forever?"

"I'm not like you, Claire. I'm not brave."

"Oh, here we go again. What's brave about being a lesbian? It's not like I chose to be. I just am." She laughs bitterly. "God, this is so stupid. All of you—you and Adrienne and everyone else—use me for whatever you need whenever it's convenient, but what about me? All I want is to be left alone and to kiss whomever I want.

"So be honest. Tell me what you want to tell me, Liv."

I take a deep breath. "I didn't print those papers; I really didn't. I think Adrienne did, but I have no proof. But I've done all this terrible, heinous shit, so it might as well have been me. I deserve for you to hate me."

I can't really make eye contact, so the bark of laughter startles me right out of my skin. When I look up, Claire is doubled over laughing. When she stops, she starts in on me. "Are you kidding me? All of the shit happening in my life is some sort of pissing contest between you and Adrienne. Are you serious?"

I half nod.

She claps her hands together. I'm wordless. Claire's not supposed to be all abrasive and cold like this. That's not who she is. She's bubbly and apologetic and easy to please. "And here I was thinking someone was trying to ruin my life but *no*. It's my two best friends trying to ruin each other's."

"Claire, I—"

She jumps up from the couch before I can finish and advances on me. "Are you out of your mind?" she demands.

She's staring right at me, every curve of her body now nothing more than another tough edge. Her blue eyes are fierce, but I cling to the knowledge that deep down, she's a marshmallow. That she let me in. When I remember that, my reply comes out honest. "Yes," I say.

And then I tell her everything.

"So you're sleeping with him and acting like you're dating, but you're not together?" Claire brushes her fingers over the mattress. The fading sun, filtered through the window, hits her hair and turns her golden.

We're sitting there, eating cookie dough like we did when we were in middle school, back when eating our feelings could solve all problems. Even though it's not that simple anymore, sometimes, when life is shit, you might as well put it behind you and eat cookie dough.

Or at least, that's what Claire says.

I laugh. "Wow, it sounds stupid when you say it like that."

"It *is* really stupid!" Claire pulls her legs up on the bed and rests her chin on her knees. "You look so happy together, though," she says, sounding like I told her Santa wasn't real.

"He's . . ." I shake my head. "He's Whit."

She tilts her head slightly, as if debating what to say. "How's the sex?"

I feel a giggle bubbling up, and my face goes red. Talking about it makes it feel more real than doing it. "It's Whit."

"I mean"—she grimaces—"so you're sort of bribing him with sex, right?"

"Ugh." I fall back on the bed, letting myself bounce up and down on the mattress. "I'm not sure which one of us that makes grosser. Anyway, now he can't even bring himself to care that I kissed Ethan. I guess I got what I deserved."

I expect her to deny it, comfort me the way she always comforts me, but instead she says, "We all got what we deserved."

"What?"

She leans down next to me on her mattress, propping her head onto her hand to watch me. I fold my arms behind my head. "We've all done terrible stuff. I'm not surprised we're finally getting it dished back at us."

"Not you," I argue. Claire doesn't deserve any of this.

"Of course I did, Liv. I've watched you and Adrienne for years. How many times have I stopped you?"

None, I think, letting the silence sit in the air.

"I've gotten so used to it," Claire continues. "Sitting quietly in the background while you two laughed about some god-awful thing. I met Adrienne in preschool. Falling into step with her was never a question because she never cared about the rules. I thought they were so important. I thought I always had to fall in line the way my family did. But she never asked me to. That felt so right.

"But it stopped being subversive a long time ago." Claire shrugs. "I don't know. I thought the two of you had my back. I thought it was worth it, to stay quiet, to stay near you." She almost laughs. "Ellie thinks I have Stockholm syndrome."

I do laugh.

"I don't want to let it go," Claire says at last. "I love Buckley. I love cheerleading and the idiots at the Rough House and eating ice cream with my best friends. But I have to because Buckley doesn't love me anymore."

"I still do, though," I say.

"I can't even decide what to think. About you and Adrienne. I want to be so mad, but I also . . . don't want to be? Like, I want this to be over." She looks at me. "Can it end now? And we be fine?"

"I don't think so," I answer honestly.

She watches me closely. I can see it behind her eyes—she's already made up her mind. "I think Whit likes you," she says as if this were any other conversation. It only hurts a little.

I snort, following her cue to drop it. "He thinks I'm a loser of the highest caliber. He can't believe he's stooping down to a girl who'll peak in high school."

"Then why would he do it?"

I stare off at the ceiling. "I don't know."

"See?" She sighs.

"We're calling it off on Friday. That was the deal."

"Ade was right, then."

My head snaps up. "What?"

"You know, she can sense stuff. She said something wasn't right with the Whit thing. That it didn't make any sense." Claire combs her fingers through her hair. "But then when she saw you together the other night, she kind of looked confused. She had that look."

"What look?"

"She wanted to know."

Claire holds the cookie dough out to me, and I break off a piece.

"She always wants to know. But I have to call it off. I'm breaking up with Whit on schedule." I've told her almost everything. Not the part I played with Mrs. Baker. Not that I'm the reason her job and her family are in jeopardy. Even I can't face that.

Claire stares at the comforter for a minute. "If you like him, why don't you tell him how you feel?"

"It doesn't work like that. I'm dangerous." I rub my fingers over the thin skin on my wrist, feeling for danger like a spark underneath. I must be. When I met Whit, he was nice and stuck-up and innocent, and now he's like every other boy who thinks sex is the least complicated thing there is. He doesn't care.

If he cared, I'd know. I wouldn't feel so small and cheap and wrong right now. I wouldn't feel so stupid for thinking he felt the same way I did. This is worse than all the Jack Daniel's showers in the world.

"Tell him," Claire says. "Tell him for me. Please."

"Yeah," I lie. *I can't*, I think. *I'm not a good person. I don't get a happy ending*.

"Come on, Liv. I need to believe in love right now."

"I know. I will. It'll be great."

She laughs and buries her forehead into my arm. Her flyaway hairs tickle me, but in that second, I don't care.

At least somebody loves me.

61

"I give up." I write it in neat script on a slip of notebook paper and sign my name at the bottom. After, I fold it up and slide it into the vent in Adrienne's locker.

Claire and I talked about it, but in the end it was my decision. I was tired of hurting everyone in my path. Really, I was just tired.

I walk out to the parking lot, slow and deliberate. Whit is standing next to his Jeep, leaning against the bumper. He straightens up when he sees me walking up to my car. "Hey," he says, his voice tentative.

"Hi," I answer.

He looks me up and down. "Are you avoiding me?" he asks.

I lean in next to him against the Jeep. "No. I was just doing this thing. That I was doing." I wonder why it matters anymore—if I'm avoiding him or if I feel anything about him at all. I've given up on beating Adrienne, and I've given up on Whit and me. I should tell him now.

"Are you okay?"

I shrug. I wish he'd stop asking, like he cares how I feel.

"Listen." He leans down toward me, talking softer as he does so. "My mom's home today, so we can't go over to my house."

I nod. Should've seen that one coming.

"So, can we go to your house and study or whatever?" he finishes. I don't know whether to be relieved or disgusted. Turns out, I can be both.

It's funny, but I think I already miss him, already anticipating the moment when this will all be over, whether it's from something I do or something Adrienne does. The thought of that moment makes me say it. "Yeah. Sure." I start to walk away to my car, then stop. Looking back at him, I ask, "Why did you agree to this?"

He glances around, unnerved, before answering. "You asked me."

"So?"

He does this annoyed head bob. "So that's why."

I take a step back toward him. "You remember that day when you fixed my hand?"

"Yeah," he says slowly.

"What did you think of me?"

He shrugs.

"Everyone saw me as this Adrienne clone," I tell him, "all wrapped up in her games and serving her every whim. I wanted—I wanted someone to know that wasn't me. That I could do whatever I wanted, be my own person. Without her."

"So I'm the only one who knows you?" he asks.

I turn my head. "I'll see you later," I tell him.

As I wait for Whit to show up at my house, I keep wondering if I really want to see him like this again. Alone, where I might be tempted to kiss him again and drive the whole thing off the rails. I start to type a text to him into my phone, staring at the empty message screen. I know I should stop this. I wait for words to come to me, hurt words or hurtful words or something.

I'm still staring at his name when the doorbell rings.

I feel self-conscious as I open the front door to my house. He asks, "Where's your mom?"

"A client meeting," I tell him. "She has clients."

He nods.

"Do you want something to eat?" I ask. "I know you like to eat after practice."

"Sure."

I walk across the living room where no one lives to the kitchen where no one eats. It's like a set on some play my mom and I have to live out.

I wonder if Whit believes it.

"Sit down," I tell him, pointing to our breakfast nook.

"You're serving me?" he asks as the chair scrapes across the floor.

I pull open the fridge, rummaging through the little Tupperware squares. "Don't I always?" I return.

"Please don't say things like that." His voice comes out flat. Even he knows I'm all bravado and bullshit.

"My mom's really into health food. Just go with it." I slam the fridge door shut, pop a top off a Tupperware full of grape salad, and pull two forks out of a drawer. Hand a fork over to Whit and sit down in the chair next to him. I fish a grape out of the Tupperware with my fork.

Complete and total silence as I chew. And then he says, "I like that picture of all of you over there."

I've never tried to kill myself with a grape before, but I think I could. If I tried, I wonder if I could get myself to choke.

The picture on the desk. Mom and Ryan and me when Aunt Kate visited last year. We'd gone to a cabin near Stone Mountain. Mom half smiling like always. Ryan looking like he was a couple beers in. And me—the picture of high school perfection.

Funny how you can capture both everything and nothing at the same time.

"Yep. It's a good one." I eat another grape.

"How old—?"

"He's twenty," I tell him before I even realize what I'm saying. "He was twenty. Now he's dead." When it catches up to me, I hate myself for not being able to react like a normal person. I'm not sure what to do. All I want is for him to ignore it, and all I can do is draw more attention. But I try to recover. "Twenty."

Whit nods. Not much he can do with that information.

"He was drunk. When he wrecked." I eat a grape. "If you were wondering." Eat another. "You probably guessed from the Jack Daniel's prank. He drank a lot."

Whit's quiet as I finish all of the grapes. Demolish them, shoving them into my mouth one by one and then all at once. They're drenched in sweet cream cheese that makes my fingertips sticky, so I bring my finger to my mouth, licking away the last of it.

I'm going to be sick. Without a doubt.

My feet slide across the floor, pushing me back slowly from the table. I stand up and stroll to the bathroom off the foyer hallway.

And I throw up. Everything. Everything in me, right down to the bones, ends up inside that white porcelain bowl. Pathetic.

I fall back against the cabinet and sit.

First, he peeks around the corner. Then he dares to come inside. Slowly, scared. He sits down next to me. I blow out a breath and lean my head back. "You don't have to stay."

"You don't do anything small, do you?" he asks.

"What does that mean?" I return.

"I don't know." He breathes. In. Out. Sighs. "Yes, I do. It's always everything to excess. If you do something, it has to be the biggest, most ridiculous thing ever. And it scares me."

I stare straight ahead. "You don't know shit."

"Olivia—"

"I have to!" I interrupt him, swallow back my pride. "I have to do the biggest thing ever because *this* might be all I have. If I get lost in this godforsaken town, everyone will forget me." I don't look at him because the thought weighs on me. "I'll be nothing."

"How can you say that?" he asks, his voice deadly serious.

"Because I saw the way you looked at me before. Like I was helpless. I always thought there was this huge world out there waiting on me, but I've been so terrified it might disappear. That I might get left here alone forever. But what if that's not the point? What if the girl who gets stuck in Buckley is exactly what I was always meant to be? What if this is who I really am, and I've been too terrified to admit it?"

"Seriously. How could you say that?" he asks me. "You're not terrified. You terrify me."

I am so cold and afraid, my teeth almost chatter. "What does that mean?"

"You're so . . . ," he tries to say, runs a hand through his hair. "Assured. It's like nothing in the world actually intimidates you. You're so much bigger than Buckley. Everything goes on around us, all this horrible stressful shit, and you don't care. And you're gorgeous and you say these things—like, sometimes you'll say something, and it'll be so simple, but it's perfect. It explains the exact thing I've been thinking. And you do the biggest things ever, and it's amazing because I'd never—I'd never *imagine* these places and these things you dream up. I'm not like that. I walk in a straight line and I follow the rules. And that's it. Without you, I never would've picked Clemson. I never would have done any of this, and there'd be nothing to make me different from my brother."

"Whit"—I turn my head, leaving our faces inches apart—"how can you not see that everything about you makes you different from your brother?"

He looks down at his lap. "What about Ethan Masters, then?"

I hold my breath. He hasn't said anything about Ethan. Not since it happened. Not since he'd started looking at me like nothing I did affected him. "What about him?"

Whit kicks out his foot. "After everything he did, you *kissed* him. He slept with your best friend, and he's the reason we had to set up this whole arrangement to begin with. You couldn't let people think you had lost the smallest bit of control. You still can't."

"Stop it," I say.

"How could you do that? If I'm so special and different from my brother—can you—would you not lie to me for a minute?" He stares across at the wall. "Do you still want Ethan?"

"It's hard," I blurt out. "No, I swear I don't, but—I don't know what I want. I'm so fucked up."

He swallows. I think I've lost him there, finally. "Do I matter to you at all?" I can see the strain on his face as he asks, like it is the worst thing he's ever had to say.

"I don't want you to," I tell him. My voice comes out soft. I don't have much left to give. "If I let you in, you'll see me. If you saw all the broken pieces and the unattainable dreams and the stupid things I tell myself, you'd be so humiliated for me. All the pettiness and the lies I've told and the people I've hurt. You'd hate me, Whit, and you'd be right. Once you hate me again, everything will be back to how it should be. I thought you'd see that."

He stares like he's not sure who I am. I could be speaking a different language. Maybe because it's the first honest thing that's come out of my mouth in longer than I can remember.

Finally, he says, "I lied."

What? I tense up.

"I've been obsessing about you kissing Ethan ever since you told me about it. You are this completely perfect catastrophe I can't pull myself out of, and I don't want to anymore. Okay? I don't want to."

I bury my face in my hands. This is what I want, and I can't have it. I should've told him I kissed Ethan and then run in the opposite direction. Why did I wait so long? "Then you're an idiot," I mutter.

"Don't fucking deflect all over me, Olivia. Tell me what you want. For once, tell me what *you* want."

I turn to face him again, my cheek resting against the hard wood of the cabinet. A breath separates us, our mouths so close we could kiss.

When he looks at me that steady, I can't do it. I can't face him. I can't tell him what I've done and lose him like this. Not if it's not on my own terms. So I look away.

God, it hurts. But what happens then? I tell him I am desperately, outrageously happy with him and we pretend none of this ever happened? Adrienne leaves him alone and he never realizes what I did?

I can't trust myself to do the right thing. And I can't trust myself with him. He could never care about the other side of me anyway. I can't ask him to love a part of me even I hate.

His voice cuts back across me. "If after everything, you can't even look me in the eye and tell me I *matter*, then this is as pointless as I always thought." He stands up, walks to the bathroom door, and stops. "You win. We're supposed to break up tomorrow anyway. Take some Pepto and lie down or something."

And just like that, he's gone.

62

The first two weeks post-Whit is nothing like life pre-Whit. I keep my nose down and stay out of the mess. Show up at school and go through the motions. Turns out it's simple, choosing to *not*.

Choosing to not play Adrienne's games, not to assume Michaela is out to get me, not to kiss someone who I bribed into dating me in the parking lot, not to antagonize Mr. Doolittle. Everything is so quiet. I'm just another face in the crowd.

Mom makes me see a therapist, and he makes me talk about Ryan. Talking about Ryan makes me sad, and when Mom asks me how it makes me feel, I get mad. At the end of my second session, I tell the therapist I think Ryan died because I was mean, and he just about scribbles himself out of his chair.

It's good progress, he says.

It's a Monday morning, and I'm standing in the hall talking to Claire. Coxie comes up to her and takes her hand, and I wish she wouldn't do that to herself—but she's told me he's the best protection she has and all I'm allowed to say is okay.

"Ethan's looking for you," Coxie tells me. He nods to the other side of the hallway, where Ethan is literally looking at me. I wave good-bye to Claire and Coxie and go to Ethan. He falls in line with me as I walk.

"Are you going to tell me what happened with you and DuRant?" Ethan asks me.

I want to ignore him, but he'll just dog me down the hall. "No." I swing my hair over my shoulder in an attempt to push him off.

"Listen, O—"

I stop in the middle of the hallway. "Stop calling me that."

He shakes his head, and I stare over his shoulder. I wish I hadn't done any of this; I wish he wasn't here.

"What's wrong with you?" he asks. "Why are you treating me like this when I'm trying to talk to you?"

There are a million reasons. Because he cheated on me. Because he watched me go down a black hole and didn't stop it. Because he let all of this happen, because everything changed after he stopped caring and now my life is this washed-out, colorless place. Except most of that isn't really his fault. "I'm sorry," I say. "I shouldn't treat you like that." Something I should've told him a long time ago.

"It's okay." And then he stops meeting my eyes, and I know something bad is coming. "Whit is hanging out with Anna Talbert. And I mean, I figure it's Adrienne's doing, but he's talking to her, too, you know?"

"What?" I ask. The cogs in my head are spinning, like I have to translate what he's saying into something that makes sense.

He puts his head down and rubs the back of his neck, looking awkward. "Anna." He glances down at me. "And Whit."

I take two seconds to decide this isn't some drunken Mad Lib, turn on my heel, and take off down the hall.

"Olivia!" I hear him yell behind me.

I should've known. I should've known she wouldn't let me go quietly into the night.

My feet carry me down the math hallway to where Adrienne's holding court at her locker. She's staring at her reflection in the mirror. Pretending to, at least. Really, she just uses it to watch the masses behind her—to see if they're watching her.

I slam the locker in her face. "Stay away from him." I speak so softly that for a second I'm not even sure she heard me. But the way she grins at her puke-green locker door like it just did something particularly nice for her changes my mind.

"Make me," she tells the locker.

I get as close to her as I can without actually kissing her. We'll definitely be drawing attention to ourselves, but I don't care. I tell her, "If you don't think he can see right through you and your games, you're seriously underestimating him."

Adrienne's hair smacks me in the face as she turns to me. "Am I?" She smiles. "Actually, maybe he can see right through me and Anna. But what's worse? Thinking he's an idiot or thinking he genuinely wants to fuck with your head using the people you hate most in the world?"

Both. "At least you know I hate you," I say instead of saying any of the rest.

Adrienne's eyes go cold. "Don't say that."

"And you know the best part?" I continue. "I don't have to pretend anymore because Claire knows what I did, okay? She's forgiven me. She knows it was an accident. She can't live with the constant backstabbing, and I can't anymore, either."

Adrienne rolls her eyes. "You still think it was a fucking accident?"

"We shouldn't have said that shit behind her back, so no, it was wrong. But I didn't want her to see it. I didn't want anyone to see it."

"I did," Adrienne says.

"What?"

"You try to expose me, teach me a lesson? Two can play that game. You had to see what a hypocrite you were. I wanted to make sure."

I step back from her. "You . . . sent out those texts from me? I didn't do it?"

She shakes her head. "O, how dumb can you be? It was for your own good so you would stop acting like such a damn wounded animal. When I realized what you did, I had to push it along. I was trying to help."

"I'm done with you," I say. "I don't need your help. Once and for all, I am going to be better. I won't sink to your level anymore."

She laughs, but there's no fire behind her eyes. She's all gone, the good part of the girl I used to love. There's nothing left.

"Why did we do this, Ade?" I ask her, my voice raw.

She looks sad, just for a moment. Lost. Then she kills that part of herself. "You don't get to quit," she says, the smirk back in her voice. "You started this. And wait until you see what I'm going to do. You thought seeing me with Ethan hurt? Just wait. You can't give up, O. You'll miss the grand finale."

She turns around like she's going to walk off, and I yell behind her, "It wasn't even real!"

She swings around. My picture will be next to *desperation* in the dictionary; kids will remember the word etched in every line of my face. "I asked Whit to pretend. None of it was real."

Everyone is listening to me.

Everyone including Whit.

"I told him. I told him I'd sleep with him if he'd pretend to date me because I knew how much you'd hate it. That was the deal. I don't give a shit about him," I finish. It was overkill in the end, but they'll buy it.

She has to buy it.

Whit stares at me, like he couldn't give a fuck if you asked him to, shrugs, and walks away.

I hope everyone tells everyone.

63

"That's not what Whit always said," I argue with Vera three days later. "He said to read the questions first, which would help me get the gist of what I needed to take from the story. He said sometimes they won't make sense."

Vera Drake is my official new SAT tutor. I cornered her in the hallway the day after Whit and I "broke up" and begged her to set me on the path to SAT success. She reluctantly agreed, so now I am with her at the country club on her break, going over verbal reasoning, and she is looking at me as though she hopes I turn into a cloud and float away from her.

"So do that," she says in that tiny voice of hers, and I swear she's almost sassing me.

"But that's not what you think?" I ask, because I still want to do it right.

She shrugs.

"What would you do?" If I have to choke an answer out of her, I think I might.

She pushes her hair back, her wide eyes on the paper. "Take notes. Go over everything. It'll help with your understanding."

My eyes narrow. "So why didn't you say anything?"

She still doesn't say anything. "What's wrong with you?" I finally ask.

"Do you think I *want* to be here?" It's barely more than a whisper. Here we go again.

"Excuse me?"

"I have to do this. I have to say yes. You don't want to hear anything I say." Her eyes are defiant, full of nerves. She's right. I did ask Vera because I knew she wouldn't say no. Some people just can't. I'm usually pretty good at spotting them.

I sit back, sighing. "I need help, Vera. So if you could give me that, it'd be great. I really don't have time to argue anymore and since I don't have Whit—"

"What happened anyway?"

"What?" I ask, distracted.

"With Whit," she replies like it's obvious. "He, like, pretty much pretends he doesn't hear your name when people say it. Like you don't exist."

"Yep." I flip a page. "I pretty much don't."

"So what happened?"

"Nothing."

"Don't you care?" she says, all casual. "It seemed like—I don't know—you should do something, you know? Say something."

I look up at her, study the lines of her face. "You don't get it."

She scribbles on the paper.

"It wasn't real," I say. "Everyone's heard about it. Everyone's heard what I said."

She's doodling on the margin of her paper. "It seems like it was pretty real to you." She doesn't even look at me, says it like it's a fact. Like she knows things about me. Like maybe I should write a terrible poem about it.

I shrug. She doesn't see it. Casually, I draw my pencil across the page. "What do you think he thinks? About me?" I glance up.

She meets my eyes. "When he finds out what you did—the Mrs. Baker stuff—he'll never speak to you again." I don't have any idea how she knows that. I feel like I should be really concerned that she just said the words *Mrs. Baker* out loud. I should be threatened. Someone like Vera, she picks things up. She blends into the walls and no one ever notices her, no one worries about gossiping in front of her in the bathroom.

Did I do that? Am I that oblivious?

I point at something on the page. "That word. *Vicarious*. I've heard that before. What does that mean?"

"It's like *secondhand*. Living vicariously through someone?"

"Oh." I nod.

"I mean, I don't know," she finally says. "I don't really know anything about it. Whit always looked—" She pauses, contemplating, her eyes on the sky. "More complete when you were with him. Like someone finally got him."

"Don't you think I'm just some 'hot unhinged cheerleader' he can tell his friends he dated once? Only good for a month and a story?"

She's still staring off into space. "How would I know?"

"I guess you wouldn't," I reply. "Why do you like Ethan so much?"

She finally makes eye contact, surprised. After a moment, her face clears and she thinks. "He always says hello to me."

"Excuse me?"

"So many people at Buckley would walk over my dead body to get to gym class on time. Ethan isn't like that. One time, I was crying in the hall and no one noticed, or cared, except Ethan. He asked me why. And when I told him, he kept talking to me. He wasn't asking to ask. He was asking to help. He's a good person."

"Even after everything he did to me?" I ask her pointedly. "You think you know him?"

She shrugs. "No. Did you know Whit? Sometimes love finds us by accident, and I think . . . well, I think Ethan's soul calls to mine," she explains, and I gag a little in the back of my throat.

But there's such sincerity, such belief and innocence on her face, it almost stuns me.

"You think Whit and I were like that? Even though he's talking to Anna Talbert now?"

Vera shrugs again.

I go back to my work, defeated.

I guess I need to ask him myself.

64

I drove over right after I finished with Vera. I'm sure Whit heard my car pull up, but he didn't acknowledge me. The trees are dancing around his secret cove as he pounds out golf balls into the distance. I sit down in the grass and silently watch him work for a few minutes. Now he captures a ball with the head of his club, pulls it toward him, and knocks it out and away. He is kind of remarkable at it.

"I don't understand why you're mad at me," I say after a while.

He sighs, without pausing. "Not mad," he mutters.

I almost believe him. Which makes me want to provoke him. Which makes me irrational. "It's better if everyone knows it wasn't real. That way, they'll leave you alone."

"Who?" he asks, hooking a ball badly.

"Everyone." I toe the grass. "You don't want them bothering you about us."

He loads up another ball. He's wearing that look—the serious one. "I don't care."

It eats away at me a bit. "At least you're interesting now."

He drives the ball straight into the ground. "I don't want to be interesting."

That I believe.

I sit up straighter. "Then what are you doing?"

He stops and drops his club right in front of him like it's useless. "What do you think I'm doing?"

Blink. Breathe. With his eyes on me, I'm hyperaware of everything: my breath, my skin, every small movement he makes. Taking off his hat and running his hand through his hair. Flexing his hand with his class ring on it. He's twenty feet away. Fifteen. Ten. Five. One. Inches.

I stand up.

His shoulders slump. He's smaller when I'm looking him in the eye. "What am I doing?" he asks, genuinely confused.

"Anna Talbert."

He scoffs. "I am not doing Anna Talbert."

"I didn't mean *doing*," I say, though I'm sure she'd like to. "I meant talking to."

"Since when do you regulate who I talk to? Especially now."

"Look, I don't know what she's up to, but I know it's something, and I know Adrienne is involved. Don't you see it? She's talking to you, probably telling you this huge sob story about what a dick her dad is and how desperate she is for attention. What do you think you're going to accomplish?"

"I don't know, Liv, but you seem to have a pretty good idea of it."

"What next? I open up my phone one day and Adrienne Maynard's sent a text of you hooking up with Anna? Can't you see you're part of their game?"

He glances up. "She was talking to me about Mrs. Baker, okay? Their families are close, and she was telling me how she was doing. So yes, I've been talking to Anna, trying to figure out how to make all that whole situation go away as soon as possible. Is that okay with you?"

I feel horrible, I do. But I can't shut my mouth. "It's an excuse. You'll do whatever they talk you into." The words sit between us, simmering, and I want to swallow my tongue.

"Because that's all I am. Some fucking idiot to manipulate for whatever you need today."

"I didn't mean that," I amend quickly.

"Yes, you did. You may not have meant to say it, but you meant every word of it. No one is a person to you." A beat. Then, "She told me you almost killed her."

I run my fingers through my hair, near tears. "God, Whit, I was such a bad person, you know that. I felt so much guilt over what happened to Anna, but it's not an excuse, okay? I know that. I think about everything I've done wrong that's led me up to this point." I blink a tear out of my eye. "I think about it all the time and wonder why I can't stop. But I always felt so much closer to being who I want to be when . . ." He waits for me to say it; I can practically see it in his expression. But I don't. I wipe the tear out from under my eye.

He almost looks disappointed for a moment. But then he goes to turn around, stopping in this space between going and gone, and says, "I thought—you sent out those texts that day and I wanted to know, okay? You were just this popular girl with no aspirations except to be popular and laugh at everyone else, and I wanted to know why you hated yourself so much. Why you needed so badly to tell me what you'd done. That was why I let it happen. You were pretty and wrong and . . ." He stops, lost. I try to latch back on to the words, afraid of where I'll be when he stops talking to me.

"You didn't care. When I told you about Ethan and the kiss, we just did it and you didn't care then." I throw it at him wildly, hoping to land on something that will make him sorry.

"I thought that's what I was supposed to do, Liv." He sounds defeated. "I thought if I made a big deal about it, it'd drive you away faster. If you knew sex was a big deal to me . . ." He trails off again, looking embarrassed.

"What, so it's not a big deal to me?" I shrug, hurt. "I'm just some kind of slut—"

"No!" he says quickly. "It's just that look you gave me when you found out I was a virgin was so embarrassing."

"That's because I thought I had taken something from you." I push my hair out of my face. "Something you'd want to save for a different girl. Someone special."

"Well, it doesn't matter now, does it?" he asks, cutting right through me. "Because you saw your opportunity to get Ethan and piss off Adrienne, and you took it." The usual barely controlled anxiety radiates off him now. I worry once he explodes, I won't know how to contain him. "And now because of you, I've got this fucked-up GPA and they're holding my scholarship and everything is a fucking disaster, Liv, so just leave me alone."

"Your scholarship?" I ask, my breath catching in my throat.

He doesn't meet my eye. "I called the coach at Clemson, and he said they're holding it for now because of my character issues." He snorts. "I have *character issues*. He says we can reevaluate in a few weeks. Mom says I should go to Duke."

"But that's not what you want."

His eyes linger on me. "C'mon, you know better than anyone. You can't always get what you want." He almost smiles.

"What if I could help?" I say. I hear my own voice tightening: same desperate Olivia.

"Help with what?" he asks.

"Your GPA! Your character! Clemson. Everything," I say. "What if—what if I tell Dr. Rickards about everything?"

Confusion colors his face. "What did you do?" he asks slowly. "What does that mean?"

I cover my eyes with my hands so he can't see me, the light slanting in between my fingers. Then he is touching me, prying them away from my face. Anger is creeping into his voice. He's smart. I know he knows. "What did you do?"

"You don't understand."

He drops my hand. He won't touch me at all anymore. "Say it."

"It was Adrienne. She told them that she saw you and Mrs. Baker and I didn't say it was true, I just—"

"Motherfucker!" he screams. I recoil because the truth hurts like nothing else. "That's the problem with you."

"What?" I ask, confused.

"You *didn't say anything*. That's what you do, Liv, because you're a fucking coward."

"Shut up," I say, head down. I feel like I'm tearing apart from the inside out. The two Olivias are colliding in a body that's only big enough for one of us. And I'm still lying. To him and myself.

"Did you put that test in my locker? Did you lie about that, too?"

I nod, meeting his eyes.

"Christ," he spits.

I hate him. Everything about him. The way he looks at me, how he sees me so small. I hate him.

"You ruined Mrs. Baker's life. I lost my fucking scholarship. God, Olivia, I'm losing my mind." He's pacing, the most contained person I know bouncing back and forth and back and forth like he'll die if he stops. "Why? Why would you do this? And don't say Claire, because that's your excuse. You love your excuses." I try to break in because it sounds like he's stopping, but he's just getting wound up. "It's not like you want to watch the world burn like Adrienne does. You know what you're doing. You do it anyway. Why?"

"How do you know I don't want to watch the world burn?" I answer defensively. "It's about my brother, okay? I know it doesn't matter to you, because you have this brother who loves you so much and you live to, like, be better than him, but I love my brother. I loved him, and I won't let Adrienne change who he was."

"Another excuse."

I take in the scene, the beautiful copse of trees and the field and this boy and this girl falling apart, and I see myself so clearly. In denial. I have to give up. I've lost. "Whit, I'm so sorry," I keep saying over and over again. And "I'll fix it" and "I want you so badly," only I can't bring myself to say it at all.

"I did everything for you!"

"I know, and I promised we were in it together. And we were, but all these things got in the way. My brother—I didn't want my mom to know and Adrienne said—"

"Is that all you got?" Whit's voice is sharp, jagged edges, his entire stance daring me.

We stare at each other, and I can feel the words, the ones I didn't know how to say before: *I want this to be real, Whit. I want you to have flirted with me in the lunch line and have taken the long way to biology every day so you could walk by my locker and have worked up the courage to ask me out and have kissed me outside my house when it was raining and I just want something normal. I want to feel like I deserve something normal and I want to start over—*

"I thought so."

"Whit—"

"Don't ever speak to me again," he cuts me off.

I watch him as he grabs up his clubs.

He turns back to me. "You are—you are . . ." Giving up, as though he could never find words terrible enough to describe me, he turns away.

"Whit," I try to say. I want to tell him that he matters so much to me, and I'll do anything—*anything*—to make this right.

But he's already gone.

65

It starts sprinkling on the way home from Whit's spot. Pretty erratic weather for the beginning of October. The thermometer sits at a ridiculous 85 degrees, begging for the end of a long summer. The smell of wet, hot sidewalk melts into the air as I walk slowly through the front door of my house, where my mom is working at the kitchen table.

Sometimes, she sits there so long, I wonder if she's melded right into the chair.

"How was school?" she asks as I run water from the faucet into a plastic cup.

"It's raining," I say, about one step up from catatonic.

Mom glances out the window. "The weatherman didn't seem to think that was ever going to happen again."

I shrug.

A million unsaid words bounce around the kitchen. A clock ticks in the background. "I need you to go to school with me tomorrow," I say.

"Why? What happened?"

I set down my cup on the counter and look at her. My face must say a lot because she slowly closes her MacBook, sits back in her chair. "Nothing yet," I tell her. "But I'm going to be in a lot of trouble, and I'd like you to be there."

"Olivia." She shakes her head. "I don't understand. Is this some kind of game?"

I almost laugh. "I—I don't want to do it alone," I say. "I have been for so long." When I breathe in, it makes a sound that might be a laugh and might be a cry, and I put my hand up to my mouth so no one will hear it. Mom shoots up from her spot at the table and puts her arms around me, and I lean my cheek into her T-shirt. "I'm sorry I'm such a disappointment."

Mom stiffens. Pulls away from me. "Why would you say that?"

"I'm not smart. Or talented. Or good at anything except ruining good things for other people, and I know you wouldn't be so miserable if Ryan was alive instead of me."

"Olivia," Mom says, touching my cheek. She's crying, too, like she did at Ryan's funeral, all red cheeked. "I know that I've failed in a lot of ways as your mother, but that's my fault. Not yours. I never thought I'd be raising two kids alone, and when your dad died . . . I messed everything up so badly."

I blink slowly. I try not to think about my dad much because sometimes I can't keep myself from blaming him. For Mom losing it, and then for Ryan losing it. I never think about who he was. Spending time on that'd be like holding on to a fairy tale. All I know about him is whispered stories Ryan told me, and I think most of them were made up as much as the ones I imagined and kept in my head.

"You're more like him than me, you know. The way people are drawn to you. You're magnetic; I've known that since you were little.

"I'm not that. You have your cheerleading and you're so outgoing, always have so many friends. I was glad you found things that mattered to you, but it wasn't what I knew. You know I'm no good with people and I was never any good with you, and then you started acting out in these erratic ways, and your brother did, too. At least I understood the way he acted out. I thought I could help him."

"Do you know how long I've spent filling in the gaps where I wanted you to be?" I finally say. "I wanted *you.* I wanted you to laugh or cry or show any sign at all that you cared." I shrug. "I always wondered how far I'd have to take it for you to care. What line I'd have to cross."

"Of course I care," Mom insists. "I'm just not good at showing it. I—I know it was so hard on you and Ryan those last years in Charlotte, when I was pulling myself back together. I had to be so careful about my balance, and that was hard. I couldn't always be what you needed." Mom pulls at her bun. She's about the same size as me, but she looks smaller right now. This is where she'd usually walk away, but she doesn't. Not this time. "I never knew that's what any of this was—this world you had with Adrienne. I always saw you . . . functioning. Not just functioning, but excelling in ways that Ryan couldn't. Fitting in. He had so many problems, and I focused so much attention on him. I wanted to help him, and I thought you didn't need my help."

My eyes water. "But I did."

"I know." I thought I'd get more satisfaction out of this when it worked. From having her look at me so intently. But right now all I see in her eyes is my hopeful reflection staring back at me. "I've tried so much since he died. Tried to be around, tried to be a mom, but I know you decided it was too late. You didn't need me anymore."

It's funny. Making her beg for forgiveness, making her understand that I've been chasing whatever love someone would throw my way for twelve years because of her, won't change anything, and forward momentum is all I have to keep me going. Right now, *she* is all I have to keep me going. And I want that. I don't want to keep blaming her for things she can't control. "I do," I finally admit. "I still do. I can't help but push at people—sometimes it's the only way I really feel anything. Because I'm so cold, like Mr. Doolittle said."

She blinks a few times, assessing me. I said too much. The cold thing—I didn't mean to bring that up. "You remember what you said to me the day you were suspended? That Ryan was the only real relationship you ever had? That he was the only one who loved you for who you are?"

I nod.

"I should've said it then, but I want you to know. Olivia, I love you. You think there's something wrong with you because feeling is hard? Look who your mother is." I shake my head, but she grabs either side of my face and holds me still. "You may be magnetic like your father, but you're guarded like me. So you understand when I say I love you more fiercely than anything on the planet, when I tell you I will do *anything* for you, they're the most sincere words that could come out of my mouth. And you know that we may be hard to break down, but when we feel, we feel harder than anyone else. Too hard, sometimes, right?"

I nod, tears spilling down my cheeks. They won't stop coming now, like a spell has been broken, like the wall in my heart has been torn completely down, and I'm nothing but feeling. White-hot feelings. All-consuming, broken feelings.

"I know—I *know,*" I say. "God, I couldn't hate you so much if I didn't love you so much, Mom. I wanted so badly to blame you for Ryan. I wanted it to be someone else's fault. That's always what I want."

She breathes deeply. I shouldn't have said hate, either. I didn't mean it. Not really. But then she says, "I should've done more for him. I let you both down." She pauses. Then, "I flew up there last year once, while you were staying at Adrienne's. I didn't tell you because I didn't want to scare you. I tried to bring him home, but he convinced me he could do it. I should've known better because I used to be able to convince myself I was okay. But I believed him, and it was the worst mistake of my life. If only I'd . . ." She trails off, looking a little lost.

"Ryan was sad," I say, and for the first time, I believe it when I say it. It's cathartic, even. Ryan was sad in a way outside of our control, and in a way we never completely understood, and he only got sadder when he left. Mom didn't feed Ryan shots and tell him to drive, and it's not karmic retribution that he crashed. He was sad, and he made a mistake. "He called me. Before he died."

Mom covers her mouth with her hand. I'm shaking all over, but I keep going. "He said he missed me, like he already knew what was coming, and I didn't want you to know." I choke over my words. "I didn't know what it meant, and I don't know what would've happened if I'd answered. If I'd talked to him and not been with Ethan." The words are so hard to get out, over the almost-sobs that threaten to completely destroy me. "It's my fault. I'm so sorry."

She puts her hands on both of my arms, gripping me hard. "Listen to me," she says, and she's crying but I've never seen her look so fierce, so in control. "It is *not* your fault. You did the best you could. We did what we thought was right, and we can't change it. You loved him so much. I think he tried as hard as he could for you. He never would've wanted to leave you behind."

"I wanted him to be okay." I draw in a ragged breath. "I want him to be here."

She's silent for a moment. "Me too."

I sniff loudly, ruining the moment, and she smiles and I smile and my heart collapses. "I've really screwed everything up," I tell her.

"Well," she says, pushing a hair back from my face, "let me help you fix it. Just this once."

"Do you think I'm trapped?" I ask. I'm dreading the answer. "In Buckley? That I'll always just be Adrienne's lackey? That I won't ever be able to feel like anyone else? That's why Whit—" I choke up all over again. I can't say Whit and think about all-consuming feelings. It hurts too much. She runs her thumb over my cheek.

"Olivia, you can do anything you want to do, be whoever you want to be. Watch the sunrise on the West Coast. Chase tumbleweeds in Texas. I know your grades aren't perfect, but not everything in life is orderly. Eighteen years ago, I thought your father and I would be raising two children in the suburbs, driving them to their first day of college, but I was wrong. I have *you*, and you're flawed and strong, and everything on the planet is ahead of you. The world is terrified of what you'll do to it. I promise. Okay?"

I can barely form the words, but I manage to nod. "Okay."

66

Adrienne always used to tell me that if you apologize for something, you're admitting you're wrong. Admitting you're wrong is absolutely the worst thing you can do. It's just another piece of her obsession with never showing weakness. How strange, that for so long, my biggest fear was someone knowing that I had feelings.

Maybe I'm contemplating the mysteries of my life because I'm about to do the scariest thing I've ever done. Mom pulls up in front of a split-level house on the outside of town. There's a playhouse on the left side of the lawn, bright pink with a white lattice trim. Mom stops the car. I feel sick to my stomach, nausea burning up and down inside my chest.

"Be direct," Mom tells me in her most professional voice. "She'll be angry. The point is to not get emotional."

I nod, staring out the window. Ironic, since I've just started to thaw out.

"Olivia. Do not get emotional," she repeats.

I look at her with a half smile. "Me? Never." Before I can think about it much more, I open the door, hop onto the sidewalk, and pound up to the house. Ring the doorbell and wait, each agonizing moment stretching longer than the last. Then Mrs. Baker opens the door, looking startlingly normal. She wears a pair of tattered old jeans, a sorority T-shirt, and her hair up in a ponytail.

"Olivia?" she asks, surprised.

"Hi," I say because I'm a dumbass. I push a piece of stray hair behind my ear. "I came to talk to you."

"Okay," she says slowly. She glances at my mom's parked car and then up and down the street like she's expecting someone to jump out at us. I can't blame her for paranoia.

"Mommy! Mommy!" A little blond girl runs up behind her, then stops when she sees me. She points. "Who is that?"

Mrs. Baker puts a hand on top of her head. "This is one of my students. Olivia. She's a cheerleader." She looks up at me. "She loves cheerleaders," she confides with a smile.

Silently, I die on her doorstep.

"Honey, go back in the den, okay?"

Her daughter nods and runs off.

"What can I help you with?" she asks, looking less bright. I start to consider that maybe she doesn't hate me. I'm probably not her favorite person by any stretch of the imagination, but she doesn't hate me. Yet. That makes things worse. It was much easier to ruin her life when she wasn't a real person. It always is.

"I wanted to let you know"—I look anywhere but at her—"I'm going to go to Dr. Rickards tomorrow and tell him that I never saw anything between you and Whit and that I'm pretty sure Adrienne made it all up. Even though obviously I don't think Adrienne is going to admit that. Without my word, they've got nothing. They'll have to let you come back to school."

"Excuse me?" she says, my words catching up to her.

"I wanted to come explain it to you that I know what I did was wrong. And"—I take a deep breath—"I want to give you all the reasons I did it, but I know it doesn't matter to you. You have all this stuff in your life that's just as important as mine. So I'm—I'm so sorry. I'm sorry for the pain this has caused you and your family. I'm sorry I hurt Whit, too. And I know he's miserable about all this."

Her face is solemn. She's not screaming or telling me I'm the worst person in the world. She doesn't have to. "You're going to be in a lot of trouble, Olivia."

"I think that's okay." I swallow hard. Shockingly, I feel much better. "I mean it'll suck, but it can't be worse than this."

"I imagine that it can't," she concedes. "I appreciate you coming clean." She tilts her head to the side. "Of course I don't appreciate you doing this in the first place. But I'm relieved to hear it from you," she admits to me.

"Tell your daughter if she wants to be a cheerleader, I can give her some tips." I smile sadly. "From an ex–Buckley High cheerleader."

"I'll do that. Good-bye, Olivia," she says, and then she steps back and closes the door in my face.

67

While I talk, Dr. Rickards scowls and Mr. Doolittle comforts me, as if proud of this breakthrough. I can't believe I ever had a bad thought about him.

Mom did most of the talking. It's a relief, honestly, for her to be so deeply involved in something in my life, even when it is something this terrible. She told me what we were going to do and lined me up behind her. Something like protection. I always thought I loved the independence her standoffishness afforded me, but God, does it feel good for someone to take the load off my shoulders. To point me in the right direction and not tell me I'm an idiot in the process. To look out for me out of nothing but love. It reminds me of Ryan.

But I do have to tell my side of the story, and it's ugly. I turn to Mr. Doolittle after I've listed my transgressions. "I'm sorry I used you. I know you were trying to help."

He waves a hand. "I'm used to it. You'll continue your SAT studies?"

"I guess." I glance down. "With Vera."

He nods and pats my leg. "Good girl."

Never heard that one before.

Mom puts a hand on my shoulder as she ushers me out and squeezes right before I open the door.

I stop for a beat and release a breath. A breath I've been holding for the past three months.

"Thanks," I say.

When Mom and I come out of the office, Claire is waiting by the door, biting her nails. She looks relieved when she sees me, as if she wasn't sure I would come out alive. Mom gives me a nod when I glance at Claire and tells me she'll wait in the car. I lean against the wall of the empty hallway before she says anything.

"Well?"

"I survived," I tell her. I blow out a breath. "Dr. Rickards will probably call you and Whit and Adrienne and some other people in to corroborate my story." I snort. "I thought he was going to have a heart attack."

Claire sucks in her cheeks. "What's he going to do to you?"

My hair catches on the cement wall behind me as I fidget around, not quite sure how to get the words out. "He said he should expel me, but given my difficulties the past few months and that Mr. Doolittle is willing to back me, he went with Mom's plan. I'll take all the classes I need for next semester online, and he'll let me graduate with our class. It wasn't the nightmare it could've been." I shrug.

Claire's face falls. "I don't want to go to school without you. I already have to cheer without you since you punched that guy." She laughs. "You're the one who keeps me from losing it here."

I tug at a strand of her hair. "Come on, Claire Bear. Everyone loves you."

"It's lonely." She closes her eyes for a minute, and it hits me just how isolated Claire feels among the people of this town. People who think there's something wrong with her, who don't understand how she didn't choose to be different. "I told Alex the other day—all of it." She opens her eyes back up. "Because he's supposed to be my best friend, and I wanted him to know that I could never feel the same way about him.

I *can't.* He told me it wasn't fair. Like I picked liking girls so I wouldn't have to like him." She sighs.

"Why'd you tell him?" I ask.

She grins kind of mischievously. "Well, Ellie was talking to me the other day. She said she'd been thinking about all the drama going on over here, and how all this hiding is kind of bullshit. I guess things are trickling through the gossip vines at Central, and Ellie says she doesn't really care what they think anymore." Claire tilts her head. "It kind of sucks it all happened this way, but she thinks we should talk about this, about us—so long as Alex was aware of the situation."

I smile at her. "That's so good."

"Yeah. Of course, I'm still not sure how it would work with my parents and everyone here . . . but only seven months till graduation, right?" she finishes with a sigh. Then she pouts. "Can I go with you? To Internet school? Please."

"I wish," I say, trying not to get all serious because I can tell she doesn't want that. "I should go. The bell's about to ring, and I'm sure Dr. Rickards doesn't want me here when the gossip breaks."

"Okay," Claire says sadly. "You know Adrienne thinks I took your side." A pause. "But she told me she was sorry about everything. She's the only person besides you who has never thought I was a joke. I need her on my side."

"I know," I answer. I want Claire to let her go, once and for all, but I can't tell her what to do. This war has always been between Adrienne and me, not her.

"I've been friends with her longer than I can remember. It's—it's safe. And I need something safe in my life right now. You get that, right?"

"Yes, Claire, I'm not mad at you. I—"

My eyes catch on something—someone—down the hall. Bent over a water fountain with a khaki-colored backpack. His eyes glance up, meet mine, and turn away.

Claire turns her head to watch Whit as he heads down a side hallway. "Do you think he'll forgive you when he finds out what you did?"

I bite into my lip and try to ignore that crushing feeling inside my chest. "No." I shake my head for emphasis. "He has to focus. Has to win another state championship. Has to get ready for college. He'll be over me in a week."

I'm staring out over the empty water fountain when I feel a punch on my bicep. I grab my arm and look down to see Claire with her hand curled into a fist. "Ow!" I yell. "What the hell was that?"

"Don't ever say that shit again," Claire says. "Whit DuRant is not too good for you. And I'm sick of you thinking that." Claire's eyes are fierce. "There's a lot of shit and a lot of shitty people in this world, Liv, I would know, but if you think for one second that you didn't break that boy's heart when he found out what you did to him, you're delusional. Why do you think he's spending time around Adrienne?"

"I don't know," I admit.

In a second, Claire's face clears and she no longer looks like a five-foot-two assassin. "Think about it." She smiles. "And call me this weekend, okay? Be good."

Still slightly scared, I nod and turn to go.

Good-bye, Buckley High.

TWO MONTHS LATER

I'm surfing through Internet pictures. Coxie had a party last night, and everyone was there. I wouldn't have wanted to be there. All the same, I miss being important.

Here's what I figure: Whit is either dating or not dating Anna Talbert. He has his arm around her in some of these pictures. I mean, it could be a friendly arm. There's all kinds of touching at parties like that.

I know Adrienne is behind it. But what if he likes her anyway?

Claire tells me nothing is going on. She said Anna likes one of the other boys who's on the golf team with Whit so that's why they're always around each other. But Whit told me before about Anna's connection to Mrs. Baker. What if . . . I guess it doesn't matter.

I haven't spoken to him in two months. And I've wanted to. Two agonizing months of wondering what he's thinking and who he's talking to and clicking through social media pictures from his college visits. I want to tell him things about my life and my therapist and being myself. I want to tell him about how stupid the verbal section of the SAT was and how I totally think I killed the math section unless I didn't.

But he has his arm around Anna and he's taller than she is so she probably loves him. That's no one's fault but mine.

My phone vibrates and I pick it up. "What's up with Whit and Anna?" I ask Claire before I say hello.

"What?" she asks.

"I just saw pictures from Coxie's party last night," I say. "They're together."

"I'm sure it's nothing," she answers unhelpfully.

Just then, an e-mail pops up on my screen. An e-mail from Adrienne Maynard. I click it open. "Watch me" is all it says. I scroll down to the attached video and inform Claire.

"Don't open it," Claire says firmly.

"Yeah," I return, "and just never know what it is. I can live with that." I jiggle my leg nervously and stare at the screen. I'm not surprised—more surprised it took her this long. After I told Dr. Rickards about our scheme to bring down Mrs. Baker and Whit, he called Adrienne in to go over her story again. Then he suspended her, on account of being sick of our shit, I'm assuming. Mr. and Mrs. Maynard pitched a huge fit and threatened to sue the school board. The school promised not to tell any of the colleges that accepted her.

I can only assume her anger has been building up all this time. It's not like it really affected her life, but Adrienne has always prided herself on never getting caught.

Still. The video is here, right in front of me. A ticking time bomb.

"This is what she wants," Claire tells me. I'd almost forgotten she was on the other end of the phone. There's a slight hysterical edge that I only barely manage to make out under my own mounting panic.

Slowly, I say, "What do you know?"

Claire takes a minute to answer. "Nothing. Not really."

"Tell me." I watch the e-mail; it doesn't move. "Please."

She sighs loudly into the phone. "That party was getting a little out of hand, okay?" She doesn't talk momentarily. "Look, I didn't stay long, so I don't know what it is, but I think it's best if you don't open it."

"I'm going to watch it," I say.

"Do you really think you should?" Claire asks.

"Yes." I click the video once but before the second click, I pause. "What if they're hooking up?"

"What?"

I am really freaking myself out now. "What if it's a video of Whit and Anna or something? It's exactly the kind of thing Adrienne would mastermind." I run my hands through my hair. The room reflects against the computer screen.

"Do you really think he would do that?" Claire asks me.

I sit in silence for a moment. Close my eyes. "No," I finally say as I open the video.

It loads up and a low-quality image pops onto the screen, all bad lighting and muffled sound. It takes a second to focus and there's Whit, playing quarters with Daniel and Anna. He chugs his beer and laughs, and Anna smiles at him in a way that makes my skin crawl. Adrienne yells at them to wave for the camera, and they all do. It cuts away. Back to Whit sitting down at the kitchen table, looking blitzed. It reminds me of Ryan in the worst way, the glassy eyes and the stuttered speech and the loud laugh that rings hollow. I run my fingers over my mouth, watching.

Adrienne is whispering to Anna. "Ask him about O," she says.

"What do you think O is doing right now?" Anna asks offscreen. Adrienne shakes the camera as she zooms in closer to him.

"Probably fucking up some other guy's life," Whit says into the camera, and I wince. I could hear the glee in Adrienne's voice, but Whit is subdued. Drunk, but unsure. He looks wrong.

"What would you say to her?" Adrienne asks, jumping in. "If she was here right now."

"Stop, Ade," someone—it sounds like Renatta—mutters in the background.

"She's right," Whit says. "She's not special. She's this girl who tears everyone down because she's got nothing of her own." Adrienne waits for him to talk again, as he sits and brings a red Solo cup to his lips. My hands shake, and I know Claire's there, breathing on the other side of the phone, but I can't remember anything but the contours of Whit's face right now, every word burning into my memory. "I still hate you, and you weren't worth it, that's what I'd tell her." Then he stops, as if having an epiphany. "I'd tell her she was beautiful and she ruins everything."

No one says anything for a second, and I can tell the entire room is listening to him, transfixed. Then I hear Adrienne whisper, "Go make out with him," but the video feed cuts off to a black screen.

I sit still, staring at the black square for somewhere between a nanosecond and the rest of time. Then Claire says, "Liv? Liv, what was it?"

I stare at the black. "I think he hates me."

"What?" she asks.

"I think he hates me because I'm me. Which is probably the right thing to do," I say slowly.

"Come on, you don't believe that. He's hurt. Why wouldn't he be?"

I'm silent.

"You tried to ruin the thing that matters most to him, even after he opened up to you. So if he hates you, look at yourself. Figure out how to convince him you're not that person. Convince all of us."

I don't want to hear Claire say that. I don't want her to think of me in that way, to distrust me.

But she does, even though we're friends, and it makes a painful kind of sense. "What if I *am* that person?"

"Then I guess we're all wasting our time." A beat. Then, "You can change it all, Olivia. I know you can."

69

The e-mail pops up at five thirty p.m. the next Sunday night.

Your SAT Scores.

My heart is going to explode out of my chest. This is the most agonizing moment of my life. I can't look at it, not right away.

So I wait until the next day. At seven a.m., I race through the halls of Buckley High, hoping not to run into someone who will kick me out. Miraculously, I don't. I fly full throttle through Mr. Doolittle's open door and run up beside him. "They're here!" I tell him.

He jumps back in shock, getting coffee in his beard. He grabs a napkin and mops it up. "Miss Clayton. You aren't supposed to be here. You need to—"

"My SAT scores. You have to tell me what you think."

He dabs away at his vest. "What are they?"

"I don't know."

He stops and looks at me. "You don't know?"

"You have to look," I tell him.

"What?"

I kneel next to him, leaning over his computer and logging into my e-mail. Without pausing for a moment to think about it, I finally open the e-mail.

There it is.

There it is.

We both stare at it for a few moments and then, without warning, Mr. Doolittle jumps up and hugs me, saying my name with so much pride, and I don't know why, but I'm crying into Mr. Doolittle's shoulder. Even if I can't go anywhere right now, someday I can go somewhere.

I can.

"Thank you," I say through my ridiculous tears. "Thank you," and it's the most cathartic moment. I worked for this and it's good for me and everyone gets a happy ending here. Others pushed me and I can prove to them it paid off, that it was worth it.

Mr. Doolittle and I spend half an hour putting together a list of admissions requirements and financial aid opportunities for the colleges I picked out.

It's amazing. Still floating on a cloud, I leave his office and run into Vera on my way out. "Vera!" I call. She turns around, her wide eyes surprised. I hug her, too, because I don't know who I am anymore. "I did it! Better than the practice tests."

She breaks into a genuine smile. "Congratulations!"

"God, I'm such a bitch, Vera," I tell her even though I'm smiling. "You didn't have to help me, but thank you."

She looks confused.

"I have a surprise for you," I say, walking away from her, backward. I'm planning as I go. "You'll see—I'll call you!" I yell, turning on my toes.

And running directly into Whit.

We both jump back. Silence fills the space between us: We both know we have to say something, but we both don't want to. We don't know how. It's like we've unlearned knowing each other.

"I did it," I hear myself say, and his brow furrows like *duh, I know what you did*, but I say, "My SATs were great. All thanks to you and Vera." I point vaguely behind me. I don't even know if she's still there.

His voice is cold. "Good job."

"It's really funny, I was in the verbal section and—"

"Look, I'm really sorry if I gave the impression we could have a conversation," he says. He doesn't walk away, though, and I start to understand what Claire said.

"You won't even listen to me." I shake my head. "You know, if you won't speak to me because your pride's hurt, then Adrienne's won."

"You're just a liar," he tells me before walking away.

A liar. Who makes excuses.

Maybe I was.

But I don't have to be.

70

Here in the South, in late fall, the cold comes out to play only at night. It assaults slowly as the sun sets, surprising you with the swift temperature drop. I pull my jacket tight around me as a breeze bites through the night, right outside the Rough House.

Every year, Michaela Verday's parents throw her the best birthday party in town, and I guess since it isn't common knowledge that Michaela's mother is sick, this year is no different. She can probably find some comfort in that anyway. Normalcy.

I wouldn't know. This year, the Verdays have rented out the Rough House for karaoke night and lax ID-ing. Of course, an invitation to Michaela's party is very exclusive.

I stand off down the side of the street, casually watching my classmates slide past the bouncers. Everyone is excited about the prospect of a party at the Rough House. Being on the list is important—it's everything.

Claire texts me that she's inside with Adrienne, Anna, and Whit. She tells me that Adrienne is definitely trying to make this Anna-Whit thing happen. The idea turns my stomach whenever I think about it. It's not that there's anything wrong with Anna, it's just . . .

Well, at least Adrienne isn't planning on screwing him herself this time.

I'm reading another text from Claire about how Coxie is desperately trying to use Michaela to make Claire jealous and that Claire feels terrible about it, especially since she wants to go hang out with Ellie at the bar anyway, when I feel a tap on my shoulder. I jump, turning around.

Ethan smiles at me. "I wish you would've let me come pick you up."

I return the smile. "Yeah. Thanks." I stand up, straightening out my dress. "How do I look?" I ask him.

"Nice," he says. Ethan never exactly had a way with words.

I cock an eyebrow.

"Before we go in, there's something I want to tell you," he says.

I step back into a shadow. "Okay."

He scratches his chin for a second before he starts. "That day in the hallway, when you kissed me, I know it was just a ploy. To make a point to Adrienne or whatever."

"Ethan. I—"

He shakes his head. "It's fine. It got me thinking. About how I was using Adrienne to make you jealous and how it wasn't fair to either of you." He scuffs the toe of his shoe against the ground. "I used her a lot, too, and I know she's Adrienne, but that really sucked of me, you know?"

I nod. "I was using Whit to make you jealous, too," I tell him. Then I add on, "At first."

"Well, it worked," he says. "But the thing I realized is—" He looks down, rubbing the back of his neck uncomfortably. "When I was sleeping with Adrienne, I was trying to punish you. For using me after your brother died and not loving me anymore. I wanted you to catch us because I wanted you to feel how terrible you made me feel. I felt all this guilt, but at the same time, I felt justified. But, even if it was Adrienne, it wasn't right. It isn't right to treat people like they're part of a game." He stops for a second, and I kind of get the feeling that he might have been the nobler of the two of us all along.

He wasn't all right, but he wasn't all wrong.

"That feeling sucks, Olivia, and I don't see how you two can do it to each other or anybody else."

"You're right," I agree. "And that feeling? I used to feel it all the time. Eating away at me. I tried to tell myself it was all right, but then Ryan died, and I knew, I just knew." I stop, shrug. "But I'm starting to get it. I'm not defined by Ryan's mistakes, but I have to start being defined by mine. I can't say 'Adrienne made me do it' or 'Ryan is dead' or all of that anymore."

"Yeah. I'm glad," Ethan says. He smiles. "And you're here to do something good. That's . . . really cool."

I return his smile. For the first time since Ryan, being near him feels natural. He steps back in the direction of the entrance. "You ready, Plus One?" he asks me.

I stop, enjoying the old feeling of mischief without the guilt. "You really think I need your invitation to get myself into this party? As if."

His brow crinkles. "So why did you tell me to save my plus one?"

I point behind him, to where Vera has shown up in a display of amazing timing. Ethan swings around, and she waves at him shyly. She looks cute in a little blue dress. Ethan gives me an inquisitive look. "We're celebrating my high SAT scores," I explain to him.

"Nice," he replies to both of us.

It's not like I have some delusion that they'll fall in love and live happily ever after. I don't even know if she'll like the party.

But getting out for an evening never hurt anybody.

"How are you going to get in?" Ethan says to me.

I shrug. "I may have cleared the whole thing with Michaela. She hates me a lot less since I replaced her tire, and I think she's looking forward to the opportunity for drama, honestly. From what I hear, getting in through the front door is all the rage these days."

Ethan snickers. "Well, ladies, shall we?" he asks, offering an arm to both of us. I take one and Vera takes the other.

"Let's," Vera says.

I smile. "Please."

71

Everyone stares as Ethan, Vera, and I walk into the bar together. Most people haven't seen me since all of my indiscretions came to light, and the fact that I'm with Ethan turns the gossip meter up to eleven. I purposely don't look at the table where Claire and Whit and Adrienne are sitting as we walk in. We all say an obligatory "happy birthday" to Michaela, who is bright and gracious to Vera, before finding a booth to ourselves.

No one else seemed to have any room.

"Is it just me or did the temperature drop when we walked in?" I ask.

Ethan smiles in that way he used to do when I said something funny but offers no response.

"Thanks again for helping me out. I know you're getting kind of ostracized because of me," I say, looking down in my lap. The truth is, I feel kind of like a jackass putting Ethan through this when he still hasn't sorted out all his feelings about the end of our relationship. Not that I have myself, but it's a closed chapter in my life. With all that's changed, I can't see myself looking back.

"I owed you one, Liv," he answers. "I'm not sure I'll ever make up for what I did."

"Thanks," I say, and I mean it.

"I'm going to go get a piece of cake," he tells me. Then he turns to Vera, who has kindly listened to all of our awkwardness without making any faces. "You want to go with me?" he asks.

She smiles and nods.

As they walk off, I notice some other football players talking around the cake table, and I figure he won't be back for a while. That's fine. I didn't ask him to entertain me.

A big man in a black T-shirt and cargo shorts is setting up a stage for karaoke. The stage is already covered in these terrible fake Hawaiian flowers that match the lei Karaoke Man is wearing around his neck. Behind the stage is a beach backdrop, epic in its ugliness.

I'm doing this. I'm actually going to do this.

"You ready?" Claire asks, sliding into the booth next to me. She sips the straw of a Coke through dark red lipstick.

"Who knew I was gonna get to do this with a romantic sunset backdrop?" I reply.

Claire snorts into her straw.

"What did Adrienne say when I came in with Ethan?" I ask.

Claire shrugs. "Not much, since I was sitting there. Whit looks a little devastated, though. Confused."

My heart twists, half glad he cared, half wishing I hadn't done it. Of course, all that could easily be Claire's overeager imagination. "What about him and Anna?"

"Friends," she says. "Definitely. Anna really was upset about Mrs. Baker. Of course, not upset enough to jump off Adrienne. And you know, I think she might actually like him, but him?" She shakes her head. "He loves you, Liv."

"Well," I begin, unconvinced, "it'll all be over soon." I glance at the stage. The man steps away from the speakers he is attaching to the microphone and nods in satisfaction. He slides over to his laptop at the DJ booth and selects something. A loud rap song fills the air, and a few people get up and start dancing. "Did you see Vera? With Ethan?"

She nods. "They're sitting over there. With Adrienne." She points and my gaze follows. Adrienne is leaning across the table, talking to Vera, laying it on thick. She looks gorgeous; she's so charming when she wants to be.

I wish she were different. I watch Whit, and he is looking at Ethan in this slightly territorial way, or at least my imagination wants to think he is. Then he glances up and catches my eyes on him.

I look away.

"All right, everybody," the man in black says from the microphone, his voice booming out into the bar, "welcome to Michaela's eighteenth birthday! We have our songbooks out for those of you ready to sing your way to fame tonight, so just head on up here and let's get this party started!" With that, he steps back to his laptop, and I say a silent prayer for his sake that he has a really, really good day job.

"This is humiliating," I say to Claire.

She looks at me for a second. "I thought that was the point."

I stand up. "I'm going."

She claps her hands together. As I make my way toward the man in black, she cheers behind me. I walk slowly, trying to force my heart to match its pacing to my footsteps. The man in black turns to me. "What song are you looking for, sweetie?" he asks me.

I cringe. "I was kind of just hoping to say a quick happy birthday to Michaela. Before everything gets started."

The man appraises me for a second. Then nods. "Okay." He picks up the microphone in front of him, flipping a switch at the bottom. My mouth goes dry. "What's your name?" he asks.

"Olivia," I mutter. "They know me," I say even softer.

"All right, folks," he says into the microphone, cutting in over the music. Heads turn in the direction of the stage, and I purposely avoid everyone's eye. "First up tonight, we have Olivia, who is here to wish Michaela a very happy birthday." He hands me the mic. "All yours, hon."

On the cusp of a nightmare, I walk onstage holding the microphone, trying one-handed to fix my dress, my hair, my life. "Um . . . hey, y'all," I begin, squinting into the spotlight shining on me and the flowers and the beach backdrop. Claire gives another cheer from our booth. I swallow. "So, I know most of you haven't seen me since I did a lot of really shitty stuff and left school, and I know you've heard a lot of rumors about how I backstabbed my friends and got showered in whiskey and asked Whit DuRant to pretend to date me, and you probably think you know it all."

I take a deep breath. "You know why I picked Whit out of all you guys, right? It's not hard to figure out—he's Mr. Everything. All State golfer, smart, and hey, I mean, check out that jaw," I go on, managing to pull a couple weak laughs out of the sympathizers in the crowd. My palm is sweating, so I transfer the microphone over to my other hand. "So, I thought I'd make Adrienne and Ethan jealous, and I thought, hell, maybe some of you guys would think I was worth something if someone like Whit could like me."

"Sit down," one of the football players yells at me.

I flip him off and continue, more determined than ever. "But the thing is, pretending to date Whit was easy. I mean, sure, I wasn't denying that he was sleeping with a teacher, but he was telling me all this funny stuff and calling me on all my shit. And that part sucked, actually.

"But somewhere along the line, it stopped sucking, and I started getting this feeling that you get when you're around *that person*. You know the one? When I was near Whit, I'd feel a bit breathless, a little lost in my thoughts, so unsure. I wanted to be the right kind of person—the kind of person he wanted to be with.

"But I think, and I never realized this before, he always knew I was the right kind of person, if I'd stop making so damn many excuses. Whit never demanded anything of me except for me to be who I wanted to be. I think that's what made the two of us so momentous together. That's an SAT word he taught me, by the way." I chance a glance at a few of the nearest faces, all of whom are glaring up at me, rapt in spite of themselves, but I don't look at the table where I know Whit is.

"Whit says I do everything like I don't care about anything," I tell them, "and maybe I do. But I figure I spent all this time in these four years with you guys holding everything in until I exploded. Knowing everyone probably hated me but never wanting to admit it to myself. Believing what I'd done to you all was what made my brother crash into a tree. Believing I could fight my way out of a corner, but that I had to fight all the time."

I push my hair back out of my face and start to look. There's Michaela, confused, as if this wasn't necessarily the drama she was expecting. Claire, smiling the biggest smile I've seen from her in months. Ethan, tetherless. Then, finally I look at Whit. Adrienne's there next to him, contempt written in her features. But Whit is just there, with nothing at all on his face.

If he fucks his world up on the seventeenth hole, he has to brush it off and keep going. It can't affect him, affect his game.

He doesn't care.

"So, Whit, this is my dumb way of saying that I'm really sorry. That I'm catastrophically sorry when I go through every day without you smiling at me or texting me a dumb joke or looking at me like you care so much that it hurts, and trying to pretend you don't care at all. I want to change it all. And what everyone is saying might be true. It probably is. You hate me and don't want anything more to do with me. That's okay. But please know, here I am in front of all these people saying that when you looked at me on the bathroom floor that day and asked if you mattered at all to me? What I wanted to say is that you *do* matter to me, every moment of every day, and nothing you do can change that. You matter so much that I maybe think I might be in love with you. . . .

"I know I would give anything to go back to that—to what we were before—and even if you reject me, I wasn't afraid to say this much. Excuses aren't going to hold me back anymore, and I won't stay quiet this time, okay?" I falter in the silence. I have to get out of here. "So that's that," I say into the mic, walking quickly off the stage with shaking hands. "Happy birthday, Michaela," I finally say, giving the microphone back to black T-shirt guy, who is staring at me like I'm an alien life-form.

I walk straight toward the table where Whit is sitting, and I'm sure everyone thinks I'm going to him but instead I turn to Anna and Vera.

"Anna," I say first, being sure to look her in the eyes. "I'm so sorry for how I made you feel. You deserved better than that, and I should've apologized a long time ago."

She stares back at me, her face blank. So, I lean over the table toward Vera. "And, Vera," I say. She watches me closely. If I say the right thing here, I might finally do some good for someone.

"Don't ever let anyone make you feel like you don't deserve to be heard, because it's bullshit. If I see you do it again, I am going to scream at you. Don't let anyone talk to you like that. Especially not me."

Then I walk away, away, out the front door and farther down the street, all the way into the shadow of a closed consignment shop at the corner. I wrap my arms around myself, cold, remembering I left my jacket in my booth. I lean into the glass window of the store, trying to catch my breath, trying to replay all the words in my head, but I'm not entirely sure what just came out of my mouth.

What I've just done.

"He's not coming," someone says behind me.

I turn around to Adrienne, holding out my jacket and strolling forward until she's next to me under the store's overhang. "I didn't expect him to," I reply, grabbing the jacket out of her hand and sliding it onto my shoulders.

She leans against a wood panel. "That was quite a performance. Confessing love at a karaoke bar."

"I wanted him to know," I say, resigned.

"Even after that video?" Adrienne asks in a disbelieving voice. "When you knew he'd reject you?"

"That's the whole point. He needed to know I gave a shit." I shake my head, pulling my jacket tighter around me. "I don't expect you to get it."

The moon steals through the torn fabric of the overhang, highlighting her hair. It shines as she gives her head a nonchalant shake. "You've embarrassed yourself in front of everyone again. How can you think it's okay to let them see you rejected like that? They go for the first weak spot they see, O; you know that."

Her tone is set for an argument, to put me back into that lonely corner and get me to try to claw my way out. Instead I smile. "I do. So there it is. Whit's my weak spot. As witnessed by God and everybody. Now you know. If you want to hurt me, use him."

"I already did," she snaps.

I stand up a little straighter. "I feel bad for you, Adrienne," I say.

"Don't. You're the pathetic one."

"You think if everyone's looking at me, they won't see you're just as clueless as the rest of us. You can't control me, and you don't want them to know."

She steps closer to me. "I've been controlling you for months." She says it with a mixture of pride and contempt. I almost laugh.

"You think this is friendship!" I spit out at her. "You still think you're doing all this for me."

"You won't survive by yourself," she tells me calmly.

"I will. I am," I promise her. "Just fine. But you . . ." I trail off. I take the jacket off from around my shoulders and drop it at her feet. "You've lost the best friend you ever had, all over your desperate need to be in control. Why did I always have to do the dirty work? Why did I have to take the fall?"

"That's just who you are," Adrienne insists to me.

"Not anymore."

I walk away then, ignoring her calls after me. They'll just be more desperate attempts to win me back. I walk away into the moonlight, a little freer. A little less scared.

72

Right before sunrise, the sky is this grayish color, still swimming in the silence and the darkness of the hours before. Every now and then, a car will drive by, someone going to or getting off from some nightmarish job. But other than me and the birds, nothing makes a sound.

I sit and wait.

The white church stares back at me, its windows dark and imposing in the grayness. But not for long now.

Mom came with me last week. I told her I wanted to see this, to kind of capture it in my memory because I wanted to imagine what Ryan saw—the beauty, the height. Something beautiful, somewhere simple.

It's been five months.

"Is this seat taken?"

The sound of another voice startles me, and I look up to find Whit standing there, looking a little sheepish, a paper bag curled into his fist.

"Yeah. Sure." I look back toward the church. I breathe for a second, louder than I mean to, as he sits down next to me, leaving a millimeter of space between our arms. "How did you know I was here?"

He fiddles with the paper bag. "I called you last night and your mom picked up. She said—well, she said I should meet you here." He unrolls the top of the bag. "I brought bagels."

"Mom loves you." I give him a close-mouthed smile as he pulls out a bagel and splits the two halves, giving me the bigger piece. They have cream cheese and everything. I bite into it without saying anything. It's kind of nice—sitting there and not worrying about what he's going to say. Just being.

"Do you know how stupid you looked in front of that Hawaiian backdrop, spilling your feelings?" Whit asks over his unbitten bagel.

I lick cream cheese off my lip. "About as stupid as you looked sitting at a table with Adrienne."

"What is it?" he asks, pointing with his bagel half. "With the church?"

"You have to watch," I tell him, biting into my bagel. "The sun will hit the very top first, at that little window cutout." I point up to it for him. His eyes follow my finger. "And then it'll start spreading down faster. Like a really great song, you know? Slow buildup and then suddenly, it hits into this crescendo that doesn't let up and the adrenaline builds and there's highs and lows, and it's—you never want it to end. You could listen to it over and over again." My hands fly in front of me as I speak, my free fingers spreading out over the enormity of the windows. I drop my hands back into my lap. "At least, that's what Ryan used to say. More poetic, of course. He'd take me to the services sometimes, but I never really knew if he believed any of it."

I glance over at Whit, and he's not looking at the church, but at me. I can't make out what he's thinking—I'd probably sound stupid if I tried—but it's nothing bad. It could be fondness, or maybe thoughtfulness. He has a little bit of cream cheese on his face, so I reach over and wipe it off his cheek. My hand leaves his face but lingers in the space between us. "Why are you here?"

"Wanted to see you," he mutters, sheepish.

"To make fun of me? Tell me to leave you alone?"

His eyes meet mine, doing that searching thing he does so well, analyzing me like the ninth hole or something. And then he kisses me. An inappropriate-for-public-venues kiss. "You're not the only one who feels trapped," he says when he pulls back. "You know?"

"No."

"Not just by this place," he says, bringing his hand up to slide into my hair. "But other stuff. Like being better than my brother, for example. Or by being part of your popularity games. Or just by who you are."

"I saw the video from Coxie's party. What you said about me," I say. Even though he kissed me, I still don't know what it means. I don't know if he's toying with my emotions or something. I want to know. I want him to tell me. "I don't blame you."

"You of all people should know a little something about wounded pride," he says. We're still so close together. He smirks, an inch from my mouth. "I'm sorry I said that stuff. I was hurt. I still am hurt, Liv. But I do want to know. If we can come back from this."

Another few beats of silence pass by.

"It's not always so bad, you know? Buckley," I tell him. "Ryan used to be so good at finding the little things that could be so beautiful, but he forgot, I think. I don't want to forget. Like you. You're beautiful in your overpriced Banana Republic, with a driver in your hands, watching a ball fade into the sunset."

He narrows his eyes. "I am?"

"And Claire and Ellie, they're beautiful, too, even when they're fighting—how in love they are, how it hurts Claire when the people she grew up with reject her, but how they make each other happy despite all of that.

"I'm not trapped," I tell him. "I thought I was. And I'm not so afraid anymore. I looked so stupid up there, but I was me, you know? In front of everybody, I was me, not who I thought they wanted me to be or expected me to be or anything else."

"You were amazing," he says.

Half a smile finds its way onto my face. "I was?"

"Did you mean what you said?" he asks, and the shy boy is still under there a little bit. He thinks I might reject him, even now.

"Most of it." I catch my bottom lip with my teeth. "I had this joke prepared about how stupid your hair was, but I forgot it when I started talking."

He laughs, kisses me again. "You know, I said I'd never speak to you again, but Mrs. Baker kind of changed my mind."

"She did?" I ask, taken aback.

He nods. "Yeah. When she came back to school, she would barely make eye contact with me, for obvious reasons, but she's got a job in a different county now. She's moving," he adds.

I stare away from the church, down at my hands, ashamed.

"So she started working with me again, and it was cool. I told her that I would cut you off for good, and she said, if you hadn't done what you did, her life would be ruined. She said she figured it was a lot of stress to be Olivia Clayton and that maybe she was too hard on you and maybe I was, too. She said she forgave you, and that if I still cared about you, that was okay." He shrugs. "That maybe it meant something."

"Like what?" I ask.

"Like that I knew who you were at your worst and your best, and I loved you the whole time," he says, turning all red and sweet. Looking at me until he's so embarrassed he has to look away.

I almost tear up. I feel free, I realize. Okay in my own skin.

I don't remember the last time that happened.

"So what does this mean?" I ask finally. "You want to date, like, for real?"

He presses his forehead against mine, in that display of intimacy we got used to when we were faking it, only this time, every second of it is real. "If I don't embarrass you too much."

"I'll still get you in trouble, you know," I respond, but the weight is floating off my shoulders and the uncontrollable butterflies he gives me are taking over from within and running into all the sides of my stomach. I let myself smile.

"I love you," he says next to my mouth.

I kiss him, grab his hand, and pull his arm over my shoulders. "Shut up," I say, nudging him. "It's starting."

After watching me a minute more, he turns to the church, where the smallest bit of sunlight hits the cutout window, taking my breath away.

He whispers it again.

Like the best songs, I could listen over and over.

ACKNOWLEDGMENTS

Olivia and co. have been with me for a long time, but there are so many other people without whom these characters wouldn't have existed. First and foremost, thanks go to my agent Diana Fox, who invested so much time in helping me shape this book, even without knowing if it would ever come together. I am so lucky she saw something in the many rough forms Olivia's story took and championed it so passionately.

My editor, Erin Stein, honored me so much by picking this book to be one of the first voices of her brand-new imprint. Her keen eye helped me to find depths to these characters I never knew existed. Huge thanks as well go to Nicole Otto, Natalie C. Sousa, and the whole team at Macmillan for making this dream a reality.

I absolutely have to mention my family, who have been so supportive throughout this process—Drew, Brenda, Will & Kyle, and everyone else in the extended Woolbright & Devore clans. Most of all to my wonderful Mama and Daddy, Bob and Pam Devore, who still don't know why I turned out this way but love me anyway.

The list of friends who have helped me get this far could be a novel in and of itself, but to Campbell, Erin, Felicia, Jamie, Meisha, Mitchel, Randi, Sarah C., Sarah W., and everyone else—I hope you found yourselves here in some way. Amanda, thanks for being such a talented photog! Rachel, Mary, and Maura, thanks for being the best coworkers a girl could ask for.

Lastly, the writer community has been my creative refuge in the world since I started writing more than six years ago. The friendships I've made stretch across so many online spaces, both defunct and active—thanks to the wonderful writers and alumni of AW, LBs, and Writer Cooler III in particular. More people have read this book than I have space to list but a huge shout-out to Rachael Allen, Erin Brambilla, Lindsey Roth Culli, Debra Driza, Sarah Harian, Rachel Simon, and Kara Thomas for their notes and encouragement. Thanks for reading this book in its many iterations and giving me invaluable feedback. And truly, thank you to anyone unmentioned who had eyes on this book—I know the list extends further back than my e-mail account, and you have all helped me to grow so much as a writer.

Most of all, thank you for reading.